THE SKY SUSPENDED

BY JAMES BASSETT

HARM'S WAY
THE SKY SUSPENDED

THE SKY SUSPENDED

BY

James Bassett

DELACORTE PRESS

Library of Congress Catalog Card Number: 68–12197
Manufactured in the United States of America
First Printing—1968

"Epitaph on an Army of Mercenaries" from
THE COLLECTED POEMS OF A. E. HOUSMAN.
Copyright 1922 by Holt, Rinehart and Winston, Inc.
Copyright 1950 by Barclays Bank Ltd. Reprinted
by permission of Holt, Rinehart and Winston, Inc.,
The Society of Authors as the literary representative
of the Estate of the late A. E. Housman,
and Jonathan Cape Ltd.
The chess classic described in Chapter Six
reprinted with permission of The Macmillan
Company from MACMILLAN HANDBOOK OF CHESS
by I. A. Horowitz and Fred Reinfeld.
© I. A. Horowitz and Fred Reinfeld 1956.

FOR OUR DAUGHTER
CINDY

Naturally, this is a story that never happened,
although it might have, and yet could, if certain
circumstances were to change. Nothing in it has
not occurred, in one form or another, since man
first waged war.
Perhaps there are some who would say that the
very size and complexity of Southeast Asia make
such a small-canvas portrait impossible. They
may be right. Others would argue that the
powerful forces now contending there are far too
deeply committed for any disengagement that
must precede an adventure of this sort.
They may be wrong.

These, in the day when heaven was falling,
    The hour when earth's foundations fled,
Followed their mercenary calling
    And took their wages and are dead.

Their shoulders held the sky suspended;
    They stood, and earth's foundations stay;
What God abandoned, these defended,
    And saved the sum of things for pay.

Alfred Edward Housman

Contents

THE SKY SUSPENDED

1

Year of the Dragon

CHIN IN HAND, not at all satisfied with his afternoon's work, Cragg glowered down at the chart spread wide across the battered desk. Thrice in the past four hours he had plotted and replotted the 800-mile route. Yet it still appeared tentative, unsure, like the quarterings of a confused bird dog in quest of a snow-covered spoor.

As a perfectionist in such matters, he was deeply troubled that the navigational aids upon which depended their course from GaiSong to Phom Than were so confoundedly sketchy. Six centuries after the Europeans arrived, two decades after a modern naval war had been fought upon, above and beneath its treacherous surface, the South China Sea remained poorly charted. And the waters along its convoluted coastline were the worst.

Suddenly, with a sweep of his arm, the good one, Cragg brushed the chart off the desk. Then he stood up, yawning, stretching, and cursing. His temper wasn't improved by the fact that the varnish on the ancient chair was stuck to his naked skin, and made the simple act of rising as vexatious as ripping off a mustard plaster.

Still brooding, Cragg pressed the offending chart flat with his bare feet, scrutinizing it from his full height, like an astronaut inspecting the dark side of the moon.

South Thietvanne's coastline curved northeastward for about four hundred miles from its river delta capital, GaiSong, before it swung due north, then slightly west, toward the North Thietvanne border where the Communists stood guard. It was, thought Cragg, like the profile of a pregnant woman, whose feet were firmly planted in the equatorial waters far below GaiSong, where her thighs joined a bulging torso. Her indented navel marked the only town worth mentioning as you went north, Dokoro, although even that was little more than a mission trading post. Phom Than, the Red stronghold, formed the nipple on the lady's generous right breast. Above were the shoulders, a slender neck, and finally a flat oriental head. Here North Thietvanne broadened to meet mainland China.

Thietvanne, north and south, *was* that woman, a fructile creature of impossible whims and dangerous moods. No man could foretell what progeny she would bring forth, whether good or evil, healthy or doomed. Indeed, her offspring was overdue, for it had been an inordinately long gestation period, starting when the French, plagued by defeat and haunted by cries of "colonialism," granted premature independence to a have-not nation ill-prepared for mere existence, much less self-ruled.

For a full minute Cragg continued to stare at the chart, absorbing its details, fixing them in his mind by that curious anatomical association. Then, amused by the odd conceit, he smiled. His large, rather uneven teeth flashed briefly behind tight-drawn lips. Cragg's smile was an evanescent thing. Some people missed it entirely. What they noticed, were his cold gray eyes, wide-set above a nose that had been fist-flattened at the bridge, an outthrust jaw, and a wiry mat of close-cropped brown hair which only now, at forty-five, was turning grizzled around the temples.

He reached for a cigar in the desk drawer, and struck a wooden match to light it. But then he paused, with the match halfway to the cigar, and looked at the girl on the bed. Shrugging, he snuffed out the flame and reluctantly replaced the cigar in the drawer. It would be ungallant of him, he supposed, to add the stench of a Manila stogie to the already foul air in the room. Although the Galleon Hotel was the architectural pride of GaiSong, and claimed to be air-conditioned, by midday you could steam clams in its fetid bedchambers.

The girl opened her eyes, lazily, and raised her tawny arms toward him.

"Come join KoKo," she invited, "for the siesta."

Cragg regarded her somberly. The girl lay against the rumpled sheets, wearing only the briefest of panties, with her thighs parted. As he looked, she slowly ran her hands down her body, tracing the outline of her full breasts, her gently convex belly, her rounded hips. She was a damned handsome article, taller than most Thiet women, and much deeper bosomed, doubtless owing to some encounter twenty-odd years ago between her mother and an amorous Frog infantryman. But Cragg was tiring of the sport.

The girl named KoKo had taken to slipping into his room during the afternoons, so that she could enjoy the dubious delights of the Galleon's air conditioning, and for an occasional bout of lazy lovemaking. The hotel, apparently, didn't mind such visitations, even in broad daylight. Or perhaps this was a special favor from the desk clerk, who had introduced KoKo to Cragg shortly after he arrived in GaiSong a month earlier. KoKo had been an eminently satisfactory partner, worth every piastre he'd invested in spurious champagne, perfume, gaudy dresses, costume jewelry, and handouts for mysterious relatives who were always in dire straits, plus the original down payment to the desk clerk. She was both fierce and tender, possessing an expertise that astonished Cragg, and quite insatiable.

Unfortunately, the idyll had lasted somewhat longer than he had anticipated, because Torgerson was taking such a blasted long time to fetch the junk *Medusa* down from Hong Kong. So

KoKo's persistent ardor had begun to pall upon Cragg, who disliked the trapped feeling that accompanied long, drawn-out affairs.

Now Cragg said: "Siesta time's *fini*, baby. And besides, it's too goddamned hot." He tugged at his sweat-drenched skivvy shorts. "I've got more work to do."

The girl's sensuous mouth formed into a pouting grimace.

"You are always working over that stupid map, *chéri*."

"It's a chart," Cragg growled. "Navymen never deal in maps. That's for dogfaces."

"I do not comprehend."

"You're not supposed to."

KoKo swung her slim legs off the bed. She walked catlike across the tacky carpet and stood beside Cragg for a moment, studying the spread-out chart. On a whim, because her innocent interest amused him, Cragg pointed out the Pregnant Lady. That seemed to interest the girl. She herself, explained KoKo, had once become carelessly *enceinte*, when the Americans occupied GaiSong, and had been forced to seek the services of a Chinese doctor.

"One learns," KoKo said philosophically. "I do not blame the American." Bending down for a closer look at Cragg's handiwork, she traced her right forefinger along the red penciled line that represented his latest attempt to fix a viable course north from GaiSong. "What are those, *chéri?*"

By way of answer Cragg gave her buttock a sharp smack with his open palm. She straightened up angrily.

"That," he said, "is what happens when cats get too goddamn curious."

"Goddamn you, Cragg."

He laughed at her savage imitation of his own speech. "Put your clothes on," he said, "and scram like a nice little girl, before I give you a real spanking."

KoKo caught the determined glint in his eye. Without any further protestation she slipped a varicolored Thai silk dress over her bare body, and stepped daintily into the high-heeled gold sandals that were balanced alongside Cragg's dusty fieldboots.

At the door she paused, half-turned, and asked quietly: "You will see me tonight?"

"Affirmative," he said. "Same place, same time."

When the door closed behind her, leaving only a trace of perfume where KoKo had been, Cragg checked his watch again. It was almost five P.M. Realization that he had been spinning his wheels since noon, fiddling with a useless chart while GaiSong took its daily siesta, made him feel unaccountably cheated. Time was one commodity, perhaps the *only* commodity, a man shouldn't waste. Nothing else mattered. Money, liquor, women, even friendships were expendable. But not time. And now he had lost five more irretrievable hours.

There was, of course, absolutely no choice. When you came to South Thietvanne, you either behaved like a Thiet and slumbered the afternoon away, or you worked behind closed doors.

Once Cragg had tried to sleep. But he awakened after a fitful half-hour, bathed in sweat, feeling more cheated than ever. So he gave it up. A few times, too, he'd gone outside during the siesta. That did no good, either, because GaiSong's murderous heat, unrelieved by the dappled green shade of the tamarind trees, forced him to slow his normal pace to a death-march crawl. As a result, the slight limp which he generally managed to conceal by walking briskly became all the more apparent.

Cragg was quietly proud of his strength and athletic prowess, and it irked him when strangers noticed his gimp right leg. He was especially annoyed if they presumed to inquire how it happened, although the explanation was simple enough, and quite honorable.

In the waning days of the Pacific War, after having survived a dozen campaigns from the Solomons to Leyte Gulf, Cragg found himself on what was derisively termed "flycatcher patrol" off Okinawa, as skipper of a motor torpedo boat. His mission was intercepting the Japanese smallcraft bent on evacuating the isolated Nip troops from coastal pockets far behind the fluid front-lines. It was uninspiring, backbreaking work, made worse by the knowledge that the adjacent fleet's larger units were taking the brunt of the enemy's suicidal last effort. Radar picket destroyers had become the *kamikaze*'s special target, as they maneuvered in the narrow offshore waters, gamely absorbing this insane punishment to safeguard the carriers. The toll in ships and men was far greater than the intelligence wizards back in Tokyo would ever realize until the war was over, when it was too late.

Cruising slowly under a fulgent July moon, shortly after midnight, Cragg's PT 387 chanced upon a whole swarm of "flies," perhaps a dozen of them, loaded to the gunwales with military refugees. Without bothering to radio for assistance, he drove into the midst of the formation, guns ablaze, only to discover that one of these presumably impotent flies was a heavily armed hornet, whose rapid-fire more than matched his own 37-millimeter bow cannon.

Nevertheless, having engaged the foe, Cragg persisted. He managed to sink the gunboat. But in the process he was twice wounded, in his right knee and left elbow, while personally conning his PT alongside the ferocious Jap. Afterward they had to pry his locked fingers loose from the spokes, and swab up the blood that was clotted beneath his canvas sneakers on the tiny bridge. By the time the medicos got around to repairing the damage, there was nothing much they could do for the shattered bones except let them knit whichever way they pleased. As a result, one leg grew permanently stiff, and one arm remained twisted.

For a while they called him "The Boy on the Burning Deck." But not for long. Once Cragg's left arm healed, his friends soon discovered that the crooked member worked like a trip-hammer thus discouraging further literary allusions.

Somewhere in his tangled flightbag Cragg found a fresh pair of skivvies, which he slipped on, and a clean cotton T-shirt. Carrying this in his right hand, he moved to the window. Automatically, he hooked his left thumb into the elastic band of his shorts, as if to disguise the fact that the arm itself was bent, even though there was nobody around to observe this slight deformity.

Cragg thrust aside the faded plush drapes, which had been kept closed to minimize the tropical heat, and peered out through the dirty glass pane. Caught by the sudden harsh sunglare, he gave the impression of being a smaller man than he was, for all his carefully distributed 175 pounds.

Once again Cragg grinned as he regarded the cardboard sign tacked to the wall beside the French window. *Défense d'Ouvrir*, it warned, reaffirming the Galleon management's blind faith in air conditioning. With the calloused heel of his right hand, using the T-shirt as a glove, Cragg hammered loose the metal lock, then cranked the window outward to a 90-degree angle. Immediately a humid blast surged against the lesser heat of the room, assailing his naked torso, as he leaned across the sill for a better view of the sodden, brown-turfed park seven stories below him.

By craning his neck at an odd angle, Cragg could glimpse the harbor, formed by the Dalagong River as it made its wide, lazy loop forty miles from the sea. He counted the moored vessels; a half dozen rusty tramp freighters, several minor warships flying various western flags, a cluster of junks that ranged from small coastal craft to great oceangoing types, and a gaggle of lightly armed units of Thietvanne's sampan navy.

He looked closer.

All that was left of the United States military force in this sadsack country were the two destroyers riding at anchor in the greasy stream. These were vestigial reminders that the United States, after spending a dozen years and uncountable dollars, had decided that the Thietvanne cause was hopeless. American troops and the Seventh Fleet were pulled out, leaving the Thietvannese to fend for themselves. Nowadays, GaiSong was merely an intermittent rest-and-recreation port, much frowned upon by the fleet medics because of its fluctuant VD rate.

Having finished counting the ships present, Cragg grunted his exasperation at what he saw. Or, rather, at what he didn't see.

This afternoon, as on all other afternoons when he had stood vigil at the illegally opened window, *Medusa* was nowhere in sight among the anchored junks. Even allowing for the southwest monsoon, which forced the clumsy old three-master to beat her way down from Hong Kong, and doubtless slowed her to a crawl, she was three days overdue. Hell. Knowing the implacability of their schedule, Torgerson should have disregarded economy and switched on the diesel. Despite its Mickey Mouse inadequacy, the two-cycle kicker could have added four knots to *Medusa's* speed, thus compensating for the headwinds that plagued southbound sailors every summer on the China Sea.

It was doubly disturbing to Cragg that the ancient Liberty ship to which he had entrusted *Mohican*—last of the motor torpedo boat Mohicans—hadn't yet reached GaiSong, either. Almost six weeks ago he had personally supervised its loading at the Embarcadero in San Francisco, helping to swaddle *Mohican* in heavy canvas so she could withstand the long deck journey, making sure the lashings were secure. The Liberty's skipper figured he might have to stop off at Manila to offload some scrap steel. But that was all. The rest of his beans-and-bullets cargo was destined for Thietvanne. So why the delay?

For a few moments longer Cragg remained in his uncomfortable position at the window, somberly watching the city emerge from its midday siesta, trying to fathom whether the bored activity of the troops in the square betokened a change of the municipal guard, or a muster preliminary to some fresh thrust against the encroaching Kongs, or the start of another coup that would give South Thietvanne its third government in less than eight months.

The rain from the previous night had left the parade ground streaked and sticky, like a pancake lightly moistened with treacle.

After a bit of confusion, the soldiers managed to arrange themselves into a semblance of order under their captain's prodding, then file across the spongy turf to the waiting trucks. Cragg noticed that their rifles were piled helter-skelter on the truckbeds. It was, he concluded, merely a guard change. The harried government could breathe easier. As for the Kongs, they couldn't have cared less about this ill-trained, ill-equipped, ill-managed company.

Now the troops were in their vehicles, squatting with shoulders hunched, eyes aimed blankly ahead, while the drivers revved the ancient motors. They rode off looking tired and already defeated.

Some correspondent had written: "The smell of blood and hate hangs heavy over the whole country." He was right, thought Cragg, although nobody seemed to be doing anything about it.

Especially the present ruler of South Thietvanne, who had breveted himself from chicken colonel to four-star rank during the last coup.

At this very instant, Cragg knew, General Trang Kwo would be lying in his king-sized bed in GaiSong Palace, pondering whether to take his helicopter to government headquarters for a spot of late afternoon paperwork, or his Rolls Royce to the Sports Club where he could get a head start on the cocktails. More than ever, today, Cragg resented the idiotic custom of the siesta. Now that General Kwo had finally granted him an audience to explain his proposition, each passing hour gave the wily bastard just that much more time to devise ways of screwing up the whole deal, or injecting into it some Asian nonsense that would render a relatively simple scheme quite impossible.

But you couldn't hurry the general.

First, he would have to estimate precisely how much was due Kwo, should he give Cragg his approval, then back it up with hard cash from GaiSong's dwindling treasury. *Quid pro* Kwo. The general's aides weren't above perpetrating this jest when they were freeloading with the foreigners in the penthouse bar of the Galleon Hotel. For the general regarded government money as his own, which indeed it was while he clung to precarious power, and he expected to gain certain personal advantages from any investment of these resources.

Swearing quietly, Cragg turned away from the window and limped back to the desk, where he had left his unlighted cigar. Absence of clothes never made Cragg feel naked. But without a cigar clenched between his teeth, lit or dead, he felt incomplete. Long ago a psychiatrist had suggested that this constant nursing of cigars by grown men was a sort of reversion to pre-weaned infancy. Maybe so. There were things, however, that even a headshrinker didn't know. A cigar provided definite other comforts, as well, such as keeping your teeth from jarring loose when you rode a PT at forty knots through choppy seas. Cragg had learned this early in the game. And since ship's-service cigars were both available and cheap, he had succumbed willingly to the habit.

Now he thrust the green-black Manila stogie into his mouth,

found a match, and coaxed the moist cigar to life. As the malodorous fumes began to fill the room, Cragg sniffed appreciatively. At its deadlevel worst, Philippine tobacco smelled better than the Galleon's bedchambers, whose unique clammy aroma derived from bad plumbing, stale perfume impregnated into the mattresses by generations of female bodies, from the responsive sweat of their men, from mildewed carpets, and from all the other unholy stenches of GaiSong itself which seeped past the hotel's loose fittings.

Cragg went back to the window.

As he watched, General Kwo's silver-colored Rolls Royce wheeled around the corner, heading west, away from the river-front palace and toward the elegant swim-and-sun enclave on the outskirts of GaiSong. The Rolls was preceded and pursued by a pair of weapons carriers. Cragg observed that the soldiers in these trucks, unlike the municipal guard, were sharply alert. They looked damned efficient, and properly so, for General Kwo had no wish to be ambushed at the Sports Club by an alley-skulking gang of Kongs, or to be mousetrapped by Thiet dissidents while he was helplessly sunbathing.

As the Rolls swept out of sight beneath the red-flowered tamarind grove, Cragg swore again. For him this meant a miserable crosstown journey in a three-cylinder Renault taxicab piloted by a hackie who would deliberately haul him five miles out of the way, just to prove his contempt for the foreign white devils.

With a shrug, Cragg returned to his B4 bag to find something suitable for the elegant Sports Club. He chose an orange-and-blue silk aloha shirt, which he had bought at the Honolulu airport during his westbound flight layover, and a pair of green Bermuda shorts. General Kwo usually set the uniform-of-the-day by wearing this same sort of off-duty mufti. Then Cragg pulled on a pair of long gray hose and slipped his feet into ankle-high suede desert boots. The mosquitoes, he thought morosely, would be orbiting like buzzards around the Club pool. He put his passport into a hip pocket and carefully buttoned the flap. Stolen American passports fetched $500 apiece on the waterfront black market even when, as in his case, they were stamped "invalid for travel to the following areas controlled by authorities with which the United States does not have diplomatic relations: Albania, Bulgaria, and those portions of China, North Korea, North Vietnam and North Thietvanne under Communist control."

Idly speculating on the world's forbidden northness, Cragg scooped the map off the floor, folded it twice, and stuffed it into an oversized manila envelope that contained the rest of his project blueprint. He didn't bother to lock the door when he left. Twice during the past week his room had been searched, Cragg knew, so he figured to make it easier for the police, or for whoever else had such morbid curiosity about his personal activities. Aside from the map plans, which he carried with him whenever he went out, there was nothing of consequence among his belongings to indicate that he might be other than what his passport said on the page labelled "descriptive data":

FREDERICK PETER CRAGG. WIFE: *none*. MINORS: *none*. HEIGHT: *6 ft. 1 in.* HAIR: *brown*. EYES: *gray*. VISIBLE MARKS: *scar on bridge of nose; ditto left elbow, right knee, both members impaired.* BIRTHPLACE: *San Francisco, Calif.* BIRTH DATE: *March 13, 1922.* OCCUPATION: *Big Game Hunter.*

On his vaccination certification, paper-clipped to the passport, it was duly noted that F. P. Cragg had been rendered immune against smallpox, yellow fever, cholera, typhus, plague, and tetanus, under conditions approved by the World Health Organization.

Since high school, nobody had ever called him Fred or Pete or anything except Cragg, a name that suited him personally and physically. But WIFE: *none* and MINORS: *none* seemed beautifully put, as did his ostensible occupation, which covered such a broad and comfortable spectrum of human endeavor.

Downstairs the desk clerk nodded a bored negative when he inquired whether there were any letters or messages in 713's pigeonhole.

"If anybody calls," Cragg said, "tell 'em I'll be back around seven."

The bespectacled clerk, who also manipulated the front switchboard, assented sleepily, as if he had just awakened from the siesta. Cragg tossed him a mock salute before he crossed the marble parquet lobby to the house telephone, where he asked the operator to ring the Sports Club. She made him repeat his instructions twice as punishment for his atrocious French before she would contact the number.

When the Club finally answered, he asked for Colonel Toyon. Cragg had to endure the stifling little cubicle for another five minutes while they flushed him out of the bar in which he was killing time until General Kwo arrived.

The colonel sounded rather miffed at having his drinking interrupted, although he became polite enough after Cragg identified himself. His cultivated British voice was a lot more authoritative here on his home ground than it had been during their talk in San Francisco, three months ago, when Paki Ningh Toyon was hard-selling Thietvanne's dubious cause. For a Thiet, the colonel spoke in an astonishingly deep tone, which was all the more remarkable when one met him in person, for he couldn't have been more than five feet tall, even in his imported elevator shoes. Most Thiets yapped like chihuahuas. It was Toyon's voice more than anything else, Cragg supposed, that had enabled him to survive the three recent governmental shakeups. The colonel greatly impressed windbags like General Kwo, who kept him around to deal with foreigners.

Toyon was a dedicated type, a zealot, of a breed that was suffering considerable attrition from South Thietvanne's ruthless barnyard power struggle. His zeal was reserved entirely for his country's welfare, with no particular regard for personal gain. This also impressed Quid Kwo. Moreover, his authentically Queen's English accent, the result of four years in a British public school and four at Oxford, was more convincing than the dandified French of his aristocratic peers who had attended the Sorbonne.

The diminutive colonel wanted to whip the Kongs with whatever weaponry and manpower he could beg, borrow or steal for the Thiets. That was why he had sought out Cragg originally. That was why, today, he kept his voice meticulously polite while speaking to this crude American whom he so cordially detested.

Toyon need not have gone to all this trouble. Cragg understood the reason for his contempt, and it didn't bother him in the least. He simply accepted the fact that the colonel was different. But Toyon's Asian-ness set him less apart from his own easy cosmopolitanism than did something else, something a lot harder to define.

Cragg thought he knew what it was. This disparity in their characters had been evident when they first chatted across the kitchen table in his Sausalito apartment. Toyon's vibrant enthusiasm for a cause which every diplomat, military expert, and armchair strategist claimed was already lost puzzled Cragg. However, despite the instability of South Thietvanne's present situation, the colonel's barrelhead offer had seemed firm enough, so Cragg played along with him.

Five thousand cash American dollars at the outset, Toyon had said, plus another five when Cragg's Mafia showed up with *Mohican* and *Medusa*. After the deed was done, and if they survived, they'd receive a final twenty-thousand-dollar instalment. Thirty grand in all.

Now Toyon was saying into the telephone: "I will meet you, Mr. Cragg, at the Sports Club porte cochere, and take you to General Kwo."

"Thanks."

"It is seventeen hours and ten minutes," Toyon said. "You will need a quarter-hour to reach the club. I shall expect you at eighteen hours minus twenty-five. His Excellency has many matters to which he must attend. Please be prompt."

Cragg grimaced. There was, also, a chasmal difference between Quid Kwo and Toyon. When he regarded them objectively, Cragg believed he preferred the general, whose cynicism wore a lot better than Toyon's perpetually hot-eyed gung-ho.

"See you later," he said.

He replaced the receiver and left the booth. On his way out of the hotel, Cragg noticed that the desk clerk was no longer somnolent, but was watching him intently through goldfish bowl spectacles.

The outside air hit Cragg like the exhaust from the stokehold of a prewar coalburner, and in the taxi it was even hotter. He felt trapped. The midget cab was an Iron Maiden, against whose metallic flanks his torturers were spraying napalm.

The intolerable heat did provide an unexpected bonus, however, for it encouraged the driver to take the fastest, shortest route to the Sports Club. This course led down GaiSong's main street past the other major hotel which, until the previous week, had been the principal hangout for second-echelon foreigners. But the Kongs had gotten wind of the fact that the Paradise was being used to billet the hired hands whom Colonel Toyon had been rounding up in the States. One evening, at the height of the cocktail hour, they detonated a 500-pound bomb in the basement, and the explosion killed twenty-three civilians in the ground-floor saloon. As yet nobody had bothered to repair the damage, or even to board up the shattered windows. Since the building itself was relatively unscathed above the third story, they moved the bar to the roof, where it should have been in the first place, and Colonel Toyon's overseas agents got busy hiring replacements for the pre-combat casualties.

Rather mordantly, Cragg supposed that this "regrettable accident," as GaiSong's controlled press termed the bombing, augmented the value of his own tardy five-man force. He mopped the sweat from his deeply creased forehead with a red bandanna and swore under his breath.

Goddamn it to hell. Where in blazes was Medusa? *Or that effing Liberty which carried* Mohican? *Or those idiots Lars Torgerson and Duke Harris and Mario DelGrado and Trump Gideon?*

Cragg scowled through the open window. The placid Thiets were going about their little businesses-as-usual, hawking stolen Yank cigarettes, vending fly-ridden pigsnouts and varnished chickens, quaffing pink apéritifs, sitting with equal impassivity on open-air barber's stools or dentist's chairs, telling fortunes by dealing cards and feeling skulls, pumping their three-wheeled pedicabs, weaving their rachitic motorscooters in and out of the traffic snarls.

Although you couldn't really dislike the Thiets, thought Cragg, only a saint could respect a people who exhibited such lazy indifference to their fate in the midst of a war that had crept, inexorable, right up to their own doorstep.

From the gaping doorway of a café, over which hung a sign promising *Le Jazz Américain,* Cragg caught the sound of raucous music. He winced. Take away the heat, the stink and the crazy costumes, and you might as well have been on the Barbary Coast of San Francisco, or in Sausalito when the Portuguese fishermen were throwing a post-Lenten wingding. It offended his professional instincts. He became angrier.

Then he smiled. Hell. After twenty centuries—of bowing to conquistadores, having been overrun by the Chinese, the Thais, the Dutch, the French and even the peripatetic British—they no longer gave a tinker's dam who ruled the slippery roost. Like their peasant brethren, they merely wanted to be left alone so they could pray in their garish temples and romance in the evening and dance the *watusi* and otherwise enjoy the fruits of western culture.

When you came right down to cases, maybe nobody had ever defeated the Thiets. What's-his-name, Kublai Khan, had tried it and had miserably failed. For this was a tough country to conquer, and tougher to keep conquered, with its summer monsoons that poured 120 inches of rainfall across the central plains, its flash typhoons, its inhospitable coastland where a man could catch malaria just by breathing deeply, its hostile mountain natives whose allegiance extended only to the gods that lived in their ancestral totem jars, its wily Mongoloid lowlanders who preferred loving to fighting and living to dying.

Crouched in the tiny back seat of his taxi, Cragg watched the saffron-togaed Buddhist monks, sour as dyspeptic owls, shamble through the crowds of happier layfolk, with their eyes fixed upon some mysterious distant goal. Like Colonel Toyon, they were idealists, although for other reasons. But unlike the colonel, they afforded General Kwo no satisfaction whatever, being contentious fellows who dabbled in backroom politics and expressed their disdain for his wicked regime by incinerating themselves on prominent streetcorners. Around these monks thronged the feckless people of GaiSong.

There were high-fashioned French ladies whose husbands still dominated the middle bureaucracy, Indian women in flowing saris with their turbanned men, Catholic priests, gaudily sportshirted Americans, blackclad Chinese and—always and everywhere—the dainty Thiet females in their silken tunics, satin pantaloons, and filmy outer skirts that were slit to their tiny waists.

It amused Cragg, and made him vaguely lustful, to see these tiny women riding sidesaddle upon the mudguards of the Vespa scooters, clutching the driver's belt, oblivious to the airstream that whipped their dresses behind them like bridal trains and flattened the blouses tight against their small breasts. Cragg recalled once having seen a replica of the Victory of Samothrace in a naval museum, her wings outstretched and her body clearly limned beneath her windswept robes. These Thiet maidens might also have been Nike goddesses, etched in miniature, personifying victories that would never come to pass.

Any one of them might make *Medusa* a magnificent bow adornment, and thereby relieve the junk's uncompromising ugliness. But whether such a lovely figurehead would also bring luck to their expedition was another matter entirely, Cragg thought, considering the almost total lack of good fortune that had thus far accrued to South Thietvanne.

An admonitory blast of the taxi's horn broke his reverie, as they swung off the main thoroughfare into a private driveway. Cragg caught a quick glimpse of pink stucco wall, topped by shards of broken glass to discourage intruders, before the cab skittered to a halt, spewing gravel. He clambered out.

It was five-forty. Colonel Toyon, who had been huddled in the shade of the porte cochere for a full ten minutes, didn't seem pleased at this delay. His rhesus monkey face was stern, and his large black eyes were brimming with reproach.

"General Kwo," he said acidly, "never appreciates being kept waiting."

Cragg grinned. "Lead on, maestro."

Clad only in a black G-string, which would have been against the law if it weren't for the fact that he himself *was* the law, Quid Kwo reclined in a strategically placed beachchair, deceptively somnolent, but alert behind king-sized dark glasses. His hairless body glistened with baby oil. He looked, Cragg decided, like a plump brown bullfrog, sitting on a lilypad, waiting for a fly to stray within reach. On a small table stood a rum collins and a box of cigars.

Behind him sat a male secretary, also in abbreviated jockey trunks, with notebook at the ready in case the general got a brilliant idea worth recording.

Without moving his bald, behemoth head, Kwo said: "It was good of you to come on such short notice, M'sieu Cragg-h." He added a noticeable aspirant *h* to the name. Then, lazily indicating a vacant chair, he invited, "Pray be seated."

Cragg struck down an impulse to remind him that their confrontation was three weeks late. Instead, he observed solemnly, "I am deeply honored, Your Excellency."

The general paused a moment while his invisible eyes pursued a tall French girl from the ladies' dressing quarters to the outdoor bar. More froglike than ever, his head swivelled ninety degrees as he monitored her passage down the entire length of the Olympic-sized pool. The French girl's round buttocks, emphasized by a flesh-colored bikini, undulated in provocative rhythm. Her magnificent breasts made her the envious cynosure of every Thiet woman present. Cragg chuckled inwardly as he thought of the way Trump Gideon might have summarized her impact upon the men around the pool: "By damn, chum, she makes things stand up that ain't got no feet!"

Nodding approvingly, Kwo flicked a signal with his bejeweled left hand. The secretary returned the nod, and, with a secret smile, arose to follow in the French girl's perfumed wake. Whereupon the general turned directly toward his guest for the first time.

"Colonel Toyon has described your extraordinary project, M'sieu Cragg-h, but I should like to hear it from the author's own lips. One never obtains quite the same effect when a story is told second-hand."

"I guess not," Cragg said. He felt in his pocket for a cigar. "Mind if I smoke?"

"Certainly not, m'sieu, provided you will accept one of my special brand." Kwo smiled wetly. "Colonel Toyon mentioned that we have this small vice in common." He proffered the box. *"S'il vous plaît."*

Cragg chose a jade-green corona. He sniffed appreciatively. It smelled like sound Havana, perhaps a residual Upmann, and he wondered how the general had come into possession of such a rare item. Still, Kwo was a man of broad-ranging interests, with friends to match. When a dictator acquired expensive tastes, he generally managed to pamper them, regardless of the trouble involved. So it was not impossible that Kwo's supply lines to Cuba had remained open, even under Castro.

The general used a gold lighter to light both cigars, first Cragg's, then his own. Cragg inhaled. It *was* an Upmann. Kwo's taste in women and tobacco passed the test.

"I brought a chart with me, Your Excellency, and a brief résumé. If you will permit me."

"Proceed, m'sieu."

Cragg spread the map across his bony knees and Kwo's fat ones. Then, referring occasionally to his handwritten notes, he began to outline the audacious plan upon which he had expended so much time, effort, and—the thought made him scowl —dwindling cash reserve. Acutely aware of the general's vagrant gaze and low attention span, Cragg kept his recital to the bare essentials.

Until the monsoon rains came in May, the Kong had pushed and plundered their way southward, along the matted jungle trails that wove in and out through *Les Montagnes Fantastiques.* But May was two months gone, and the rainforest defiles had become so mired that even the hill natives avoided the Crazy Mountains, as the Thiets' white advisers called them. Always, hitherto, this season of wild rains and sudden storms had been accepted as an annual act of providence by the GaiSong government. If the Kong couldn't maintain their overland supply lines, it was plausibly argued, they wouldn't be able to fight. Ergo: a welcome breather for the hardpressed Thiets, time to mend the barricades, to rebore the cannon, to recruit fresh troops.

But this year, regrettably, the Kong didn't cooperate. What had been mere suspicion in early June became a confirmed fact before the month ended, as coastwatchers reported unusually heavy offshore junk traffic along the route that curved southward from Communist Phom Than to the no man's land just above GaiSong, in the Dalagong River delta.

True, there had always been a certain amount of illicit shipping here, which the landbound Thiets seemed powerless to halt. Unloaded after dark, these contraband weapons vanished like the Kong themselves into a region of miasmic swamps and flooded rice paddies, inhabited mainly by peasants whose ties to GaiSong were tenuous at best, and more often than not a matter of outright defiance. Periodically, without much success, South Thietvanne's sampan navy launched forays into this impossible territory. But their range was limited, and their .30-calibre machineguns proved of scant use against the thick-planked junks. Nor was it deemed feasible to board the Kong ships, whose fierce crews outnumbered those of the largest patrol sampans by better than ten-to-one.

By July, when Cragg arrived in GaiSong, the pattern had been clearly established. The Kong were moving in recognizable convoys. As these convoys grew, first three, then five, then as many as a dozen vessels to each sea-train, the erstwhile dream of monsoon peace became a nightmare.

"You can't lick these bastards by hitting them after they've reached the delta," said Cragg.

Kwo's obsidian eyes narrowed behind the protective lenses. He smiled frostily. "What exactly do you propose in lieu of 'hitting these bastards' at the Dalagong mouth?"

Cragg touched the chart with his right forefinger, indicating the Kong capital, Phom Than, which lay about fifty miles above the dotted line that demarcated the two Thietvannes. "Here's their breeding ground, Your Excellency. An animal, *any* animal, is most vulnerable when it's mating. To put it another way, we should jump them while they're organizing their next convoy."

Colonel Toyon, who had been listening in immobile silence, suddenly remarked in a funereal tone: "Our intelligence believes it may total fifty ships."

"If that's the case," said Cragg, "once they leave Phom Than they'll be unstoppable by anything less than a Seventh Fleet destroyer division."

The general hefted his rum collins and gazed profoundly into the glass, as if it were a crystal ball.

"At last accounts," he said, "the American Seventh Fleet had sixty warships in the South China Sea. Whereas you, M'sieu Cragg-h, expect to accomplish your purpose with only two." Kwo's glistening face lost its false joviality. "*Two!*" he snorted. "An outdated motor torpedo boat and a Hong Kong junk."

Cragg exhaled a rich Havana smoke puff. It mushroomed for an instant in the dank air like an atomic cloud, until it was dissipated by a stray breeze.

"That," he said, "is the essence of the whole scheme. Even if you had enough ships for a full-scale offensive, Your Excellency, they'd never reach Phom Than without getting clobbered. Hell, the Kong haven't much air strength, but what close-range stuff they've got is pretty sharp. MIG fighters. Twin-engined Ilyushin bombers. They're just itching for a chance to play with their Russian toys."

"But your ships," Kwo taunted, "could achieve this miracle?"

Cragg hunched a bony shoulder. "I've never believed in fairies, Santa Claus or miracles. That's why I'm still here."

"You would enter Phom Than harbor with this mismatched pair," Kwo persisted in his heavily sarcastic voice, "and destroy the enemy's convoy?"

"That's the approximate idea, Your Excellency. The Germans got away with it at Scapa Flow in 1940, didn't they?"

Kwo slumped back in his chair and made an explosive sound that might have been laughter. "But, my friend, Captain Prien's lone submarine slipped into the British base without being seen. Beneath the surface."

"We can't submerge," Cragg conceded. "But we'll get into Phom Than."

"And like that U-boat," the general demanded incredulously, "you expect to return alive?"

"Is there any other way?"

Kwo ignored the sarcasm. With a grunt, he hoisted himself upright in the sagbottomed chair, planting his elbows squarely upon his outspread knees, so that his glistening face came level with Cragg's.

"Beyond all these questions of doubtful strategy, m'sieu, there is another issue entirely. Thietvanne has never engaged mercenaries to fight its wars."

"When the French were here," said Cragg, "they had the Foreign Legion."

Kwo snorted in disgust. "*Les Français!*"

"People fighting for their freedom usually accept whatever help is available," Cragg said. "Especially when their back's to the wall."

"The way the Spaniards accepted your Abraham Lincoln Brigade in the 1930s, I suppose?"

"More or less."

"But those men," said Kwo, "enlisted for a cause. For glory."

Cragg looked pensive. "In thirty years all the glory has gone out of war. I've seen it go. Haven't you?"

Remembering Dien Bien Phu, where he had lost many good friends among the ten thousand taken prisoner by the Vietminh, the general nodded. "True. There is no longer any glory. War has become only a business."

"Besides," asked Cragg, pressing his advantage, "what was Colonel Toyon doing in San Francisco last April—lining up lute players for a gamelan orchestra?"

"In Thietvanne terms, that was long ago." Kwo blinked his gelid eyes twice, very slowly. "And our treasury was much fatter."

"Does the price tag bother you?"

"Thirty thousand dollars," said the general, "is a large sum of money."

"It *was* thirty, Your Excellency, when Colonel Toyon made the first down payment. But inflation has set in. Also wear-and-tear. Now it's fifty thousand. But I'll throw in *Mohican.* It's all yours."

Cragg inspected Kwo's impassive countenance, as if testing the effect of his outrageous gambit. The oily face remained bland. Kwo said: "European mercenaries in the Congo, m'sieu, earn less than four hundred dollars per month."

"Plus seventeen-a-day when they're in rebel territory," said Cragg. "And their next-of-kin get twenty thousand dollars insurance. Posthumously."

"Colonel Toyon informs me that you are a bachelor," Kwo observed in his soft voice, "without any dependents."

"What about my crew?"

"Your crew—I believe they're called 'Cragg's Mafia'—seem to be equally unencumbered."

Cragg glanced sourly at the silent colonel. "He's compiled quite a dossier."

"I like all the facts," Kwo said comfortably, "before I make a decision."

"You get what you pay for," Cragg shrugged. "Nothing more."

"Nor less," amended the general, sitting up straighter in his chair. "However, Colonel Toyon tells me these fellows of yours are rather special. And that you, M'sieu Cragg-h, were a famous hero in the American war against the Japanese."

"Hardly," Cragg growled.

Kwo abruptly extended his fat right hand. "Shall we consider it done, my friend?"

Disbelieving, Cragg echoed, "Done, Your Excellency?"

"Done, m'sieu. Approved. Ratified. And now, as you would phrase it, let us 'shake' upon the arrangement."

Cragg took the general's soft moist palm in his own dry fist. It had been too goddamned easy, he thought, the way Quid Kwo capitulated after taking such elaborate pains to downgrade the strategy, the equipment, and the probable outcome of his wild scheme to invade Phom Than. However, now was hardly the time to probe Kwo's motives, beyond making damned certain there were no undeclared jokers hidden in the stacked deck. During the few weeks since Toyon visited him in Sausalito, not only the five thousand given him as an advance payment had gone down the tube, but almost five thousand more out of his own small hoard: flying the Mafia brethren to Hong Kong, buying the junk *Medusa,* and outfitting her for the beat southward to GaiSong. Yet beggars can't be choosers, Cragg told himself bitterly, particularly where mendicancy is a way of life.

"My terms are satisfactory?" asked Cragg, releasing the general's limp hand.

"You drive a hard bargain," Kwo acknowledged. "But we will not argue. Twenty-five thousand U.S. dollars now, including what you have already been paid. Another twenty-five thousand when you return." He emitted a froggy sound. "Alive!" Kwo gestured to his aide. "Give M'sieu Cragg-h the envelope, Quang."

The secretary thumbed the combination lock on his dispatch case, opened it, and drew out a bulky manila packet, which he thrust at Cragg. Then he added a second, thinner, envelope to the first.

"You may inspect them," offered the general, "if you wish."

Cragg inspected the bulging envelope casually. The currency was arranged in neat bundles of $100 bills, each with its original thousand dollar wrapper.

"Our handshake was adequate guarantee, Your Excellency."

Kwo smiled. "As further assurance for both of us, M'sieu Cragg-h, I have detailed Colonel Toyon to accompany your mission, as the government's official representative."

Cragg cast an inquiring look at the little Thiet officer, who appeared somewhat less than enchanted with his assignment. Yet the order plainly came as no surprise to him, for Toyon's only response was a philosophical half-shrug.

"Good to have you aboard, colonel," Cragg said reluctantly.

The general interceded. "After all, I hold Colonel Toyon responsible for many things, including his original suggestion to my predecessors that the Free Republic of Thietvanne should 'buy' armed assistance. And—" with a guttural laugh, "for overruling my doubts about this preposterous adventure. It seems only right, does it not, that the colonel should test the medicine he recommends so enthusiastically?"

Whatever enthusiasm Toyon felt for the project, thought Cragg, was kept under careful wraps. In fact, his evident distaste for joining the Mafia matched Cragg's own coolness at the prospect of accepting him as supercargo on a desperate expedition whose every member would have to pull his own weight, perhaps literally, before the goal was reached.

Cragg estimated Toyon's bandy-legged thinness. Dripping wet, he'd probably weigh less than a hundred pounds. But again, this was no time to start an argument. It was axiomatic among the GaiSong diplomatic corps that Quid Kwo never took a stance without good and sufficient purpose, even though his surface reasoning might seem illogical. If the general wanted a watchdog aboard *Mohican* or *Medusa,* so be it.

Suddenly Cragg pitied the scrawny little colonel, thinking of the beating he'd take when *Mohican* battered her eighty-foot hull against a frontal sea. Jeep-riding along a rutted Thiet trail in search of Kong guerrillas was kindergarten stuff by comparison.

"We can always use another expert hand, Your Excellency."

"True," Kwo said. "Your five men are not enough. You will need more. And Colonel Toyon's first duty will be to recruit them for you." The general sighed. "It has become increasingly difficult to find trustworthy supporters, M'sieu Cragg-h. Strangers to GaiSong can make grave mistakes, even fatal ones, in choosing their companions."

"You're very solicitous about my welfare," Cragg said.

"Your welfare is now our investment." Kwo stood up. "Incidentally, m'sieu, we have received word from Radio Dokoro that your ship, *Medusa,* refueled there four days ago. She should arrive at GaiSong tomorrow."

"Why wasn't I notified earlier?"

"Because," the general said in his enigmatic fashion, "we prefer to keep our information about coastal shipping movements secret. The Kong pay well for such intelligence.

"But *Medusa* is my ship!"

"Four days ago, M'sieu Cragg, I made a private decision to engage your services. Technically, therefore, she joined Thietvanne's navy on that date."

Before Cragg could shape another protest, Colonel Toyon broke his long silence.

"As soon as I dress, Mr. Cragg, I will take you back to the hotel. You would be most foolish to travel alone with all that money."

After the Sports Club's chlorine-scented heat, it was a luxurious pleasure to sprawl back against the soft leather seats of the Rolls Royce, and breathe the air-conditioned chill, while the uniformed driver maneuvered them adroitly through the traffic. He chose the long way home, Cragg noted, along the Dalagong River, rather than cutting directly across town. This brought them past the sampan slums, where generations came into being, lived, loved, then died after spawning new generations. In the early dusk, Cragg could make out the crimson glow of charcoal fires, a few of the ten thousand that burned in GaiSong, tended carefully in braziers on the wooden deck. Some of the sampan dwellers were bathing, a few fished, but most were merely passing time, staying alive, until night fell and they could lose themselves in slumber.

In the darkening countryside beyond the city, there would be millions of others crowding into their misnamed "fortified hamlets" after a day in the fields, with equally scant concern for what tomorrow might bring, other than the unvoiced hope of survival. In the current euphemism of the Thiet government, these areas had been "cleared," and the Kong brought under "control." But few believed this. Especially in the hamlets.

Cragg sighed. Not that it mattered a tinker's dam. But as a professional, he hated to see failure compounded.

On the far side of the commodious backseat, Colonel Toyon remained quiet, as if lost in his own mournful thoughts. He hadn't spoken a word since ushering Cragg into the car. Now they were approaching the hotel by way of the tree-shrouded boulevard that extended from the waterfront to the municipal park where the soldiers had gathered earlier.

Cragg interrupted his reverie.

"You told General Kwo that my men weren't concerned about their next-of-kin," he said. "What about yours, colonel, since you've also been elected for this job?"

Without turning his head Toyon replied in a dead voice: "My wife and daughter were killed last summer in a Kong ambush five miles outside of GaiSong, when they were returning from a swimming party. Like you, Mr. Cragg, I am quite alone."

"Sorry."

The colonel did not speak again until the Rolls halted in front of the Galleon. Then he said curtly: "I shall meet you in the lobby at seven o'clock in the morning, and we will set about assembling a crew."

"Thanks," Cragg muttered, as the car door slammed shut.

He limped into the hotel with the manila envelope clutched

beneath his crooked arm, bid good evening to the perpetually grinning desk clerk, and took the elevator to the penthouse bar. The sun was damned well over the yard arm. It was time for a whisky. Several, in fact, because when *Medusa* arrived, he would have to go on the wagon as a stern example for the Mafia's drinking set, Lars Torgerson in particular. Once the crazy Swede started boozing, he became a devil, a threat to anyone who crossed him, and a downright menace to navigation.

The Galleon's top-floor saloon was called the Poopdeck, an unlovely name that dated back to the American occupation. But the sobriquet had stuck, thanks to the continuing patronage of well-heeled Yankee traders, Seventh Fleet drop-ins, and itinerant entrepreneurs like Cragg himself. Tonight the bar was jammed, as usual, with male and female vultures, hovering around the fringes while Thietvanne lay dying. They had a splendid vista of the wounded country from this twelfth-story perch, through plate glass windows spanning all four sides. On a clear day they could see smoke puffs from mortar fire in the brushlands beyond the city limits, and at night the artillery bursts made a nice effect.

Cragg ordered a scotch-on-the-rocks with a lemon twist.

After it came, he toyed moodily with his drink, jabbing at the peel with his swizzle stick, watching the ice slowly melt, as he ruminated upon his curious dialogue with General Kwo. From somewhere Cragg recalled that this was the Year of the Dragon in Thietvanne. Last year it had been the Wolf. Next would be the Pig. There was a lesson, he supposed, in this neat bit of escalation: first the sly wolf, then the firebreathing dragon, and after that the carrion swine, rooting what they could out of their thirty percent investments before they fled to Paris by way of their Zurich banks. He wondered idly, then, how Colonel Toyon stayed so goddamned thin among all this easy loot.

When the second drink arrived, unconsciously aping General Kwo's earlier gesture, Cragg held it aloft and peered through the amber liquid, toward the aircraft warning beacon that revolved atop the Government House. Nobody ever shut off the lights in GaiSong. After all, the real war wasn't yet being fought in these streets, and the Kong had no planes capable of raiding the city. So why make life unnecessarily miserable. *Hein?*

Cragg decided to get drunk.

He had plenty of time. KoKo didn't do her striptease at Le Coq d'Or until twelve, and he'd be damned if he'd sit around a sleazy nightclub all night, inhaling stale tobacco smoke, having his ears assaulted by rock-and-roll music, and all the while fending off Le Coq's importunate bargirls. KoKo was billed as the Flower Girl. A red rose, clutched between her teeth, comprised her ultimate costume. Le Coq d'Or, whose inappropriate name provoked much ribaldry among its male clientele, was another legacy of the departed Americans, who had left behind *le jazz* and *le striptease*. An earlier administration had tried repressive moralism as a substitute for national morale. But it hadn't worked. Under General Kwo there were no holds barred. Literally.

By ten P.M., however, solitary drinking began to pall. So Cragg signed the chit and went back down to the street-level café for a ham sandwich and a cup of rotgut French coffee. Partially sobered, he stopped at the front desk to have the clerk lock his money-filled envelope in the safe, before going to Le Coq d'Or.

"Don't they ever give you a night off?" Cragg asked.

The desk clerk shrugged. "It is my own choice, m'sieu. When one has a large family to support. . . ." He hefted the envelope appraisingly, as if to evaluate the contents, in a manner that left little doubt that he guessed what was in it. "Does monsieur wish a receipt?"

"Would it serve any useful purpose?"

"No." The desk clerk grinned slyly. "If I were a dishonest man, a receipt would not matter. I would simply take your money and vanish."

"But sometimes it pays to be honest, doesn't it?" suggested Cragg.

"Sometimes, m'sieu."

Cragg tossed him a mock salute. "Then we understand each other, my friend."

"*Vraiment,*" agreed the desk clerk, "we do. In many ways. You will be at the usual place?"

"Check."

"And later, perhaps, you wish supper served in your room?"
The desk clerk paused. "À deux?"

"Okay."

Annoyed by the desk clerk's bland assumption, feeling somewhat hemmed in, Cragg left the hotel. It was pleasant outside,
after the overripe atmosphere of the Poopdeck and the coffee
shop. So he decided to walk the dozen blocks to Le Coq d'Or.
When he got there, the floorshow had already started, and a
bottle of scotch, ice, and two glasses were on the table they
always saved for him in a far corner of the room, beneath a fake
palm tree.

Cragg poured himself a stiff drink, lighted a cigar, and tried to
ignore the Cockney emcee's cornball bawdiness. Having seen the
show more than twenty times in the past month, he could
anticipate every dirty line. Moreover, the emcee was a determined master of the single entendre, and his act didn't improve
with age.

Shortly before KoKo was scheduled to appear, the maître-
d'hôtel threaded his way among the postage-stamp tables to
where Cragg sat, bearing obsequious word that a lady desired to
speak with him.

"Did she give a name?" Cragg asked, not really caring, since he
had never bothered to learn the identity of the casual women
he'd encountered in GaiSong, other than KoKo herself.

"Mlle. Denise Legére."

"I don't know her."

"Shall I say you are not here, m'sieu?"

"But somebody has obviously told her that I am."

"Doubtless."

"What the hell. It might help shorten the war. Send her along."

The maître-d' bowed and departed. Cragg took another swal-
low of scotch. Then he turned his attention toward the wide
entrance. Several unattached women sauntered into the twilit
room, surveying the scene boldly, and found vacant chairs either
at the bar or at the minuscule tables. They were *vraies Gai-*

Songeuses, svelte, coiffeured, Eurasian. But they weren't searching for him.

Finally, after minutes had elapsed, Cragg saw her. She entered the room hesitantly, as if she didn't belong there, and stood near the archway for several moments. Cragg stared incredulously when the maître-d' pointed in his direction.

Even from that distance and in that dim light, Mlle. Legére looked very young, very small, and very dowdy. Nor did this initial impression improve as she drew nearer. Cragg regarded her with undisguised contempt. She was wearing a duncolored dress, cut like an old-fashioned linen duster, which did nothing to lessen her plainness, and she was carrying a leather shoulder-strap bag. Closer scrutiny confirmed that Mlle. Legére also wore black cotton hose and scuffed brown boots that reached halfway to her hidden knees.

If this appalling churchmouse was seeking companionship, Cragg told himself bitterly, she had crept into the wrong pew.

Mlle. Legére halted beside him.

"You *are* M'sieu Cragg?'" she asked timidly.

"On advice of counsel—" he began, then stopped. She wouldn't understand, anyway. "Guilty."

Mlle. Legére slipped into the booth alongside him, primly smoothing the drab skirt over her knees. She sat quite still, watching him. Her unrouged lips parted in a tentative way, as if she had meant to say something but thought better of it.

Cragg said, "Whisky? Cognac? Martini?"

"Tea, if you please."

"Straight?"

"I beg your pardon, m'sieu?"

"Skip it." He summoned the waiter, relayed her order, and instructed him that tea actually meant *tea* in this odd instance. "What brought you here?"

"I went to your hotel, and the man at the desk informed me that you often come to this place."

"The bastard talks too much."

Mlle. Legére seemed unruffled. "Please do not blame him. I told the man it was a matter of utmost urgency to the mission."

"Mission?"

"Dokoro Mission," she explained. "They say you are taking a ship there. I wish to accompany you."

"Who says I'm going to Dokoro?" Cragg growled.

Mlle. Legére's right shoulder raised in a Gallic shrug. "One hears many things in GaiSong."

"Specify."

"Colonel Toyon, whom I have known for many years, told me that he has begun to enlist a crew for your ship, m'sieu. He suggested that I speak with you."

The waiter's sudden appearance with the tea forced Cragg to contain his angry reaction to this breach of security. He paused while the service was arranged, and until Mlle. Legére had poured herself a steaming cupful. She lifted it to her lips, regarding him steadfastly across the rim, waiting for him to speak.

Cragg studied her for a moment. Mlle. Legére set the cup down. He saw that her right hand was deeply tanned. It looked very capable. And so, he realized, did her small chin, which the girl held resolutely high as she returned his candid stare. It wasn't a bad chin, really, albeit a trifle too square for Cragg's taste. Long ago he had learned that you could squander an inordinate amount of time and effort on women with determined chins, without accomplishing anything very constructive. He didn't suppose, either, that stubborn Frenchwomen behaved much differently from their American counterparts.

Cragg said mildly: "Assuming your information is correct, this won't be a holiday cruise for female schoolteachers."

Mlle. Legére's eyes widened. They were a smoky blue, he noted, the color of beach glass that has been tumbled countless times against tidal sands, then tempered by the sun.

"How did you know I teach school?"

"Sheer genius," Cragg admitted. "It had to be that. Or else playing nurse at the mission hospital."

"But I am not a tourist, m'sieu. And it is most urgent that I return to Dokoro." She moved closer, and her low-pitched voice took on a pleading quality. "Last Monday I came to GaiSong on the shuttle plane to buy medical supplies. Since then the Kong guerrillas have rendered it impossible, with their mortar fire, to land at the mission airstrip."

"Can't Colonel Toyon help you?" Cragg asked. "He seems to be a good friend."

"Colonel Toyon assisted me in procuring the medicines," Mlle. Legére said, "but he cannot arrange for their shipment."

"Then why pick on me? Why not try your luck with the regular supply junks? They travel up the coast all the time."

"Nothing has reached Dokoro for eight days, m'sieu. It has been declared an active combat zone by the government. The junks no longer put in there."

Cragg regarded the girl's earnest, upturned face while he considered her last statement. An essential phase of his plan hinged upon replenishing their basic supplies at the mission enroute to Phom Than. If Dokoro was in trouble, so were the Mafia. Although they could always live off the land, where food was concerned, oil to keep *Mohican* going would be unavailable elsewhere, short of Phom Than itself. Yet General Kwo had made no mention of any unusual developments at Dokoro.

"For a schoolmarm," he opined bleakly, "you run a damned efficient intelligence network."

Whatever reply Mlle. Legére intended for this remark was lost in the fanfare that signaled the grand entrance of the Flower Girl. While the off-key piano, bass fiddle and electric guitar played their version of Minsky drag, KoKo performed her dance. It was a simple bit of terpsichore, entirely ritual, which brought the girl to her ecdysiastic climax in less than ten minutes. But it sufficed. The Coq d'Or resounded to masculine applause as KoKo stood tall and straight in the muted spotlight, arms outstretched, dark aureoled breasts heaving, sweat glistening on her shaven torso, as if she were lashed against an invisible crucifix.

Cragg had continued to smoke stolidly during the brief act. He did not clap when it ended.

"You do not appreciate this dance?" Mlle. Legére observed him with almost clinical interest. "The others find it quite exciting."

"I've caught it before," Cragg said, "twenty-seven bloody times."

"She is a very beautiful woman."

"Obviously."

"Do you know her well?"

Cragg drew deeply on his cigar, exhaled, and gave Mlle. Legére an ironic glance through the billowing smokecloud. "Why not ask the desk clerk that question, too?"

Suddenly the girl seemed embarrassed by her own presumption. She fumbled with the handle of her teacup, half-raised it to her lips, and set it down again. "*Pardon*, m'sieu. I am being unspeakably rude."

Cragg smiled fleetingly. "As a matter of fact, the lovely lady will be here damned soon herself. Maybe you can get the answer firsthand."

"It was a stupid question," protested Mlle. Legére. "Now you are making sport of me."

When KoKo arrived a few minutes later, Cragg introduced Mlle. Legére as an acquaintance from upcountry. KoKo gave the French girl a shrewd appraisal. Then, finding nothing to arouse her competitive instincts, she chose a seat between them on the semicircular banquette.

"Scotch, Cragg."

"Naturally," he said with elaborate emphasis. "Isn't it always?"

"Always," KoKo agreed complacently. She loosened the silk peignoir which was adhering to her moist body, and fanned her uncovered breasts. From her belt she drew the symbolic rose. "Here is your reward."

Cragg accepted it indifferently, and tossed it toward Mlle. Legére. "A souvenir," he said, "of a wild night on the town."

His studied disinterest sparked KoKo to sudden wrath. Pushing back the table, she stood up, and trod viciously on Cragg's right instep with a spiked heel as she drew free.

"Goddamn you, Cragg!"

"You're repeating yourself, *chéri*. That's what you said this afternoon."

"Go to hell!"

Without a backward glance KoKo stalked off toward her dressing room. Cragg watched her go, shaking his head in mock sorrow, while he massaged his bruised foot.

"Does that answer your question?"

Mlle. Legére nodded in amazement. "Truly, she must be a very old friend, m'sieu, to fly into such a rage over nothing."

"KoKo's an artist." He laughed. "That gives her a license to be crazy."

"Perhaps if I were more like this woman," Mlle. Legére began, then stopped, leaving the cryptic sentence unfinished.

Cragg looked at his watch. "It's damned near twelve-thirty. She won't come back." Yielding to a whim that surprised him, even as he voiced it, he added: "Why not join me for dinner?"

"There are no cafés open in GaiSong at this hour."

"I've got a champagne supper for two waiting at the hotel."

"Oh." Mlle. Legére regarded him with great solemnity, biting her lower lip, before she asked in a low voice: "Is it permitted?"

"Among old friends," said Cragg, ironically, "the Galleon permits almost anything."

"I see." The girl looked down at her worn boots, then up at Cragg, as if she also were caught off guard by some sudden caprice. "It would be a disappointment for you to dine alone after having made such careful arrangements. N'est-ce pas? I accept your gracious invitation, m'sieu."

His enthusiasm had already waned. "Eating alone never bothers me."

"But the champagne?" she chided. "One cannot toast oneself." She paused. "Besides, I have not eaten all night, searching for you. I am quite hungry."

"Okay," he said ungallantly. "Let's roll."

At her insistence they stopped first at the small *pension* where Mlle. Legére was staying, two blocks from the Galleon. Cragg had to wait in the cabbage-smelling parlor while she repaired her *toilette*. The absurdity of what he was doing, and the grim prospect of spending several hours with this pathetic church-mouse, had put him in a vile temper by the time she reappeared twenty minutes later.

Cragg was more irritated than pleased to discover that she had made an effort to relieve her drab attire, and to do something about her equally plain face. She was wearing a necklace of twisted coral, and a pair of gold earrings. Had he been less annoyed, he might have been touched by the sight of these trifling adornments which underlined, rather than mitigated, the dowdiness of her travel-stained costume. The simple beads did, nevertheless, draw attention to the undeniable truth that Mlle. Legére's neck was proudly arched, and delicately shaped. Her ears were set close to her head, the way he liked them. She had tinted her lips with a pale pink rouge.

Cragg had to concede that the overall effect was an improvement. Mlle. Legére could pass muster in a crowd. As she took his arm, he caught the aroma of a subtle perfume.

For once the desk clerk was neglecting his sentry duties, dozing behind the marble-topped counter, when Cragg escorted Mlle. Legére into the deserted lobby. It was necessary to awaken him.

Anticipating the man's surprise, Cragg explained: "KoKo made other plans. So I've invited another guest."

The desk clerk recovered quickly. "The Galleon is most honored, Mlle. Legére." He bowed. "I trust you will find the supper to your liking."

"Thank you."

"Everything has been prepared exactly as you ordered, M'sieu Cragg."

"Good."

After the elevator door closed behind them, Cragg demanded: "Did this fellow know your name when you came here earlier?"

"No."

Cragg scowled. "He's a goddamned nosey bastard."

"Hotel clerks in GaiSong have many sources of information. Moreover, it would not have been difficult for him to learn the identity of a visitor from Dokoro."

"But why the hell should he care?"

"Perhaps," she suggested in a demure tone, "he is attending to the interests of Mlle. KoKo."

Cragg glanced at her sharply. But the girl's face was a picture of innocence. "Here's seven," he growled. "It's where we bail out."

As the desk clerk had promised, everything seemed in readiness for a proper tête-à-tête. There was a magnum of noble vintage Mumm's icing in a silver bucket. The napery that swathed the card table was patched in a few places, but it was the best the Galleon could offer. When the copper warming shells were removed, the broiled partridges looked succulent, and not really as akin to GaiSong pigeon as Cragg had feared. Three slim tapers, set in an ornate candelabra, tempered the gloom, and for the moment the room had lost its air of stark impersonality.

Cragg was pleased to discover that the villainous brown habit that he had assumed to be Mlle. Legére's dress was actually a sort of duster, which she discarded once they entered the hot little chamber. Beneath it she wore a tan linen skirt and a white silk blouse. If not fashioned by Dior, these at least complimented her slim figure. He supposed the girl's unprepossessing outer garment also served as protective coloration, like a chameleon's, to safeguard her against the perils of a hostile jungle. Or even the more intrusive menace of GaiSong's backstreets.

While Cragg busied himself uncorking the wine, she tuned his transistor radio to the all-night music-and-news station. The saccharine outpouring drowned out the whir of the air-conditioner.

Cragg poured champagne into the longstemmed goblets and handed one of them to Mlle. Legére.

"Cheers," he said.

The girl touched the rim of his glass with hers. "I shall drink," she said, "to your charity."

"What do you mean?"

"To your benevolence in accepting me aboard your ship," she amended.

"You'd better sit down," said Cragg, "while I put you straight on a few things."

Without comment, Mlle. Legére took her place opposite him at the table, and sampled the partridge. It was obvious that she was genuinely hungry. Cragg allowed her to eat in silence for several minutes before he spoke again.

"What makes you think I'd waste valuable cargo space on a woman?"

Mlle. Legére opened the battered purse which she had slung across her chair. She laid a crumpled roll of Thiet currency on the tabletop. "Here are seven thousand piastres," she said. "They are worth a hundred American dollars. Would they not compensate for that cargo space?"

"Even if I were running a passenger service, which I'm not, it wouldn't be enough."

"It's all I have, m'sieu."

"Seven thousand piastres might pay for the cubic footage you'd occupy, and for the food you'd consume, but not for the trouble you'd cause." He gave her a deprecating grin. "You see, we don't carry separate facilities for women, either in *Mohican* or *Medusa*."

"So!" she exclaimed. "You have not one, but two ships, m'sieu!"

"Both of them full."

"But—"

Cragg thrust the banknotes back into her open purse. "You've also been assuming that I'm going to Dokoro. Why should I risk it if other civilian crews won't?"

"Because you are not a civilian," said Mlle. Legére. "You are working for Thietvanne."

"More gossip from Colonel Toyon?"

"It is a fact, *n'est-ce pas?*"

"Okay," Cragg agreed. "We'll stipulate. I'm one of General Kwo's hired hands. A mercenary. And that's all the more reason why I can't haul passengers. This is going to be a goddamned rough party. Toyon's enough deadwood. I don't need any more."

Mlle. Legére took a sip of champagne. Her smokeblue eyes watched him unswervingly. Finally she said: "Since I was a little girl I have traveled to Dokoro many times by sea. I know the coast better than I know the streets of GaiSong. Truly, you need me."

"Like I need a hole in the head," he snorted. "Which is what I'd damned well have if I took you along."

Mlle. Legére leaned toward him across the narrow table. The gesture caused her breasts to strain against the thin silk of her blouse. Cragg viewed them appreciatively.

"I am qualified for anything, m'sieu."

"That covers a multitude," he said, "of sins."

She straightened in the chair, flushing, but there was no retreat in her expression.

"Possibly," she murmured, "if I were more like Mlle. KoKo.
. . ."

Cragg laughed. "That's a hell of a quaint notion. But what you
don't get through your noggin is that once we leave GaiSong it's
goodbye to fun and games. Everybody works."

"I have always worked, m'sieu."

"At what, *bébé?*"

"I have already told you," she said patiently. "My father directs
the hospital. My mother supervises the nursing staff. I assist
them. And I teach in the mission school."

"Can you cook?" Cragg asked.

"Yes. And I can catch the fish that must be cooked. Further-
more, I can mend your sails, and if there should be shooting, I
can also be of use."

"Firing an M-14 rifle?"

"No, m'sieu. I have never learned to handle weapons. But I
have had much experience with the wounded." Mlle. Legére's
face was grave as she added: "At Dokoro we treat many persons
for injuries from poisoned stakes that cut through their shoes,
and those who have been shot from ambush. Their numbers
grow. That is why I came to GaiSong for medical supplies."

Cragg rewarded her with an ironic grin. "Maybe you do have
hidden talents." Again he caught the sweet aroma from her
sweptback hair, fragile as the girl herself, as she pressed forward
once more, beseeching his consent.

"You will take me?"

"Christ!" He pounded the table with his clenched fist, hard
enough to make the champagne goblets jump. "Give a man time
to think!"

"Yes, m'sieu," she said meekly.

"See me tomorrow," he roared. "Maybe the hangover will
soften my brain. Maybe I'll go stark raving mad and say Yes."

Mlle. Legére arose. She put on her linen duster, slipped the
purse containing the rejected money over her left shoulder, and
stood motionless for an instant, staring down into his angry face.

"Believe me, M'sieu Cragg, you would not regret it."

Cragg said nothing. He watched morosely as she made her
way to the door, with her head held high, stepping gracefully in

her ridiculous boots. After she had gone, he remained seated at the table, scowling at the half-eaten food, and muttering small impotent curses. There were certain days when Cragg knew that his luck could not fail him, that he would live forever. But this was not one of them.

Then he got up, limped to the desk, opened the lower drawer, and pulled out a bottle of scotch.

As Mlle. Legére had said, it made no sense to drink champagne alone.

2

"We All Have
a Beached Look"

ALTHOUGH IT WAS Cragg's turn to play host that spring, the Mafia convened under circumstances quite unlike those that surrounded any of their nineteen previous reunions.

For one thing, there was the cryptic navalese telegram which Cragg had sent to each of them: "Big Deal Cooking on Front Burner. Volunteers Needed for Extra-Hazardous Duty involving Foreign Travel. Addressees of This Dispatch Are Hereby Designated Same."

For another, there was the news that Cragg had somehow managed to come into possession of an authentic World War II vintage PT boat, named *Mohican II*.

Under ordinary conditions, they would camp in the barren little three-room flat over Cragg's fishbait-and-tackle shop that stood on pilings above the landlocked waters of San Francisco Bay, consume a prodigious quantity of liquor, grill the fish they caught off the pier, sleep on surplus Army cots when the infrequent need arose, then wake up refreshed and ready to damn the world's eyeballs all over again.

The Mafia was a sort of Last Man's Club. Originally, disregarding expense and distance, they had flocked together from every part of the country. Places like Fort Smith, Ark., Springfield, Mo., Amarillo, Tex., Walla Walla, Wash., McCloud, Minn., and even Machias, Me. There had been eleven of them, at first, the full crew of Lieutenant (junior grade) Frederick Peter Cragg's PT 387. Then attrition set in. Now only five were left, including Cragg, who continued over the years to be the Mafia's *de facto* chieftain. If he'd stayed in the Navy, as everybody had expected, Cragg would be a four-striper by now, they reasoned, and therefore outrank the hell out of them.

But Cragg hadn't stayed in.

For a man who had survived four years of almost constant action in the South Pacific, the Philippines, and the Ryukyus, with a Navy Cross and three Purple Hearts to prove it, peacetime duty seemed unbearably tame. Cragg wrestled with shoreside red-tape for eighteen months, before he liquidated his naval career and pocketed $3,000 in combined leave and separation pay.

At twenty-four, he enrolled at Berkeley under the G.I. Bill, intending to complete his interrupted college education. But mainly he majored in poker, minored in crapshooting, cursed the gimp knee and elbow that kept him out of football, and watched his grades steadily decline. When the mood seized him, he would rent a sailboat and spend a solitary day duelling with the great bay's tricky winds and crosscurrents.

After one of these excursions Cragg quietly packed his belongings in a duffelbag, and exited from the dormitory with the merest handflip in the direction of his cramming roommates. He limped across campus to the interurban depot and caught the bus for San Francisco, where he checked into the Mark Hopkins. He had never before stopped at a luxury hotel. The impulse to do so now struck him suddenly, just as the bus reached the apex of the Bay Bridge's soaring span, and he saw the fabled towers of the city burst into view, silhouetted against the dying sun.

The room cost him twenty dollars a day. But it was worth the price, thinking how Pop Cragg would roar and hoot and slap his skinny thighs at the thought of a saloonkeeper's kid hobnobbing with all those rich bastards at the Mark, if he were still alive. But Pop had died in 1943, a month after his son went overseas, so he never saw his son's Navy Cross or the Purple Hearts. These would also have pleased the little Dane, who had doubled as bouncer at his saloon, even though he weighed less than 145 pounds with a full whisky bottle brandished in each fist.

Cragg inherited his own peculiar brand of independence from this rugged old warrior, who let it be known that he feared neither God, Man, nor the Devil, in whichever order you chose.

Despite their conformity in this regard, however, Cragg and his father were vastly different in another non-physical way. Cragg was a drifter, whereas the old man stayed resolutely *put*, immovable, in his dank little Mission Street saloon. Pop Cragg had a curious set of values, which apparently satisfied his meager needs. Despite his inarticulateness, he managed to get the idea across to the boy who seemed so loath to assay his own "values" (whatever in hell *they* were) and who was so unconcerned, or unaware, that he lacked something, a compass, a rudder, which might change him from a drifter into a purposeful mover.

Pop Cragg wore no man's yoke.

True, he'd married a tall, strapping, black-haired girl whose antecedents dated back to the Spaniards who explored the California coast. Once in a while he granted her the privilege of bossing him around the hamburger joint that replaced the saloon when Prohibition was decreed. But not often. After Repeal, with the bar reestablished, Pop Cragg took complete command, leaving his wife free to devote her full attention to bringing up their sole son and heir. Then, shortly after the boy's thirteenth birthday in 1935, she died during a flash epidemic of Asiatic flu. Young Cragg's inheritance from his mother, like the legacy of independence he later received from the old man himself, was something that could not be probated. She gave him her splendid physique, her dark features, her governable temper, and her ancestral love for the sea.

By the time Cragg reached high school he had developed a fierce competitiveness, which he vented by playing football with youngsters half-again his weight. Cragg liked bodily contact sports. And he soon learned that mere heft wasn't the answer to superiority on the field. There were certain tricks of the trade which counterbalanced one's lack of pounds, if a fellow was both quick and clever. What the referee didn't see, didn't count. Nor was this considered cheating, under the ground rules that prevailed south of Market Street, where only the fittest survived.

So Cragg ran with the gang, hot-rodding along the back streets in an old Model A he'd wrangled from an automotive junkman, flouting the cops, jeering when authoritarian adults described the bleak future that awaited him and his whole disorderly crew. Yet Cragg broke no *big* laws. He simply disregarded the niggling small ones, the social regulations which he viewed as the component parts of a vast straitjacket.

Nevertheless, to the amazement of his teachers, Cragg passed all his subjects and entered the state university. He endured college for two years, enough to qualify him for naval officer-training when the war started, but not enough to give him the foggiest notion of what he wanted to do after he earned his degree.

Cragg was more contented in the Navy than he had ever been before. Even the stern discipline imposed during the basic ninety-day-wonder period at Northwestern, and later at PT school on Narragansett Bay, appealed to him.

For the first time it made sense to take orders. When he got to the Solomons, Cragg ran what navy men like to call a taut ship, demanding absolute obedience from his men, while giving them a full measure of justice in return. Off duty he was their egalitarian comrade, helping to scrounge torpedo alcohol for illegal celebrations, and otherwise making it plain he was a commoner at heart.

Together Cragg and his men helped write a brief, brave chapter of naval history. In the process, they came to love their eighty-foot plywood boat, as one comes to love an exotic foreign car despite its many idiosyncrasies, or an uncomfortable home with a breathtaking view. Even during the final months of the Guadalcanal campaign, when the boat was vermin-ridden and battle weary, they regarded her as a thing of great beauty, confident that she could still deliver a torpedo attack at forty knots ("faster when goosed").

Before it was over, Cragg's Mafia had fought at Guadalcanal, New Georgia, Bougainville, Leyte Gulf and Okinawa. They won a Presidential Citation as part of a squadron that helped derail the Tokyo Express. They picked up another for their role in the desperate drama of Surigao Straits, when the Nips roared down upon an obsolete American fleet with a superior force of battleships and cruisers. Three crewmen received Silver Stars, five got Bronze Stars, all of them achieved Purple Heart distinction. And Cragg himself was personally awarded a Navy Cross by a tired admiral who had debated at some length whether a court-martial wouldn't be more appropriate, considering the Mafia's notorious habit of going it alone rather than in consort, as the Good Book required.

After V-J Day, while they were hanging around Okinawa and gloating over their plethora of separation points, Cragg's Mafia used to speculate what a magnificent idea it would be to purchase a surplus PT boat from the grateful government, and set up shop for themselves. They could hire out on a charter job. Or fish. Or hunt for treasure. Or, they exulted, latch onto some nice little private gook war and show the natives how *real* sailors operated.

But the fantasy lasted only long enough for the Mafia to reach San Francisco, telephone home, and scatter to the four corners of a vast country that found itself suddenly, hectically, at peace. At their first reunions they recalled the dream, and indulged themselves in a brief moment of nostalgia for what might have been. But it was soon forgotten. . . .

. . . Cragg had stayed at the Mark Hopkins for three weeks, reveling in the luxury of breakfasts in bed, dining at elegant establishments like Ernie's and Amilio's, getting quietly drunk when the mood seized him, and walking off his hangovers in the brisk morning air.

It was late June. San Francisco is always lovely in June after the fog lifts around ten A.M., leaving the skies wine-clear except along the seaward horizon where the cloudbanks muster while awaiting another nightfall. Out of his window facing the harbor, Cragg could see the big, white Pacific liners detach themselves from their piers, swing into midstream, then head slowly toward the Golden Gate, passing the homebound vessels as they departed. Occasionally a gray warship, her repairs completed at Mare Island or Hunter's Point, would ease silently past the Embarcadero and stride west, with a gathering bone in her teeth, like a lean watchdog on the spoor of an intruder. And always, among these naval and pleasure craft, there steamed the workaday freighters and tankers, deep-laden for their foreign missions, which had suddenly assumed a new significance in that early summer of 1950 when the North Korean Communists had struck across the 38th parallel.

One afternoon, having arisen very late, Cragg showered, shaved with extra care, donned his newest sports jacket and flannel slacks, and went down to the Navy recruiting office at Civic Center. In his lapel, for the first time, he wore the tiny blue-and-white enameled bar that signified the Navy Cross. As he approached the duty officer's desk, Cragg took special pains to minimize his limp, and he kept his left thumb hooked in his coat pocket while he shook hands.

"I want to sign up," he said.

The two-striper, whose own service ribbons testified more to stateside longevity than to combat bravery, eyed Cragg's Navy Cross emblem with undisguised respect.

"Is your commission still active?"

Cragg shook his head. "I stayed in service for eighteen months after the war," he said. "But when I got out, I sort of let things lapse." He grimaced. "Hell, lieutenant, you know how it is. They send you a lot of papers, and sometimes you forget."

"It shouldn't matter," the two-striper soothed. "Not when you've got a Navy Cross in your record."

"*Muchas gracias.*"

"Bring your records around tomorrow," the recruiting officer said. "Meanwhile we'll run you through a quick physical."

Cragg did his best with the navy medic. But once he had stripped down, and stood naked under the doctor's cold professional stare, the unhappy outcome was never in doubt.

"Can you run on that leg, Mr. Cragg?"

"Sure."

"Let's give it a whirl."

Cragg stepped briskly across the linoleum floor, sweating despite the room's clammy chill in a valiant effort to unhinge the locked knee. It didn't work. The doctor looked thoughtful. Perhaps, he suggested, the Bureau of Naval Personnel would waive this infirmity and ignore the crooked arm, if Cragg didn't mind a shore billet.

"No thanks, doc." Cragg remembered the landlocked two-striper parked on his widening backside out in the reception hall. "It's sea duty or nothing."

So it was nothing.

Oblivious to the five P.M. fog that was beginning to roll down Lombard Street as he left the recruiting depot, Cragg punished his treacherous leg by slogging all the way back to the hotel. He was bone-weary by the time he'd finished the twenty-block hike. And that night he spent almost two hundred dollars on a riotous tour of the North Beach dives, winding up in an Italian cathouse where the girls said a prayer for him after he drunkenly told them about his troubles.

Next morning Cragg discovered that he had less than ninety dollars left out of his original stake. Since it was only Thursday, and he'd been paying by the week, this was just enough to clear his hotel bill and leave four bits for the bellhop who wrestled his duffelbag downstairs.

"Check my gear," Cragg said. "I'll come back for it later."

Then he dragged his gimp leg uptown again to Civic Center, made an application for a G.I. business loan, and took a job slinging hash until the Veterans' Administration could process his claim. For seven weeks he lived in a Turk Street fleabag while the bureaucratic wheels ground slowly. At this crucial juncture, the Mafia showed its mettle by providing written assurances concerning the character, integrity and know-how of one Frederick Peter Cragg, former naval person, who was seeking a few thousand inconsequential dollars so that he could buy a small fishbait-and-tackle shop in Sausalito, Calif., which he had spotted for sale during a random prowl of the lower Bay.

Eventually the check arrived.

Cragg moved into the minuscule apartment above the store, acquired a few sticks of furniture, and began savoring the kind of life he'd dreamed about since he was a kid. At first it was pleasant, and immensely satisfying, to accommodate the sport-fishing trade during the long bright days. When night came, he would generally hit the sack and lie there smoking a good cigar, reading history, and listening to the waves slapping against the barnacled pilings. Except for the presence of an occasional woman who'd stay with him for a while, cooking his meals and darning his socks, until the arrangement assumed such a comfortably enduring aspect that he was forced to breach their unspoken contract, he lived alone. These liaisons always ended in that fashion.

After he managed the down payment on a diesel-powered tuna clipper in which he often traveled alone, far beyond the Farallones, Cragg was away more often than he was home. For a week at a time a flyspecked *Gone Fishing* sign would dangle from the knob of his store's sagging front door, while trade went to hell. He couldn't have cared less.

Cragg deliberately courted storms. At the shop, his shortwave radio remained tuned to the marine weather station. When word came that the Beaufort scale indicator was climbing from a gentle breezy three toward a spine-tingling six or more, he'd reach for the *Gone Fishing* sign. At twenty-five knots, the wind would be whipping the open sea between the Gate and the Farallones into foam-crested waves, after which would come the heaving slag mountains and the cutting spindrift. Cragg's wharfside neighbors, who figured he must have lost a few marbles in the war, tapped their skulls knowingly whenever he prepared his craft for another one of these solitary expeditions. They even invented a permanent "ghoul pool," subscribing five dollars apiece, with the pot earmarked for the man whose guess came closest to the sad hour when Cragg didn't return from one of these idiotic adventures.

But their money-backed forebodings left him as unmoved as their earlier concern for his cavalier business habits.

In the summer of his fourth year as a charter man Cragg stumbled one morning upon an advertisement in the *Chronicle*, listing a refurbished PT boat for sale. It had been the prized possession of a wealthy sportsman from Pebble Beach, now dead, whose estate wanted to unfreeze this anachronistic floating asset. Called *Mohican*, it was on display at the Monterey Yacht Club. Price: $20,000.

More out of curiosity than with any real intention of buying the craft, Cragg drove down one afternoon to the beautiful little community in his Morgan for a first-hand look. It seemed incredible to him that any authentic PTs remained after all these years. Most of the World War II types had been burned on the distant Pacific beaches, after having been cannibalized of their useful gear. A PT is too transient and fragile a thing for mothballing. Their ribs were cracked, frames bent, planks wormy, keels broken, timbers rotten. Those few that had been ready for overseas shipment, or which remained on the assembly lines, enjoyed a brief butterfly existence as civilian toys.

Unlike the heavier Air Force rescue boats, however, the PTs proved to be rather impractical as yachts. Their oversized motors sent fuel costs skyrocketing, and their rugged behavior, once they reached blue water, held scant appeal for Sunday sailors.

Now, in the waning sunset, Cragg studied this last of a once-proud breed. For all her elegant disguise, *Mohican* looked much like the boats Cragg himself had commanded, as she rode gently on the untroubled surface of a backwater slip. The slightly convex main deck swept eighty feet from blunt fantail to sharp prow in the same clean, remembered fashion. There was the same outward flare to her classic flanks, from chine to gunwale, and a hint of speed kept under close leash.

Cragg slowly circled *Mohican* on the slatted boards that adjoined the U-shaped shelter, frowning, pursing his lips, as he surveyed what had been done to her utilitarian topside.

The compact clutter of weaponry had been stripped away. In lieu of her original four torpedo tubes, midship .50-caliber machineguns, after 20-millimeter cannon, and smoke-pot at the stern, *Mohican* displayed a vast assortment of sportfishing gear: stainless steel mechanical chairs, trolling platforms, a tall mast for spotters who'd be on the lookout for swordfish and marlin, and above all that a radar rig which far surpassed the wartime PT's primitive search gear.

The changes wrought belowdecks were equally drastic. *Mohican* was immaculate. With a slight pang, Cragg recalled his own patched boat, forever stinking of mildewed mattresses, volatile fuel, human sweat, and the noisome leavings of the rats and roaches that inhabited her bilges. *Mohican* smelled like a new car, leathery and polished, and she was nobly air-conditioned.

Cragg could find only one obvious concession to practicality during his tour of her working spaces. Although *Mohican's* late owner could easily have afforded the hundred-octane gasoline which her original three Packards drank like so many twelve-cylinder alcoholics, they had been torn out, and replaced by a pair of four-stroke Caterpillar diesels. These durable engines warmed up fast, didn't use much water, and consumed a low-grade fuel oil available wherever trucks were found. If this metamorphosis had reduced *Mohican's* top speed from forty knots to a bare twenty-plus, so that she could no longer expose her stepless bottom at full throttle, it had also given her a comfort and a dependability which her elder sisters never enjoyed. Moreover, her normal 500-mile cruising range was greatly enhanced. There was another compensation, Cragg knew, for this loss of glamor. The Packards were supposed to be overhauled and groomed every 500 hours, like racing colts, whereas the Percheron diesels ran virtually forever.

Meditatively, Cragg made his way forward along the narrow passage from the engine room, through what had once been officer's country amidships, past the minuscule galley, to the beamiest area in which a wartime crew would have lived. Here, instead of the ten-by-fifteen cabinful of pipe-berths *Mohican* had once carried, was a lordly teak-paneled stateroom, with a pair of double beds, thick white carpets, stereo hi-fi, and an array of handsome built-in cabinets, including a bar.

Cragg scowled at the stateroom for a long moment, before he

clambered stiffly up the ladder that led to the charthouse. His stricken look vanished, as he caught sight of the most completely equipped navigational center he'd ever seen on a craft of *Mohican's* size. The eight-by-ten cubicle contained enough electronic gear, radar, sonar, and Loran to insure a safe voyage through any waters of the world, charted or not.

Silently cursing himself for profligate folly, aware that he would have to sell his faithful clipper, Cragg walked up the ramp to the boatyard office and wrote a down-payment check for this preposterous bauble.

Thanks to an alert stringer for the *Chronicle,* the purchase of a quondam PT boat by a former PT skipper did not go unnoticed in the San Francisco press. It created a minor sensation, and a certain amount of good-natured nonsense was scribbled about the incongruity of an ex-naval hero hauling fatcat sportsmen around the Bay aboard such a hopelessly neutered warcraft. There were pictures of Cragg in his wrinkled khakis, taken on Guadalcanal an aeon earlier when some forgotten admiral pinned the Navy Cross to his sweatdrenched blouse. And there were photographs of the latter-day Cragg, looking more than a little sheepish at all this unsought publicity, even though it was good for his charter business.

Late that same night, while he was dourly studying his likeness in the paper, Cragg's bedside telephone rang.

"Colonel Toyon here," said a strange, precise, very deep British voice.

Cragg tried to recall where he might have met a Limey colonel, but couldn't, unless it had been at some rear echelon South Pacific base during the war. Maybe the colonel was a relic of those days, a former liaison joker.

"What can I do for you?" Cragg asked. Then, rendering due privilege to the colonel's invisible rank, he added, "Sir."

"Would you mind terribly if I dropped around to your digs tonight?"

Cragg checked the wind-up alarm clock on his nightstand. "Hell, colonel, it's damned near twelve. Can't whatever-it-is wait till morning?"

A slight pleading note modified Toyon's *basso profundo*. "My business," he said, "is rather urgent."

When a Britisher rates his affairs as rather urgent, Cragg knew, it's generally an understatement of the case. "Okay, colonel. Be my guest." He yawned. "Where are you now?"

"At the Fairmont."

"Oh, Christ!" That meant an hour's wait while Toyon blundered his way out of town, across the toll bridge, then down into Sausalito's ill-lit and crooked streets. "Give me an idea of what's up. Maybe we can deal by phone, if it's a charter job or something like that."

"Unfortunately," said the colonel, "this is a matter which must be discussed in person. Also in private."

Cragg sighed. "All right. But make it snappy, colonel. This has been a rough weekend. I'm pooped."

"My car is waiting," said Toyon. "I shan't be long."

He wasn't. At fifteen-till-one, while Cragg was drawing nourishment from his second cup of bourbon-laced black coffee, the downstairs doorbell rang. Cragg padded to the top of the landing in his bare feet.

"It's unlocked," he called. "Bust in."

At that, the door opened quickly, and a diminutive figure stepped into the hall. Dressed in somber civilian garb that made him seem smaller than he was, the intruder could not have been more than five feet tall. From his superior vantage, Cragg stared down at the strange little man, who paused for an instant at the foot of the stairs, clutching a heavy dispatch case and boldly returning his incredulous gaze.

"Who in hell are you?" Cragg demanded.

As if amused by Cragg's discomfiture, smiling, the visitor climbed halfway up the short staircase before responding to the surly challenge. When he spoke, it was in the same unmistakable British voice which Cragg had heard earlier on the telephone: "Colonel Paki Ningh Toyon, sir, representing the Free Republic of South Thietvanne."

Cragg relaxed. "Sorry, colonel. You fooled me. I was expecting something in tweeds." He proffered his right hand. "Welcome aboard."

Toyon shifted the dispatch case and reached for Cragg's outstretched palm. His delicate countenance had turned grave, almost apologetic, as he followed his bathrobed host into the apartment.

"When I was a boy," he said, "my parents sent me to England to be educated, rather than to Paris, where most Thietvannese go for their schooling. My father was much impressed by the 'playing fields of Eton' legend."

Cragg led his visitor into the kitchen. He offered no comment, but waited for Toyon to come to the point. The colonel, however, seemed content to let the matter rest, while he busied himself with the contents of his dispatch case.

"Care for a drink?" Cragg offered. "Coffee, maybe, or something stronger?"

"Coffee, thank you."

Toyon drew out a map. He spread it across the grease-stained table that served Cragg as a between-meals desk, then stood back with his fist against his small chin, like Hamlet contemplating poor Yorick's skull.

Almost dreamily, in deep and measured tones, Toyon murmured: "It has been a beautiful country."

"Why the past tense, colonel?" Cragg asked, as he poured the coffee. "Even a war can't destroy geography."

Toyon's narrow shoulders fluttered. "Thietvanne is like a woman who has been raped. She will never be the same again."

"You mean, she might have to bear somebody's bastard?"

Toyon nodded. "You put it rather crudely, Mr. Cragg. But that is how it may indeed transpire. If we lose this war. . . ." His melancholy voice faltered.

"Thietvanne's coastline reminds me of a pregnant woman," Cragg said suddenly.

Surprised, Toyon turned back to the chart, studied it briefly, then said: "That had never occurred to me. But it is indeed true. I see her quite plainly." He shrugged again. "However, I did not travel here to waste your time talking about this map."

"So I'd imagined, colonel."

"If you agree to a proposition I am prepared to make on behalf of my government," Toyon said, "we can resume our topographical chat in a better context."

"Proposition?"

"I am offering you a job, Mr. Cragg, at a handsome salary."

"Doing what?"

"Defending the cause of South Thietvanne."

Cragg smiled. "That sounds fine, colonel. But all I know about your 'cause' is what I've read in the newspapers, or seen on television. To be brutally frank, it leaves me goddamned confused."

"Civil wars tend to be confusing," said Toyon. "After a hundred years there are people who still dispute the causes over which your own Civil War was fought."

"Sure. But you're talking about Americans arguing with other Americans. Thietvanne's one hell of a long way from Sausalito, colonel, and we don't even hold a second mortgage on your real estate any more. We've pulled out. Remember?"

"This I know." The diminutive colonel gave him a sad glance. "Perhaps I should start by explaining why I came to you in the first place."

"That might help."

Toyon extracted a copy of the morning *Chronicle* from his dispatch case. It was folded to the story about Cragg's purchase of the PT.

"I read this while I was waiting at the airport for my Pan American connection to Hong Kong."

"So?"

"So I canceled my reservation and searched out the remarkable Mr. Cragg." The colonel paused. "For the past three months I have been endeavoring to enlist—hire, if you prefer—qualified people for my country. Specialists who possess the skills we lack, and who can fill the gap created when your military advisors were withdrawn. In particular, we need men with nautical expertise."

"You mean," Cragg translated, "there's a dirty job that calls for deepwater sailors."

"Precisely." Toyon indicated the map. "These markings in red describe our dilemma, Mr. Cragg. They show the supply route used by the Kong, and the positive sightings of major movements which our coastal watchers have reported to us."

Bent over the chart, Cragg counted twenty-three scarlet X's. "That's a hell of a lot of contacts, colonel."

"It is worse than you imagine," said Toyon. "Those four larger circles denote convoys, escorted by heavily armed junks, which have begun to supplant individual shipments in recent weeks." He handed Cragg a list. "Here is an accounting of the equipment taken from the only Kong ship our forces have been able to destroy. This vessel sank in shallow waters, so the cargo was saved."

Cragg took the typed memorandum. Among the catalogued items were ninety-seven tons of ammunition, arms and supplies; more than a half-million rounds of small-arms ammo; fifteen hundred Mauser rifles; almost a thousand submachine guns; several hundred pounds of medical goods, plus a smattering of newer weaponry benchmarked by the Red Chinese factories. It was, Cragg admitted, a damned impressive haul.

"Very sticky," he said. "But where do I come in?"

"During the Pacific war a similar crisis arose, did it not, when the Japanese provisioned their forces through a system of close-in convoys much like this?" Toyon picked up the *Chronicle* and read a paragraph aloud: "'Lieutenant Cragg received the Navy Cross, second in valor only to the Congressional Medal of Honor, for heroism in a drawn battle with a heavily armed enemy supply flotilla. Although gravely wounded, he remained at the wheel of his damaged PT and—'"

Cragg snorted. "Ancient history, colonel."

"History repeats itself. Different times, same problems. Until today, I was not aware that any of these—what d'you call them?—'mosquito boats' remained in existence. In Washington they told me that four prototypes of a newer model had been built a few years ago, but I was unable to learn their whereabouts."

"Those were scrapped in '56," Cragg said. "Besides, they had aluminum hulls instead of mahogany. Hell. All that exposed metal would've made them mousemeat for radar pickets."

Toyon's luminous eyes were aglow with anticipation. "It was a most fortunate happenstance for me, Mr. Cragg, coming upon this article."

"But it also might prove expensive. Charter contracts run skyhigh nowadays, particularly when you're talking about something that's six thousand miles from home base. And there's always the off-chance that maybe I'd lose my whole investment because of a misplaced Kong shell, to say nothing of my neck in the bargain."

"Surely the holder of a Navy Cross is not afraid?"

Cragg rubbed his chin meditatively. "You bet your ass the holder of a Navy Cross is damned afraid. I'm just figuring the angles, in case we start talking turkey. Like where would I find decent crews, guys willing to risk their necks, or the armament we'd need to put *Mohican* on a war footing."

"We will take care of those matters."

"Balls!" Cragg regarded him scornfully. "Maybe you can dig up the weaponry, colonel. But I'm sure as hell not going to sail with a bunch of meatheads who don't know a taffrail from a taffypull."

Toyon was unmoved. "In this engaging recital of your wartime career, there is mention of the 'loyal band of brothers' who served aboard your boat. It also discloses that you gentlemen hold a reunion each year about this time."

"Are you suggesting that Thietvanne wants to hire the whole package—chief, *Mohican,* and all the Indians?"

"Yes."

"Assuming they'd buy in, that would really skyrocket the price."

"We are prepared to pay."

Cragg made a rapid computation. "Thirty thousand?"

"Yes."

"You'll furnish the hardware?"

"Yes."

"And pay the cost of shipping *Mohican* to GaiSong?"

"That also."

"You make it sound like a damned attractive business venture. Better than hunting sharks."

Toyon repeated his elegant shrug. "It is only fair, Mr. Cragg, to remind you that Thietvanne is a war zone. There would be no insurance for your boat. Nor," he appended, "for your next of kin."

"I'm an unmarried orphan," Cragg said, "without even a bastard to my name."

"What about your comrades in arms?"

"The Mafia understands minor details."

Toyon looked pleased. "They must be very brave men."

Cragg shrugged. "They are."

"Excellent." Toyon refolded the map. "May I ask, sir, are you interested?"

"Once we've agreed on the basic terms of a charter, I never haggle over details with a client. You've got yourself a deal, colonel." Cragg reached for the whisky bottle. "So let's drink on it. Then we'll start plotting against the heathen Kong."

Toyon's lips parted in a wide smile. "As a good Catholic," he said comfortably, "I can now join you in such a toast."

It was five A.M., and growing light above the mist-shrouded eastern hills, before they finished. Out of the parley emerged a bold plan which, carried out effectively, could stymie the insurgent convoys. Blessed with extraordinary luck, it might even deal the Kong a blow from which they would not recover for many weeks, long enough for the desperate Thiets to regroup their outmaneuvered forces.

An integral part of the stratagem involved the purchase of an ocean-going junk for use as protective coloration, and for carrying reinforcements, during the long, hazardous run up the coast. This was Toyon's idea. He said there were dozens of such stalwart craft available in Hong Kong at amazingly cheap prices. Cragg accepted the proposal willingly, provided Toyon would make the necessary arrangements.

Thereupon Toyon suggested that Cragg proceed to GaiSong at his earliest convenience, to line up a crew for the junk and get *Mohican* restored to military status, while his Mafia cohorts fetched the clumsy junk down from Hong Kong. The colonel expressed sincere regret that he wouldn't be able to accompany his new American ally on the expedition itself, because of the confining nature of his duties as special aide to General Kwo, who was (said Toyon) a most demanding fellow.

"Don't apologize," Cragg soothed. "Hell, naval operations aren't meant for the army anyhow." He grinned. "You'd probably get seasick."

"I do," the colonel acknowledged glumly.

Before he left, Toyon gave him a certified bank draft for $5000, neatly typed, and made out in the name of Frederick Peter Cragg.

"You were awfully damned sure I'd buy, weren't you, colonel?"

"Not really, Mr. Cragg. But I had high hopes, and precious little time to ponder the matter before the Wells-Fargo people closed their doors at three o'clock yesterday afternoon. You are not offended?"

"No," said Cragg. "I'm not offended." He folded the check and slipped it into the pocket of his bathrobe.

Predictably, it was Lars Torgerson who arrived first, already more than two-sheets-in-the-wind after a bibulous midmorning flight from Minneapolis, full of the combative gung-ho he always displayed whenever something brewed that might develop into a nice, man-sized, groin-kicking donnybrook. Torgerson's physical appearance suited his name. He was a brooding Norse giant with rufous blond hair which had started thinning a bit at the crown, and pale blue eyes that seemed forever bloodshot, either from drinking too much or from staring too long at the naked sun. He had been quartermaster of their PT during the war, a boatswain's mate first-class, and a natural helmsman. The Mafia called him "the poor man's Leif Ericson." It was a lasting source of regret to Torgerson that Cragg had been forced to assume the controls in their climactic engagement off Okinawa, thus depriving him of the joy and the glory which was his due, merely because a Jap shell exploded too close to his face, temporarily blinding him. Anybody who dared, or who didn't have good sense, could pick a fight with Torgerson by reminding him how Cragg had relieved him that wild night, even though the skipper was damned near a basket case himself at the time. Few did. During the war years, Lars Torgerson's berserk temper was notorious from Noumea to Manila, and the passage of time hadn't improved it. His central incisor was missing from his upper jaw, where he'd stopped a flung marlinspike in 1943, and he still spat dangerously through this toothgap when he wanted to see how the wind was blowing.

Those who knew Torgerson best had learned something else about this idiosyncrasy. It could also signal the onslaught of one of the big Swede's mercurial rages. That was the way, he rumbled, a *man* cleared the goddamn decks for action. If Torgerson spat between his teeth on a windless day, you ducked for cover.

Lars was currently in the process of getting divorced from his third wife. Or, rather, she was divorcing him, on the starkly evidential grounds of cruelty. He had a regrettable habit of slapping her around with his mammoth right palm, she testified, whenever he drank too much, which was roughly every night that he was home. In self-defense, Torgerson could only point to the fact that he wasn't home very much, and that she was damned lucky he kept his hand unclenched. Had he given this snivelling creature the fisticuffs she so richly merited, there wouldn't have been any need for a divorce. Only a quick funeral.

Like Cragg, he had tried a few odd jobs around Minneapolis before he discovered that civilization wasn't ready for him. Then, as an antidote, Torgerson drifted southward to the Florida keys, where he found intermittent work as a deckhand for the yachting crowd who brought their gleaming playthings down from Long Island Sound and the Chesapeake when winter came. But it was gruelling, demeaning labor, and Lars much preferred to spend his time skin-diving, for which there was no monetary reward whatever. He grew proficient in this dangerous art, set a few records, and wound up dead broke. Whereupon Torgerson ambled north again, irresistibly drawn to the land of his forebears, to become a guide for the peripatetic millionaires who hunted in upper Minnesota's lake country. Somehow this didn't strike him as carrying the same badge of servility that polishing yacht brass did, since all men were rated equal in the wilderness. Moreover, he was curiously popular with these sportsmen. In a masochistic way, it seemed, they liked to be whittled down to size by this roughhewn character who didn't give a fingersnap for their money, and whose outlook on life was so bluntly honest. Besides, as products of a matriarchy, it was pleasant for them to listen while Torgerson aired his views about women, and more particularly, about his several wives.

At Cragg's suggestion, Lars Torgerson hit the sack before lunchtime, to sleep it off before the rest of the Mafia dropped anchor and the serious drinking got under way. Although he went to considerable pains, normally, to demonstrate that they were no longer Navy, and that rank, such as it was, belonged to a dead past, Torgerson went to bed like a docile sheep. There were moments when Cragg's cold stare, boring into the Swede's pale blue eyes, had an unsettling effect on him, and dashed icewater over his temper before it could fairly ignite.

About an hour later Duke Harris arrived by cab from San Francisco International Airport. He made his customary sedate entrance after giving three precise knocks at the door of the waterfront shack. He came up the stairs carrying the battered *Gone Fishing* sign in a kidgloved hand, and clucking with mock disapproval.

"Highly mendacious, Leftenant Cragg. Unbecoming an officer and a gentleman, to lead one's friends astray in this fashion."

"That's to frighten off the civilians, Your Lordship. Put the goddamn thing back where it was."

"Aye, aye, sir." Harris trotted downstairs and rehung the sign on the doorknob. From the lower hall he saluted elaborately. "Mission accomplished."

"Sir," Cragg prompted, grinning.

"*Sir!*"

This small parochial joke never failed to amuse the Duke, whose ancestry (he claimed) could be traced in Burke's Peerage, if you could stand the fine print, from Runnymede to the Queen's last Honors List. Of course, you wouldn't find the name of Calvin Harris there, specifically, owing to a slight bar-sinister complication that attended his birth. Actually, said the Duke, he'd fled the Old Country when he was seventeen to avoid embarrassment, either for himself or for his putative father. Truth was, Harris had run away from a Liverpool orphanage, and even now, in moments of stress, his fastidious English gave way to the Merseyside argot.

At forty-six, the Duke was the oldest of the surviving Mafia, a wiry man, the sort you saw in those photographs of the Dunkirk evacuation, who'd always had their teapots and their Primus stoves handy, no matter where, during the war. He was almost eggbald now, with only a hint of lank dark hair on the stern of his odd-shaped skull. This gave him a malevolent Pickwickian look. Duke Harris had been radarman on their PT. ("Hell, we Limeys invented that bloody miracle, you know!") When he wasn't watching for bogies on the screen, Duke doubled as cook in PT 387's cramped galley.

After World War II, he had drifted into radio repair work, and then television, in Pelham, N.Y., because the town sounded "so godawfully British—but believe me, sir, it isn't!" The Duke achieved only limited success as a TV fixer. But it was enough to keep him in Earl Grey's gunpowder tea, provide carfare to Long Island where he attended the Sunday cricket matches, and finance a yearly tweed suit from a tailor he knew on Bond Street. Harris was an old maid bachelor in the best Henry Higgins tradition, who deemed every man a gentleman until proven innocent. And he credited his modest commercial attainments to the fact that "you Yanks will do anything for a bloke who can talk through his nose without movin' his bloody lips."

Daintily, deliberately, the Duke peeled off his gloves. Then he reached into a waistcoat pocket and extracted five plastic toothpicks, which he inspected with grave concern.

Cragg leered. "I didn't suppose you toffs ever used anything as crude as a toothpick."

"We don't." said Harris. "These are my counters."

"So?"

"Each of these utilitarian objects represents a martini consumed on that hideous aircraft enroute hither from Kennedy Airport. Remember, leftenant, when one prepares to enjoy a hangover, it is most distressing not to know the extent of one's Original Sin."

Unlike Lars Torgerson, who traveled tourist, Harris had bought deluxe accommodations for his flight. If one can't go first-class, he observed, one shouldn't go at all. He had other cogent apothegms. Such as: If a thing's not worth doing, it's not worth doing well. And: You don't have to generate good ideas, because any idea worth a damn will generate itself.

The remaining Mafia pair didn't come by air at all, but by transcontinental bus, journeying together. Rumpled, unshaven, smelling of dried sweat, they bounded up the stairs, clamoring for cold brews before Cragg could wrench the apartment door open.

Mario DelGrado finished his can of beer in three convulsive gulps, before setting down the scuffed valise he carried in his left hand, and then asked for another.

"Damn, that's good!" he marveled. "Believe me, it's a long frigging haul from the Jersey meadows, *amici.*"

Cragg punched open a fresh can. "How's good old Hackensack?"

"Lousy." Mario's ferocious brows knit together above his magnificent nose. "Four families trying to scratch a living off a hundred acres, raising too little produce and too many *bambinos.*"

"What's the DelGrado population now?"

"Seventeen," Mario said morosely. "Correction. Make that eighteen. I forgot to count myself."

Cragg nodded his sympathy. He had visited the truck farm, years ago, when Mafia met there for its annual reunion. Even then it had seemed woefully inadequate to support the DelGrado family's growing needs. Now that Mario's brothers and sisters were married, with offspring of their own, it must be a hopeless case, a sort of transplanted Appalachian poverty belt. Only Mario, the eldest, had held the line against the birthrate explosion, although this was a tragedy in itself. Shortly before going into the Navy in 1942, he'd married his highschool sweetheart, and when he returned home on leave after bootcamp, she became pregnant. Eight months later Mario got a letter from his mother telling that Sophia had died in premature childbirth, and that his son, the prime heir to the DelGrado hundred acres, was stillborn.

Cragg well remembered the morning when the bitter news arrived. They'd just completed their shakedown tests off Pearl Harbor aboard PT 387, which had, *mirabile dictu*, been built at Bayonne, N.J., across the mudflats from Hackensack. They held orders to join Halsey in the South Pacific. They were proud as hell. They were Cragg's Mafia. And it was Mario DelGrado, whose squat, dark physique belied his placid Mediterranean nature, who gaily coined this sinister name for their eleven-man crew. Mario said his grandfather had once belonged to the

Black Hand in Sicily. The old man used his sardine boat in those days to transport the dread brethren on their *vendettas* against the Palermo authorities. But that was how it went back in the 1890s. Now most of the DelGrados were law-abiding land-lubbers, who wouldn't presume to argue with traffic cops.

Mario disappeared for a full week after receiving his mother's message, leaving Cragg the untidy alternative of reporting him as A.W.O.L., or covering up. To the Mafia's quiet delight, Cragg chose the latter. They were organized into two-man posses, with stern orders to find Mario before the squadron commander dis-covered he was missing, or before they embarked in the LST that would ferry them across the Pacific to ComSoPac's headquarters at Noumea.

It was Cragg himself, teamed with Torgerson, who located the errant crewman in a Catholic church on the windward side of Oahu. For six days Mario had lived on prayers and pineapples. Having now made his peace with God, he said solemnly that he was ready to rejoin the holy war against the Japs.

After that, Mario always wore a crucifix around his tunsized neck, instead of the regulation dogtags. But Cragg made no effort to enforce the rule. Since dogtags were chiefly a device for identifying corpses, anyhow, and if Mario didn't care whether his next-of-kin got the remains, what the hell difference did it make? That was his personal business. As long as the guy tended to his engineroom duties as Motor Mechanic First-Class, and occa-sionally spelled Harris in the galley when the Duke's foul Limey cooking began to spur talk of mutiny, he could wear whatever jewelry he pleased. Knowing Wop cuisine helped, because spa-ghetti and Spam were plentiful in those days, whereas Brussels sprouts and roast beef weren't. Mario sprang from a long line of culinary improvisers. The Duke didn't.

Cragg said, "Toss your gear into the bedroom, fella, so you can drink with both hands."

Then he turned to the tall, slim, elegant man who accom-panied Mario, and who was watching them both in silent amuse-ment. The newcomer fastidiously wiped the last foamy flecks of beer from his graying moustache. He bowed.

"Greetings, *mon capitaine.*"

"Mario's a commoner," Cragg chided. "He's supposed to take the bus. But I'm downright surprised at you, Trump."

"That's because you don't dig the danceband racket, sir. We always go Greyhound. When we've got work, I mean."

"Things a little rough?" Cragg asked compassionately.

"Rougher than a cob. Goddamned teen-agers don't want genuine music anymore. Just a guitar and a bongo drum. Or a jukebox."

"Maybe you should switch to bourbon, Trump. It'll stand up better to your manly tears."

The dapper man gave a nonchalant shrug, "Hell, skipper, I'm not complaining." He peered around at the others. "Seems to me we all have a beached look."

Cragg saw no reason to argue the point. As usual, Ambrose Gideon was right, in his annoyingly offhand fashion. The last of the Mafias were indeed a drydocked lot. *Item:* an improvident charter boatman. *Item:* a drunken northwoods guide. *Item:* a dilettantish TV repair artist. *Item:* a Jersey carrot grower. *Final Item:* this broken-down orchestra leader.

With an inward wince, Cragg remembered the offhand way he'd assured Colonel Toyon that the Mafia would regard his dangerous mission "as just another job." He recalled, too, how the colonel had complimented him upon the bravery of these selfsame men. Yet they were tied together, he and his erstwhile subordinates, by common bonds that transcended war service. None of them boasted any real outside ties, beyond Cragg's Mafia, or any visible success in postwar life. However negative such bonds might be, they nevertheless existed, and were strong, in the age-old tradition that misery loves company.

Gideon, at forty-one a year older than Mario DelGrado, epitomized their doleful plight. Inevitably, he had been nicknamed The Trumpet, a sobriquet which was soon reduced to Trump, after the Mafia discovered that he had been a hornblower in a hotel swing combo. Even in those days Gideon wore a moustache, to conceal the fact that he was under age for this kind of work. Trump Gideon ran PT 387's gunnery department, with special responsibility for the 37-mm. barge-busting cannon that was mounted on the forecastle deck. His assignment was somewhat akin to bossing a volunteer hook-and-ladder company, because the task of firing the smaller weapons devolved upon anybody who happened to be free when an engagement impended. It was assumed that all hands knew enough to handle a simple .50-caliber machine gun. All hands did. The Mafia wore a string of gunnery E's (for excellence) as proof of their skill.

After the war ended, Trump drifted back into commercial music. But with dancehalls folding, with the youngsters who had been their mainstay now rocking and rolling to jukebox tunes, a few big name outfits grabbed what little trade remained. Although his fifth wife, Marty, was reaching limited fame as a television singer, having graduated from bands, Trump Gideon didn't feel he could hang around much longer as a useless appendage to her chariot. So he was in the market for something —hell, anything!—that might restore a bit of the style he'd damned near forgotten he was once accustomed to.

Despite urgent pleas, coupled with threats of positive mayhem, Cragg refused to talk about his mysterious telegram, or his acquisition of *Mohican*, until Mario DelGrado finished preparing dinner. That took almost two hours. It featured lasagna, topped by a savory red sauce that was brewed with especial loving care in honor of their last post-victory banquet aboard PT 387. In the interim, while they waited, the Mafia drank themselves into a pleasantly receptive mood.

When they were surfeited with food, and after Mario's final triumph, a jug of brandy-laced café espresso, was carried to the table, Cragg banged for attention with his spoon. Immediately the Mafia sprang to exaggerated, respectful attention.

"I've accepted a charter job," he announced, "that's too big for me to handle alone. So I'm calling for volunteers."

Duke Harris raised a quizzical eyebrow. "Sight unseen, leftenant? Sealed orders—all that sort of rot?"

"Negative. You'll be told. But it's a goddamned ticklish proposition. Any leaks could blow the whole thing skyhigh."

"Proceed, skipper," drawled Trump Gideon.

Bluntly, succinctly, leaving out the dramatic flourishes, Cragg relayed his conversation with Colonel Toyon, and showed them the map he had sketched from memory after the Thietvannese departed. They listened without further comment, almost critically, until he exhibited the $5000 check.

Whereupon Lars Torgerson rose ponderously to his feet, towering above the small table, his cheeks flushed with excitement. As he spoke, Torgerson accentuated each word by slamming his fist against the scarred board.

"By God," he bellowed, "that's the best flogging news I've heard since the Japs bombed Pearl Harbor!"

Gideon reached for the bank draft. "Is this chit for real?"

"It's certified, fella."

"Then count me in."

Cragg glanced toward Harris. "What about you, Duke?"

"We British have a proud history of volunteering to untangle other people's messes." Harris favored them with his bland Pickwickian smile. "On the other hand, being only a transplanted Briton, I guess I'm entitled to a few simple reservations."

"Such as?" Cragg growled.

"Why the devil did you pick a godforsaken place like Thietvanne to bring the Mafia back to life?"

"Several reasons. For one thing, Duke, even though they might throw crooked dice, it's the only crap game in town. Nobody else has a decent war going. At least, not yet to the point where they're yelling for help. Also, it's familiar territory, in a crumby sort of way, like the stinking Southwest Pacific, where we fought the Big One. Same weather. Same jungle. Same devious native types."

"Sounds frightfully appetizing."

"Beggars," intoned Cragg, "can't be choosers."

Duke traced his hand thoughtfully across his gnarled skull. "Thus spake the inexorable voice of truth. As a qualified beggar, *leftenant*, your humble servant options to enlist for the rigged crap game."

"Thanks." Cragg aimed his attention at DelGrado, who was sitting across from him, immobile beneath the naked overhead light, his swarthy face moistly shining. "You're the anchor man, fella."

Mario's white teeth flashed. "Unless you're nuts about boiled rice, you'll be needing an experienced Wop chef."

"Good." Cragg's voice abruptly resumed the command authority they all knew so well. "At first light tomorrow we'll take *Mohican* out for a test run to see how much you lunkheads have forgotten about PTs. . . ."

3

No Lesser Breeds

Prodded out of his deep slumber by the telephone's imperative ringing, Cragg dragged himself upright in bed and groped through the semidarkness toward the sound. His reaching hand knocked the instrument off the cradle, so he was forced to fumble around the gummy carpet until he could locate it again. Cragg groaned. Bending down, he discovered, accentuated the headache which had gripped him the moment he opened his eyes. He also became conscious of a vague malaise, perhaps the forerunner of dysentery, somewhere in the region of his solar plexus.

It had been an abysmal, tactical error, Cragg conceded grimly, trying to drown his annoyance at Mlle. Denise Legére with all those straight scotches. Now he had a monumental hangover, a sore gut, and the still unresolved problem of what to do about this importunate French girl.

As he picked up the phone, Cragg peered at the luminous dial of his wristwatch. Five bloody A.M. He snarled something suitably ungracious into the mouthpiece. A soft female voice responded without rancor, and for a startled instant he thought it was Mlle. Legére, ready to resume her plea at sunrise. But it wasn't.

Solicitously, ready to protect a guest against needless intrusions at such an absurd hour, the hotel operator purred: "Will you accept a call, M'sieu Cragg?"

"Who is it?"

"The harbormaster, m'sieu, with an urgent communiqué for you."

"Put him on."

"But he speaks only French," the operator warned.

"In that case," Cragg said, "you're hired as my translator. One hundred piastres for three minutes."

"*Merci.*" He heard her address the harbormaster in rapid-fire French, then pause briefly, while she transcribed the message. After a moment the operator came back on the line. " 'The Liberty ship *Vesper* anchored in port one hour ago,' " she quoted. " 'Her captain desires that M'sieu Cragg report aboard at his earliest convenience to assist in removing certain deck cargo consigned to him, so the hatches can be freed for further unloading. The captain awaits a prompt reply from M'sieu Cragg. He is in Berth 12-B.' "

In spite of his throbbing head, Cragg grinned at the Liberty skipper's eagerness to get rid of *Mohican,* after the inordinate time it had taken to reach GaiSong in the first place. Yet that was understandable. Nobody wanted to stay in this godforsaken port any longer than absolute necessity required, because of the evil weather, the malarial mosquitoes, the predatory vermin, and the constant threat of waterfront Kong pirates staging a raid. It suited Cragg, however, to lend his personal assistance to the unloading, rather than leave the thin-hulled PT to the dubious mercies of native stevedores, whose deliberate clumsiness at cargo handling was an open scandal.

"Have the harbormaster relay word that I'll hustle down there *tout de suite,*" he said.

The operator giggled. "*Oui*, M'sieu Cragg."

"As for yourself, *bébé*, you've earned your hundred piastres. They'll be at the front desk."

Cragg swallowed three aspirin for his hangover, and chased them with a pair of brown Entero-Vioform tablets for his queasy stomach. Then he limped downstairs after trying vainly to rouse the all-night elevator boy. The thin rain had started again, and the dawn was buried in a scrofulous gray waste that matched his foul mood.

It took him forty minutes to reach the Liberty by taxicab and sampan. When he came aboard, Cragg found that a deck gang had already begun to lift *Mohican* off her chocks, preparatory to lowering the craft over the side. As he feared, she showed several ugly scars where the cargohooks had grazed her flanks, and the sling that was being secured around her stepless bottom seemed woefully inadequate to sustain *Mohican's* fifty deadweight tons.

In a bullhorn voice that carried all the way to the bridge, Cragg called an immediate halt to these clumsy proceedings, thereby fetching the captain angrily below to see what in Tophet was the matter.

"This is *my* ship, mister, and I'll thank you not to issue orders to *my* men."

"But this boat," Cragg said in an icy voice, "happens to be *my* property. It's a damned delicate hunk of machinery. Your clowns are treating it like a Sherman tank."

"I want that hatch cleared inside of a half-hour."

"It'll be cleared," growled Cragg, "as soon as I decide you've got that boom properly rigged for hoisting, and not one second sooner."

The captain took a menacing pace forward. "How would you like to swim ashore, mister?"

"And how would you like to have this bucket of bolts interned in GaiSong for the next six months?" Cragg retorted. "It might interest you to know that you're dealing with official Thietvanne property now. General Kwo wouldn't care to have *Mohican* report for duty in more than one piece. He's got plans for her."

"Quid Kwo has bought your frigging boat?" the captain asked in an incredulous tone.

"In a manner of speaking."

Still suspicious, yet afraid to risk the off-chance that Cragg was telling the truth, he capitulated grudgingly. "All right, I'll give you sixty minutes to dump your toy into the water. *Comprenez?*"

Cragg grunted. "Better double that, captain. I want to count the guest silver before we part company."

But it was almost eleven before *Mohican's* hull was finally settled with great care into the muddy stream. She remained tethered to an outslung boom for another sixty minutes while Cragg went below to test the engines. At length he appeared topside again and waved toward the captain, who was standing on the freighter's bridgewing, impatient for his unwelcome guest to depart so the sampan lighters could start receiving their loads.

"Everything's shipshape," Cragg called pleasantly.

"Then shove off, mister."

"My pleasure, sir."

Cragg flung him a parting salute as he inched his throttles forward. The deck crew released *Mohican's* bow and stern lines. Gathering speed, she swept effortlessly in the direction of the Thietvanne naval landing, a half-mile across the somnolent river.

At ten knots *Mohican* handled well, answering the rudder like a tame elephant heeding its mahout's bare heels. Cragg listened critically to the steady thrum that emanated from the engineroom thirty feet aft of his tiny exposed bridge. There were no misfires, no false harmonics in the workhorse beat of the twin diesels.

Alone aboard this miniature warship-to-be, performing the dual role of captain and crew, Cragg experienced a special sense of power, a strange lift, that was far different from the simple feeling of physical isolation he had known during his *Gone Fishing* interludes off the Farallones. Suddenly he was aware of the absolute command authority that would soon be his to dispose however he wished. What caused this renascence of a deep and heady emotion he hadn't felt for over twenty years, he could neither have expressed in words, nor defined satisfactorily to himself. Perhaps it was the smooth heft of *Mohican's* wheel under his clenched fist, as she plowed a steady furrow

across these coffee-brown waters, that summoned it back. Already
he was contemplating the changes that must be wrought in
Mohican, to make her the fighting lady her designers had originally intended.

That might also explain it.

Above and to starboard of the boat's control superstructure, in
place of his electrically operated marlin chair, Cragg planned to
mount twin .50-calibers. Forward, where the deck flared to a full
twenty feet of beam, he wanted 40-millimeter cannon capable of
inflicting mortal wounds upon the thin steel or thick wooden
hulls of the enemy vessels that would confront them at the climax
of their journey north, if not a damned sight sooner. This broad
deck was barren, now, save for an oversized life raft from which a
five-piece swing band had once played for moonlight dancing on
the forecastle. Amidships and aft, of course, he would fit other
armament to supplant the gaudy sport-fishing gear with which
Mohican was presently burdened.

But Cragg had long since concluded that little could be
accomplished belowdecks to make her resemble his old command, other than to hang bunks in the owner's pretentious stateroom, and strip away all the gimcrack paneling and gallimanfry
that looked so fine on yachts, like cathedral gargoyles, but which
on a man-o'-war would be absurd, if not downright disastrous,
during an engagement.

Cooled by the gentle breeze that eddied past the waist-high
cubicle from which he conned the boat, Cragg guessed he felt
better, a little less hungover, and ready for the intricate business
of coming single-handed alongside the shabby pier a few hundred yards ahead. As the mist cleared from his brain, that curious
awareness of incipient power seemed also to increase.

Just for old time's sake, it might be fun to go barreling into the
Thiet navy dock at 40 knots, the way they used to climax a
successful Slot cruise, then throw her into reverse a split-second
before she crashed. He listened once more to the engine drum-
beat. Still sweetly regular. So what if she couldn't match the
breakneck speed of her wartime sisters? No matter. Thanks to the
tender care Cragg had given *Mohican*'s four-stroke Diesels since
rescuing her from pampered exile, she could generate a respect-

able 15 knots, hour after hour, in foul weather or fair. Scared, he figured, she might turn up 20. Which was damned comforting assurance when you scrutinized the eastern horizon, out where the paddy-fields met the China Sea, and saw the dustgray scud that harbingered the summer monsoons.

Cragg lowered his sights to squint through the slight river haze at the quay where, he observed, a dozen-or-so nondescript natives were drawn up in a semblance of military array. Since his was the only craft approaching the Thietvanne navy dock, he supposed they were waiting to honor his arrival. Then, to his chagrin, he saw Colonel Paki Ningh Toyon standing at the head of this tatterdemalion band. Even from that distance, the colonel looked annoyed as hell.

Suddenly Cragg remembered. He'd been scheduled to meet Toyon at seven A.M., so they could go crew-hunting together, and now the church bells were sounding high noon. He sighed. It was obvious that the colonel, unwilling to brook delay in this urgent personnel mission, had done the job himself.

Cragg said, "Oh, Christ!" in an audible voice as he edged *Mohican* closer, ready for chaos to break out when these raw recruits tried to help. Toyon flicked a sign. With an astonishing display of skill, they warped the boat against the dock, dropped collision fenders and made fast the bow and stern lines. The colonel watched with impassive mien until *Mohican*'s engines went dead. Then he stepped briskly aboard.

"As usual, Mr. Cragg, you are late. Tardiness is a most regrettable habit."

"Also as usual, my dear colonel, I rediscovered that nothing is ever simple in GaiSong. Even if I hadn't forgotten our date, which I unfortunately did, there wasn't a goddamned thing I could do about it." Cragg surveyed the platoon of small brown men who were swarming across *Mohican*'s decks with freshwater hoses and swabs. "I see you've been busy."

Toyon nodded. "These are splendid fellows," he said proudly. "They know the sea."

"Fifteen," Cragg counted. "You must have cleaned out the whole hiring hall."

"These are fishermen. They volunteered for this duty without asking where they were going, or when, or why."

"Fifteen bloody messengers-to-Garcia," muttered Cragg.

"Pardon?"

"A corny American figure of speech, colonel."

Cragg studied Toyon's volunteers more closely. Most of them were typical Thiets, fragile-boned, tiny, clad in the inevitable denim pullovers and black pantalons, and wearing either kerchiefs or conical straw hats to shade their heads from the emergent sun. From having watched them at work, however, he knew their amazing strength. Like ants, they could move several times their own inconsequential weight by combining sheer animal thrust with clever uses of levers and counterbalances. Somehow they always managed to wrangle their huge bamboo fishtraps up from 100 fathoms, and get them aboard the sampans, without spilling so much as a six-inch reef bass. They were, Cragg admitted grudgingly, the exception that proved his rule: when it came to hard work, most Thiets would rather crawl under the nearest banana tree, open their mouths, and wait until Newton's Law took effect.

Toyon seemed to divine his thoughts. "These men will fight."

"What makes you so sure?"

"They all come from a fishing village several hundred kilometers north of here, called Han-tsu, where ninety-seven Thietvannese were massacred during a Kong raid. Ten lost their wives. Eight lost both parents as well. And many returned home to find their children murdered." Toyon paused. "See that chap with the black eyepatch?"

Cragg stared in the direction of the colonel's pointing finger, at a taller-than-average Thiet who was busily shining the brass fittings around the forward charthouse windows. Suddenly aware that he was under inspection, the man stopped his scrubbing. He grinned broadly. Despite the friendly grimace, his dark betel-stained teeth and the clumsy patch over his left eye gave him the evil look of a Malay pirate.

"I'm glad he's on our side," Cragg said generously.

Toyon signaled the Thiet to carry on. "That man, Akim, chanced to be in his village when the enemy arrived. He fought very hard, trying to save his wife and children." The colonel paused for a moment in melancholy introspection, thinking of his own murdered family. "The Kong left Akim for dead, after searing both his eyes with redhot stakes, but he miraculously recovered the sight of his right one. It was a splendid tribute to the Dokoro Mission hospital," added Toyon, "and to the surgical abilities of Dr. Legére."

"Legére!"

"You have heard of our famous doctor?"

"I've met his daughter."

"Ah, yes. The charming Mlle. Denise." A faint smile lightened Toyon's habitual gloom. "But where did you encounter her?"

"It's a damned long story, colonel, and I think you know most of it." Toyon looked inquiring. "She tracked me down at Le Coq d'Or. After that I took pity on the little wren, and we had chow in my digs at the Galleon."

"Why pity, Mr. Cragg?"

"The lady wants to hitch a ride to Dokoro."

Toyon made a humming sound through his pursed lips. "So! What did you tell her."

"I was just drunk enough to say she could drop around again this morning."

"Like myself," Toyon observed dryly, "she may possibly think you have—what is that delightful Yankee phrase?—'stood her up.'"

"Not the mademoiselle," Cragg growled. "She'll stick around till hell freezes over. You can depend on it."

"D'you plan to take her along?"

Cragg gave the colonel a hard glance. "Maybe it would be better at that, considering all she knows about this expedition, thanks to you. Maybe it's not safe to leave her around where some Kong agent might get next to her at a Sunday night prayer meeting."

"I trust Mlle. Denise implicitly," said Toyon. "And I would do anything within my power to assist Dr. Legére."

"So I gather."

Although Toyon seemed unperturbed, his voice took on an acid note. "There are *certain* women in GaiSong, my dear friend, who would not hesitate for a moment to reveal their boudoir secrets, if they were sufficiently tempted. Some of them, indeed, are paid in advance for such intelligence."

Cragg abruptly shifted conversational course. Indicating the scrubbing, polishing Thiets, he said: "Their credentials sound impressive enough. But that's no guarantee they'll hang tough when the shooting commences."

"Again you have my personal assurance," Toyon stated in his sepulchral tone. "These men will not fail. They would die first."

"Agreed."

The colonel stared for an instant, as if trying to fathom precisely what Cragg meant, yet offering no comment upon this cryptic remark. Instead, he turned to his men, and issued a brusque order in Thietvannese. The one-eyed Akim made a monosyllabic response that Cragg assumed to be the native equivalent of "Aye, aye, sir!" At Akim's relayed command, six fishermen broke off their topside chores, and ascended the ramp to the unloading area, where a small truck was parked beside Toyon's jeep. They returned carrying two rifles apiece, slung yoke-fashion across their narrow shoulders.

"While we are gone," promised the colonel, "nothing will happen to this boat."

Cragg leveled a dubious glance at *Mohican's* sentry detail. He would much have preferred to remain aboard himself, blueprinting the changes necessary to ready her for combat duty, while awaiting the arrival of *Medusa.* After Torgerson and the others reached GaiSong, he'd set up a watch, quarter and station bill whose primary function during their brief stay in port would be *Mohican's* physical security. But now he had no choice. Toyon was eager to get started on the long list of material items which must be pried loose, like so many pearl oysters, from the reluctant warehouses of Thietvanne's hard-pressed military establishment. To accompany him, Cragg would have to entrust *Mohican* to Akim and his baker's-dozen associate pirates.

For a moment, he weighed the alternative of staying behind and letting the colonel forage alone. But he immediately rejected the notion. Confronted by a tough-talking Thiet supply sergeant, Toyon would settle for mortar launchers when what they really wanted was a 75-mm. cannon; or he'd come back with a smoke-pot in lieu of the flame-thrower nozzle Cragg intended to bolt beneath the big gun's barrel, or a walkie-talkie instead of the shortrange radiophone that was essential for communication between their two ships. Toyon might be a topnotch diplomat, a persuasive bargainer among peers, but Cragg had serious reservations about his grasp of soldierly fundamentals.

"Okay, colonel, she's all theirs." He gave Akim a final searching look, and imagined he felt the tall Thiet's invisible eye returning his speculative gaze. "As a special favor to me, though, you might suggest that now's as good a time as any to start dying for the Cause, if anybody tries to sabotage *Mohican*."

Toyon's gray lips tightened in a mirthless smile. "I already have, Mr. Cragg," he said with quiet dignity.

"Good. Then let's roll."

Because Cragg's gut was bothering him again, they stopped at the Galleon Hotel before moving along to the artillery dump, so he could pick up a supply of anti-dysentery pills. Toyon walked into the lobby with him. And there they found Mlle. Legére, perched on the edge of a brocaded chair beside the elevator, her feet set primly together in their absurd halfboots, smokeblue eyes fixed unswervingly upon Cragg, as he limped across the long room. It was, Cragg told himself sourly, the day when payment for all his sins of omission came due. First Toyon. Now this.

Mlle. Legére stood up.

"I have been waiting for you, M'sieu Cragg," the girl said in a reproachful tone.

"Colonel Toyon would tell you that's the story of my life. Making people wait." He frowned. "You don't discourage easily, do you?"

"In this unhappy part of the world," Mlle. Legére murmured, "one learns the virtue of hope. Often there is nothing else."

Cragg took a step toward the elevator. His stomach hurt. He needed another brown pill very badly. "Thanks to the colonel, here, I've suddenly acquired a full crew. As a matter of cold fact, we're already two *men* over complement," he added with careful emphasis.

Mlle. Legére pursued him anxiously.

"Please!" she urged.

At the elevator door Cragg stopped. He appealed to Toyon, who had been observing the tableau, saying nothing.

"You've appointed yourself our chief recruiter, colonel. What in hell is *your* opinion?"

Toyon did not hesitate. "I would say, take Mlle. Legére with us."

"Even considering what we're up against?"

"Precisely for that reason, sir. Oh, my fishermen know the coast, perhaps better than she does. But she knows the people. As we travel north we will encounter many tribes to whom the name Legére is a conjure-word. Believe me, Mr. Cragg, the mademoiselle's father is a well-loved man."

"I don't follow you."

"Our purpose," Toyon said in his didactic voice, "is reaching Phom Than intact. We number exactly twenty, do we not, counting my fifteen and your five? If we permit ourselves to be distracted along the way with minor skirmishes, with useless battles, we may never reach our destination. Or if we do, we may emerge too weak for the final assault. Do you follow me, sir?"

"Closer," Cragg admitted. "But I'm still lagging."

Toyon continued: "My forte is diplomacy. At one time I represented South Thietvanne at the United Nations. I speak four languages, and five native dialects. But those people of the north, who inhabit the country around Dokoro Mission, converse in strange tongues that even I cannot understand. Khmer. Fragments of the more exotic Chinese idioms. Laotian. And here and there a pidgin which makes no sense whatsoever to an outsider." He indicated the girl. "Mlle. Legére, I am told, is fluent in nine dialects."

"Ten," she amended demurely.

Cragg edged away from the elevator, to let its operator answer an insistent summons from some distant upper floor. "Sweet talk doesn't guarantee neutrality. Suppose there's fighting? People getting killed. What then?"

Mlle. Legére lifted her chin a perceptible degree. It was, Cragg noticed again, an incongruously square, determined chin, that would tolerate damned little nonsense.

"Last night I told you my mother taught me the art of nursing.

At Dokoro one must constantly be prepared for casualties, to heal the wounds of those who have been hurt in the guerrilla warfare."

"So these things don't frighten you?"

"I did not say that, Ms'ieu Cragg."

As if baffled by a problem beyond solution, Cragg suddenly spread his powerful hands in a parody of Gallic surrender. "Okay. I yield to the colonel's judgment. But I don't like it one damned bit."

"Perhaps Mlle. Legére should sign a release," Toyon suggested ironically, "absolving you from liability in the event of an unforeseen accident."

Cragg snorted. "Everything about this foul-up is unforeseen, colonel. That's the charm of it." He jabbed the elevator button. "Okay, miss. Come along. At this stage of the ball game, everybody works, and nobody gets paid, except room and board. You can start earning your salt as captain's yeoman."

"Pardon?"

"We'll set up shop in my room, to keep things out of the bureaucracy's clutches, and preserve what little security is left for this crazy expedition. You'll handle phone calls, take messages, run the office, while the colonel and I go scrounging after equipment."

Mlle. Legére asked solemnly, "Am I also expected to live here, M'sieu Cragg?"

"Hell, no! This is a business proposition. Strictly, positively, definitely, absolutely. After hours you'll go back to wherever you crawled out of when you first latched onto me. Comprenez?"

"Yes," she acknowledged in the same low-pitched, husky tone which Cragg had found so disconcerting at their first encounter. "I comprehend."

"Incidentally," he said, "we can't go on calling you Mlle. Legére for the next three weeks. There won't be time. So we'll skip the formalities. Your official name, for the ship's company roster, is Denny." He grinned. "And mine's Cragg."

"You have no Christian name?"

"Just Cragg."

"Very well—Cragg."

They left Denny sitting at the desk, pecking away at the antique portable, trying to transcribe the outlandish names of the fishermen whom Toyon had hired to flesh out *Medusa's* skeleton crew.

"We'll be back at seven P.M.," Cragg said. "Meanwhile, if you get hungry, call room service. The food's lousy, but it's better than starving to death."

Denny smiled. "Is that why you take those brown pills, Cragg?" "Probably."

"They are without merit," she declared firmly. "I will bring you something that really stops the pain."

"Thanks, Miss Nightingale." Cragg handed her the room key. "Keep the door locked. . . ."

During the remainder of the afternoon, until the GaiSong warehouses began bolting their gates and shuttering their windows against the night-prowling Kong, they went from arsenal to arsenal in search of the weaponry Cragg needed.

As patiently as possible, sitting beside Toyon in the jeep, he explained how an eighty-foot torpedo boat could, given judicious care and by stripping its extraneous gear off the deck, accommodate a startling array of firepower. What he needed, said Cragg, was a pair of twin .50-caliber machine guns, installed on either side of the waist-high bridge, for engaging targets dead ahead. Toward the bow he'd install a 40-mm. cannon, and couple to it a mortar of twice that bore, which the same gunner could aim simultaneously, and with reasonable accuracy. On *Mohican's* squat fantail, there would be a cannon, perhaps a 75-mm. Long Tom, if their foraging turned out well, linked to a goodsized flamethrower that fed from the pressure fuel tank in the lazaret. (Fortunately *Mohican* had been converted to diesel, said Cragg, or else this lethal combination wouldn't be practical.) Amidships it would be nice to have a brace of rocket launchers, to round out an armament mix he'd come across in an article about "Patrol Guerrilla Motor Boats" in an old *Naval Institute Proceedings*. But Cragg guessed they mustn't expect miracles. He would settle for an additional 40-mm. machine gun, which his

World War II veterans could doubtless manage a lot better, anyhow.

"Why the flamethrower?" Toyon asked.

Using both hands to illustrate his point, Cragg detailed the tactics of a situation that would most likely confront *Mohican* in the ultimate stage of her mission. His right hand, representing the PT boat, drove straight toward the thumbside of his left hand, which represented an enemy vessel. At this juncture, said Cragg, they'd be blasting away with their machineguns and the 40-mm. cannon, keeping the foe off balance while they closed for the kill. Then the *coup de grâce* would be administered by the flamethrower after they'd damned near boarded the Kong, or at least come within short-range spitting distance. It was, Cragg admitted, a new and unorthodox concept. But it made a lot of sense.

As for *Medusa*, she would be rigged in such a fashion as to make her appear an ordinary, seagoing, fishstinking, cluttered junk. He intended to pattern her after those British Q-ships that raised such havoc with the Nazi raiders in the early 1940s. Cragg envisioned six .50-caliber machine guns along each side, firing from concealed ports in her stout wooden flanks, plus a 40-mm. cannon high on her East Indiaman poop, which would be completely hidden by the gaggle of chicken coops, trailing lines, and sundry accouterments that made a Chinese junk a home-away-from-home for her crew. If he could, he intended to emplace a similar cannon on *Medusa*'s triangular foredeck.

At seven-thirty, well past the intended hour for relieving Yeoman Legére, they adjourned their search, having amassed roughly half of Cragg's inventory. The smaller weapons had been easy to obtain. But the 75-mm. cannon and the flamethrower proved to be items which only field commanders could requisition without a personally signed order from General Kwo. And mortars were out of stock entirely.

So Toyon said he would drop Cragg at the hotel, and then bung along to Government House, where he'd relay their difficulties to the general. When they sortied next morning, he would have all the necessary papers for the other items, including a

Patton tank, if Mr. Cragg decided during the night that this, too, was indicated.

"I might take you up on it. We could lash a tank to *Medusa's* welldeck and—" Cragg broke off, laughing, at the sight of Toyon's anguished grimace. Somewhat stiffly after almost six hours spent cruising GaiSong's potholed streets, he debarked from the jeep and waved goodbye. "Hell, colonel, forget the Patton. I'll settle for that Long Tom and a barbecue torch."

Toyon looked relieved. "Until tomorrow, Mr. Cragg."

"Roger." As the colonel moved to depart, Cragg detained him with a final request: "There's one more item we'll need—a full set of combat swimming gear." Toyon's relief became puzzlement, so Cragg added: "It's for my executive officer, Torgerson, who's a damned fine skindiver, among other things. You can never tell, colonel, what uses we might find for underwater equipment."

"Please write down the specifics," Toyon said resignedly.

Cragg scribbled a catalogue of the essentials: neoprene foam rubber wet-suit, gloves, face mask, sheath knife, swimfins, special life jacket, oxygen units, and explosive materials for constructing bangalore torpedoes.

"That should cover it."

Toyon took the list. "Very interesting," he said, leaving.

Denny's low-pitched voice, muffled by the door panel, answered his rataplan knock. *"Qui est là?"*

He grimaced at the unyielding, paint-flaking door. *"C'est moi, bébé. M'sieu Cragg. Ouvrez!"*

The key turned briskly, and he stepped inside as the door swung open. As usual, it was furnace-hot in the sealed room. But somehow it wasn't the same as Cragg had remembered it from the previous afternoon, before his visit to General Kwo, when he had finished charting the Mafia's course up the Thietvanne coast. The girl's subtle perfume gave it a living presence, softening its ugliness, cloaking its dubious past.

"I have finished all the typing," she said.

"Good."

"And when you did not return, I went to a pharmacy and

purchased this for you." She proffered a bottle of greenish-white liquid. "You must use it."

Cragg eyed the unlabelled concoction doubtfully. "What's in the stuff? It looks godawful."

"Bismuth. Paregoric. Anise. Certain other healthful ingredients."

"Do I have to drink it straight?"

"*Comment?*"

"Without even a slug of bourbon?"

Denny smiled. "Yes, M'sieu Cragg. As you say, straight."

"The Cragg's straight, too, without the monsieur. Remember?"

She nodded soberly, but with a hint of amusement in her eyes. "How do the American sailors respond to an order from their superior? Aye, aye, sir!" Then, demurely, she added: "Cragg."

He limped to the sagbottomed bed and sat down heavily. "To hell with house rules, baby. Let's open up and invite in some of that lovely fresh air." He stretched his long body full length upon the rumpled bedspread.

"Aye, aye, sir," Denny repeated, starting for the window.

Cragg saw that she had taken off her clumsy boots. In her black cotton hose, Denny's feet looked very small, and her legs much too slender for the mansized tasks he supposed she must perform at Dokoro Mission.

He yawned. "Black stockings don't do a damned thing for a female, you know, unless they're nylon mesh."

Denny didn't reply immediately. She appeared totally engaged with the rusted crank handle. When she spoke, there was a curious note in her voice, that might have betokened embarrassment, or irony, or self-deprecatory humor. Unable to see her expression, however, Cragg couldn't be sure.

"At Dokoro," she said, "one does not wear nylons because of the mud."

"I'll buy you a pair for formal dinners aboard *Mohican*." Cragg said. "It's a real clean boat."

When she turned toward him, she was smiling once more. "But I am only the cook, *mon capitaine,* and cooks do not come to the table with their masters."

"The Mafia's democratic," he said sleepily, "where women are concerned."

Denny padded across the room. She picked up the bottle which he had set on the bedstand, unscrewed the cap, and poured an inch of syrupy medicine into a glass.

"Drink," she commanded.

With a groan, Cragg obeyed. He pretended to gag. Then he collapsed in mock anguish, shutting his eyes against the overhead glare. It had been a long day. Unaccountably, he found himself impelled to relate his experiences to this strange, resolute girl, to confide in a way that surprised himself, even as he was describing all that had happened since the hotel operator called him at dawn. From her straight chair at the desk, Denny listened attentively. She laughed from time to time at some absurd observation about Thiet chicanery, or Colonel Toyon's oddball anglicisms. But mostly she seemed content to let Cragg ramble.
. . .

He awakened suddenly, aware that the room was very quiet, and raised himself on one elbow. His wristwatch showed eleven P.M. Except for the twenty-five-watt bulb that shone pallidly from the student lamp, and a thin finger of moonlight probing through the open casement, it was quite dark, almost funereal. Denny was at the desk, asleep, with her head upon her folded arms.

Cragg got up. Aside from a slight stiffness in his joints caused by the unaccustomed bronco tactics of Colonel Toyon's jeep, he felt better than he had for days. His gut no longer ached. Although this might mean only a tenuous truce with the dysenteric amoebae, he was grateful for the surcease that Denny's medicine had given him.

He shook her gently by the shoulder. "Reveille, Yeoman Legére."

With a shamefaced grin, like a sentry caught slumbering on duty, Denny sprang to seated attention on the uncomfortable chair. Cragg looked down at her. "Why did you let me sleep?" he demanded accusingly.

"You were tired, Cragg."

"And now I'm hungry. That stuff of yours worked. It's the first time I've craved a decent meal in a week."

She peered at her own masculine wristwatch. "But at this hour—"

He interrupted. "They'll still be serving at that crazy river-boat restaurant. I know the place, I've been there as late as two A.M., when it's still jumping."

"I have heard about the Happytime," Denny said doubtfully, "although I have never been there."

"What did you hear?"

"Many strange things. It is reported that Lian Huk, its owner, has amassed a fortune selling black market food and liquors to the foreigners and their women, perhaps with the connivance of the government."

"Not perhaps, baby. Positively. They're all in cahoots. Like packrats, they stash away everything that's lying around loose, plus a hell of a lot that isn't."

Denny nodded in melancholy agreement. "When I tried to purchase medicinal brandy for Dokoro Mission, I was told that none was available, that the Thietvanne field hospitals had taken the entire supply. It was the same when I asked for grain alcohol, until Colonel Toyon exerted his influence."

"Naturally. Lian Huk 'distills' his own gin aboard the Happytime. For him it's an act of patriotism, seeing that the martini crowd doesn't go thirsty. After all, some of his best customers are local V.I.P.s, and if he doesn't keep 'em properly oiled, how can they keep on fighting the war?"

"War!" Denny's chin lifted scornfully. "These men are not fighting. They are dividing the estate, while their country bleeds on its deathbed."

"You feel pretty damned strongly about it, don't you?"

"Yes, Cragg. Damned strongly." She stared up at him angrily, as if he, too, were among the spoilers. "You will learn for yourself, soon enough, why I am bitter. Once we reach Dokoro. . . ." She paused, shrugging her slim shoulders, and did not continue.

With a hint of irony in his voice, Cragg said: "You're an exceptionally noble citizen, Denny, in a world full of complete and utter bastards, if you'll excuse their baptismal name. Frankly, I don't like Lian Huk, either, but sometimes a man's appetite outweighs his scruples. What's more," Cragg said, "if we don't eat his steaks and drink his booze, somebody else who's a lot less deserving will. So in the long run we wouldn't have accomplished a damned thing, would we?"

Rising, Denny reached for her dusty cloak. "Very well. I shall go with you. But I will not share Lian Huk's stolen food and liquor."

"Maybe I'll have what's left on my plate put in a doggie bag," he said, "so you can eat it when nobody's looking."

"*Comment?*"

"Doggie bags are a quaint offshoot of the affluent Yankee society. Nobody goes hungry. Not even Rover." He grinned. "While you're using the facilities, I'll crawl out of these beat-up khakis and into something more elegant for the occasion." As Denny started for the bathroom, with the brown garment draped over her arm, he added slyly: "Will you do me one huge favor, mademoiselle?"

"Yes, Cragg."

"Belay that goddamned Mother Hubbard. When I buy the nylons, I'll also pick up a nice mink stole."

Denny replaced the offending coat on the back of the desk chair. She blushed. "In Thietvanne one does not wear furs," she said in a hurt tone.

"Tonight you won't even need a tulle shawl." He inhaled the warm, moist air from the illegal window. "It must be ninety degrees outside, with enough humidity to float a battleship."

"You are ashamed of my costume," she insisted.

Caught off balance at this unexpected display of feminine pique, yet amused, Cragg sought to mollify her. "When you're wrestling mosquitoes upcountry," he acknowledged lamely, "it must be a damned useful outfit. But here in town—"

Denny interrupted in a cold voice, "Here in town the women dress to please those *bastards* you mentioned a moment ago, and to keep their minds off a war that neither of them, male or female, will admit exists."

Cragg spread his huge hands in a sign of total surrender. "For God's sake, wear the thing. I couldn't care less."

Without further comment, Denny marched into the bathroom and slammed the door. Ten minutes later she emerged wearing fresh lipstick, her luxuriant dark hair carefully combed, and a tentative smile on her small face. She held out her left hand, like a schoolgirl waiting to be escorted into the promenade line of a formal ball.

"Let us proceed, Cragg."

He took her arm. Marveling at its muscular firmness, he led her toward the hall, away from the shabby room, away from the chair upon which lay the purposefully forgotten cloak. In recognition of the moment, Cragg himself had donned a khaki flight jacket, and put on a necktie.

For a judiciously applied 500-piastre note, Lian Huk found them a table on the choice outboard side of his refurbished paddlewheel steamer, with a fine view of the moon-drenched Dalagong River. It was, like all of the tables at the Happytime, quite small, designed for clandestine leg-feeling as much as for the economics of Lian Huk's shrewd operation. Cragg cramped himself against his chair to avoid a frontal collision with Denny's knees. He ordered a Dubonnet for her and a double scotch-on-the-rocks for himself.

"Make it genuine scotch," he instructed. "Not that lousy Jap stuff. And bring us a couple of your best steaks. Rare."

Lian Huk departed humming a wordless Thiet tune, cheerfully confirmed in his belief that this tall, lanky American was indeed a live one (to use the Yankee's own colorful argot) despite the dowdiness of the French girl who accompanied him. No matter. *Chacun à son goût* (as the French said) when it came to women. Personally, Lian Huk preferred them cut more along the classic pattern, blonde, highbreasted, callipygian, with what the discriminating Americans called a come-hither look in their mascaraed eyes. Lian Huk employed a dozen such houris aboard the Happytime. They drank expensive ginger ale from refilled Veuve Cliquot magnums, made explicit love beneath the gaudy paper lanterns on the verandah deck, and often went home with their aroused customers after the bar closed at four A.M.

"That man," Denny said distastefully, "reminds me of a coral snake."

Shifting his legs, Cragg extended them cautiously on either

side of his companion's chair, without disturbing her. "Lian Huk is the resident bastards' favorite boy. And the taxes he pays on his Happytime income—at least the part of it they can nail him with—makes this their favorite money tree."

Cragg gazed downriver toward the broad, looping roadstead where the cargo vessels were anchored. In the light of the effulgent moon it was possible to watch the gantry cranes unloading the few ships that had found berths alongside the inadequate docks, and to glimpse the tiny locomotive towing its string of flatbed cars along the gravel strip which paralleled the sluggish Dalagong, hauling precious military freight to the Thiet warehouses. It was a primitive operation, remindful of the South Pacific days, when an earlier conflict had engulfed a French colony called New Caledonia. The capital of that island was Noumea. Its twelve thousand inhabitants treated the war effort in much the same cavalier fashion which GaiSong's two million reserved for their own present crisis—as an annoyance to be overcome, or better yet, transformed into a profitable enterprise.

Denny was speaking again.

"When you invited me to dinner, Cragg, I behaved abominably, did I not?" She gave him a rueful smile. "Perhaps it is because I am an emotional woman. For that you must forgive me."

"Emotion is a woman's privilege," Cragg said.

"Don't men ever succumb to emotion?" Denny asked in an innocent tone.

He uttered a harsh laugh. "Not if they want to survive in this godforsaken jungle."

"Thietvanne?"

Cragg paused to let the waiter place their glasses in front of them. "Thietvanne. Berlin. Israel. Cyprus. Vietnam. Korea. Hell, anyplace, including my own dearly beloved California. They're all populated by man-eating tigers." He sampled his scotch. It was almost genuine. "Tigers can't afford emotion, and neither can the tiger-hunters. The only neurotic tigers I've ever seen were the ones in the Fleishacker Zoo, pacing their cages and wondering where the hell they'd gone wrong."

Denny's air of innocence seemed to heighten. "Wasn't it pity that made you change your mind about giving me a passage to Dokoro? And isn't pity a valid emotion?"

"Pity didn't have a damned thing to do with it," he growled. "It was a practical decision. You can handle a necessary job. So you're part of the crew."

"Thank you, Cragg."

"Don't thank me, baby. Thank the fact that you can communicate in ten gook dialects."

"It would help," Denny said earnestly, "to refrain from calling them 'gooks.' Even in the remotest hamlets, these are human beings, who feel as deeply about life as you or I." She lifted her glass to eye level and studied the roseate wine for an instant. "Perhaps more deeply, Cragg."

"Freely translated, I suppose, even the primitives are entitled to their emotions?"

"Yes." Denny took a dainty sip of her apéritif. "Familial love. Affection for the small acre upon which they were born, and where they will doubtless end their days, despite its natural hostility."

"What about the other billion hectares beyond their own little plot?" Cragg demanded. "Do they also love those enough to die for them?"

"It has been so many years since this war began," said Denny, "that a whole new generation has grown up, unaware of how the struggle began, or why it must continue."

"Wouldn't they be as well off if the Kong won?"

"No, Cragg. Because then they could not even regard that simple acre as home. We try to teach them this in the Dokoro Mission school. But it is difficult. When one is little, he cannot easily picture how it would be to have nothing."

"You're waging a losing fight, baby."

"Perhaps."

"Why don't you quit before it's too late?"

Denny regarded him somberly. "Why did *you* volunteer for this losing game?" she countered.

"Hell, I didn't volunteer. I was drafted."

"I do not comprehend."

"Maybe drafted isn't the right word. Toyon ran after me, waving a fistful of dollar bills, and I couldn't escape."

"You are very cynical." She stared out across the placid river, toward the low-lying distant shore where an occasional pinprick of light delineated the Kong guerrillas' bold encampments. "How far away is San Francisco?"

"Six thousand miles."

"Then surely it must have been more than money that brought you here."

"I'm just a red-blooded American boy, I guess. Adventure appeals to me."

"Unless one believes in a cause," Denny said softly, "it is wrong to kill."

"But *you* believe the Thiets are on the side of the Lord, don't you?"

"Yes."

"So what difference does it make, whether I'm officially baptized in the faith, or whether I merely play for the team that owns me?" He took a drink. "Look, in the States a guy from Alabama can play football for a team in New York. That doesn't make him a New Yorker. He probably hates the place. But he's loyal to his bosses, as long as they pay him well."

Denny frowned. "This isn't a game, Cragg."

"Hell, war's the best participant sport that was ever invented."

"Then it was invented by the Devil himself!"

"Granted. So were a lot of businesses. That's why non-involved types like myself are better equipped to follow ground rules without getting confused." He added ironically: "And without getting the basic issue all fuzzed up with emotionalism."

"What *is* the basic issue?"

"Staying alive, and winning."

"But even a professional might die in this 'business' of yours, Cragg," she murmured.

"Everybody's dying from the moment they're born. It depends on how much you want to live. Me, I started dying forty-five years ago. So it doesn't matter, does it, when the axe falls?"

"That's immoral."

"How old are you?"

"Twenty-three."

"Then you're almost half as dead as I am. Except you don't realize it, because you've been inoculated with a lot of silly ideas." As Cragg finished speaking, the waiter eased noiselessly alongside them, bearing two sizzling steak platters. He arranged them on the table with a flourish. Cragg reached for his fork and knife. "Let's stop yakking, and eat this ill-begotten food."

During their talk, Cragg's attention had been diverted from the river. Now he addressed himself single-mindedly to his meal, unaware that Denny was ignoring his command to eat. Instead, she was gazing through the plate glass window, as if searching for logical words with which to counter this crass philosophy.

Thus it was that the girl saw her first, breasting the sluggish current like a vestpocket East Indiaman, carrying herself with a bogus dignity that belied her clumsy lines, which were softened and attenuated by the moonglow.

In a surprised voice Denny said, "What a curious circumstance, Cragg, to see a Chinese junk flying your American flag."

He put down his knife and fork.

Obviously under power, since she did not bother to tack against the offshore breeze, the approaching vessel was quite close, and despite the uncertain light, *Medusa*'s three-quarter silhouette was unmistakable. She looked immeasurably better than Cragg remembered her from Hong Kong. Her rigging was taut. Her raked masts were properly stepped. And her fresh canvas sails would be the despairing envy of every junk captain in GaiSong harbor, once the sun rose.

Caught in the bright beam of a searchlight mounted upon her commodious poopdeck, the flag rippled from the mainmast pinnacle traditionally reserved for the weathervane pennon that denoted a junk's home port. Cragg's heavy brows knit in annoyance. Considering her mission, it was highly irregular for *Medusa* to be showing the United States colors at all, much less after sundown. This unseemly touch of bravado, he guessed, was the combined decision of Lars Torgerson, who couldn't resist a practical joke, and of Duke Harris, who had probably found the legalism that justified it. Such as Article 710 of Navy Regulations, which specified that "under no circumstances shall an action be commenced or battle fought without the display of the national ensign." But it played hob with their urgent need for anonymity at this delicate juncture.

"That's the other ship of my elegant hired fleet," Cragg grunted. "She's crewed by idiots."

Still scowling, he continued to watch as *Medusa* drew parallel with the floating restaurant. At this close range he could see the great, villainous, squinting Evil Eye painted on the portside of her blunt bow; and he saw the four men on her concave deck, preparing the ninety-foot craft for anchorage. Torgerson himself stood at the horizontal spoked wheel, a triumphant Viking, keeping her rigidly on course among the clutter of sampans that plied the Dalagong on their mysterious night errands.

As Cragg turned toward Denny, ready to amplify his dour remark about the Mafia's behavior, a thunderclap explosion ripped apart the Happytime cafe.

In that unearthly split-second, the sternwheeled pleasure dome was transformed into an inferno, raked by shrapnel, by lethal shards from the burst windows, by splintered segments of flooring, by bulkheads and furniture, all of them propelled across the ruined salon like the debris that follows in a tornado's wake.

Cragg found himself flattened against the minuscule dance floor, alongside the girl, miraculously uninjured except for a gash over his right eye. Instinct kept him where he was, with his crooked left arm laid protectively across her shoulders, while the screaming survivors of the blast milled toward the inadequate exits that led to the weather deck. Denny did not move. He supposed that she was dead. Yet he continued to protect her against the roughshod feet of those who sought imagined safety beyond the flaming, shattered room.

Suddenly a second explosion, greater than the first, sent its concussive wave across the shambles. There were more screams. Then the anguished voices stopped. In the comparative quiet that followed, Cragg heard only the dry crackling of flames, and the sound of the Happytime's ancient superstructure breaking up.

He raised his head cautiously.

Between the heaped tables and the gaping holes that had been doors lay the bloodied corpses of the recent merrymakers. They were flung about in the careless attitudes of discarded rag dolls, clothing ripped from their bodies, naked limbs crushed and severed. Some of the diners had been killed at their tables, struck by poniards of steel from the initial bomb. Owing to the freakish path of the concussion, they were still sitting upright in their chairs, with their wine goblets unbroken. Among the scattered bodies, a few wounded Happytimers were starting to move, now that the worst had passed.

It was the ultimate scene from a mad artist's diorama of Hell.

The Kong terrorists had employed a particularly devilish stratagem, exploding the first bomb to cause a stampede in the crowded room, with a follow-up charge that slaughtered those who survived the initial carnage. During the war Cragg had been witness to a similar act on a narrow jungle trail outside the PT camp at Bougainville. The enemy had constructed his frightful weapon from a Claymore mine, a device that spews an arc of knife-sharp fragments for fifty yards or more. Like the double-edged Scottish sword whose name it bears, the Claymore lops off heads, dismembers, disembowels, scything to ribbons everything and everybody along its lethal pathway.

On Bougainville, the target had been American marines, combat veterans inured to battle, hardened to the possibility of sudden death. On the Happytime there were no marines. True, a few stray Yank sailors from the tincans out in the harbor had drifted into the place with their Thiet girlfriends. But the rest were civilians, noncombatants.

Cragg nudged Denny with his good right arm. She made a faint whimpering noise, stirred, and rotated her face toward his painfully, as if it hurt to move.

"Are you all right?"

"I think so." Denny stared over his shoulder in horror. "Oh, blessed Mother of God. . . ."

Slowly, like a somnambulist rising out of bed, she struggled to her feet, before Cragg could offer his hand.

"You'd better wait till a doctor has a chance to check you over," he said, "you never know about blast damage."

Denny shook her head. "No, Cragg. I must help."

Resolutely, in a manner that allowed no interference, she walked across the bloodstained deck and began administering elementary first aid, as the first wail of ambulance sirens keened through the shattered hull.

At that holocaustic moment, when all capacity for shock had been drained, Cragg was not at all astonished to see Torgerson and Mario DelGrado burst through the jagged door frame of the outboard exit. Torgerson arrived first. Looming big against the night sky, baleful in the crimson gleam of the unchecked fires, Lars might have been a chance witness at the last skirmish of Armageddon. But his huge Scandinavian face betrayed no awe at the scene before him. It was contorted with the berserk rage that gripped him whenever something beyond his own brawny ability to prevent occurred within his sight and hearing, or happened to him, personally.

Suddenly Torgerson spotted him.

"Jesus H. Christ!" he bellowed. "It's Cragg."

"What's left of me, fella."

Torgerson's furious look had eased into a semblance of concern. "You okay?"

"Minor cuts and bruises," Cragg said. "I'm damned lucky."

DelGrado looked around the room and instinctively drew a cross against his grimy T-shirt. "I had the binocs trained this way when it all began," he said in a wondering tone, "watching all the people have fun. When we were about two hundred yards away, I saw these two guys with black boxes climbing aboard from a little sampan. It seemed funny so I kept looking—"

"And a few minutes after that," interrupted Torgerson, "this frigging orange crate blew apart like a ten-inch salute. It was a hell of a welcome you laid on for us, skipper."

"Duke Harris figured they could use some help fighting fires," DelGrado added simply. "That's why we high-tailed over."

Torgerson said, "He and Trump have already got the pumps working, *Medusa* should be pouring riverwater into the furnace any second now."

"It's a damned nice try," Cragg said, "but it won't do much

good. Nothing can save this bucket. She's sinking." He peered toward a distant corner where Denny, barely discernible through the acrid smoke, was assisting an ambulance crew. "Main thing is to get the wounded out of here before they drown."

Torgerson saluted. "Aye, aye, sir."

Hobbling painfully, Cragg led them away from the area of the dead, to that section of Happytime's saloon where most of the maimed were concentrated. His crippled right leg felt worse than usual. He guessed it had borne the brunt of his fall when the explosion flattened him against the deck.

Twenty minutes later their rescue work was finished. Out of the eighty-seven persons whom Lian Huk listed as patrons that night, forty-eight had been killed instantly. Five others died later at the Thiet army hospital. The remaining thirty-four would survive, after a fashion, to mourn their lost kin and curse the Kong. Nobody ever found the saboteurs who triggered the massacre. It was assumed that they, like the *kamikazes* of an earlier war, had immolated themselves in their own bomb blast.

Less than a quarter-hour after the second explosion, the gutted hulk settled upon the muddy bottom of the Dalagong, with most of the dead still aboard.

Cragg was the last to jump across the widening gap between the two vessels as *Medusa*, abandoning the hopeless task, edged clear. In those final moments he had looked in vain for Denny. But she was nowhere in sight. Aware that nurses would be desperately needed, Cragg supposed she had gone with an ambulance to the hospital.

Now he made his way aft from the junk's deep waist, past the small teakwood cabin which had replaced her original owner's tarpaulin shelter, and thence up the sharp incline to the galleon-like poop. Lars Torgerson, his face blackened, pale brows singed bare, had resumed his rightful place at the wheel. Normally two men were required to turn the mammoth rudder. But Torgerson gloried in his single-handed ability to swing the heavy wooden spokes without human assistance or recourse to the steering tackle. Impelled by her sturdy one-cycle diesel, *Medusa* was again headed upstream at six knots, aiming for the mooring which GaiSong's harbormaster had allotted them by radio an aeon ago, before the trouble began.

Cragg collapsed gratefully into a canvas chair.

Despite his near-exhaustion, however, he gave the clumsy craft a swift professional scrutiny, before closing his eyes to let Trump Gideon bathe and bandage the ragged gash on his forehead. She was, he decided, about as shipshape as any junk could expect to be, from her lyre-backed stern to her ridiculously flat prow, below which hung three mammoth anchors. His cursory appraisal had uncovered no evidence of preparations for *Medusa's* clandestine armament. Even the chicken coops and pig cages that were secured against the stern panel, above the creaking rudder, looked natural. They'd make ideal cover for the 40-mm. cannon which Colonel Toyon's men would bring aboard tomorrow, as would the heaped-up pile of manila hawsers on the bow.

With a twinge of disloyalty, it struck Cragg that *Medusa*, for all her gaggle of gear, was actually more of a ship than *Mohican*, although she measured only ten feet longer than the eighty-foot PT, and was four times slower. Yet she evolved from a nautical lineage whose unbroken ancestry went back almost fifty centuries, whereas the PT wasn't invented till World War One. Legend related that ancient Cathay's Emperor Fu Hsi, who believed himself the result of a union between a water sprite and a rainbow, had ordained the construction of the original junk in 3000 B.C. No matter. By Marco Polo's time, the Chinese were among the world's smartest sailors, with an inflexible seafaring code that still serves as the model for many a naval regulation.

"The captain becomes a king when he is at sea," reads this basic bible. *"Even if he is young, he must be considered an old man as long as he is head of the vessel."*

Feeling his age, and more, Cragg cast a final glance along *Medusa's* broadwaisted deck, spread below him like the courtyard of a medieval castle. Lashed across the cabintop was the seventeen-foot motor whaler he had insisted they buy in Hong Kong. Somewhere along the line they might need an auxiliary smallboat, he said, either to rescue some damned fool who fell overboard, or to implement the crucial stage of the plan which, as yet, was still vague in his mind. Although *Mohican* herself carried an inflatable liferaft, capable of sustaining twelve men, its sole propulsion, other than paddles, was a half-baked sail assembly. At best, this crude device guaranteed four sidewise miles for every five the raft moved ahead. "It flew," Cragg paraphrased saturninely, "on a wind and a prayer."

Wearily, then, he shut his eyes, and let Trump Gideon go to work on his wound with an alcohol-dipped swab. Later they'd gather around the messtable for one of Mario's bellypleasing dinners. There would be time enough to break the news about Colonel Toyon, the Thiet crew, and Mlle. Denise Legére. . . .

Like a pale silken scarf across a woman's bare shoulders, a mist had draped itself along the surface of the tepid river, as the atmosphere grew imperceptibly cooler during the hour it took DelGrado to prepare their meal. Through the haze, dimly perceived, there was a curious cloud formation that seemed to rise directly out of the setting moon's polar cap. Still glowing, but reddish now that it lay so close to the horizon, the moon gave the appearance of a world in flames, and the upward curving cloud might have been the vestigial remnants of a thermonuclear explosion. Below it, in a northerly direction from GaiSong, other lights were visible, which had nothing to do with the city's nocturnal life. These flashed, went dark, then flashed again. They marked the cannonading in the delta country at the foot of the Fantastic Mountains, where Thiets and Kongs were locked in combat along the approaches to the capital, less than forty miles away. As he sensed, rather than heard, the heavy gunfire that caused the distant bursts, Cragg's desire to leave GaiSong became more urgent.

From the metropolitan side of the Dalagong, carried by the feeble offshore breeze, wafted the city's omnipresent stench. It was a melange of odors generated by too many peasant refugees crammed into too little living space, and by open-air cookery whose only substance was brown rice and the noxious *nuoc mam* fish sauce. Tonight it was made worse by the lingering aroma of charred wood and flesh which drifted across the water from the restaurant hulk.

Doomed GaiSong stank like death itself.

And yet its people were going about their nocturnal business as if nothing had happened. The savage momentary excitement had faded along with the dwindling wail of the ambulance sirens. In its wake remained only the briefest memory of a pain that came and went, which none could cure, and which therefore must be accepted as Buddha's will. Although GaiSong's fatalistic reaction to the bombing was expectable, it was also deeply perplexing to Cragg, as he stared across the narrow expanse that lay between *Medusa* and the tranquil city.

Shaking these random impressions from his bandaged head, Cragg turned to face his companions.

The four men were squatting cross-legged around a lowslung oriental table that DelGrado had placed on the welldeck. Replete after a hearty dinner, warmed by the Chianti which Mario had produced with such a flourish from his galley locker, they had lit cigarettes and were now quietly blowing smoke at the insect swarms. They seemed quite unaware of the incongruous image they evoked, here in the midst of a war-that-wasn't. After all, it hadn't bothered them to feast on the beaches twenty-five years ago, and it didn't concern them now.

Torgerson spoke first. Indicating the muffled gunflashes, he observed in the judicious tone of a first-night critic: "It's coming awfully goddamned close, skipper."

Cragg nodded. Perhaps his purpose would be better served if he approached the subject obliquely, rather than frontally, as he had intended. "If this were San Francisco instead of GaiSong, they'd be scrapping over who gets to boss San Quentin. That's how goddamned close it is, fella."

Torgerson pondered this geographical analogy for a moment. Then he rumbled: "If we hadn't bugged out like the goddamned Frogs did a few years ago, these people might've had a chance."

"Obviously *our* guys figured they didn't," said Cragg. "At least, that's how the Big Brains calculated the odds, after trying everything in the book. Advising. Bombing. Ground support. Hell, mister, somebody's got to blow the whistle when it needs blowing."

"Remember Guadalcanal?" Torgerson demanded hotly. "And how these same Big Brains damned near pulled us off that crazy island?"

"Sure I remember. Probably they would have in another week or so, considering the losses the marines were absorbing. But that was a different kind of war, and a different kind of enemy, who stood and fought when you tracked him down." Cragg spat contemptuously over *Medusa's* highrailed side. "These Kong are a different breed of fanatic. They hit hard and run fast. Like tigers. For some oddball reason, they want to live so they can fulfill their mission, which is delivering GaiSong to their rulers in Phom Than, all neatly wrapped up in butcher's paper, when the rains stop."

"If tonight's a sample there won't be a ruddy lot left to put under the tree."

"Assuming GaiSong holds out till Christmas, you mean."

"It'll hold," Cragg opined solemnly. "The Kong haven't started moving down in force. Not yet. This is just the advance guard, the probing action. They're waiting for their weapons buildup before they holler for the main body."

"How soon will that happen?"

"Toyon's intelligence jokers claim it's just around the corner. Maybe a few weeks. Maybe a couple of months. No more." Cragg reached into the breast pocket of his jacket for one of the Havanas from the box General Kwo had given him. Before lighting it, he glumly inspected the crumpled cigar, surprised to find that the fragile tobacco cylinder had fared even worse than his own gimp leg during the fall. After he'd gotten it drawing reasonably well, Cragg resumed: "That timetable speedup explains why Quid Kwo was willing to boost our take. He's counting damned heavily on us."

In his nasal voice, Duke Harris drawled: "If it weren't considered such frightfully bad luck, old boy, we should rename this preposterous vessel. Something like *Kwo's Last Straw*." He smoothed the strands of lank hair across his eggshaped skull, trying to discourage the mosquitoes that hungered for his moist, bald scalp.

"We've taken that chance already," Cragg reminded him. "This scow started life thirty years ago as *Lotus Blossom*."

Torgerson's ribald laugh boomed across the table. "Hell, there's only one kind of luck. Bad. And it's caused by plain stupidity. Good luck isn't accidental. It's what you make for yourself."

Cragg saw his opening. He asked sardonically: "Did you figure on bringing us 'good luck' when you barged into GaiSong harbor like a Star Spangled advertising blimp?"

"Flying the flag was Duke's idea," Torgerson muttered.

"So naturally you bought it. Very cute. Very public-spirited." Cragg tossed away his smoldering cigar. "Also very stupid. Especially when you topped it by playing Good Samaritan with half our goddamned navy."

DelGrado asked in a disbelieving voice: "You mean we shouldn't have lent those poor devils a hand?"

"I mean exactly that, Mario. Until we start north, it's not our fight. By getting involved, you guys have blown skyhigh what little cover we've been able to preserve. And Christ knows it wasn't much to start with."

"In all the confusion," said Harris, "I doubt whether anybody noticed the ruddy American flag."

"Balls! Nothing escapes the Kong. Kwo can't transfer a corporal's guard from GaiSong to the delta without striking sparks. Those babies have eyes like horseflies, in the back of their shaved heads. They notice everything." Cragg let the Mafia wait in silence while he limped from the rail to the cushion where he had been seated during the meal, and cupping his chin upon his upraised left knee, he studied them each in turn, the way a sniper might estimate an array of prime targets before taking careful aim.

Only Torgerson appeared undaunted by Cragg's fixed stare.

"So we pulled a boner," he acknowledged. "Chalk it down to the fact we've been away from the game too long. We're out of practice."

Cragg grimaced as he recalled how his own offhand comparison of battlefields and playing greens had been received earlier that evening. "This isn't a game," he said, consciously echoing Denny's words.

"Anyhow," muttered Torgerson, "it won't happen again."

"You'd better be bloody well positive it won't, laddie-buck." Cragg glanced at his wristwatch. "As of right now, zero-one-five, I'm issuing all the orders. *Comprenez?*" After a short pause, he made a gavel of his clenched fist, struck the table, and declared in a parliamentarian tone: "There being no objections, the motion is hereby carried."

Even the unrepentant Torgerson looked relieved. From long experience, the Mafia knew that Cragg had forgiven their blunder, although he would never forget it. Repeating the same mistake, or one remotely like it, would bring his Jovian wrath down upon them like a thunderbolt from Olympus. There would be no escape for the wicked.

Shortly after daybreak, Cragg explained, the fifteen-man crew would report aboard *Medusa*. They would bring with them machine guns and cannon for immediate installation in accordance with a sketch he'd leave with Trump Gideon. As a security precaution, he added with more than a hint of sarcasm, the Thiets had been instructed to conceal this weaponry under stocks of bananas and breadfruit. Cragg hoped nobody would tell them to go screw, figuring they were bumboat peddlers, when their sampans came alongside.

"How will we know we're dealing with the right guys?" asked Gideon.

"No sweat. Their strawboss wears a black patch over his left eye. His name is Akim. He's an ugly customer, bigger than the rest of 'em, but Toyon trusts him." Cragg gave Torgerson a crooked glance. "As exec, you're also personnel officer. So it'll interest you to know that the colonel handpicked the whole batch while I was getting *Mohican* unloaded."

"Maybe we ought to shanghai the son-of-a-bitch and let him nursemaid his gook buddies," Torgerson snarled.

"That won't be necessary, fella. Thanks to General Kwo, Toyon is all ours for the duration. Or till death do us part." Cragg's wry look vanished. "Incidentally, we don't call them 'gooks,' I've been informed. While they're with us, we'll treat them like Yank sailors. No better, no worse. Remember, you're officers and gentlemen, now, by Act of Congress. The goddamned Thiet congress, of course, which meets every other Friday in Quid Kwo's hip pocket." He regarded Torgerson speculatively. "As a simple rule-of-thumb, mister, you might try coddling them the same way I coddled you back in the South Pacific, when you were striking for chief."

Torgerson held his comment to an insubordinate belch, but Cragg let it pass.

So Duke Harris stepped into the breach. "In the process of liquidating the Empire," he said mildly, "we British have discovered that there really aren't any lesser breeds without the law, Rudyard Kipling to the contrary notwithstanding."

Cragg gave his qualified approval to this statement. "Taking Colonel Toyon for a starter, let's proceed on that theory. This is his country. He's ready to die for it, and at damned low pay. So are his men. If anybody cares, Toyon and his one-eyed friend, Akim, have something else in common. Their families were murdered by the Kong." Embarrassed at the solemn response to his revelation, Cragg announced in an offhand manner: "We also have acquired a new chef."

"What's wrong with my cooking?" DelGrado protested. "Too much chili in the meat sauce? Too little basil? Too much garlic?"

"Nothing, Mario. But you're going to be damned busy with other duties. Like keeping *Mohican's* diesels pumping for the next three weeks."

Gideon said mournfully, "When I was traveling with the band, I ate Missouri catfish, Philadelphia scrapple, Texas tamales, and even Arkansas sowbelly. I guess I can live on Thiet garbage."

"Dry your tears, Trump," Cragg soothed. "This is a genuine French chef, trained by the great Escoffier himself."

DelGrado's dark eyes widened in respectful amazement. "Where'd you find him?"

"Not him. *Her.*"

Torgerson exploded. "Jesus H. Christ! A woman! Have you lost your everlovin' marbles, skipper?"

"Maybe," Cragg admitted. "But there wasn't any choice. Toyon wanted her, and he outranks me. You might say he's sort of her sponsor."

"You mean," Torgerson demanded angrily, "we're under a goddamned gook's command?"

Cragg ignored the forbidden epithet. "Only till we shove off. Toyon's jurisdiction stops at the water's edge."

This didn't satisfy Torgerson. "So where do we billet the colonel's lady?" he glowered. "In the chicken coops on deck? Or with the pigs?"

"Neither. Mademoiselle Legére draws *Mohican's* private stateroom." As if astonished by his own abrupt decision, Cragg paused, then added lamely: "Besides, she's not the colonel's lady."

Torgerson contrived an exaggerated leer. "Okay. So she's one of Captain Cragg's women."

"Repeat negative. She's nobody's woman," Cragg chose his words carefully, "although she does happen to be a lady. Matter of fact, she's a schoolteacher. We're giving her passage back to Dokoro Mission, where her father runs the hospital. It's that simple. She knows nursing, too, plus being a damned fine linguist. Which means she's a little extra insurance for us."

"You make this female sound like a real jungle doll," Torgerson grumbled.

"Triple negative." Cragg looked over his right shoulder toward the smoldering ruins of the Happytime. "When I last saw her, after the explosion, she looked more like Florence Nightingale on a Crimean battlefield, only smaller. And a hell of a lot busier."

"I gather the lovely lady was your date tonight, old buddy."

"She was."

Torgerson sounded pensive. "What d'you reckon is the feminine for Jonah?"

4

Plot a
Straight Course

BY DAYBREAK THE RELENTLESS cycle of torrential rains and false reprieves was threatening again. All along the eastern horizon where the China Sea met the marshy lowlands there hovered a dark cloud mass, like the afterbirth of a destroyer squadron's smokescreen, ragged, dirty, slowmoving. In flight from such unpropitious weather, even the gulls were deserting the coast to sample the easier life of the brackish Dalagong. After them came the pelicans, lumbering behind the smaller, swifter seabirds in echelon formation, rigidly disciplined as carrier bombers.

Although he knew that the previous day's respite from the monsoon downpour was only a temporary boon, for which he should have been grateful, Cragg greeted the drab dawn with a curse. It would rain by noon, he decided, scowling through *Medusa's* rigging. He swore again, more loudly. If Colonel

Toyon's monkeys ran true to form, they'd arrive late, work with maddening slowness, and run for cover when the storm hit, leaving the job half done. That could mean a full day lost, perhaps more, in getting *Medusa* outfitted. Meanwhile *Mohican*, having been assigned second priority for tactical reasons, awaited the ministrations of this same dubious crew.

For the tenth time since he came aboard *Medusa* at five A.M., an hour earlier, Cragg peered in the direction of the commercial quay where Toyon's sampans would load. He checked his watch. It was now five-thirty. If the little buggers didn't show in another five minutes, he would go below and slake his sorrows in a mug of DelGrado's jet-black coffee, along with the rest of the Mafia who had begun preparing *Medusa* for her transformation long before dawn. They'd done well. The ratty sheets of tarpaulin that dropped from the mizzenboom, and which would conceal the stern guns until Trump Gideon got them emplaced, looked plausible enough, like impromptu rainshelters. A similar contrivance screened the midships and bow sections.

Cragg hoped that the Thiets would exhibit as much appreciation for camouflage when they carried the equipment aboard, and remember they were stocking *Medusa* with bananas, not weapons.

He need not have worried.

At five-thirty-four, with barely a minute remaining of the allotted grace, the lead sampan pulled away from the wharf and headed for the anchored junk. It was followed by two others. Cragg gave a small sigh of relief. Since neither trucks nor stevedores were in evidence around the loading area, he deduced that Toyon had arranged to bring the guns down from the warehouses after sunset, and hide them in the sampans during the safest predawn hours. The colonel had shown commendable security judgment, besides saving a worrisome amount of time that might otherwise have been spent manhandling this heavy gear in the broad gray light of day. The deep-laden boats approached *Medusa*'s outward side, where they could accomplish their business in relative freedom from prying eyes ashore. Impressed, Cragg felt a glow of respect for the inscrutable little man.

Toyon came aboard first. He looked grim, more harassed than ever, as he ceremoniously shook Cragg's hand.

"I trust your technicians are prepared to install this equipment," he said in a funereal voice.

"Hell, they've been standing by since five A.M." Cragg regarded him amusedly. "Why the sudden rush?"

"During the past twelve hours," said the colonel, "certain unforeseen developments have made it most essential that we leave at the earliest possible moment."

Cragg quoted a well-remembered bit of navalese. " 'When in all respects ready for sea, proceed on duty assigned.' " He shrugged. "Except for these popguns, and taking on fuel and water, *Medusa* is ready, colonel."

"What is your best estimate of the shortest time required to accomplish these things, Mr. Cragg?"

Trump Gideon stepped forward. "That's my department, sir." He preened his neat gray moustache thoughtfully. "With luck, we should be finished by tonight. Around midnight, I'd say, considering we have only four guys available, and we can't use floodlights."

"I quite understand the necessity for working in the dark, Mr. Gideon. But there is no reason to be shorthanded." In rapid-fire Thiet, the colonel addressed the one-eyed Akim, who had fetched the second sampan alongside, and was now directing its unloading from *Medusa's* welldeck. Without interrupting his labors, Akin replied by holding up three fingers. Toyon looked pleased. "You shall have competent assistance, my friend. Three of these men are trained mechanics. Akim will detail them as soon as the boats have been emptied."

Gideon appealed doubtfully to Cragg. "Is that okay with you, skipper?"

"At this point, whatever the colonel wants, he gets. Right now it happens to be speed." Cragg gave Gideon's skinny rump a whack that propelled him toward the stern where a 40-mm. cannon had already been hoisted onto the poopdeck in its protective sheathing of bananas and breadfruit. "So pour on the coal, fella." When he turned to confront Toyon again, his jocular mood was gone. "That takes care of *Medusa*. But what about the special gear I ordered for *Mohican*?"

"Everything you requested will be at the dock this afternoon."

"Including my Big Bertha and the flamethrower?"

"Yes."

"That's fine. Except for one other minor item. We can't begin work on the PT until Gideon winds up here."

"On the contrary, Mr. Cragg. A detachment of specialists from the GaiSong ordnance depot will accompany the equipment." Something akin to a smile flickered across Toyon's usually somber face. "General Kwo has decreed that they are to work around the clock to render *Mohican* 'in all respects ready for sea,' as you so colorfully phrase it."

Cragg pondered this unexpected news for a full minute before making any comment. His instinctive reaction was to reject the Thiet ordnance men, however skilled they might prove by local standards, as too clumsy to tamper with *Mohican*'s delicate fittings. Not even Gideon had ever laid a hand on his precious property. He'd planned to supervise her armament personally, managing the tricky stuff himself, allowing Trump to wield blowtorch and welding iron only in those places where it didn't count. Maybe this was foolish. Maybe this was how a surgeon behaved when his own child needed a difficult emergency operation, and there was nobody around he could trust. Nevertheless that's how it stood. Still and all, when he came right down to bedrock, what recourse did he have? *Mohican, Medusa,* the Mafia, even Cragg himself, were now the official property of the Thietvanne government, lock, stock and commandeered gunbarrel, totally subject to Kwo's whims.

There was, of course, one shred of comfort. Once they left GaiSong, proceeding north under strict radio silence, it would be different. For then if Quid Kwo got no acknowledgment of his future orders, how could he be sure they've been heard in the first place.

"What broke the logjam, colonel?"

"Last night's bombing," said Toyon, "and the discovery of an enormous cache of Kong weapons—a veritable arsenal, sir!— hidden at a coastal village fifty miles above Dokoro Mission."

"Aren't these bombings getting pretty commonplace?"

The colonel shook his head, looking sad. "Until now, perhaps, our people have been fortunate," he said. "This marks a new

enemy tactic. One can only assume they have begun to import a
fresh supply of special weapons." Toyon drew a memorandum
from the breastpocket of his immaculate uniform jacket. "Twelve
more so-called Claymore mines were found when we raided
Hung Roa yesterday," he said, consulting the paper. "Also 3,500
rifles, one million rounds of small arms ammunition, 20,000 stick
grenades, a half-ton of TNT plastic charges, 2,000 mortar shells,
500 anti-tank grenades of a variety that has only recently been
manufactured by the Chinese." He returned the dispatch to his
pocket. "Under monsoon conditions such a major shipment
could never have reached the Kong along their overland trails."
He added gloomily: "Their coastal buildup has now commenced
in earnest, and it will increase by geometric rather than arith-
metical progression before the rains stop."

"You could be right, colonel."

"I *am* right, Mr. Cragg, believe me. Our evidence is unassailable. The Kong's packtrains abandoned the mountain passes a
fortnight ago. They have taken to the sea."

"And you're still convinced that one good hard strike against
Phom Than will stop them?"

Toyon recognized the question for what it was, calculated
rhetoric to test his faith in Cragg's audacious stratagem. "It is
your plan," he countered. "Do you still believe so?"

"No," Cragg said candidly. "I don't. But it'll jolt the bastards.
Confuse them. Make them cautious. Which means they'll have to
slow down, figuring we might have more stashed away where
this came from, if they don't want to get mangled again."

"Would your plan change if I told you that the convoy
assembling at Phom Than numbers at least fifty ships, instead of
the fifteen we originally anticipated?"

"Is that the latest scuttlebutt?"

Toyon blinked his remarkable eyes in puzzlement. "Scuttlebutt?"

"Rumors, colonel, from the intelligence mill."

"These are not rumors," Toyon said. "Thiets may not always be
eager warriors, sir, but they have an immense capacity for
espionage. I would stake my life on this information."

"Yours and mine both, colonel, along with twenty others."

Cragg gave a valedictory thought to *Mohican,* and to the Gai-Song ordnance plumbers who would soon be swarming over her fragile hull. Then, squaring his shoulders, he said resignedly: "Okay. Ready or not, we'll roll within twenty-four hours, even if it means finishing the job en route." He called to Torgerson, who was moodily inspecting the unfurled mainsail for telltale signs of mildew. "That'll have to wait, fella. We're going ashore for a strategy powwow, because the war's started a little ahead of schedule." Cragg turned. "You, too, colonel. Have your people notify us at the Galleon Hotel when *Mohican's* gear arrives."

It was hardly eight A.M., but the Eurasian desk clerk, with a benign smile, reported that Mlle. Legére had procured M'sieu Cragg's key almost thirty minutes ago, and had repaired directly upstairs after ordering a pot of tea sent to the room. He assumed it was acceptable to M'sieu Cragg, permitting her this privilege, since the mademoiselle had been here before, and was manifestly a cherished friend. M'sieu Cragg growled that whatever Mlle. Legére wanted she damned well could have. Whereupon M'sieu Cragg beckoned to his two companions, the ugly Scandinavian giant and the small Thiet colonel, and limped ahead of them to the elevator.

The desk clerk waited until the lift door clanged shut. M'sieu Cragg was indeed a bizarre man, given to strange goings-and-comings at impossible hours, and possessed of curious friends. His association with Colonel Toyon, who was reputed to be General Kwo's most trusted adviser, capped a most interesting roster. And the presence now of Mlle. Legére had begun to give meaning to certain things that the girl Koko had relayed after her last matinee with M'sieu Cragg.

Information of this sort, the desk clerk mused contentedly, shooting his grimy cuffs, could prove most useful to a poor devil with four hungry children, whose salary at the Galleon was 5,000 miserable piastres each month. He reached for the telephone.

. . .

At the sound of Cragg's familiar tattoo against the louvers, Denny opened the door immediately, and stood aside to let them enter. She was again wearing that abominable linen duster, Cragg noted, although she had discarded her equally horrendous boots.

"You needn't have punched the time clock so all-fired early," he said.

"*Comment?*"

"Skip it, *bébé*." Cragg turned. "Meet my exec, Lars Torgerson. He's a damned fine sailor, but he's also apt to behave like one when he's ashore. So watch out for him. He bites."

Torgerson gave her a wolfish grin that exposed the frontal gap where an upper tooth was missing. "Pleased to meet you, miss." He clasped Denny's hand with his mammoth paw, peering down into her startled face. "Don't worry about getting bitten. Hell, you're not *big* enough to eat."

"That is most reassuring." As Torgerson slowly released her hand, she added with a demure smile: "Although I do not believe what Cragg says about you, m'sieu, after observing your gallant behavior last night. It was a noble deed, to risk your life in such a fashion."

"It was boneheaded foolishness," snapped Cragg, "that damned near cost us the ship." He clumped across the room to the desk and unlocked the middle drawer where he kept his chart. "Now let's quit swapping bouquets and go to work."

Unabashed, still grinning, Torgerson followed after him. "You didn't do the girl justice," he said softly. "Take it from a connoisseur, skipper, there's a hell of a lot more female underneath that crazy smock than meets the untutored eye. I might work up an appetite yet."

Cragg flushed. "I hadn't noticed."

"I'll bet!"

"Stow it, mister." Suddenly these sophomoric crudities annoyed him more than usual. "She's strictly off limits. Savvy?"

"Yes, sir!" Torgerson agreed with exaggerated meekness.

"Good." Cragg unfurled the map. "Here's the finished plot. Memorize it. I'll have Denny make a copy. But you've got to know it cold, from GaiSong to Phom Than, all eight hundred miles of it." He paused. "And back again, fella, *if* we're lucky."

He motioned for Toyon and the girl to move closer so they, too, could study the chart while he outlined the Grand Design, upon which he had lavished so many hours of vexing labor. As soon as she was outfitted, hopefully before sun-up tomorrow, *Medusa* would depart, thus gaining a half-day's leeway over the swifter *Mohican,* and insuring that nobody would tab them as a pair. Each midnight thereafter they'd rendezvous at the points indicated on the chart by red X's: *Alfa, Bravo, Charlie, Delta, Foxtrot, Golf, Hotel.*

Cragg interrupted himself to explain for Denny's benefit that these were postwar alphabetical designations approved by the western Allies, which supplanted the old American signaling phonics: *Able, Baker, Charlie,* etc. Purely by coincidence, he observed, the letter *H* represented Dokoro Mission. In honor of this occasion they would change Point *Hotel* to Point *Hospital.*

The check points (Cragg went on) were one hundred miles apart. He had arrived at that exact figure simply enough, by computing *Medusa's* average rate-of-advance on a twenty-four-hour basis. By day the junk would remain well out of land range, under sail, using her diesel only if she fell behind schedule. She'd proceed under power all night. Meanwhile *Mohican,* traveling only after dark, would log a steady twelve knots. Before each dawn broke she would make for some convenient cove, and lie doggo until the next nightfall.

Once they reached Point *Hospital* (he continued) both vessels would wait offshore while *Medusa's* whaleboat reconnoitered Dokoro Mission before the PT slipped into the little harbor and refueled. *Mohican* would then ferry a deckload of diesel oil out to the junk.

Weatherwise, their blessings were a mixed bag. Although the monsoon rains would make life damned uncomfortable, keeping everyone below most of the time, they'd also provide some insurance against snoopers on the beach. Moreover, the moon had already begun to wane. By the time they reached no man's land, a hundred miles or so beyond Dokoro, it should be full darkness.

Cragg glanced around, first at Torgerson, who was silently moving his lips in an effort to absorb the unfamiliar nomenclature, then at the inscrutable Toyon, and finally at Denny. She was frowning at the map. "Any questions?"

Torgerson shook his blond, balding head. "Later," he muttered.

"Colonel?"

"None."

"Denny?"

The girl lifted her critical gaze from the map. "Certain of these rendezvous points appear to have been most carefully selected, Cragg, since they lie opposite suitable anchorages." She touched a forefinger against Point *Delta*. "Here, for example, is a good one. Although I do not admire the Frenchman who owns this plantation at Bien Goa, I believe that he can be trusted. He would doubtless aid us with supplies. But the others puzzle me."

Cragg was well aware of the faults that plagued most of his sites. Because of the inflexibility of each day's run, there had been no choice but to spot each X equidistant from its neighbor. Like the denouement of this haphazard adventure, they'd have to play these midnight get-togethers by ear, hoping the PT's short-range radar could locate *Medusa* in case some emergency required a change in the prescribed rendezvous. They would also make it standard operating procedure to send *Medusa*'s whale-boat ashore to reconnoiter before committing *Mohican*.

So Cragg saw no profit in elaborating upon the simplistic method by which he had arrived at their midnightly fixes. "What's wrong with the Frenchman?" he sparred, giving Point *Delta* a mock-serious scrutiny.

"One hears so many strange stories about M'sieu Panache that some of them surely must be true," she said cautiously.

"Such as?"

Denny hesitated. "I do not wish to gossip, Cragg."

"You'd better clue me if we're going to sample Bien Goa's hospitality."

With manifest reluctance Denny said: "M'sieu Panache inherited this plantation from his father more than twenty years ago. He has never married, yet he has many children." She shrugged delicately. "Of itself that is perhaps not unusual. Once there were many such Europeans in Thietvanne. They lived like natives in the remote areas, or on the beaches. But these were not men of substance, and they became absorbed by the very people among whom they dwelled."

"I gather that our individualistic friend hasn't been melting-potted."

"No," said Denny, "he has not. M'sieu Panache somehow continues to exist both as a Frenchman and a Thiet, growing his crops without interference and dispensing them to whoever wishes to buy."

"What sort of crops?"

"Originally Bien Goa raised only tea and rubber." She stared down at the chart. "But now a certain number of hectares have been set aside for opium poppies. It is this harvest which guarantees M'sieu Panache immunity from the Kong. The rebels collect all that he produces, take the flowers to Phom Than, process the juices, and return the powders to GaiSong, where they are sold by the underworld. Opium," she mourned, "is a destructive weapon as old as China itself."

Cragg said doubtfully, "But you still think this Panache fellow can be trusted?"

"He is, after all, a Frenchman." She looked up. "He has always been good to the mission. Often he lent us supplies. And we know that he has helped assure that the Kong respect Dokoro's status as a sanctuary, by interceding in our behalf."

"In that case, why didn't you ask Panache for the things you needed? His plantation is a hell of a lot closer."

"Because Bien Goa has no airfield." Denny's face clouded. "And it is highly improper for a woman to go there alone."

"You didn't have any such scruples about visiting GaiSong," Cragg said.

"GaiSong is a city, whereas Bien Goa is M'sieu Panache's private kingdom."

"Where even a Frenchwoman mightn't find herself immune from the loyal Frenchman?"

Colonel Toyon intervened. "From the viewpoint of the Thietvanne government, much that transpires at Bien Goa is most distressing. Officially we wish it were not so, for Panache condones the practice of certain customs on his plantation which have long been forbidden. But sometimes one must reach an accommodation with a lesser evil, in order to preserve a greater good. Let us, therefore, categorize this man as an unmoral person who serves an essential purpose."

Torgerson had been listening without comment. Suddenly he exploded a harsh laugh.

"What's so goddamned funny, mister?" asked Cragg.

"Nothing." Torgerson's mirth subsided. "Unless it's these screwball new designations." With a spatulate thumb he ticked off the last three rendezvous points after Dokoro Mission, reciting the distasteful words in a prissy voice: "*India, Juliett*— for Christ's sweet sake—*Kilo.*"

"You had a question," Cragg reminded him.

"Aye, aye, sir. Coming back to the Phom Than caper, how big is this Kong fleet we're supposed to knock out?"

"According to Thiet intelligence, it's more flotilla than fleet. The colonel figures about forty cargo junks."

Torgerson loosed another guffaw. "Hell, that's peanuts."

"Sure. Only four-to-one odds," Cragg conceded. "And besides, *Mohican's* guns should cut 'em down a notch, especially if those jokers are saving most of their weapon space for freight."

Toyon's lugubrious voice dissented. "I am afraid that you are being unwarrantedly optimistic, my friend. The Kong are not stupid. They will be armed."

"Ever whistle past a graveyard, colonel?"

"No, Mr. Cragg."

"Nevertheless, that's what I'm doing. Whistling. It's a lot cheaper than getting drunk to boost your morale."

"Perhaps," said Toyon, "I myself should practice this curious habit."

"Why not? I tried yoga once. It's no better." Cragg dropped his bantering mood. "So much for the lyrics and libretto. Now let's talk about typecasting."

During the sleepless night just past, Cragg explained, he'd devoted a vast amount of serious thought to personnel assignment, always starting from the inescapable premise that there would be no opportunity to train Toyon's fifteen men before they shoved off. Now that the schedule had been advanced by twenty-four hours, barely enough time remained to get a rough idea of

what basic talents each Thiet possessed, such as gunnery, engine
mechanics, seamanship, and the like.

Toyon coughed politely. "My men were carefully chosen, Mr.
Cragg. I can tell you that six of them, including the three
ordnance specialists who were detailed to assist Mr. Gideon,
understand automatic weapons. Seven have served in junks. Two
are acquainted with motors. And one cooks food in the European
style."

In a surly aside Torgerson muttered: "We're up to our arses in
cooks—Frog, Wop and now Christ-only-knows-what."

"That's fine." Cragg ignored his exec. "But do any of these
paragons speak English?"

"Regrettably, sir, very little."

"Torgerson will command *Medusa*. Unless you have some
valid objection, colonel, I'd appreciate your help running his
crew. He'll need an interpreter to relay orders." Cragg smiled
compassionately. "You should know that a junk rides a damned
sight more smoothly than a PT, and that we've got a bitchkitty of
a rugged trip ahead of us."

Toyon took no offense at this tacit assumption of his land-
lubberliness. "It is true, Mr. Cragg, that I am not a good sailor," he
said. "One facet of British culture which I neglected to polish at
Oxford was love of the sea."

"Then it's all settled. The others will ship with me in *Mohican*,
plus two gunners and a deckhand from your outfit."

Cragg glanced at his exec. Torgerson was weighing the pros-
pects of operating *Medusa* with an all-native crew and a seasick
Thiet army officer, bleakly aware that he had no alternative. Of
the five Mafias, only Cragg and he were qualified to skipper the
cumbersome junk.

"Don't I even rate *one* of the guys for company? Mario? Duke?
Trump?"

"Negative, fella. Mario is my engineer. Duke's got his hands
full with all that electronic gear. Trump's nursing the 75-mm.
Long Tom."

Torgerson jerked his thumb toward Denny. "What about her?"

"Sorry. As the captain's yeoman, she's indispensable. We also
need an interpreter." Then, taking pity, Cragg promised: "But

don't worry, fella. From time to time I'll spell you personally, after we've set up a routine."

"Thanks a bundle," Torgerson said bitterly.

"Anyhow, we'll all wind up in *Mohican* when it's over."

Toyon's liquescent eyes widened. "Why is that, Mr. Cragg?"

"Even assuming *Medusa* survives, we can't use her for the voyage home. We'd never make it. She's too slow. Once the dirty work is done, colonel, we'll have to haul out of Phom Than as if the devil himself was on our tail."

"But that means carrying twenty-two persons in *Mohican*," Toyon protested.

"It's an old story for PTs. They've been workhorses ever since Corregidor. You'd be surprised what they can crowd belowdecks. Besides," Cragg added stolidly, "we won't be carrying twenty-two on the return trip."

"No?"

"Don't forget casualties, colonel. . . ."

By dint of inhumanly hard driving, with Torgerson supplying the bullwhip and Gideon the technical reins, they managed to complete *Medusa's* armament a full hour before the Saturday midnight deadline. Cragg nodded his grudging approval at their handiwork.

"It'll have to do," he said.

Torgerson took the accolade in stride. "We've got a hell of a battlewagon here, skipper. J. P. Jones himself would've loved the bastard." Wiping the sweat from his balding pate, he added: "I'll stack her up against any goddamn canoe in Central Park."

Cragg dismissed the irony. "After you finish loading stores, you can knock off for the rest of the night. But I expect this bucket to be under way at dawn. Understand?" He turned to Gideon. "Take a break yourself, Trump. We'll get cracking on *Mohican's* gear at the same time, when we can see what the blazes we're doing."

"I think," opined Gideon, "that this historic commissioning rates a modest wetting-down ceremony. Don't you, bossman?"

"Maybe I'm a horse's ass for agreeing," Cragg said, "but go ahead. You've had a long haul from Hong Kong. Just keep it under control." He gave Torgerson a sharp glance. "Savvy, mister?"

The exec made an impious gesture with his right hand. "Cross my black heart and hope to crap out if we break our Boy Scout pledge."

Gideon preened his moustache. "They say GaiSong used to be a lovely liberty port. Better than Sydney."

"It's changed," said Cragg, "for the worse."

"But there *are* females in town. I've seen 'em through the prison bars." Gideon wiped his hands daintily on a piece of oily waste. "You pioneered this oriental pearl, sir. I trust you'll guide our faltering footsteps."

"Negative. I've seen all I need to see, and done all I need to do. You're on your own."

"At least," Gideon pleaded, "drop a few names."

"Try a dive called Le Coq d'Or. If you mention me, they'll only charge you triple for the drinks. And the hunting isn't too bad."

"Nice clean game?"

"Government inspected." Cragg eyed them coldly. "Better take DelGrado and the Duke along as chaperons."

As Trump Gideon described it later, the imbroglio was just one of those things that evolved, like primitive man. They hadn't really intended to get into a brawl. Nevertheless it had happened, and now they were all remorseful as hell because Cragg had been forced, in the interests of preserving his crew intact for their dawn departure, to bail them out of the mess.

Initially they had repaired to the Galleon's rooftop Poopdeck, for a few lubricative belts, as a warm-up to the business at hand. Here they had encountered a singularly unsympathetic, not to say downright hostile, audience when they sang a few close-harmony ditties from World War Deuce. Ballads like *Gorblimey* and *I Wanted Wings*. It wasn't so much the bawdy lyrics, Gideon recalled, as the sheer volume which seemed to offend the natives. Made brusquely aware that their talents were not appreciated, refused further drinks, they embarked forthwith on a pub crawling circuit which ultimately fetched them to Le Coq d'Or.

At first they were greeted warmly by the tall Thiet maître-d', who vowed that any friend of the estimable Captain Cragg was a friend of his, *parbleu!*

Somewhat less than cold sober by this time, the Mafia was

promptly engulfed by importunate waves of dark-eyed houris, whose hints of forbidden pleasures after Le Coq folded its gaudy wings at four A.M. were matched only by their capacity for fake champagne. And since this was a weekend, the Mafia was further treated to a unique performance by a stupendous doll named KoKo, who struck Torgerson as precisely the type he'd been seeking all his mother-loving life. By reason of seniority, he elected to take over the KoKo detail.

That was, in retrospect, their basic tactical error.

Having had more experience than his brother Mafians in such matters, it even then occurred to Gideon that Mlle. KoKo might enjoy a special relationship with management, or at least rate a higher fee than the price of a magnum of ginger ale, mislabeled champagne. It seemed likely, too, that the *première danseuse* might resent being cast, as it were, in the role of a filly in a claiming race. Arrangements for such a liaison, Gideon suspected, had to be worked out more diplomatically, perhaps through the maître-d' himself.

But such subtleties eluded Torgerson, who was a man of direct action.

As KoKo passed the Mafia's ringside table, en route backstage to get some clothes on, the Swede reached out with a brawny paw. She halted, glaring down at him, and brushed off his restraining hand.

"*Cochon!*"

Torgerson grinned joyfully. "A broad with spirit!" he exulted, grabbing for her again.

At that instant KoKo spat squarely into his leering face. Torgerson responded by driving the hard husk of his right thumb into her naked buttocks.

"Some goose," he grunted, "for the sauce."

Outraged, KoKo straightened up like a suddenly unflexed bow. She reached for a convenient champagne bottle, and smashed it over Torgerson's sunburnt head. It shattered beautifully.

Still grinning, disregarding the blood that gushed from his split scalp, Torgerson seized the dancer with both hands. He flipped her prone across his knees and began to administer a sound spanking.

KoKo screeched.

As the maître-d' started toward them, accompanied by a half-dozen stalwart aides, Gideon, Harris and DelGrado leaped to their feet. Until that moment they had been sitting quietly, like spectators at a bullfight, admiring the exec's technique. Now, resignedly, they cleared the decks for trouble.

Gideon swept the cloth off the postage-stamp table, sending an array of bottles, glasses and silverware crashing across the floor in the path of the oncoming foe. Whereupon DelGrado picked up the table itself, and heaved it at the maître-d', who was leading the pack. Harris dived for a light switch affixed to a nearby pillar, the location of which he had filed away in his electrician's memory, for possible future emergencies.

Although this didn't extinguish all the house lights, it reduced the already inadequate wattage to the point where the ensuing scrimmage took place in a dim, blue, cavelike atmosphere, that heavily favored the night-visioned Mafians.

Within seconds the maître-d' found it wise to beat a temporary retreat. Four of his troops had been rendered *hors de combat* by Torgerson and DelGrado, who were holding the bridgehead behind a heap of shattered tables on the perimeter of the tiny dance floor. Gideon and Harris defended the flanks and rear. Bare-torsoed now, brandishing his hamlike fists in the sepulchral gloom, Torgerson was a truly menacing figure, calculated to make the lesser Thiets pause before resuming their attack.

KoKo, having fled when hostilities commenced, screamed futile encouragement from the sidelines.

"*Tuez les bâtards! Tuez! Tuez! Tuez!*"

The maître-d' gave his star a withering look, and shouted something to the bombazine-clad cashier, who was hovering near the arched doorway. The cashier nodded. Returning to her teller's booth, she picked up the telephone and dialed.

Torgerson correctly interpreted this byplay. "They're hollering for reinforcements," he bellowed. "Let's roll!"

But the maître-d' had anticipated just such a breakthrough attempt. As the Mafia drove a salient toward the porticoed entrance of the dance hall, Le Coq's entire kitchen gang surged around the corner. There were six of them. They were armed with butcher knives and meat cleavers, which they seemed quite capable of using. Even Torgerson was impressed. Like a cautious lion tamer, holding a broken chair against his chest, he slowly gave way. DelGrado, Gideon and Harris fell back simultaneously, until the Mafia quartet was once more grouped behind its furniture barricade.

Torgerson set the defensive pattern by scooping up the broken champagne bottle with which KoKo had wreaked her revenge earlier. He flourished the lethal weapon at the advancing kitchen detail, like a boarding cutless, and they slowed perceptibly. When the other Mafians positioned themselves alongside him, similarly equipped, the Thiets halted.

Duke Harris took advantage of the lull to make a temperate suggestion: "We'd jolly well better start advancing, *mes amis,* to the rear." He motioned toward a red-glowing *sortie* sign beyond the deserted orchestra dais.

Torgerson nodded. "Okay. All engines astern full."

Very coolly, walking backward in a kind of reverse skirmish formation, they made for the exit, pursued at a respectful interval by the nightclub attendants.

Gideon was the first to reach the door. He groped for the knob in the semidarkness. "We'd better separate," he said, "and meet later at *Mohican.*"

"Check," Torgerson said.

But the door, warped tight by the tropical dampness, refused to budge. So the Swede put his burly shoulder against the panel and shoved hard. It burst open, catapulting Torgerson into the cul-de-sac alley behind Le Coq d'Or and, as it immediately turned out, into the waiting arms of a dozen Thiet MP's, who had surrounded the club after their alert by the maître-d'.

Torgerson struggled free, fists flailing, as the other Mafians came through the sprung door. For a wild few seconds the four of them resisted. But they were soon forced into the bottleneck, and held at bay with leveled rifles. Although the MPs had been disinclined to employ firepower against the belligerent Yanks thus far, it seemed likely that further opposition might drive them to it. Despite a savagely aching head caused by the butt of a Thiet pistol, Gideon perceived this with great clarity. He said to Torgerson: "The Lilliputians have got us tied down, Gulliver. Let's arbitrate."

The exec shrugged his battered shoulders. "Okay. You talk to the little friggers."

Gideon hoisted his arms in token surrender. He looked across the menacing MP ranks at the maître-d' who was watching the melancholy tableau from the doorway.

"It would be well for everyone," Gideon suggested placatively, "if you'd ring Captain Cragg at the government wharf, and explain what's happened."

The maître-d' stepped forward. "Why Captain Cragg, m'sieu?"

"He's our fearless leader."

"Why did you not inform me that you were more than merely friends of the captain?" the maître-d' asked in an aggrieved tone.

"You never gave us a chance," said Gideon, massaging his bruised skull.

The maître-d' conversed in rapid-fire French with the MP platoon sergeant. Then he announced: "You will be allowed to telephone your captain, m'sieu. If he agrees to take custody of the prisoners, and pay for the damage you have caused to Le Coq d'Or, the military police will let you return to your ship, without filing official charges." The maître-d' regarded the pent-up Mafia curiously. "It appears," he concluded, "that you have a certain immunity from prosecution. . . ."

Medusa slipped her moorings at daybreak, almost six hours before her scheduled departure time. Watching from shore, as she picked her way past the larger vessels berthed in midstream, Cragg noted that the junk's camouflaged armament was in reasonably sound shape to withstand the beating it would take during the northward journey. In fact, he thought wryly, *Medusa* was a damned sight readier for sea than the man who commanded her. When he'd bade Torgerson goodbye fifteen minutes ago, the Swede was suffering the tortures of hangover hell. His empurpled right eye had swollen tightly shut, giving him a weird Moshe Dayan look, and he wore a bandage like a caul over his broken head.

Yet Torgerson somehow managed to twist his split lips into a horrible smile.

"You were wrong," he croaked. "GaiSong's still a great liberty town. Alongside this burg, Sydney's a goddamn pink tea R-and-R port."

Cragg was not amused. "Treasure the memory, mister. It'll have to last you one hell of a long time. And it's going to cost you four hundred bucks out of your mustering-out pay."

As *Medusa* pulled away, Torgerson raised his bandaged fist in an obscene gesture that only Mario DelGrado could have properly appreciated. Cragg made no response.

Behind him, just then, he heard the bells of the ancient stone cathedral, summoning the Catholic faithful to early morning worship. The sound was strangely comforting. Although he was not a religious man, it occurred to him that this happy combination of churchly music and promising weather could be a good omen. At least, thought Cragg, the Thiets on board *Medusa* might construe it as such, for the rains that had impeded their all-night labors had once more abated, and there was a golden hue to the lightening dawn which bespoke another break in the monsoon.

Cragg fervently hoped so. Aside from its salutary effect on the crew's morale, a day of decent weather would permit his two ships, particularly *Medusa,* to engage in some sorely needed on-the-job training. There had been no chance for a shakedown cruise, much less the week-long intensive rehearsal he had planned for them.

At seven P.M. *Mohican* edged away from the Thietvanne naval pier, with her weaponry only half-emplaced. But the departure could not be further delayed if they were to make the initial midnight rendezvous at Point *Alfa.* On this first night out it would be unwise, Cragg decided, to keep Torgerson waiting forty miles off the Dalagong estuary, milling around in the darkness, wondering what in hell was cooking with *Mohican.* Anything could happen under those conditions. At best, the clumsy junk might wander so far off course that they'd waste a full night searching for her. At worst, there was always the likelihood of a stray Kong privateer blundering across *Medusa,* and capturing her before Torgerson could organize his peagreen crew for a fight.

Point *Alfa* lay eighty-odd miles from GaiSong. At 15 knots, *Mohican*'s standard operating speed, they should arrive on target no more than an hour late, Cragg figured.

Fortunately, there was no nonsense about revving up the PT's diesels. Her twin engines required precious little water, and what they did need heated quickly, transforming steam into workhorse energy that drove the pistons through their endless cycle. Speed was controlled by increasing or limiting the amount of fuel sprayed into the cylinders at the top of each firing stroke, where the air had been compressed to 500 pounds per square inch. In sequence, the husky pistons plunged downward, and on the next upthrust they forced the waste gases through the exhaust valve. These were primitive contrivances, thought Cragg, alongside the wartime Packards. But they had their saving graces. Instead of tanks filled with volatile 100-octane ethyl, you carried non-explosive oil. *Mohican* was ready to move at a moment's notice. And after that she'd keep going hour after hour, until her cylinders sucked empty air. Moreover, the economical diesels would make it possible to reach Dokoro Mission, replenish, and have ample fuel in their bunkers for the climactic round trip to Phom Than and back.

Assuming everything went well at Point *Alfa,* they would leave the junk behind and proceed at 15 knots to *Bravo,* where Denny said there was a reasonably secure anchorage. If this indeed proved safe, Gideon could finish his ordnance chores before they left again at sundown. It should not be an impossible task. The principal item, the 75-mm. cannon, was already bolted to the fantail, along with the flamethrower assemblage.

As *Mohican* stepped down-river, gathering speed, there was a dampness in the night air that signaled the end of the monsoon truce. Cragg had the wheel. From his vantage on the minuscule bridge, behind the cramped chartroom where Duke Harris was double checking their course, he sniffed the moist atmosphere. It smelled, he decided, like a mausoleum pried open by vandals bent on stealing a corpse. As if aware of this desecration, the churchbells had gone silent, giving way to the jukeboxes that would wail from now until four A.M. in the taxi-dance stews along the receding waterfront.

In a complacent mood, forgetful of the emergencies for which he was hoarding them, Cragg took one of General Kwo's choice cigars from his shirtpocket. He made it a practice to include a Havana among his ration of Manila cheroots, on the offchance that a crisis might occur before he could slip below where he kept his precious supply.

Cragg lit it with loving care. While he was savoring the fragrant smoke, Denny emerged through the hatch that led from the crew's dayroom. For an instant she stood in the narrow passageway between cabin and bridge, tightly gripping the steel splintershield, as if uncertain of her balance.

"Is it permissible to join the captain at the wheel?"

Without removing his gaze from the river, Cragg said it was. "While we're still in friendly territory," he added magnanimously, "you can even talk to the motorman. Later it will be different. This telephone booth gets a little cramped when we go into action."

"Thank you."

He puffed contentedly on his cigar. Then: "Mario says he went with you to six o'clock mass."

"Yes."

"The cathedral chimes gave *Medusa* a nice send-off. I was listening. They sounded a lot better than the aloha music the Hawaiians play when the big liners leave Honolulu."

"That is something I would not know," she said. "But my prayers also went with her."

"And what about us?"

"Mario prayed for *Mohican*'s safety."

"Didn't you?"

Denny let the faint slipstream breeze cool her cheeks and ruffle her dark hair for a moment before replying. "On the very first morning that I heard you were in GaiSong, I began a novena to St. Francis Xavier for the success of our expedition. This was the ninth day."

"Our expedition?" Cragg repeated. "Nine days ago I'd have clobbered anyone who suggested there'd be a woman aboard *Mohican.*"

"Your accepting me," Denny said softly, "was also contained in my novena."

"I see." He studied her profile in the pallid glow of the binnacle lamp. "But why Xavier?"

"For excellent reasons, Cragg." She turned toward him, her smoke-blue eyes shining. "They call St. Francis Xavier the Apostle to the Indies. More than four centuries ago he served the Church as a missionary in this part of the world. Although it cannot be proved, my father believes that St. Francis once stopped at Dokoro on his journey from Ceylon to Japan." Denny smiled. "And did you yourself not come from San Francisco?"

"Close enough," Cragg admitted.

"*Voilà!*"

For a long time after that, they both watched the river. On the starboard side of the broadening stream they could dimly make out the suburban mansions, dark and deserted now that their wealthy owners had fled to the dubious shelter of the city. Once they saw, or imagined they saw, the distant flicker of small arms fire off the port bow, where the salt marshes began. And once they were hailed by a patrol sampan of Thietvanne's freshwater navy, heading upstream. But it passed out of earshot before either boat could establish satisfactory rapport, and was soon lost to sight. Although he could hardly blame him, considering the woeful combat disparity between the thirty-foot sampan and the eighty-foot PT, Cragg was surprised at the Thiet commander's refusal to give chase.

By nine-thirty, an hour before they were due to reach the Dalagong estuary, the murk sweeping in from the China Sea had turned to rain, gentle at first, then cold and drenching. With a firmness that brooked no argument, Cragg ordered Denny below for the night. Once they reached open water, he said, *Mohican's* amiable behavior would change for the worse, along with the weather.

"You'd better practice getting your sea legs in broad daylight," he added, "so we could rescue you if you fall overboard. Accidents can happen to the best of sailors, and I don't want to risk losing you quite yet."

"Am I so valuable, Cragg?"

After considering this ingenuous question, he answered in a way that betrayed mild astonishment at his own words. "As a matter of fact, baby, you are. As things stack up, we'll need your advice on the coastal layout. Also your linguistic talent." He paused. "And maybe another novena once we leave Dokoro."

"My father and mother will join me in that," Denny said gravely.

Cragg gave her damp crown an avuncular pat. "Pneumonia can be as fatal as drowning. *Dépêchez-vous!*"

"What about you?"

"I'm waterproof." As Denny started to leave, he called her back. "On second thought, have Mario send up my oilskins and a mug of black java."

While Cragg was waiting, Harris poked his head inquiringly through the open charthouse door.

"D'you plan to keep our present rate-of-advance, skipper?"

"Affirmative."

"In that case," said Harris, "we should pick up *Medusa* by radar at about 0030, range ten miles, and close her by 0115, depending on sea conditions."

"And on Torgerson's ability to hold his damned scow on station," Cragg added.

"Should I contact him by TBS after we've got *Medusa* fairly on the screen?"

"Hell, no! It'd be just our luck to have some goddamned Kong junk eavesdrop us with a walkie-talkie."

Harris disappeared back into his cave. Cragg turned to greet the Thiet messenger who had arrived with the foulweather gear and the coffee. It was one of the deckhands. He balanced the steaming mug on the ledge alongside the instrument panel. Then, like a medieval squire proffering a suit of armor to his knight, the Thiet solemnly extended the bulky garment so Cragg could get into it without taking both hands off the wheel.

"Thanks," Cragg muttered, pleased by the tiny man's unexpected initiative. Bracing the wheel with his warped left arm, he wriggled into the graygreen oilskin trousers, then allowed the Thiet to help him with the jacket. The messenger stepped back a pace, showing betel-stained teeth in a grin of approval, and produced a longbilled canvas cap from the hip pocket of his own tattered dungarees.

"Mister Mario wishes the captain to have his lucky hat," he said.

"My compliments to Mister Mario. I'd forgotten all about this crazy chapeau."

"He found it in Hong Kong junk when you flew to GaiSong." The Thiet's horrible red grin widened. "He say charm hat means good luck fortune for whole ship."

"Well, we survived the Big War," admitted Cragg. "Maybe the magic still works for the little ones."

"Now I bring coffee."

As the Thiet handed him the cup, Cragg asked: "What's your name?"

"Loo."

"Where'd you pick up English?"

"Dokoro Mission school," the Thiet said proudly. "From Mlle. Legére." His face grew sad. "My wife also learned English there. She spoke most beautifully. And when the Kong raided our village, they cut her tongue out because of it, and so this talent caused her death."

"Sorry, fella."

Loo nodded. Then he brightened, as if a happier thought had struck him. "Your ship travels well, *mon capitaine*."

"Ever handle the wheel?"

"Many times," Loo said enthusiastically. "Sampans. Junks. And once, long ago, a small steamship that traveled from Bien Goa to Phom Than, before the Kong became our enemy."

"Swell. Suppose you take over while I drink this jamoke." Cragg noticed the other's scrawny, half-naked torso. "After you go below for some raingear."

But Loo had already slipped past him, and was reaching eagerly for the spokes. "Thiet sailors live with monsoon," he said with simple dignity. "Never wear raingear."

"Okay, fella. You're the doctor."

After relinquishing the helm, Cragg took a half step down the charthouse companionway and set his coffee on the deck, confident that Loo couldn't get himself into any trouble during the next few minutes. At this juncture, where the river joined the sea, the Dalagong was ten miles wide. It would be good to relax, even briefly, before they encountered blue water.

When he had drawn up their watch, quarter and station bill for this first night's operation, Cragg made the spartan decision to keep all of his men on continuous alert. Denny would be permitted to retire to the owner's plush stateroom. But the Mafia, with their three native crewmen, were ticketed for a twelve-hour stint. Nobody would be relieved until *Mohican* herself was safely bedded down, and thoroughly camouflaged, in the hideaway cove near Point Bravo. Even then they'd catch only a few hours of sleep, because Cragg intended to resume work on the boat's armament by midmorning.

Trump Gideon and the Thiet ordnanceman were spending their watch in the eight-by-twelve dayroom, which raised a sort of camel's-hump abovedeck between the bridge and the stern, fitting together the disassembled weapons. Above the noise of the wind and rain, Cragg could occasionally hear the Thiet's singsong voices, and Gideon's own baritone making a valiant effort to pierce their impenetrable language barrier.

They were nearing the visible boundary line between the river mouth and the limitless sea. Despite the gloom, Cragg could make out where the muddy waters of the Dalagong met the darker open expanse. Hoisting himself stiffly off the ladder, he lurched around the splintershield and into the bridge cubicle. His crippled leg was bothering him, as it always did when the weather turned foul.

"You're relieved, Loo."

Although the miniature helmsman's stained teeth were chattering from the damp cold, he surrendered the wheel reluctantly, as if loath to go, after giving the spokes a final caress.

"This is indeed a good ship, *mon capitaine*."

"Yes," said Cragg. "It's a damned good ship. Now you hop below, crawl into dry pants, grab a mug of coffee, and report to Mr. Gideon. He needs your help getting through to his gunnery friends."

Grinning his pleasure at this new responsibility, Loo departed, with his skinny right arm raised in an approximate salute.

Mohican heralded her entrance into the China Sea by giving a sudden, upward surge as she breasted the first offshore swell. Then the fifty-ton PT seemed to settle down, pacing easily through the tall crestless waves, the way a trotting mare might compensate for a hillocky track.

The luminescent hands of the panel clock showed 2300, an hour until midnight, as Cragg swung the wheel to port. The fickle weather had, for a wonder, cleared slightly, until it now permitted a few grudging miles of visibility from the bridge. He turned briefly astern for a farewell glance at the receding delta coastline. There was no sign of life. Even the lighthouse that stood guard on a coral spit at the Dalagong's mouth was blacked out. Friendly vessels never attempted the upstream passage after sundown, and none save the most foolhardy would dare these changeable shoals in an effort to reach the sea once night fell.

Cragg resumed his forward vigil.

If *Medusa* were on proper station, she should be about thirty miles away. He braced his shoulders against the steel sheathing, with his canvas-shod feet well apart, to make himself as comfortable as possible for the long grind. His night glasses felt heavy around his neck, and his webbed gunbelt was cutting painfully into his hips. Cragg prodded through the swaddling folds to shift the position of the belt, which carried his Colt .45 automatic and a ten-inch sheath knife. But he rejected an impulse to rid himself of the weapons, for that would mean hanging them in the charthouse where they would be inaccessible if a sudden need arose.

To be sure, the automatic was a clumsy weapon, inaccurate beyond a few yards. But at point-blank range its bullets could stop a charging bull, or a determined Kong trying to board *Mohican*. The sheath knife was a SeaBee product, made in the Solomons out of an old jeep spring. He kept the blade honed to razor sharpness for severing fouled lines, or the flesh, tendons and bones of a human limb.

At 0030 Harris reported a radar contact about three degrees to port, slightly inshore from *Mohican*, and eighteen miles distant.

It was obviously the junk, faithfully on station, because the blip wasn't moving. Cragg trimmed the wheel. After another half-hour on this course, Harris announced that the range had closed to ten miles, which brought *Medusa* close to visual sighting under the improved weather conditions. Cragg hooked his left elbow over a wheelspoke, and with his right hand trained the night binoculars upon the place where the junk should come into view.

At almost the exact second that Harris called, "Range nine miles," a pinprick of light appeared on the restricted horizon, went off, then winked again.

Cragg peered through the glasses for a full minute to make sure his eyes hadn't tricked him. He saw the light twinkle several times more, in a series of long and short flashes which could only mean that somebody was making deliberate signals from the junk. But they weren't couched in Morse code; and the light itself, rather than beaming toward *Mohican,* was aimed toward the mainland.

Cragg cursed softly.

He had issued orders for a total blackout by both ships, from sunset to sunrise, during the northward haul. Whatever the explanation, therefore, it was an unpardonable security breach on Torgerson's part, letting some ham-handed clown fiddle around with a signal lamp. Unless, of course, Lars wasn't aware of what was happening aboard his own ship. Without turning, Cragg bellowed for Gideon and Harris to join him on the double.

Duke reached the bridge first. "What's the problem, old boy?"

Cragg gestured toward the flickering light. In the brief interval since his first startled glimpse, it had come within naked eyesight range. From all indications the illicit signalman was perched in *Medusa*'s upperworks, probably at the crotch of her mainmast, hidden by the sail, where he could function without being detected from the poopdeck. It had to be sabotage.

"We've got trouble, gentlemen," he said. "I think somebody's chatting with the enemy."

"Son of a bitch," muttered Gideon, staring.

Cragg began to wrestle with his foulweather gear. "Peel me out of this goddamned straitjacket," he instructed Harris, "then hustle your tail below and ask DelGrado to goose those engines of his like they've never been goosed before. Tell him I want twenty knots." To Gideon he said quietly: "Better unlimber the Long Tom, fella. We might have uninvited guests before the night's done."

"Check."

Harris shucked the oilskins in five seconds flat. Cragg cinched his gunbelt a notch tighter.

"You might also warn the girl to stay below for the rest of the night," he said, "unless I order all hands to abandon ship."

Almost five minutes elapsed before DelGrado managed to coax *Mohican*'s twin diesels into stroking at top speed. In that interval the mysterious light blinked only a few more times before going dark. If its operator were indeed sending his signals from the sixty-foot level of the junk's mainmast, they would be visible for a good dozen miles. Assuming the recipient to be a Kong vessel, moreover, it would take the foe at least an hour to intercept *Medusa*. By then, Cragg figured, he should have his own ill-matched, ill-equipped pair as ready for this premature action as they'd ever be. With major luck, or a miracle, the surprise which the Kong were intending for their unsuspecting quarry might be reversed.

He listened critically as *Mohican*'s engine thrum grew a decibel noisier. Then he grinned. Good old Mario must have used a cattle prod for a goosing stick.

When they had closed to less than a mile, Cragg could hear the barnyard sounds that came from *Medusa*'s poopdeck. Chickens clucking. A disoriented rooster crowing five hours before the sun rose. And the pig which Torgerson had tried to veto, but which Toyon had insisted upon as a final touch of verisimilitude, was bewailing its fate from the narrow cage. To another ship approaching her in this fashion, the junk could have been any one of a hundred such bumbling, innocent craft that plied the coastal waters of Thietvanne. She lay motionless on the turbid sea, motor idling, rhomboid sails slatting, as *Mohican* came nimbly alongside.

Even before the collision fenders were in place, Cragg gave the helm to Harris, told him to keep the others aboard, and clambered up the rope ladder that had been lowered from *Medusa's* waist. Torgerson accosted him jovially as he hoisted himself over the cumbersome rail.

"Glad to have company, skipper. It's lonesome out here."

"We may have a damned sight more company than you expect, mister."

Cragg brushed him aside and headed directly for the base of the mainmast, where he stood for a moment, peering aloft through the tangled rigging. At the juncture of the mainyard and the tall pole he could make out a shadowy, immobile figure, stretched full length along the upperside of the sharply canted spar, and taking full advantage of the concealment offered by the sail itself. This phantom could not possibly have been detected from astern.

With Colonel Toyon and Akim in tow, Torgerson left the wheel with a substitute and stomped across the deck to join Cragg. "Something wrong with my rigging?" he asked testily.

"Plenty."

"It looks four-oh to me," Torgerson said, "for a frigging junk."

"Take a harder look." Cragg pointed. "Right where the yard's bent onto the mast."

Torgerson scowled upward, briefly silent, like a resentful schoolboy. But an instant later he exploded with a leonine roar. "Whoever you are, get your ragged ass down here before I blow it to bits." He drew his automatic, a twin of Cragg's, and aimed carefully. There was no response, by voice or movement, from the man on the crosstree.

Toyon observed reasonably, "The fellow doesn't speak English, you know."

"He'll understand."

Cragg took over. "Belay it, fella. You'll never wing him from here. Besides, I want the little bugger alive. He's been signaling to somebody, and we'd better find out who're his playmates."

Torgerson holstered the pistol reluctantly. "Okay. You're the boss."

Cragg unbuckled his own gunbelt and tossed it to Akim after removing the sheath knife, whose naked blade he slipped into his trouserband. He reached for the mainmast shroud. "I'm going to bring our friend down for questioning." Then he started aloft, making good time despite his stiff leg, like a huge cat prowling along a windswept branch.

Torgerson turned to Akim. The one-eyed Thiet was carrying his most prized possession, an ancient bolt-action rifle, with which he shot seagulls that rested in *Medusa's* rigging and befouled the deck during the run down the Dalagong.

"Cover him," Torgerson snapped, pointing.

Even before the colonel translated, Akim nodded compliance, and raised the heavy weapon to his skinny shoulder. The gun muzzle followed Cragg's wary approach toward the huddled figure on the crosstree. In the four minutes it took him to reach his quarry, there was no further sound from below. They watched, fascinated, as Cragg moved within arm's length.

The man on the crosstree seemed to be shrinking away from his pursuer. Then, abruptly, as if he had reached an irrevocable decision, he rose to his feet. Making no effort to steady himself by grasping the mast, he stood there, swaying slightly, like a circus aerialist poised on a high wire.

Torgerson yelled, "He's going to jump!"

In that split-second Cragg acted. He made a lurching tackle, caught the man's ankles, and managed to drag both himself and his prey against the V-shaped gaff, where they remained wedged for an instant in a tangle of flailing arms and legs. The captured man screamed once. Thus, as suddenly as it had begun, the brief encounter ended.

Cragg's hoarse voice called out. "You'd better come on up, Lars, I'll need help with this guy. I had to knife him. He's in no shape to come down by himself."

When they finally wrangled the man below, and sat him none too gently upon the deck, he was still conscious, but bleeding profusely from a deep wound in his naked belly, just above the beltline of his stained dungaree drawers. He lay on his back, staring up blankly into the formidable faces of Cragg, Torgerson, Toyon and Akim. His blood spread in a widening pool on the planks beside him.

"It's a bad cut," said Cragg. "He can't last long."

Toyon nodded. Kneeling over the stricken man, he spoke a few Thiet words and was answered by a weak return nod.

"He will talk."

The interrogation continued haltingly for several minutes, with Toyon asking brusque questions, then placing his ear close to the man's mouth to catch the whispered responses. At length he seemed satisfied.

"Finished, colonel?"

"Quite finished, Mr. Cragg." Toyon nudged the motionless form with the toe of a polished boot. "He is dead."

"What's his story?"

"It is the same old tale," said Toyon, "The Kong bribed him with the promise of safety for his family, if he would keep them informed of our whereabouts." The colonel's voice grew melancholy as he recounted the defection of a crewman whom he had personally selected. "They gave him a signal lamp, which he concealed until we reached Point *Alfa* tonight. Since he was assigned to the morning watch, he was permitted to sleep on deck. This made it easy for him to slip away after the others turned in. By ascending the foremast and crawling back along the mainbrace, he was able to accomplish his purpose without being observed."

Cragg made an impatient gesture. "The little bastard had us boresighted at Point *Alfa*. D'you reckon he had other fixes, too?"

"If the Kong did not intercept us at *Alfa*," said Toyon, "they intended to make a further attempt at *Bravo*."

"Or points north, I suppose?"

The colonel looked glum. "Doubtless."

"Then we've got to wind it up here." Cragg slammed his balled right fist into the cupped palm of his left hand. "Did the bastard clue you on how many Kong are involved, and what's on their minds, exactly?"

"It is only one ship," said Toyon. "But it is a very large one."

"Goddamn it! How large?"

"One of the biggest. A seagoing junk, and heavily armed. It carries fifty Kong. They are specialists in the art of grappling and boarding. They intend to capture *Medusa,* and hold the survivors as hostages."

"They'll be disappointed," Cragg growled. "There won't be any survivors, whichever way it goes."

He motioned to Torgerson. Together they walked to the starboard rail to confer with Harris, DelGrado and Gideon, who were clustered on *Mohican*'s convex foredeck, staring upward, anxiously waiting to learn what had happened.

Cragg was already considering a workable counter-strategy. With so few pieces to play, he knew, it had to be a simple game, like one of those mate-in-three clichés. Essentially, the Kong ship must be knocked out of action before she could close in upon *Medusa*, where her superior manpower would easily overwhelm Torgerson's twelve untested Thiets. (No, make that thirteen, Cragg thought dourly, if you counted Colonel Toyon, whose own military prowess was still moot, despite his icy composure.)

But Chinese-built junks were damned hard to sink. Their four-inch teak planking, which withstood the ravages of hullboring teredos, was equally impervious to medium-caliber gunfire. Cragg remembered the Nip barges in the Solomons. They had kept moving despite a thousand rounds-or-so of .50-caliber poured into their hulls by the prowling PTs, and sometimes it took a valuable torpedo to finish the job. But *Medusa* had no torpedoes. Nor did *Mohican*.

With her newer, better-kept diesel, it would be simple enough for them to cut and run. Yet flight would merely postpone the encounter which was bound to follow once these Kong notified their coastwatchers that the quarry had temporarily escaped. Then stealth would be impossible, and they'd have to run a gauntlet of seagoing enemy marauders from Bien Goa to Phom Than. Any subsequent engagement might well be fought on the Kong's own terms.

It was useless to think of returning to GaiSong. That avenue was now closed for the same reason.

Thus the alternative was bleakly obvious. In naval parlance, the foe must be sought out and destroyed, promptly, ruthlessly, utterly, while the Mafia still had a slight element of surprise, some small initiative. This was the sort of directive Halsey used to give his Third Fleet commanders on the eve of battle. It was Cragg's order now.

They would ignore the fact that the Kong had them outnumbered two-to-one in bodies, while concentrating on the happier fact that they themselves could match two vessels, however small, against the enemy's heavier one. After dallying at Point *Alfa* for another hour, to bring the Kong ship firmly in sight, *Medusa* would proceed eastward, adjusting her speed to the pursuer's, luring him away from the coast. When it came, Cragg hoped, the battle would be joined beyond all visual range of the shore, so that even the gunflashes couldn't be observed.

As guarantee against any slipups, Torgerson would send a man aloft with a blinker light, and dupe the Kong into believing their turncoat hireling was still on the job, transmitting his simplistic location fixes.

During this delicate chase, *Mohican* would maneuver to flank the enemy by hustling north, then swinging around from the west. Throughout, Duke Harris would keep his radar trained on the two junks. If the margin became too narrow for comfort, he'd take a chance that nobody in the area was radio-equipped, and instruct Torgerson by TBS to pour on a little more coal.

All in all, they must deal their cards the way they did in the old PT base poker games, like riverboat gamblers. But if things broke right, they should be able to stage their fireworks display somewhere below the outer horizon. In short, Torgerson must string out the contrived stern chase for at least three hours.

It was now 0100. Under this schedule, zero hour would be 0500, which meant they'd have the additional small comfort of a dawn sky, and lessen the chance of having their gunflashes monitored by prying shoreside eyes.

Cragg finished sardonically: "Otherwise it'll be all over the local papers in the morning."

Torgerson grinned his gaptoothed grin. "Hell, we're going to have a goddamned turkey shoot."

"Or," amended Cragg, "a sitting duck roast. With you on the spit." He reached for the Swede's great fist. They solemnly shook hands. "Any questions?"

"Negative."

"Happy hunting, fella."

Cragg hoisted his stiff leg over the rail, turned, and started down the ropeladder. DelGrado had the PT's engines going smoothly before he hit the deck, and Trump Gideon was already casting off. He took the wheel. *Mohican* uncoupled gracefully, like a ballet dancer quitting a clumsy partner, and moved north at twenty knots.

For the next hour Cragg found himself prey to a host of illogical worries, and all because their stratagem seemed to be unfolding without a flaw. He would have preferred some minor foul-up, a delay in the Kong closing the ten-mile gap, perhaps, or some temporary failure in communication between *Mohican* and the presumed spy in *Medusa*'s maintop. Remediable snafus were normal, even expectable. Perfection wasn't. As *Mohican* followed her parabolic course, however, the periodic radar contacts relayed from the charthouse confirmed that the junks had almost conjoined, that Torgerson had suddenly pulled free, that he had begun his spurious flight.

After that, from a safe distance of eight miles, *Mohican* shadowed the slow-moving vessels.

Torgerson dealt out his crooked deck with excruciating care. Once the Kong got within sniffing distance of *Medusa,* near enough to make them think they could call the pot. But Harris barked a warning into his radiotelephone just as machinegun fire burst from the enemy's grasping prow. Torgerson replied jauntily that he'd given the Kong a deliberate nibble so they wouldn't get discouraged enough to break off the chase.

Shortly before 0500 the moon, which had been etching a silver electrocardiogram across the ebony scroll of the sea, packed up its equipment and disappeared through a dark trapdoor in the lower sky. Covered by the ensuing blackness, all the more intense because of the predawn hour, *Mohican* wheeled south for her surprise rendezvous with the overconfident foe.

Cragg called to Harris. "What's *Medusa*'s range?"

"Five miles."

"Tell Lars we'll show our hole card in fifteen minutes."

"Roger."

He glanced toward the fantail, where Gideon and his two Thiet gunners were making precise last-minute adjustments to the 75-mm. cannon.

"Got your Long Tom ready, fella?"

"Ready as it'll ever be." Gideon's tone was more urbanely bored than usual. "Problem is, will I be able to aim this bastard without a decent fire-control system?"

"We'll close within three hundred yards," Cragg said. "At that range you can toss the stuff with your bare hands."

"Sure. If these jokers feed me the ammo fast enough. Our ensemble hasn't rehearsed, you know. The melody may sound ragged."

With an imperturbability he didn't feel, Cragg said: "Hell, Trump, we were all raw-assed reserves once. Remember? This is good on-the-job training for your little gremlins."

Gideon's reply was a disgusted snort, audible across the forty feet of windswept deck that separated the two men.

Cragg gave his attention once more to the task of conning *Mohican* toward the burgeoning pinpricks of light that marked the spot where Torgerson had finally let the Kong move in for their expected kill. From this distance, a fraction over four miles, the yellow tracer streaks from *Medusa's* three portside .50-calibers were plainly visible. An instant later two heavier explosions originated near the same source. These would be her 40-mm. bow and stern guns, also firing to port.

Cragg gave a jubilant yell. Torgerson had managed to bring his vessel athwart the Kong junk, thereby insuring himself that the enemy would be too preoccupied with untangling himself to observe *Mohican's* rapid approach.

He hoped that Gideon was watching the impressive broadside laid down by *Medusa's* native gunners. It might restore his faith in Thietvanne.

Before *Mohican* passed the halfway mark in her race to join the assault, the Kong managed to uncross the *T*, and Torgerson no longer held the advantage. As the junks converged, the superior enemy firepower made itself disturbingly evident, probing for soft spots in *Medusa's* stout hull, raking her eighty-foot deck, forcing her exposed 40-mm. crews to take shelter. There was one shred of comfort. As yet the Kong's shooting evidenced more quantity than quality.

Cragg shouted into the engine room speaker tube: "Got any

more knots up your sleeve, Mario? Torgerson's in deep trouble."

"Christ knows. I'll give it a try."

"Good boy." Cragg pushed hard against the spokes, as if his own bodily pressure could impel the PT ahead faster, and cursed the day her fatcat owner had ordained removal of the lovely Packards. He was rewarded by a slight lift in the diesel tempo. "Goose 'em again, fella!"

Even at 22 knots it took *Mohican* another eight minutes to reach the fringe of the worsening encounter. *Medusa* was burning in several places as a result of the foe's voluminous tracer fire. These blazes still seemed minor. But Cragg knew they would prove fatal unless Torgerson's pinned-down crew were soon set free to quell them.

When Cragg judged that he was within five hundred yards, he swung the wheel hard to starboard, and *Mohican* veered sharply, presenting herself in three-quarters profile to the enemy junk. At this extreme short range, the Kong towered in the darkness like a British man-o'-war, twice the PT's length, her vast flank looming as unassailable as a medieval castle wall.

Cragg looked over his shoulder.

Gideon had the Long Tom trained, awaiting a slightly better angle before opening up. Two degrees right rudder sufficed. As *Mohican* swung broadside, the 75-mm. cut loose with a thunderclap roar, slamming its high explosive point-blank at the Kong's waterline, directly amidships. Cragg signaled DelGrado to throw both engines into reverse. *Mohican* slushed to a crawl. She halted briefly, while the inexperienced gunners coaxed a fresh shell into the loading mechanism. Ordinarily the Long Tom was semi-automatic, capable of thirty rounds per minute. But Gideon, unwilling to risk a jammed weapon, had elected to use this cumbrous single-shot method.

With painstaking care, the way an outweighed boxer sets about to conquer a huskier but less skillful opponent, *Mohican's* formidable cannon went to work. Caught off guard, the Kong confusedly tried to shift their own machineguns from starboard, where they had been engaging *Medusa,* to this threatened portside. But they were too late. From his almost stationary platform, as the PT lay idling, Gideon pumped twelve brass-jacketed HE projectiles into the behemothic junk, aiming always for the same spot. Within a few minutes, the enemy craft began to list, slowly at first, then more rapidly as water flooded her breached carcass.

A baker's-dozen shells ruined the Kong.

Whipping unimpeded through the hole that had been blasted by its predecessors, the lucky thirteenth burst in the Kong's cavernous hold, sending whitehot fragments into an ammunition stowage locker. Immediately there was a much louder explosion, and afterward a sudden silence, followed by the shrill cries of the Kong sailors as they massed along the canting port rail, ready to leap into the sea.

Desultory machine-gunning resumed from *Medusa*, hidden somewhere in the smoke beyond the stricken junk. It continued for a minute or two, then ceased. Torgerson had obviously decided to let *Mohican* handle the mop-up while he extinguished the fires that were still smoldering among the tangled gear on his welldeck.

Cragg got the PT underway once more, and put another hundred yards between himself and the burning, sinking enemy. Through his binoculars he looked on impassively as the Kong abandoned ship. They dropped in tight clusters over the side. There was no attempt to launch lifeboats, assuming the Kong had any, and those who could swim paddled away from the gutted vessel toward the bobbing flotsam. The last to leave merely stepped from the deck into the embracing water, for by then the junk lay almost on her side.

Trump Gideon left his gunnery post to join Cragg in the bridge enclosure. His teeth gleamed startlingly through the powdergrime that blackened his handsome face. Gideon's smile was that of a man awaiting deserved credit for a job well done.

"The goddamned Swede was right," he exulted. "We had a turkey shoot."

"You did okay, Trump." Cragg hesitated, wishing to say more. It had been too easy. He knew that nothing else connected with their mission would be this simple again, so beautifully fitted into place, so flawlessly consummated. But now was not the time to raise such doubts. "How were your gunnery assistants?"

"They'll make out."

Cragg nodded quietly. It had started to rain again. He stared across the murky waste that separated *Mohican* from the struggling men in the water. Then: "Take the wheel, will you? I'm going to hit the TBS for a few words with Torgerson."

"Aye, aye, skipper."

Duke Harris had *Medusa* on the circuit when Cragg entered the charthouse.

"Torgerson got off with minimum casualties," he crowed. "Two chaps creased by bullets. Nobody killed. The Kong must be bloody poor marksmen."

"People get rattled when their plans screw up," Cragg said. "Kong are no exception. They'll act a lot sharper next time." He reached for the microphone. "Is Torgerson still on?"

"Yes."

Cragg pressed the talk button. "Lars? Listen to me goddamned sharp. This is a firm order. I want you to go after those bastards in the whaleboat."

Despite the imperfect quality of the TBS, which gave voices a thin metallic timbre, Torgerson's surprise was unmistakable. "Rescue the little friggers?"

"Negative." Cragg shut his salt-rimed eyes. "Take along a couple of BARs. Shoot to kill. I don't want any survivors."

"No prisoners?"

"None. Savvy? None at all."

"Check."

"We'll be bugging out now, fella. If this lousy weather holds, maybe we can make the beach without getting spotted." Cragg replaced the mike on its hook. "Plot a straight course, Duke."

Then he groped his way slowly, laboriously, back to rejoin Gideon on the bridge. *Medusa* was already lost to sight in the rain squall. But a brisk crackle of gunfire told him that Torgerson's crew had commenced the methodical slaughter of the Kong, picking them off one by one from the deck, even before the whaleboat was lowered. Cragg massaged his stiffened elbow. It was indisputably true. Nothing came easy anymore, including the issuance of death sentences for fifty defenseless men caught between the Devil and the deep black sea.

Yet what earthly choice had he?

Cragg heard a faint noise in the darkness behind him. He turned. It was Denny. She was wearing an oversized set of foulweather oilskins. They rustled as she walked.

"You're supposed to stay below," he reminded her harshly.

Denny edged into the cubicle beside the two men. "Mario said we have won the battle. So I disobeyed you, Cragg, and came up here to help with the wounded."

"There are no wounded."

"What about the Kong?" she asked. "Surely they must have sustained many injuries when their ship was sunk."

Cragg gestured into the rainswept void behind *Mohican*. "Do you hear anything?"

Cocking her head over the side, Denny listened intently for a moment. Then she faced him with a puzzled frown. "It is the sound of guns," she said. "But why are they still firing?"

"Because," he informed her coldly, "I told Torgerson to kill every last Kong."

Denny's small hand tightened on the rail. He saw her knuckles whiten. "But that is murder, Cragg."

Cragg shrugged a tired shoulder. "*C'est la guerre, bébé.* I'm sorry. But my heart doesn't bleed very easily for the Kong nowadays." He thrust her roughly aside and pushed toward the exit. To Trump Gideon, on silent duty at the helm, he growled: "Can you hang tough for a couple of hours while I grab some sacktime?"

Gideon regarded him without emotion. "Sure thing, skipper."

"Thanks." Cragg made a particular effort to step normally as he left the bridge. "That Thiet seaman, Loo, handles a wheel pretty damned well. I'll send him up." He gave Denny a curious look. "Loo told me he and his wife were students of yours. His English isn't bad. Maybe we should find out how *he* feels about turning the other cheek. . . ."

5
Blind Man's Buff

TWO DAYS PASSED without incident. *Mohican* slipped quietly into her assigned hideaway each morning, while *Medusa* forged ahead to the next rendezvous. Trump Gideon finished his ordnance work before their second union at Point *Bravo*, and pronounced the PT ready to tackle anything short of an armed cruiser. Duke Harris had begun conferring with Denny on what lay beyond Dokoro Mission, when she wouldn't be available for topographical advice. Mario DelGrado improvised a system for baking pizza in the butane oven of his miniature galley stove. All went well.

Watching them, holding a light rein but saying little, Cragg was pleased by this mounting evidence that the Mafia had not lost its wartime efficiency.

His satisfaction was marred, however, by Denny's behavior since the sanguinary action off Point *Alfa*. From the moment they headed shoreward after the skirmish, the girl had studiously ignored him. On the rare occasions when she spoke to him at all, her remarks dealt with such impersonal matters as the advisability of certain coves and river mouths for *Mohican*'s daylight sojourns, the technical dialogue which she made possible between Gideon and his Thiet gunners, or the menu which she and Mario now jointly prepared.

After forty-eight hours of this glacial treatment Cragg found himself getting edgy. It annoyed him to discover that, for the first time in years, he felt cramped on an eighty-foot vessel which boasted every creature comfort a man might need, including an air-conditioner for use at the boiling zenith of the Thietvanne day. Perhaps, he brooded, trapped was a better word.

As Denny made it increasingly plain that she preferred his absence to his presence, Cragg responded with evasive action of his own. He spent longer periods than necessary poring over Harris' plotboards in the charthouse, and when Gideon and the girl discussed ordnance with the Thiets, he would disappear below, there to lie upon his transom berth, staring glassily at some book plucked at random from the small paperback library he'd brought from the States. In this absurd fashion, alternately skulking and hiding, he kept their contacts to a barely civil minimum.

Eventually, Cragg supposed, Denny would snap out of her mood, and see the futility of punishing him for having shown no mercy to the Kong survivors. Meanwhile it made damned little sense to reason with an unreasonable female, to explain patiently again why neither side of a ruthless war could afford to give quarter to its enemy. To such logic Denny's mind was shut tighter than a dogged-down porthole.

Yet what really bothered him, Cragg conceded, was the fact that he over-reacted to her curious ill humor.

Take tonight.

Mohican was tethered at her mooring a few yards offshore from a mangrove swamp which Denny said should render them safe from any sudden guerrilla attack. Once he'd conned the PT several miles up the winding stream, and seen how the gnarled trees sent their reptilian roots down to the very edge of the brackish river, Cragg agreed that she was right, as usual. This weird tangle provided a dense natural cover. Behind it stretched a quagmire which not even the Kong could penetrate. Under such relaxed circumstances, with two hours remaining before their sunset departure, the Mafia had decided to eat a decent meal for a change in the leisurely quiet of the wardroom mess. Denny set five places at the pulldown table that dominated this alcove off the amidships companionway. Mario prepared enough chicken cacciatore for all hands, including the grinning Thiet crewmen who were waiting topside for this unexpected largesse.

When dinner was ready, Gideon broke out a bottle of Chianti from the cold locker. Still working at the cork, he strolled aft to bang on Cragg's door.

"Chowtime, skipper."

Perversely, then, Cragg snarled that he had a lot of things to do. If they'd be kind enough to fetch him a plate, he'd eat at his desk.

"Okay, bossman. Suit yourself. But you're missing a swell party. Listen." Gideon held the Chianti bottle close, so Cragg could hear the festive pop as the cork came free. "Dago red. Our next-to-last jug."

"Drink it in good health, mister. Just bring me some iced tea."

Even to his own ears, the words sounded petulant, boorish, and Cragg turned away guiltily from the locked door. He glowered at his reflection in the wall mirror. The lean, weathered countenance glared back at him like the face of an ungracious stranger. He thumbed his nose. Then he observed aloud: "You, Cragg are a goddamned horse's ass. Shape up or ship out!" Thoughtfully, no longer frowning, he reached into his desk safe and chose a Havana from the half-empty gift box. When it was well lighted, he blew a rich smoke ring at the outer bulkhead across the tiny compartment.

It was almost six P.M., less than seven hours until their rendezvous with *Medusa* at Point *Charlie*. Lars Torgerson, he knew, would be tickled pink at being relieved from his despised duty, even temporarily, and would gladly swap his foul-smelling command for a civilized night aboard *Mohican*. Actually, this wasn't a spur-of-the-moment decision on Cragg's part. Since leaving GaiSong, he had wanted to get the feel of the junk, to acquaint himself with her seaways, so that he could more intelligently fit the awkward craft into the pattern of their final assault on Phom Than. Now seemed as good a time as any to swap horses with Torgerson. Better, in fact, Cragg concluded self-righteously.

He grinned.

Mlle. Denise Legére would be equally astonished, if not as pleased, with her temporary assignment to *Medusa*. Since he also intended to give Colonel Toyon a brief respite, the girl would have to go with him to the junk as interpreter. Remembering Torgerson's hungry look, it occurred to him, too, that Denny's presence could distract Lars from the proper performance of his duties if she were left on the PT. All in all, Cragg figured, he had rendered a scoutmasterly judgment.

Quite pleased with himself, he stubbed out the Havana, and cut off the smudged end with a pair of nail scissors. He put the unsmoked segment into his shirtpocket for later use, unlocked the door, and ambled down the passageway to join the others at dinner.

"Even an old salt," Cragg said blandly, in response to their inquiring glances, "is entitled to change his mind."

Denny received her orders with remarkable aplomb. If it pleased Cragg to have her interpret for him on *Medusa*, very well. Was that not one of the reasons why he had so generously permitted her to sail with them? What difference, then, where she served him? *Mohican* or *Medusa*, it was all the same to her.

She had packed all her personal gear in her one worn shoulder-bag. But when he offered to carry it, she politely refused his assistance. Cragg bowed and stood aside as she started up the tall ladder. Once Denny was well embarked, however, he moved to steady the swaying lines. Her booted feet moved resolutely from rung to rung, hesitating only an instant before each new upward step, until she reached *Medusa*'s rail. There she was met by Torgerson himself who had left his precious wheel when Akim reported that Mlle. Legére was paying them a surprise visit. Before she could object, Lars extended both brawny arms and swiftly hoisted her across the waist-high barrier.

Watching from below, Cragg caught a brief glimpse of pale flesh above dark hose, as her body was flung upward. Denny would be furious, he knew, although she would have shown a lot more provocative thigh if Torgerson had let her climb the rail without help.

On his way up the ladder, Cragg managed to compose his face into an expression of suitable gravity, and when he finally swung his own long legs over *Medusa*'s rail, he was every inch the naval commander, brusque, stern, businesslike. Quickly, making it clear he wished no argument, or even discussion of his proposal, Cragg explained why he and Denny were aboard.

Torgerson offered one tentative suggestion. Mightn't it be a good idea, he asked, for him to stay and explain a few of the junk's eccentricities?

"This bucket talks only heathen Chinee," he added, aiming his gaptoothed grin at the girl. "You'll need an interpreter for that, too."

Colonel Toyon intervened. With an ironic smile he observed: "Mlle. Legére speaks both Mandarin and Cantonese."

"Okay." Torgerson surrendered easily. "But never say I didn't warn you, skipper."

Cragg nodded. "I won't. Main thing you've got to bear in mind, fella, is that when I'm in *Medusa,* you're in *Mohican.* And vice versa. Savvy?"

"Check."

"Good. Now I want you and the colonel the hell out of here within ten minutes."

"Doublecheck. Just as soon as we can throw a few little things together. Razor. Toothbrush. And clean skivvies in case we get caught with *our* pants down." Torgerson leered at Denny, and laughed uproariously when she blushed. Then he jabbed his thumb toward the idly slatting mainsail. "Remember that old saying, skipper, about familiarity breeding contempt? By tomorrow morning, when you've come to know *Medusa* real well, you'll want to spit in her ugly painted eyes. She's a real bitch!"

Torgerson swept them both with a last, derisive look as he went below.

For the rest of the night Cragg held the junk steady on course-045, due northeast, to keep well away from the Thietvanne coast. The monsoon, blowing out of the southwest, drove *Medusa* at a fairly decent clip. Several times during the post-midnight hours their trailing log registered better than eight knots. Contrary to what he had expected from Torgerson's sour remarks, the deep-bellied vessel behaved almost like a lady. She obeyed the helm with a minimum of protest, and seemed generally content to accept his will. Perhaps it was the junk's ponderous, rolling motion that recalled for Cragg the Pregnant Woman of his chart, and the way her nubile upper thighs described a vast curve between Point *Charlie* and (the aptness of the term charmed him) Point *Delta*.

Despite the wind, the night was warm, once the rain stopped. Denny had refused to sleep in the master's cabin on the quarter-deck. Now, alternately dozing and waking, she lay upon a pile of waterproof cushions which Akim had arranged for her beside the wheel. Some emergency might arise, she said, that would require Cragg to issue a sudden order. She wanted to be available.

"I can point my finger at anything I want done," he said, "and yell. Even Thiet sailors understand that kind of language."

Nevertheless she stayed.

By three A.M. the last cumulus traces of the storm front had vanished, leaving the cleanly arched sky filled with a myriad of bright stars. Denny forgot her weariness. She sat up, staring into the night, elbows propped against the cushions. Cragg heard the soft rustle.

"You look like Cleopatra queening it on her Nile barge," he said.

"Is that a compliment, Cragg?"

"Yes."

"Then I thank you." Denny did not press the subject. Instead she asked, pointing. "What are those three brightest stars, upper-most in the heavens, toward the east?"

Cragg peered up at the lustrous sky. "The largest is Vega," he said. "It forms a triangle with Altair and Deneb. Look closely. Inside the triangle you can see the Northern Cross."

"They are beautiful. And very peaceful."

"Also useful," he appended. "We couldn't locate Dokoro Mission without them."

While she remained silent, watching, Cragg sketched the rest of the summer firmament, which seemed to grow more luminous as the night waned. He showed her Sagittarius the Bowman, and the square shape of Pegasus beyond the Northern Cross itself, and Orion's shining belt near the celestial equator, and immovable Polaris upon which man based his first real navigational technique.

Denny smiled. She stretched in lazy catlike fashion, and lay back upon the damp cushions, with her hands clasped beneath her head. The innocent gesture brought her breasts into sharp outline beneath the sheer silk blouse. Cragg regarded her amusedly, intrigued by the situation. Nearby, in their wicker cages, the barnyard fowl were making slumbrous noises, and a definite stench wafted from the pigpen. Yet the girl seemed oblivious to either the strange sounds or the homely smells.

"Come here," he said, beckoning.

She moved closer to him, without speaking, and obediently set her back against his chest. Even when Cragg folded both his arms around her, she did not protest. Still amused, he casually insinuated his right hand into the V-neck of her blouse, beneath her brassiere, and cupped her left breast. He felt the nipple harden at his touch.

Unhurriedly, almost indolently, Cragg withdrew his hand and brought the girl around so that she faced him. For a long moment he studied her intent face, like a connoisseur appraising a valued acquisition. Denny met his gaze without flinching.

"Goddamn," Cragg said wonderingly.

Then, abruptly, he kissed her. He sensed her body stiffen, and her soft lips were cold against his opened mouth.

"Okay," growled Cragg, "if that's how it's got to be."

As if to punish her, to prove the folly of passive resistance, he thrust her downward to the deck. Pausing for an instant, heavy upon her, he waited to see whether she would finally try to repulse his crude attempt at rape.

She did not.

Emboldened, Cragg eased himself aside and drew the linen skirt above her thighs with one hand, while keeping her shoulders imprisoned against the hard planks with the other. He felt the pliant flesh beneath his probing fingers. But Denny remained motionless, unresponsive, her smokeblue eyes fixed on the far-away stars.

As whimsically as it had come upon him, Cragg's lust faded. He kissed her again, very gently this time, and arose to a kneeling posture. Denny made no effort to rearrange her clothing. In the dim light her naked thighs gleamed palely, defenseless, until Cragg himself pulled down her skirt, covering her nudity.

"Why didn't you fight back?" he demanded. "Everyone else does—even those who just pretend they don't want it."

"Do they?" she murmured. "I thought perhaps this was to be a partial payment for my passage to Dokoro. Wasn't that what you intended?"

"Hell, no! I didn't intend a bloody thing," he said disgustedly.

Denny gave him an odd smile. "You are a difficult man to comprehend."

"Sure. Like the goddamned Sphinx." He lurched to his feet. As he stalked away, he announced bleakly: "I'm going to relieve Akim at the wheel. You'd better get some rest."

Her low voice pursued him. "Goodnight, Cragg." He did not reply.

Soon, lulled by the soughing of the wind in the sails and the faint creaking of *Medusa's* upperworks, Denny fell asleep. She did not awaken until daybreak.

It was an elemental sort of dawn, heralded by the crowing of the caged rooster on the fantail. The eastern rim turned coral pink, then brilliant crimson, and after that gaudy preamble the sun shot out of the sea like a molten cannonball, rising fast into the cloudless sky. But for Cragg, hunched over the starboard rail, moodily savoring his first Manila stogie of the new day, there was neither joy nor glory to be derived from this familiar spectacle. In the short moment before its birth the embryo morning had a malignant blood-red quality. The sky was too unnaturally blue for such an early hour, the sea too calm.

But for Denny, rubbing her eyes to clear away the myopia that comes from deep slumber, it was a landsman's dream of beauty.

"What a magnificent morning, Cragg."

He turned slowly toward her. She was standing erect, smoothing out the wrinkles in the drab duster which had served her as a blanket during the night. Nothing in her guileless countenance suggested that she might wish to speak of his clumsy attempt at seduction. Having spent the predawn shaping a proper answer to the girl's inevitable recriminations, once she'd found time to brood over his behavior, Cragg was perplexed, even annoyed, that she now chose to let the matter drop. He had planned to comment scathingly on her presumed innocence as being more feigned than real, and to assure her that he did not make a habit of snatching candy from infants, even when such sweets were proffered so enticingly.

In a louder voice, as if she thought he hadn't heard her initial greeting, Denny called: "*Bon jour*, Cragg."

He gestured with his cigar at the baleful sun. "Don't count on it. Even where the weather's concerned, *bébé*, beauty is only skin-deep."

Denny stepped lightly down the sloping deck and joined him at the rail. If there was any double meaning to his churlish observation, she seemed unaware of it, as she inquired earnestly: "What is wrong with this beautiful morning?"

He explained the ancient truism that red dawns usually spell trouble before the day ends. She nodded understandingly.

"A storm?"

"Sooner or later."

He smoked silently for a minute. The tobacco cloud floated aft, borne on *Medusa*'s six-knot slipstream. Because the wind had diminished first to a mild breeze and then to a dead calm, the junk was wholly dependent on her diesel. Taking advantage of this lull, Cragg whistled a couple of the Thiet sailors up to the poopdeck, and set them working the big horizontal wheel. Their respectful attention to the binnacle card made it obvious that he had also managed to fix in their minds the course *Medusa* must follow.

Denny was impressed by the way the junk's wake streamed aft in a clean white line, straight as an arrow's flight. She sighed. One day soon it would point toward Dokoro.

"Are you hungry?" Cragg asked.

"A little."

"Then let's go see what Akim's cannibals have dreamed up for breakfast."

Denny said reproachfully: "The Thiets were never cannibals."

"That's a goddamned relief," he said, "everything considered."

She did not smile. "You are a blasphemous man, Cragg."

Suddenly, no longer nettled, he laughed at this solemn pronouncement. "Sailors, soldiers, and especially marines swear a great deal. But the words don't mean a god—a bloody thing. It's their safety valve."

"Don't you believe in Him?"

Startled by her unexpected question, Cragg sought momentary refuge behind a weak counterproposal. "Is this the missionary talking, mademoiselle?"

"I am only a teacher, not a missionary. But your soul does interest me, Cragg."

"Maybe I haven't got a soul."

"But you are a man of heart. If a man has a heart, he must surely have a soul."

"What makes you think I have a heart?"

"Because you are here in Thietvanne."

Cragg motioned toward the cabin. "You'd make a swell chaplain, *bébé*. Now let's eat."

When they had finished breakfast, Cragg left the girl on deck and went below for a thoroughgoing inspection of *Medusa's* cavernous interior. Her hold was dimly lighted by three kerosene lanterns that swung on gimbals attached to the overhead beams. Except for an afterspace just large enough to house both the diesel engine and a charcoal galley, it was a single compartment, about the size and shape of a slightly rounded boxcar. He approved the snugness of the bulkhead that separated this area from the smaller room, and he paid mental tribute to the ingenuity of the Chinese, who had invented watertight marine doors, along with gunpowder and moveable type.

Cragg probed the forward-canting mainmast with his sheath knife. Its soundness, further testimony to Chinese genius, was the result of prolonged burial in damp earth. This process gave the pine column a granite consistency, yet left it pliant enough to withstand a typhoon.

He felt the teak beams which supported the overhead decking. They had been shaped with adzes that never missed a stroke, then plane-smoothed by hand. The spikes that held them together were fashioned of wrought iron.

Painstakingly, methodically, Cragg checked the bilge pumps, sampled the brackish water in the oaken barrels, examined the ammunition stowage, poked into the dried stores locker, and even tested the rope hammocks where the off-duty watch slept like tree-dwelling animals.

He saved the engine room until the last. Although the diesel was silent now, it looked reliable enough, and he saw that the simplistic machine had received affectionate care from the two-man black gang. It gleamed dully in the semidarkness, as the result of much oiling and polishing.

He gazed speculatively around the half-empty cargo space. *Medusa's* hold was designed to accommodate more than fifty tons of bulk freight, such as finished cotton and silk goods, or bagged rice, which the Hong Kong merchants could sell in nearby countries where trade with Red China wasn't banned. Occasionally vessels like *Medusa* hauled more strategic items, aviation gasoline and explosives, though these shipments were a rarity in normal commerce, owing to the fire hazard. Of course, the fatalistic Kong took their chances, losing quite a few junks in the bargain, because they had no choice.

As he started forward, Cragg was struck again by an idea that had come to him when he inspected the too-tightly compacted ammo bins, and which had been germinating in the back of his mind ever since. It was a unique notion, unorthodox in the context of modern naval warfare, yet as old as the art itself.

In the short time it had taken him to diagnose *Medusa's* internal organs, the weather had worsened more than Cragg would have thought possible. Leaving Denny and Akim behind, he hurried aft to the poopdeck, where the twin helmsmen were already having trouble. Cragg lent a hand, and the three of them fought the junk back on course-045. To guarantee that she wouldn't stray again, he detailed two more of the huskiest Thiets within earshot to help steady the reluctant wheel. All this he did before Denny arrived, windblown and breathless, to resume translating. Sheer lungpower, Cragg had found, enabled him to penetrate the language barrier, at least enough to create understanding when the message was fairly obvious in the first place.

Free for a moment, he ducked into the cabin for a precautionary look at Torgerson's barometer. Its downward quivering needle showed 29.60, a sure sign that they would be engulfed by the storm front before the afternoon waned.

But the sea and the sky were themselves the most ominous portents of the violence to come. Where the long waves broke close by, the water was an odd brownish color, that of stale beer, and the more distant seas along the narrowing horizon looked even dirtier, more roiled. Taken in conjunction with the grisly sky, which had closed down upon the lone ship like a giant fist, the whole effect was one of elemental menace, heightened by the repressive quiet that marked this phase of the gathering storm.

For the rest of the morning, as the cold wet wind's velocity increased, Cragg held *Medusa* under full sail. Shortly before noon he summoned her diesel into action in a further valiant effort to reduce the mileage between them and Point *Delta* before the tempest hit. But by one P.M. the junk's laboring behavior forced him to reef canvas, and an hour later he reluctantly gave the word to drop the mainsail, leaving *Medusa* to challenge the gale with what remained of her shortened garb on foremast and mizzen.

Back at the wheel once more with the two Thiet helmsmen, Cragg kept a worried eye on these straining remnants of sail, silently cursing himself for having been fatuous enough to release Torgerson for a pleasant holiday aboard *Mohican*. Already he felt grave doubts for the proficiency of his native crew, whose whitened glances betrayed a growing fear each time they had to inch their way forward to make an adjustment in the sheets, or to lash down some item of deck equipment that threatened to cut loose.

Yet Cragg could hardly blame them. Despite his superior wisdom and experience, the tumultuous waves, and the wind that howled against *Medusa's* skintight canvas, were disturbing even to him.

One circumstance, nonetheless, favored them. The wind was

blowing from directly astern. Thus, running before the gale, she proved more than able to maintain her scheduled advance until nightfall. It wasn't much of a sunset, Cragg conceded grimly, but rather a gradual loss of what little visibility they had enjoyed during the waning afternoon. As the graygreen murk gave way to impenetrable blackness, he ordered down the last few square yards of the truncated mizzen. This was a necessary precaution. Caught by an emergency, fumbling in the rainswept dark, Cragg was afraid his nervous crew might take so long to drop this essential sail that they'd lose a mast before the chore was half-done.

After that, finding her stability much impaired, *Medusa* labored through the huge following seas with only the diesel to hold them roughly on course.

Cragg's best estimate of their average speed was a meager four knots, slower when the junk was climbing the flank of some unseen wave-mountain, eerily faster as she plummeted down the nether slope. He guessed, too, that they had another thirty miles to travel before they would reach the approximate vicinity of Point *Delta*. At four knots, this meant seven and one-half more hours of numbing torture, and a rendezvous delayed at least until three A.M.

Cragg turned to Denny. The girl had stoutly disregarded all previous suggestions that she take shelter in the master's cabin. She had allowed herself to be bundled into foulweather gear, however, and now she was crouched beside him at the wheel, grasping a freshly rigged lifeline with one hand, shielding her eyes against the rain with the other. He had to shout to make himself heard above the tumult.

"It's time for you to go below!"

Denny's wet face peered up at him from beneath the jutting sou'wester cap. Her small jaw, Cragg noted, was outthrust. She seemed ready to treat this implied command exactly as she had responded to his earlier hints.

Her mouth framed the stubborn words that were lost in the storm: "But I prefer to remain here, Cragg."

He laughed rudely. "Look, baby, it's fine with me if you want to drown yourself. But that'll have to wait. Right now I've got a special job for you. Something I should handle myself, but can't, because I've got to keep this crazy bathtub from filling up."

When Cragg's roar subsided, Denny touched her temple in Gallic salute, and formed with her lips a suddenly obedient "Aye, aye, sir."

He beckoned her closer. "Listen carefully. There's a voice-radio set on the cabin transom. Switch it on and give the tubes a few seconds to warm up before you take the microphone off its hook. Press the talk button. Then, once every minute, I want you to call, '*Medusa* to *Mohican*,' loud and clear. Maybe Duke Harris will hear you the first time. Or maybe you'll have to keep calling for a couple of hours, because we're still a hell of a long distance away, and this TBS doesn't have much range. But don't get discouraged. Whatever you do, don't quit. Understand?"

"Yes, Cragg, I understand." Denny made a vain effort to dry her face with an oilskin sleeve. "At Dokoro, it was often my duty to operate the mission radio. Yours should not be too much different."

"Okay. When you raise *Mohican*, tell Harris they're to proceed directly into Bien Goa without waiting for us at Point *Delta*. We'll follow as soon as this goddamned storm will permit."

Cragg now concentrated on the increasingly difficult task of guiding *Medusa* through the opaque darkness. They were no longer traveling northeast. To fetch them into Bien Goa at the earliest possible moment, he had shifted from course-045 to 340, slightly west-of-north, which brought the gale against her slab-sided port flank. Cragg kept his gaze fixed on the luminescent binnacle. Each time the junk's ninety feet of bare-sticked hull was caught in a trough of the now-quartering sea, the magnetic compass card spun wildly, as much as a dozen degrees.

For two hours he fought the storm and the ship in this manner, cursing them both, grimly aware that their painful forward progress was equalled by their lateral slippage, yet powerless to do anything more about it. He could only trust that the Thiet engineer hadn't been thrown against a bulkhead by the impact of a sudden wave, and knocked senseless, thus removing him from supervision over the all-important diesel. If the faithful engine died for lack of its shepherd's care, Cragg knew, they were also dead. Stone-cold, mackerel dead.

But somehow it stayed alive, and the single screw kept turning. There were excruciating periods when an abnormal wave-crest tilted *Medusa's* stern skyward, causing the freed propeller to chew noisily upon empty air. Each time Cragg held his breath, alert for the sound of cracking metal that would signal a broken drive shaft.

In the midst of this single-minded duel, Denny's abrupt reappearance came as a surprise, for he had forgotten about her. She followed the lifeline up the slippery deck, then stood beside him at the wheel for several moments before he was conscious of her presence.

"M'sieu Harris finally responded," she said. "He took your message to Torgerson, who sends word that they will do as you have instructed."

Cragg looked at his watch. It was ten-forty P.M.

"You had the devil's own time reaching *Mohican*, didn't you?"

"It was not easy. But when we achieved contact, M'sieu Harris said he 'read me five-by-five.'" She asked proudly: "Is that not good?"

"*Très bien.* Like hollering down a rainbarrel." Cragg gave her a tired grin. "Funny thing. Women's voices carry better over the air than men's, especially under bad atmospheric conditions." He studied her pale, drawn face. "Now that you've finished that job, I have a new one for you."

"Yes, Cragg?"

"Turn slowly around, go back where you came from, and hit the sack."

She frowned. " 'Hit the sack?' "

"Crawl into the captain's bunk. Close your eyes. Speak a bedtime prayer for a heathen monster named *Medusa* and its heathen skipper. Don't you poke your little nose out of that cabin until I sound the all-clear." He shut off her incipient protest. "That's a flat order, baby. Scram!"

Denny flicked her pink tongue at him in a classic gesture of womanly defiance. But she left without further protest.

It was nearing three A.M. when *Medusa* arrived somewhere off Bien Goa. Although the storm had abated slightly, and the sea was noticeably calmer, visibility continued from nil-to-poor.

Cragg figured he could see ahead for about a quartermile. But even this was a rough estimate, for the rainswept night gave him nothing upon which to take a fix with the simple stadimeter that also served as a gunnery rangefinder. Regretfully, he indicated by sign language to one of the Thiet helmsmen that he wanted Denny awakened and brought aft.

She arrived promptly, looking fresh and composed, and eager to help.

"We've got a damned ticklish exercise ahead of us," Cragg explained. "I need you on hand to pass my orders to these jokers."

Denny nodded.

"Akim will take over here in a couple of minutes. Have him break out the rest of the crew. I want everyone on deck, except the engineer and the cook."

"Yes, Cragg."

"Meanwhile, ask my friend here, the tallest one, to act as bow lookout. He should keep his eyes especially peeled for underwater objects. If he spots anything, tell him to sing out loud and clear, so you can shoot the word to me, *pronto*."

Denny interpreted this for the Thiet, who turned inquiringly toward Cragg with a comment of his own.

"He wishes to know what manner of objects might be seen in this vicinity," she said.

"Coral reefs," Cragg snarled. "The chart shows a whole bloody forest of the stuff along the coast, filled with coralheads that grow within a few feet of the surface. They can rip a hole in a ship's bottom like a bowie knife slicing sowbelly. There's a clear passage into the lagoon, about 150 meters wide, but I'm damned if I know exactly where it is—" he grimaced, "or even where the hell *we* are right now, other than a couple of lousy miles offshore in the general area of Bien Goa."

Sobered by this information, the helmsman-lookout started forward, just as Akim arrived. They exchanged a few words in Thiet. Thoughtfully, then, Akim adjusted the piratical black patch on his eye which had come askew during his four uncomfortable hours in a forecastle hammock, before he addressed himself earnestly to Cragg. His horrendous smile was missing. He obviously found no joy in their immediate plight.

Taking *Medusa* into Bien Goa in this kind of weather (Denny translated) was the height of folly. Wise sailors entered the Frenchman's lagoon only by day, or when a full moon showed where the surf broke along the barrier reef. Akim was personally acquainted with a dozen Thietvanne skippers who had come to grief on these treacherous shoals, and he would prefer not to add himself to such a melancholy list. However, if Captain Cragg persisted in this mad venture, they should place a leadsman alongside the lookout on the bow. His positive soundings would be a useful adjunct to the other's unlikely visual sightings.

Cragg gave his approval, albeit doubtfully, in full awareness that while one heave of the line might indicate a safe thirty fathoms, a split-second later *Medusa* could impale herself upon a coral stalagmite only a few feet from where the lead had touched down.

"Akim can throw the line himself," he said, "if it'll make him any happier."

The one-eyed Thiet was on his way forward before Denny could finish translating. Cragg reached inside his sou'wester for a cigar.

It was moist and crushed. But now that the rain had dwindled to a thick mist, he was determined to enjoy his first smoke since early evening, as solace during this brief interval between emergencies. Even mercenary captains, Cragg thought saturninely, deserved an occasional morale builder.

The inevitable crisis developed sooner than expected. He had barely coaxed the mangled cigar alight, and drawing after a fashion, when Akim yelled a warning from his invisible post.

Denny reported: "We have now reached the edge of the reef. It is shelving fast."

Cragg leaned hard against the horizontal wheel, and *Medusa* swung slowly to starboard. It was his intention to parallel the shoal, probing cautiously, until he located the minuscule gap which gave access to Bien Goa's tight harbor. Cragg knew that this was risky business. But the deplorable vagueness of his chart left him no alternative, and the phrases printed opposite the Bien

Goa barrier were more admonitory than useful. Three of them read: "Shoals break in heavy seas. Reef dry at mean low tide. Foul ground." Two others simply noted: "Wreck."

Under normal conditions, the entrance would be marked with a pair of lights. But conditions were not normal at Bien Goa, and they hadn't been for ten years of guerrilla warfare.

For the next quarter-hour, while Akim's soundings fluctuated between twelve and twenty fathoms, Cragg waited hopefully for the bow lookout to announce a surface sighting. But none came. There was no word, either, from the pair of lookouts posted on each of the three masts. Worse, more annoying, his own normally acute vision had been so impaired by the long night's vigil that even nearby objects, such as the winches on the welldeck, seemed blurred and unreal. *Medusa's* powerful searchlight merely accentuated the opacity of the night, stabbing vainly, but finding only more gloom. From all he could learn by sight and sound, the reef might have been a million miles distant.

Then, suddenly, Akim shouted again.

"It is shallower," Denny relayed in an imperturbable voice. "Seven fathoms."

Cragg tried again to pierce the murk with his saltrimed gaze. Dimly, uncertainly, he thought he could make out something to port, an undulant gray line, where the sea had been so uncompromisingly dark. At almost that same instant the topmost lookout shrieked from his perch on the maintruck.

Denny reported calmly: "He has seen waves breaking. The reef is very near. Perhaps fifty yards."

Before Cragg could swing *Medusa* hard-to-starboard, away from the menace, the barrier had moved alarmingly close, and he was able to make out where the surf pounded against its outermost coral fringe.

He cupped an ear. The steady, almost metronomic wave-beat might have been reassuring to anyone listening from inside the lagoon, for it meant that the heaviest seas had subsided. But to Cragg it signified only that the most hazardous phase of their journey had now begun. Somehow he must contrive to remain within sight of these breakers, whose ghostly substance provided the sole clue to the reef's whereabouts, while seeking the channel that lay a few miles ahead. It would be a damned tricky job, Cragg realized, keeping *Medusa* on a safe parallel course to the shoal, with less than a hundred feet of maneuvering room. It left no margin for error. The slightest miscalculation would spell disaster for the clumsy junk, and for everyone aboard her.

Cragg reached for the bandanna he always kept in a hip pocket, and blotted the nervous sweat that was beginning to trickle down into his eyes. He thought enviously of Lars Torgerson and *Mohican*. Thanks to Duke Harris' radar, the PT should have experienced no trouble whatsoever locating the gap in the coral. Right now the Swede bastard was probably sleeping off an illicit hangover after a night of Monsieur Panache's vaunted hospitality.

With a small curse, Cragg jammed the bandanna back into his trousers. He pulled at the bill of his lucky cap and blinked once more in the direction of the reef. Then, as a blind man guides himself along a sidewalk by warily tapping his cane against the curb, alert for the sudden void that signals an intersection, he began to steer *Medusa* through the night. Barely a stone's throw to port, the surf showed as a pale line in the otherwise total blackness, like a light streak on a photographic negative. At any moment, Cragg knew, the line would abruptly disappear. Where it ended, they'd find the lagoon passage.

After that, a simple leftward spin of the wheel should direct them into Bien Goa harbor.

For the next ten minutes Cragg traced a curving course along this strange guide-strip. Once he thought he detected a rift. But it was either an optical illusion, or a place where the sea poured through some minor flaw in the reef, for the line reappeared almost immediately. All the while, from the bow, Akim tolled his singsong litany of the depths beneath *Medusa*'s eight-foot draft. They held reasonably steady at about five fathoms.

Cragg wished he could free himself from the helm long enough to light another cigar, or that Denny were a man so she could light it for him. Anyway you looked at it, he brooded, this was one hell of a lubberly way to make a landfall.

An outcry from the maintop snapped his reverie.

Denny said: "He reports an opening in the reef. It is so wide that he cannot see where the surf resumes."

"How close are we?"

She called to the lookout, who answered at once. "Perhaps two hundred meters," Denny translated.

"Good."

Cragg made a fast computation. Assuming the spotter was accurate, this would total slightly more in honest yardage, 220-or-so, which meant proceeding for another two minutes on their present course before *Medusa* came abreast of the entrance.

"I want a third man on the wheel," he told Denny. "When I say *'maintenant!'* the three of us will have to crank that blasted rudder to port faster than it's ever been cranked before. Make damned sure they understand."

"Yes, Cragg."

She summoned a Thiet deckhand from the rail, where he had been staring in rapt dismay at the booming surf, and relayed Cragg's order. The Thiet nodded comprehension as he joined his fellow helmsmen. They both looked at Cragg, half-smiling, plainly confident for the first time during the fearful night that Buddha had indeed heard their prayers for deliverance.

But Cragg had tallied only four of those vital seconds when *Medusa*, without warning from the lookouts on bow or main-mast, struck an underwater obstacle. There was a ripping, grinding, tearing noise deep within her bowels as the junk hit hard, hung up for an excruciating instant, then slipped clear. When she gathered headway once more, Cragg sensed a mushiness of movement, a curious drag, that was abnormal even for the clumsy *Medusa*.

He deliberately let another five seconds pass. The junk's unaccustomed behavior grew worse. Cragg swore aloud. It wasn't necessary for him to inspect the damage to know what had happened. At this ultimate moment before she would have been home free, *Medusa* had impaled herself upon one of the coral-heads that stood guard at the entrance to Bien Goa, and her breached hull was letting tons of seawater into her hold.

How much or how fast he could only guess.

Cragg spared a grateful thought for the tight bulkhead that

separated the main compartment from the engineroom. At least *Medusa* still had power. She was continuing on course in strange, wallowing fashion although her progress was noticeably slower. He made another rapid calculation. At this rate it should take about twenty seconds to reach midchannel, where he could relinquish the wheel and give his full attention to damage control. Provided, he told himself bleakly, *Medusa* would cooperate by staying afloat that long.

Cragg turned toward Denny. The girl was sitting on the deck, dazedly massaging a bruised elbow.

"Are you okay?"

"Yes, Cragg." Denny struggled to her feet. "But what of the ship?"

"It'll survive, baby." He pointed to Akim, who had rushed aft from his useless station on the bow, and was anxiously awaiting further instructions. "Tell Akim to take a half-dozen men below and see if they can't poke a few fingers in the dike. Also warn the engineer that he's not to open his bulkhead door under any circumstances. We're already bleeding bad enough."

Akim chose six seamen, barked a brief order, and hustled them off, like native lambs being chivvied off to a barbecue pit.

Pessimistically, under his breath, Cragg wished the Thiets good luck. They'd need it. Then he cast a critical glance forward, past *Medusa*'s barren mast and depressed bow, at the place where the surf gleamed once more in the translucent darkness.

"*Maintenant!*"

Under the combined thrust of the three sweating helmsmen, the horizontal wheel spun, the great notched rudder churned through the water, and *Medusa* began drunkenly to turn. The immense new weight sloshing around in her hold caused her to respond less readily than Cragg had planned. She needed all the room there was, but she made it, with a few yards to spare before the coral rose again.

Cragg removed both hands from the spokes, and flexed his stiffened fingers.

"This bucket is aimed straight for the beach," he told Denny. "I want her kept that way. Make sure these fellows get the message."

"Even if we run aground, Cragg?"

"Until we run aground," he growled. "Junks are like landing craft. Sometimes they need their faces rubbed in the mud." He waited until Denny passed the order. Then: "Better grab something solid just before we pile up. Next time you fall down you might break one of those pretty little legs."

Medusa plowed on.

From his recollection of the chart, Cragg estimated they had roughly three miles to negotiate across the circular lagoon to the Frenchman's plantation headquarters. The shallow beach was composed of soft sand. If they reached it, *Medusa* would be snug as a beached LST, adjacent to decent repair facilities. If. That was the operative word. If. He smote his left palm with his right fist. The junk's overworked diesel had been driving them at six knots when they rammed the coralhead. Now they were reduced to a paltry four.

Cragg lifted his hand to test the breeze. It was fairly stiff, and blowing across their port beam. This quartering tack was ideal for *Medusa*. Under full canvas she might pick up another three-to-four knots, disregarding her swollen condition, and reach the distant shore.

Cragg darted a glance around the sloping poopdeck. Only four Thiets remained unoccupied. They were huddled against the stern rail beside the smelly fowl cages, immobile, frozen, waiting for the junk either to founder, or to smash herself to pieces upon the beach. He beckoned them forward.

"Hoist the sails," he commanded. "Every goddamned rag of 'em!"

Denny translated. Despite their predicament, Cragg was amused that her small voice could convey such a large measure of authority.

Stirred out of their torpor, the four deckhands moved with surprising alacrity, and managed to get the sails placed before *Medusa* had covered another blundering half-mile. Once more at the helm, Cragg felt the pace of the waterlogged craft quicken as her slatted canvas bellied. They would, he decided, make it after all.

"Have one of the boys train the searchlight dead ahead," he instructed Denny, "so our host will know that we're here."

Medusa pummeled her steel-tipped nose hard against the fine white sand, and kept thrusting until fully one-quarter of her keel was out of water.

Hercule Panache himself led the welcoming party along the beach from the thatch-roofed pavilion, a half-mile distant, where he and the Mafia had been sweating out the junk's arrival. Cragg watched them coming. He'd been right on one count, wrong on another. Although Lars Torgerson was magnificently looped on Monsieur Panache's cognac, the big Swede was still ambulant, with his hangover several hours away.

Cragg scrambled down the careening starboard flank. He dropped tiredly to the soft ground. Torgerson lurched toward him, grinning idiotically, and flourishing a longnecked bottle at the splintered hole in the junk's bottom.

"By God, skipper, you sure as hell should've kept old Lars with you, from the looks of things."

Too exhausted to debate the issue, knowing the futility of reprimanding his drunken exec at this moment, Cragg accepted Torgerson's outstretched hand. "It might have made things easier," he agreed enigmatically, "all the way around." Then he greeted the others.

Monsieur Panache removed the soiled topee from his egg-bald head and bowed deeply.

"It is my pleasure," he intoned, "to welcome you to Bien Goa, captain."

Cragg peered at the Frenchman's seamed and leathery face, seeking whether these matter-of-fact words were genuinely meant, or merely a mask for his true feelings. Derision, perhaps, at the ridiculous plight of the foolish American officer. Or Gallic irony. Or both. But Panache seemed quite sincere.

"Thanks," Cragg grunted. "I'm afraid we're presenting you with a few unexpected problems."

"Here," said Panache dryly, "we are accustomed to dealing with the unexpected."

"So I hear."

The planter was in his late fifties, a squat, rugged, brutish sort of man, ferociously spadebearded, with a skin that resembled old mahogany. Caught in the uncompromising glare of the searchlight, his cheeks showed deep smallpox pits.

"Ah," the Frenchman cried out suddenly, baring his great white teeth in a formidable smile. "At last you are honoring Bien Goa with your presence, Mlle. Legére. I offer you a special welcome on this unexpected occasion."

Denny gazed down at him without emotion. *"Merci, M'sieu Panache,"* she said in a level tone.

Torgerson tossed aside his cognac bottle and reached for a rope that was suspended from the poopdeck. "I'm going up to rescue the fair maiden from this crumby derelict," he announced delightedly, as he started to hoist himself aboard the junk.

But Denny was too quick for him. Before Torgerson could reach her, she slid down the side, fell, and landed unceremoniously at Cragg's feet. For an instant she sprawled on the beach, her damp clothing disarrayed, while he grinned down at her.

Hercule Panache replaced his topee. "Let us all proceed to my house for a cup of hot tea. The dawn is near. You need sleep, Captain Cragg, before embarking upon your arduous repairs."

6

"Morituri te Salutant"

R ELUCTANTLY, YET UNCONDITIONALLY, Cragg surrendered to the bone-deep fatigue which had brought his mental
and physical resources to such a low ebb that any attempt to pass
judgments, until he could replenish his strength, would be utter
folly.

As if drugged by the Frenchman's hot green tea, he slept for
five dreamless hours. He awoke with the sun burning against his
face through the mildewed netting that gave only dubious protection against the tropical insects whose bite carried everything
from malaria to elephantiasis. Because the anopheles mosquito
thrived along the Thietvanne coast, Cragg had ordered the Mafia
onto an atabrine diet, despite their loud protests that they had
been rendered immune by the tons of the stuff they'd swallowed
during the war. Now, as he looked at his watch, he noted
distastefully that his own skin was beginning to take on that old,
familiar ochre hue.

It was eleven A.M.

Glancing about the open-sided hut, in which his cot occupied a position of honor nearest the front steps, Cragg saw that he was alone. All the others, he supposed, were dutifully carrying out their various assignments, while he slumbered like a mudbound native sow. Even Torgerson—blast his sodden soul!—had somehow managed to get cracking. Earlier, in that numbed interval before exhaustion overtook him, Cragg had been on the verge of throwing the book at his second-in-command. Torgerson knew that once they embarked on a mission liquor was tabu, especially for himself, as a confirmed though intermittent alcoholic. Nevertheless he couldn't resist the sauce. And when drinking was coupled with open-handed hospitality, of the sort dispensed by Hercule Panache, the Swede had no conscience whatsoever.

"In the wartime Navy," Cragg might have charged, "you could be shot for getting drunk on the job."

But this sure as hell wasn't the Navy (as Torgerson might justifiably have rebutted) and any resemblance between the Frenchman's jungle plantation and the wartime world they'd inhabited in the 1940s was purely coincidental.

Cragg dug the last granular vestiges of sleep from his eyes with a ruthless fist. He scowled across the busy compound, where Monsieur Panache's laborers were engaged in stacking huge clots of latex alongside the smoke shed. In the few hours since the rain had stopped, the ground had already dried out, and their bare feet stirred miniature dust clouds as they worked. It was villainously hot. Forgetting the natives, Cragg felt a small stab of compassion for his four crewmen, who were also caught in this fierce midmorning heat, racing to get *Medusa* repaired for the next leg of their journey. With little enough to gain from their present efforts, or from what would follow, the Mafia was displaying singular devotion to duty.

An itch on his bare chest made itself known. Cragg scratched at the place, vaguely hoping that the bug which had penetrated the net-defenses wasn't malarial, and then groped for a Philippine cigar in the shirt that lay where he'd flung it across the foot of the cot. He lit the cigar. It tasted the way the smoke shed smelled, acrid, foul, and rubbery.

Cragg crawled out of the enveloping net, dressed in a hurry, and left the sweltering hut. He was immediately accosted by a small, grinning native, who had been crouched in the shade of a coco palm, patiently awaiting his emergence.

"Papa Panache ask you come for lunch."

Cragg shook his head. "Tell Papa Panache that I've got other fish to fry. Thank him. Kiss him on both cheeks. Not now. Maybe later."

But the native persisted. "Papa Panache ask—" he began again. This seemed to be his only English, memorized for the occasion.

"Okay, okay." Cragg lifted both arms in token surrender. "Lead me to papa, sonny, if you must."

Calling himself *papa*, mused Cragg, was probably one of the Frenchman's paternalistic whimsies, although the strong likelihood existed that Hercule Panache actually was the progenitor of half the Bien Goa population, if rumors could be trusted. Certainly Denny believed them. In their few idle moments aboard *Medusa*, the girl had told him a great deal about the planter, a lot of it unfavorable, and much of it unbelievable.

"'These are *my* people,' claims M'sieu Panache," she reported scornfully. "In truth, many of them are, for M'sieu Panache takes his pleasure where he finds it, and often. He has not one wife, Cragg, but many native women. He is like those ancient Annamese emperors, who fancied themselves poets, and who chose the fairest maidens to serve in their palaces."

"Strikes me the old buzzard leads a damned full life," Cragg said in an admiring tone. "Also a slightly charmed one, considering the rugged spot he's in, sandwiched between the Thiets and the Kongs."

Denny's smoldering distaste for Papa Panache erupted. "This abominable creature thinks that he understands the natives. By living like an aborigine, he imagines that it is possible to make them love him. Love!" She spat out the word. "He believes also that the tides of war can wash across Bien Goa and leave him personally untouched, since he deals equally with both sides."

"Maybe he's just being practical," Cragg suggested, "like any other smart Frenchman."

Denny flushed angrily. Her lip curled. "M'sieu Panache is the very essence of practicality, Cragg. When GaiSong government invited all the villages to join in its fortification program, he did not bother to send regrets. Instead of surrounding Bien Goa with sharpened bamboo stakes and barbed wire, as directed, M'sieu Panache surfaced the roads that lead into the jungle. He claims that such improvements make it easier to reach his rubber trees. Nevertheless, they also facilitate the Kong's traffic from the seacoast, during those periods when the enemy controls this province."

"What about Dokoro Mission?" asked Cragg. "Does your father ask for an I.D. card before he'll treat a native for the yaws—or a gunshot wound?"

Denny gave him a scornful look. "That is a different matter. My father is a humanitarian, not a profiteer."

"But patching up a Kong guerrilla so he can fight again has the same overall effect as giving him a brand-new rifle."

"You will never understand such things," she said in a suddenly restrained voice. "And they cannot be taught, Cragg."

Hercule Panache met him at the broad, doorless entrance to the plantation's *grande maison*. He was wearing a brocaded oriental skullcap in place of his topee.

Without regret Cragg tossed aside his half-smoked cigar and limped after him into the cooler interior of the low-ceilinged house, which was much like the thatched guest hut, except for its greater size, woven partitions, and opulent Hong Kong furnishings. During his tour in the Solomons, twenty-odd years earlier, Cragg had visited a number of deserted plantations. Tropical architecture, he concluded, was an art form that stubbornly resisted change, and far more durable than the casual stuff of which it was made.

"I am honored, Captain Cragg," said Panache, as he ushered him toward the dining room.

"You are very kind to uninvited guests," Cragg replied. "I hope we won't outlast our welcome."

The Frenchman bared his formidable teeth in a responsive smile. "Your assistant, M'sieu Torgerson, announces that he will complete his repairs by tomorrow noon."

"Won't it embarrass you to have us camped on your doorstep for another twenty-four hours?"

Panache shrugged a burly shoulder. "If you are concerned lest the Kong take umbrage at my harboring two Thiet naval vessels, captain, pray set your mind at ease. We have, shall I say, an arrangement."

"So I've been told."

"Doubtless by Mlle. Legére," Panache observed in his urbane, slightly accented voice, preening his beard. "She has consented to join us for luncheon, along with Colonel Toyon."

Abruptly, like a dropped Buddha, he plumped himself in front of the Japanese-style table. Cragg followed suit although his stiff right leg was ill-adapted to floorsitting.

Panache clapped his fat palms. Immediately a diminutive Thiet girl, clad in a flowered cotton sarong, glided through the archway from the pantry. She was pretty, almost beautiful, with delicate Eurasian features. As she bent down to place a handsome cloisonné teapot and two fragile cups before them, Cragg noted pleasurably that her breasts required neither support nor embellishment. Unlike those of the GaiSong women, they were palpably real.

"This is Marie," said Panache with obvious pride. "My Number One girl."

Marie accorded Cragg an ageless smile, bobbed her small head, and silently departed. She was, he guessed, about sixteen.

"I assume that Mlle. Legére has revealed many other things about me," Panache went on.

"Some."

"Mlle. Legére is a strong-minded young woman. She holds certain definite opinions, not all of which are necessarily correct. But no matter." Panache heaved a dramatic sigh. "Regrettably, she retired to her couch before I could press for reciprocal details about *you*, Captain Cragg. One likes to know his guests, if only to cater more intelligently to their special tastes." He peered into the teapot, gave an approving nod, and filled the two cups. "However, your chief officer, M'sieu Torgerson, proved most useful in supplying the information that a proper host needs."

Cragg sampled his tea before making comment. It was robust,

yet subtly aromatic, with a fragrance whose identity eluded him. Finally he observed: "Cognac is an effective lubricant for some tongues, isn't it?"

"This was particularly rare cognac," Panache said equably. "It is called the brandy of Napoleon."

"You'd have succeeded just as well with gin," Cragg grunted. "How much of his guts did the drunken Swede spill?"

"Very little, actually. Only that you are engaged in a mysterious enterprise on behalf of General Kwo's government, which has to do with interdicting arms shipments by the Kong. Despite the liquor, your associate grew rather cautious when I exhibited too great an interest in your *modus operandi.*" Panache took a critical sip of tea. "It is too heavy with jasmine. I must admonish Marie to be more careful." He dabbed a trace of moisture from his beard. "In the unhappy years when my compatriots were fighting the rebels, I became a student of guerrilla warfare. Somewhat detached, perhaps, yet nonetheless a genuine academician. For that reason, I am always interested in fresh techniques. Your adventure intrigues me greatly."

"I thought you didn't care which side wins," Cragg said, "as long as it doesn't interfere with business."

Panache loosed another sigh. "One is forced to live with one's reputation. That is mine. Like yourself, I am a mercenary. With me, it is simply a question of commerce. True, I deal impartially with both North and South. Otherwise I would not be in business, as you have rightly pointed out. But this reality does not preclude my hoping that the Kong will be defeated in the end. If you were a Frenchman, you would understand such matters." He shrugged. "Or even an Englishman. Consider Hong Kong, where the British trade regularly with the Red Chinese. That, too, is a marriage of convenience, *n'est-ce pas?*"

"What about the opium poppies you grow here?" Cragg demanded. "Are they also part of this 'reality'?"

"They provide a further guarantee of immunity," said Panache. "It was not my choice in the beginning, to plant such a detestable crop. But I have permitted it to expand." Suddenly grave, he added: "More than opium can be harvested from these fields, *mon capitaine.*"

"For example?"

"Intelligence data. My peasants who traffic with the Kong learn many useful things. They pass them along to me. And I radio the pertinent facts to GaiSong in a code we devised many months ago." Panache gave Cragg a saturnine look. "You seem astonished. It is possible that Mlle. Legére did not divulge the full extent of my secrets."

"It's barely possible," Cragg admitted. "But I am surprised— damned surprised—that you'd tell all this to a total stranger. What makes you think I can be trusted with information that might cost your neck, if it ever leaked?"

"Sometimes," said Panache, "one simply knows these things."

"Instinct?" Cragg's tone was mocking. "Honor among mercenaries?"

"Perhaps. You have sold your services to a cause which I share, captain, regardless of what Mlle. Legére believes. Each of us has his own way of accomplishing this goal. Mine may be less direct than yours. Yet it has the same purpose." Panache impulsively thrust out his right hand. "I wish you luck, my friend. But make haste. So little time remains."

They shook hands solemnly. It was evident the Frenchman's sybaritic ways did not bar him from physical toil. He had a powerful grip, and his palm was heavily calloused, despite its fleshiness.

"Maybe it's already too late," Cragg said.

Panache waggled his bald, burnished head. "Not for what you have projected. And if your plan succeeds, the clock will stop for a few precious moments, and they may find a new source of courage in GaiSong. Enough," he added with sudden scorn, "to keep the bell from tolling Thietvanne's final hour."

"Then the Swede *did* spill his guts."

"Do not blame M'sieu Torgerson. I have known the details of your mission for more than a week. Intelligence is a two-way street. Colonel Toyon himself notified me when you chose Bien Goa as one of your daylight hiding places." Panache laughed. "Point *Delta*, is it not?"

"Toyon also talks too goddamned much."

"On the contrary, the colonel is far more dedicated to his

country than General Kwo. He feels a sense of urgency for your undertaking that one finds difficult to describe."

"Let one try."

"Very well. Colonel Toyon knows that Kwo has made certain tentative overtures to Phom Than. The general is a badly frightened man, whose fears have been heightened by the sound of artillery outside the gates of GaiSong. If he concludes that it might save his skin, and preserve some element of his valuable dictatorship, Kwo may submit to a truce parley." Wryly, wearily, Panache finished: "France agreed once to such a conference. Your country encouraged us. Remember? So did many others. But it did not work then, and it cannot work now. The Communists are an exceedingly large camel to allow inside one small grass hut. While Kwo is arguing a cease-fire line, they will continue to advance, until there is nothing left to arbitrate."

"When is Kwo supposed to take his dive?"

"Pardon?"

"How soon does Toyon think he'll toss in the towel, roll over, give up?"

Panache glanced toward the door. "No doubt the colonel would prefer to answer that personally."

Toyon stood between the divided shellbead curtains at the dining-room portico. For an instant he remained there, regarding them quietly, before walking across the matted floor. Then he sat down, still without speaking. The underslung table might have been devised for his tiny, simian figure. He pushed his short legs beneath its red lacquered top, and nodded when Panache asked whether he wished tea while they were awaiting breakfast.

"Well," growled Cragg, "what about Kwo?"

In his deep-toned voice, whose British accents contrasted with Panache's higher-pitched Gallic inflections, Toyon said deliberately: "Everything hinges upon the outcome of our assault against the Kong's convoy base at Phom Than. If we can fulfill this assignment, the general may take heart. But," he went on, "it must be a spectacular victory."

Panache interposed dryly, "Your 'fleet,' captain, seems ill-equipped to attack such an armada."

"General Kwo felt the same way," Cragg said, "until we convinced him otherwise."

"Of course." Panache clapped his hands to recall the serving-maid, who materialized out of the pantry like a nubile djinn. She vanished almost as abruptly after Panache announced that they would not delay breakfast any longer for Mlle. Legére. Turning again to Cragg, he said: "Since you are not a novice in the art of war, one assumes you have evolved a strategy to correct this tactical imbalance."

Cragg gave him a searching look. "Trying to solve that riddle has cost me a lot more sleep than the storm we just came through. But I think there's an answer." He drummed his knuckles against the tabletop, lightly, the way a pensive judge might toy with his gavel, while mulling over some thorny point of law. "It's a hell of a long shot, though, with about the same odds as getting Double-O on a crooked roulette wheel."

Panache, who had been examining the tea-leaf dregs in the bottom of his cup, suddenly glanced up. "And if the ball drops into the wrong slot, captain?"

"Then the house wins," said Cragg. "Maybe they'll be generous, like the management at Monte Carlo, and give us a pistol so we can blow out our brains."

"You are an extraordinarily brave man."

"I'm a plain goddamned fool, with four other goddamned fools as friends, and—" Cragg inclined his head toward Toyon—"a fifth goddamned fool as a 'volunteer' on this excursion." The colonel accepted the dubious accolade in gloomy silence. Cragg continued: "The solution came to me one night after we left GaiSong, when it was too late to lay in the supplies we'll need to pull it off."

"Where do you propose to obtain these items?" Panache asked.

"Here," Cragg said, "or at Dokoro."

"What is required?"

Cragg recited promptly: "A dozen barrels of pitch, two hundred pounds of sulphur, a few barrels of slowburning black powder, fifty gallons of kerosene, a dozen sticks of dynamite, caps, and whatever other arsonist materials you've got lying around loose."

Panache stroked his massive beard. *"Formidable!"* he breathed. "But these things are not easy to procure in our isolated part of the world. Nor would those who possess such treasures surrender them freely."

"What about you?" Cragg demanded.

"Most of what is needed will be found in my warehouses," said Panache. "I doubt, however, whether Dokoro could supply you. A medical mission does not employ explosives, or combustible fuel, in the same manner as a plantation."

Cragg glanced at Toyon. "How's the expense account, colonel? Can we pay?" The Thiet officer nodded gravely. "Will you sell, monsieur?"

"These stores are not for sale." As Cragg half-rose from his seat, starting to redden with anger, Panache continued in a firm voice: "But I should be happy to donate them to *our* cause, captain."

Toyon began, "On behalf of the Thietvanne government, sir, may I offer grateful—"

The Frenchman brusquely shut off his thanks. "I am not interested in the gratitude of GaiSong's rulers. My only concern is making it somewhat more possible for this gentleman to achieve his Double-O."

"You've helped," grinned Cragg, reaching across the table to shake hands with Panache for the second time. "The original odds were 1000–to–one. Now they're merely 999 against us."

"That suffices," Panache said.

Their conversation halted while the native girl, Marie, skillfully served breakfast. There were yellow papayas, soft as custard, and topped with quartered limes; slices of palm-smoked bacon, crisply broiled, which gave the lie to the canard that all Thiet pigs sprang from tough primal stock; tiny pullet eggs shirred to a golden-brown in fresh butter; fluffy bread made from some nutlike, fine kerneled grain, then lightly toasted; exotic fruit preserves; and a rich dry sauterne which Panache identified for them as *Château d'Yquem* 1955—"a year that was as splendid for Bordeaux wines as it was disastrous for French colonialism."

They were spooning earnestly at their papaya when Denny entered the dining room. She had obviously devoted considerable care to her morning toilet. Her dark hair was piled up in an elaborate *grande dame* fashion, a style unfamiliar to Cragg, who preferred the windblown naturalness Denny had displayed aboard ship. But he noted with more approval that her moist lips were slightly rouged, as on the night of their visit to the ill-starred Happytime, and that her slim legs were encased in the nylons he'd bought for her in GaiSong that same eventful day. When Denny brushed past him, Cragg discovered, too, that she was again wearing a provocative trace of scent.

After exchanging brief greetings, she motioned the three men back to their places, then took her designated seat at the table, sinking gracefully upon the cushion that served as a chair. Panache turned away his intent gaze, disappointed, as Denny's knees fled beneath her modest skirt. Catching the Frenchman's glance, Cragg felt unaccountably annoyed.

Lifting his wineglass, Panache proclaimed in an exaggerated tone that was better suited for a Parisian salon than for a plantation messhall: "To the confusion of our enemies!" He extended his goblet toward Denny, who touched hers against it with obvious distaste.

"I was not aware, M'sieu Panache, that you acknowledged the existence of a common foe."

He smiled at her, unruffled. "As Captain Cragg has learned, Mlle. Legére, I am something of an enigma, even to myself."

The rest of the meal proceeded in relative silence. Cragg ate hastily. He was anxious to check the Mafia's progress with *Medusa*. When he finished, Cragg excused himself, and got clumsily to his feet, announcing that he would see them later.

Panache stayed him for a moment. "Since tonight will be your last chance to sample peaceful pleasures for many days, I have instructed my people to prepare an authentic Bien Goa festival in honor of your visit." He flourished his wineglass. "Actually, *mon cher capitaine,* it is a simple matter of advancing our national Liberation Day from Friday week. My little ones were delighted when I told them we shall observe it eight days early."

Cragg detached himself from his logistical worries with a visible effort. "What the hell 'liberation' do the Thiets have to celebrate?" he asked ungraciously.

"Even an enslaved race may boast a proud history," said Panache, "and Thietvanne is not yet in chains. The Feast of Quyen Dhu dates back more than a thousand years, to the time when a man bearing that name drove the Chinese out of this country, and began for his people a millennium of freedom." Panache let a slight but significant silence elapse. "At least, captain, to the degree that freedom is ever recognized in Southeast Asia."

Colonel Toyon took up the theme. "It might astonish you, Mr. Cragg, to learn how certain aspects of Thietvanne's honorable past resemble those of your own Thirteen Colonies. Fourteen hundred years before Quyen Dhu ousted the Manchus, our forebears fled China and made their home here. Like the New England Pilgrims, they made friends with the natives—Proto-Malayans—to produce a somewhat darker race. I, myself," Toyon added with quiet dignity, "can trace my ancestry to the fourth century before Christ."

"As for changing the festival date," Panache said, "this presents no problem whatsoever. Peasants do not concern themselves with Gregorian calendars. They count the days, weeks and months by the cycle of their rice crops, whose gestation period matches that of a human being, from the moment the earth is impregnated until it is ready for harvest." The Frenchman chuckled softly. "Do you play chess, my friend?"

Cragg was surprised at the seemingly irrelevant question. "Yes. But what has chess got to do with all this?"

"Much," said Toyon. "Quyen Dhu himself was a renowned chessplayer. It is recorded that he calmly finished a chess match before he led the Thietvannese against the oriental oppressors, just as England's Sir Francis Drake completed his round of bowls before sailing against the Spanish Armada."

Panache caressed his beard, looking ruminative. "Custom requires that a chess game climax the night's festivities."

"It sounds pretty goddamned wild."

"I promise you, sir, that *this* game will not prove boring."

After making only the briefest amenities for the fine meal and the coming night's entertainment, Cragg left. Denny's eyes followed him to the door. Then she also arose. It was necessary for her to repair the damage which the storm had inflicted upon her wardrobe, she explained, before they sailed for Dokoro.

Cragg stopped to light a cigar at the bend in the trail that descended by gentle stages from the plantation buildings to the beach. It was one of General Kwo's Upmanns, a belated tribute to the elegant breakfast which he had dismissed in such cavalier fashion. While he lovingly coaxed the cigar alive, he let his gaze rest on the placid lagoon, which had seemed so ominous in the storm-swept darkness of the previous night. Viewed in the tropical sunlight, it was serene as the upper reaches of San Francisco Bay on a rare windless day, a two-mile ellipse, a giant palette, gleaming with every shade of blue and green in the cosmic spectrum.

Long ago, Cragg remembered, there was another lagoon much like this one in the New Hebrides, where the Mafia had conducted their final shakedown trials with PT 387. The same sort of ramshackle fishing boats, with the same red lateen sails, had paraded across its glassy surface enroute to the barrier gap. And the same kind of smaller craft, hewn from the same palm boles, had carried the traptenders to the waters above the sudden depths inside the reef, where their egg-shaped bamboo boxes were moored with rattan cables, already filled with bonita after lying there since daybreak. It had been an absurdly peaceful scene, then, in the whirlpool vortex of a conflict that meant nothing whatsoever to the Melanesians. It was no less incongruous, now, on this troubled coast of Thietvanne, where the natives asked only a modicum of freedom to fish, to till their rice paddies, and to raise a few pigs and chickens, as their ancestors before them in those ever-shortening periods between incomprehensible wars.

Like that PT 387 of old, *Mohican* rode serenely on the bosom of the lagoon, a hundred yards or so offshore. The men working upon her deck seemed very small from where Cragg stood.

Along the far edge of the shimmering expanse the Thiets' grass huts appeared to sprout from the water on tall stilts. Coco palms arched above them. These were productive trees, with old names like *sao,* and *dan,* and *ban lang,* much prized for their rich oil.

Beyond the huts and the palms stretched an expanse of savannah grass, perhaps ten miles wide, leading upward to the Fantastic Mountains, their peaks dark against the midday sky.

It was reliably reported that big game abounded in those rain-forest slopes. Cragg exhaled a mournful, smoky breath. He would have liked to select a pair of high-powered rifles from *Mohican's* arsenal, invite Torgerson along, and spend the remainder of the week hunting tigers. But that was impossible for several reasons, of course, even if the Kong hadn't been prowling the jungles.

Regretfully, he swung his gaze toward the eastern horizon, and saw that the storm front through which they had passed was still lingering far out at sea, despite the inshore calm. Cumulus clouds were piled heaven high, precariously balanced on the warm lower air, and where they met the tropopause they took on a menacing look, as if some strange and violent chemistry was taking place within their swollen whiteness. Cragg started walking again. The rankest amateur meteorologist could guess tomorrow's weather. It would be stinking lousy.

Notwithstanding, *Medusa* and *Mohican* must sail at "the earliest practicable moment," as the Navy would say.

Puffing savagely at his cigar, Cragg limped along the path that paralleled the lagoon, kicking occasionally at the dark volcanic sand. As he approached the place where the junk was undergoing repairs, he could hear the Thiet's singsong voices, and the sound of their rough carpentry.

Medusa lay much farther out of the water than she had been when Cragg abandoned her shortly before dawn. With grapnels hooked into the high ground, stout ropes attached to the deck winch, and sheer brute force, they had manhandled her a good fifty feet up the beach, like a giant land crab, until her entire hull was exposed. Then Torgerson had careened her to starboard once more, and placed chocks against *Medusa's* bottom, in a manner that made the wound in her forequarter easily accessible. Two of the Thiets, woodworking specialists, were fitting a piece of mahogany over the hole from the outside, using crude hatchets and adzes to shape the irregular patch. Soon, Cragg noted, it would fit perfectly. An application of caulking compound should finish the business of rendering *Medusa* seaworthy.

But his satisfaction was short-lived.

Near the downward hogcurve of the keel another Thiet, his face hidden from Cragg's view by the great wooden fin, appeared to be setting fire to the junk's stern with a blowtorch. Only the man's ragged dungaree pants and naked torso were visible. He was alternately spraying acetylene flame against her portside, pausing, letting the slightly charred surface cool for an instant, then repeating his extraordinary performance.

Cragg yelled, "For Christ's sake, knock it off!"

A puzzled Thiet face, half-covered by an enormous pair of welding goggles, peered at him from beneath the smoking keel.

"*Bon jour, mon capitaine.*" The man put down his torch. He exposed a horrendous set of betel-stained teeth. "Is there a difficulty?"

It was Loo, the English-speaking Thiet, who had demonstrated such unexpected skill at the helm during *Mohican's* first night out of GaiSong.

"What the hell are you doing?"

"Meestair Torgerson order these barnacles removed. So I obey."

Loo picked up the blowtorch and aimed another fiery burst at the hull. Upon closer scrutiny, Cragg saw that the blackened areas were places where marine growths had been burnt to a quick crisp, rather than sections of charred timber.

"Does Mr. Torgerson know you're building a bonfire to delouse this bucket?"

"Delouse?"

"Forget it. Where is the exec?"

"Inside the bucket," said Loo, proud to have added a new Yankee word to his vocabulary. "Performing the inspection."

Cragg shot him a dubious look. "Take it easy with that flamethrower, mister," he said starting up the ladder that was braced against *Medusa's* upper flank.

As Loo once more hoisted the blowtorch aloft, the muscles in his skinny arms tightened. But the heavy instrument did not waver. He called over his shoulder: "Do not worry, *mon capitaine.*

Chinese sailors always burn barnacles in this fashion. Never hurt junk. They taught me their special magic at Hong Kong shipyard."

Although the seacocks had been wide open for hours, draining the hold, water was still ankle deep in the after-section of the breached cargo department. Cragg's temper did not improve as he sloshed doggedly through the bilge in quest of Torgerson, who was reported in conference with the Thiet motor machinist. That interminable breakfast, his latest brush with Asian technology, and too little sleep were the cause, Cragg decided, all the more vexed at his self-discovery that he was indeed in a foul mood. But Panache had merely been acting the proper host, and Loo was doing a fine job. As for sleep—hell!—how much did Edison ever need? Or Einstein? Or Dr. Schweitzer? Or the astronauts? Five hours out of forty-eight was ample for any grown man.

With sudden irrelevance, Cragg's thoughts turned to Denny, as he had last seen her, ineffably cool, contained, perplexing, and so goddamned *female*. In her calm presence, for some incomprehensible reason, he acted like a tangle-tongued idiot, taking refuge behind masculine crudity, hoping to prod her into a reflexive demonstration of simple womanliness. Rather guiltily, then, Cragg recalled how the girl's smokeblue eyes would widen, darken, and her small jaw clench whenever he made a remark that was deliberately aimed to shock. Denny could not know, of course, the effect upon him of her own low-keyed responses to such nonsense. Or the way in which he was moved by a sudden glimpse of her elfin figure, and inexplicably stirred when she stood close to him.

Cragg felt the chill from his water-soaked feet creeping upward, ready to assail his crippled knee, and he swore softly. Hell. There were certain callow notions a man must put aside, once he disappeared over the goddamned hill. Forget them. Behaving otherwise would stamp him as an unvarnished, obsolescing fool. He swore again. It was, he told himself sourly, a good thing they'd deliver the girl to her parents at Dokoro four days hence, before temptation really set in, and breached his avuncular defenses for the second time.

With a vicious kick of his good left leg, Cragg forced open the engine-room door.

Torgerson greeted him casually, unabashed at having been caught in the act of lighting a forbidden cigarette in the machinery compartment.

"Glad to have you aboard with us commonfolk, skipper. How was breakfast at the castle?"

"Conversation, mainly."

Cragg gave Torgerson a cold glance. The Swede's eyes were bloodshot and the cigarette trembled perceptibly as his hand guided it toward his lips. There was a two-day growth of dirty blond stubble on his sunburnt face. But he responded to Cragg's coolness with a mocking grin.

"Did *petite chérie* manage to make the scene?"

"Yes."

"Damned shame about the storm," Torgerson sympathized. "It must have loused up your honeymoon."

"Go to hell!" Cragg changed the subject. "How's the repair job coming?"

"We should have everything squared away for an early afternoon departure tomorrow."

"Good." Cragg decided to repay the exec's sarcasm. "Sometimes an alcoholic conscience makes a guy work harder, doesn't it?"

"Remind me never to get stoned on brandy again," Torgerson groaned.

"I won't have to, mister. There isn't going to be any next time. Consider it a final order. Savvy?"

"Okay, teacher."

Cragg turned toward the Thiet motor mech, who had remained at respectful attention while they were talking. "What about the power plant?"

"This joker understands engines a lot better than he does English. DelGrado thinks he's a goddamned bush genius. In spite of the clobbering it took, it's still four-oh, thanks to his black magic."

"And the deck guns?"

"Trump checked 'em out an hour ago. Aside from a few sprung fittings they're in pretty fair shape. He's on *Mohican*, now, futzing around with that crazy flamethrower of yours."

"Good." Cragg thwacked Torgerson's broad shoulder. "Nice workout for the Mafia, fella. Just like Guadalcanal, isn't it, patching up damage with wire, spit and shoestring?"

"Hell, *Mohican* didn't catch any trouble. We missed the bad part. This scow absorbed most of the punishment." Torgerson trailed him through the hatch and into *Medusa's* dank hold. "Now what's the exercise?"

"Whenever you're ready we'll start loading cargo."

"Cargo?"

"Affirmative. Papa Panache is donating a couple tons of special gear to the cause."

As he limped toward the ladder, Cragg catalogued the pyro-technic assortment which the Frenchman had promised to supply. Torgerson listened in amazement.

"You sound like a frigging arsonist."

"Maybe I am."

"What the devil are you going to do with all that stuff?"

"We'll use it," said Cragg, "on targets of opportunity."

This cryptic explanation, Torgerson knew, would have to suffice. As Cragg had unnecessarily reminded him, it *was* the 'Canal all over again with a two-striper maniac dreaming up nutty schemes, issuing blind orders, and the Mafia discovering the hard way what really cooked after they'd gotten their tits caught so deep in the wringer there wasn't any turning back. Sometimes, when Cragg felt in a generous mood, he might lift the curtain an inch or two, and give them a rough preview of the night's plot. But that didn't occur very often. Mostly the cold son of a bitch kept his own stubborn counsel, on the theory that one guy scared crapless over the gory details of the next mission was enough. So why should that one guy, namely Cragg, spread panic by revealing how PT 387 was going to invade (say) Choiseul harbor single-handed and bag a tincan before the Nips woke up? Why, indeed, aside from the obvious fact that the

Mafia didn't scare easily. It was downright hoggish of Cragg to enjoy the pleasures of anticipation, like a secret drunkard, while leaving his subordinates only the thin gruel of unconfirmed rumor. If a guy was expected to help with the crash landings, Torgerson believed, he should also participate in the takeoffs.

"You're a cagey bastard, aren't you?" he said belatedly, and rhetorically, after they had reached the open deck.

Cragg grinned. "Isn't that DelGrado," he countered, pointing, "over there with all those people?"

Torgerson scowled toward a grassy knoll, beyond the beach, atop which stood the flower-garlanded ruins of a small temple. In the forecourt several natives were preparing to roast a wild boar. They had dug a large pit beneath a palm tree, partially filled it with smooth rocks, and were raking redhot coals over the stones. Stripped to the waist, his rugged torso almost as brown as theirs, Mario DelGrado appeared to be supervising the task.

"Sure. That's the Wop, all right, showing 'em how we barbecue a pig back home." Torgerson glowered. "One big, happy family on a goddamn Jersey meadows picnic."

Cragg headed for the exterior ladder. "See you later, Lars. I'm paddling out to *Mohican*. Maybe Duke's picked up some fresh scuttlebutt from GaiSong."

As he had expected, Harris was huddled over his shortwave set in the cubbyhole chartroom, a halfdeck below the PT's bridge, engrossed in electronic eavesdropping. Most people involved with radio, notably announcers, impressed Cragg as being compulsive talkers. But Duke was a compulsive listener, endlessly seeking some informational tidbit which would provide the missing link, the ultimate word on the Word, that might clarify whatever hairy situation happened to confront them at a particular moment. It had never disturbed him in the way Torgerson used to be bothered, that Cragg refused to divulge the advance details of their nocturnal adventures in the South Pacific. Nor did it concern him now. Duke maintained that tactics was the captain's business. On the other hand, as a cardcarrying ex-subject of Her Britannic Majesty, he himself claimed an Englishman's birthright to dabble in strategy, at least hypothetically, and to form his own private conclusions about the overall conduct of any war, including one fought upon this godforsaken China Sea.

Duke had a padded headset clasped over his knobby skull like a pair of outsized earmuffs, a rapt look on his Pickwickian face. He was fondling the selector dial with the nicotine-stained fingers of his right hand, while he adjusted the fluctuant volume with his left. Beside him, wearing an auxiliary pair of earphones, sat Toyon. The colonel's expression was more melancholy than ever, and he was making notes on a yellow scratch pad.

Neither man heard Cragg enter the cubicle. He stood behind them for an instant, peering at Toyon's unintelligible scrawl. Then he tapped Harris on a bony shoulder.

Duke glanced up. After disengaging his headset, he said: "We're monitoring Radio Phom Than, skipper. Those blighters are beaming their chatter directly into South Thietvanne, using local frequencies. Seems they're trying to impress any villagers who own radios, as well as the local chiefs and the merchants, with the futility of further resistance." Duke indicated Toyon's notes. "He'll run through it for you."

The colonel removed his earphones. In the tone of a reluctant judge pronouncing a death sentence, he carefully paraphrased the notes he had written down in Thiet. His precise Oxford speech made a mockery of Duke Harris' mixture of Yankee and Liverpudleian accents.

"The Kong appear confident," he said, "to the point of braggadocio. They are broadcasting matters which we have previously obtained only through intelligence sources. Troop numbers and disposition. The extent of their supply flow. And," Toyon added in a quick burst of scorn, "even the target of their final drive to 'free our enslaved brethren.' "

Cragg asked casually, "The coastal delta above GaiSong?"

"How did you know this, Mr. Cragg?"

"Intuition, colonel. Plus simple logic. Now that they've got General Kwo wavering, they want to toss their Sunday punch. GaiSong is your country's glass jaw. So naturally they'd concentrate their full force in that area. And since they're ready to move by sea, the delta's the best unloading spot." Cragg motioned toward the colonel's pad. "Did their confessional include the convoy buildup?"

Toyon nodded grimly. " 'Like tall trees in a copra plantation,' " he translated, " 'our many-masted armada grows upon the azure waters of Phom Than harbor, receiving the sinews of war which will soon enable our heroic soldiers to crush the evil oppressor.' "

"Was any deadline set?"

"Unfortunately, much of the broadcast was marred by heavy static. I did hear mention of the Feast of Quyen Dhu, but the context was not altogether clear. Perhaps it was merely coincidental."

" 'Liberation fleet,' " Cragg mused aloud. " 'Liberation Day.' " He snapped his fingers. "Christ! It makes sense. The Kong might just try something like that, as a crowd-pleaser, to show the world what wonderful bighearted bastards they really are."

Toyon blinked his dark, aqueous eyes. "The festival is only eight days away."

"I know. Our schedule calls for hitting 'em on Thursday, which means we've got exactly one, lousy, goddamned day's margin, if *Medusa* can sail tomorrow." Cragg gave the colonel a speculative frown. "Do you reckon your ever-lovin' general can hang tough for a whole week? Or will he start hollering uncle before we get there?"

"I have ceased to predict what General Kwo will do," Toyon replied frigidly.

Duke Harris cut in. "If it's any comfort, skipper, the blighter went on the air himself last night, advising the faithful to 'gird themselves for terrible new privations' unless some honorable way is found to end the war."

"That's no comfort," Crag growled. "Besides, I've already heard the same lament from Panache. The guts of it, anyhow." He twisted his tall frame toward the chartroom door, bumped his close-cropped head against a low beam, and cut loose an exasperated curse. "Keep tuned to Phom Than. Maybe they'll drop us a clue."

Massaging the bruise, which had already started to swell, Cragg ascended to *Mohican's* narrow deck. On the fantail, he saw, Trump Gideon and his Thiet gun crew were bunched around the 75-mm. cannon. He hobbled aft to find out what the hell they were doing.

As he came abreast of the metal shield that housed the stern 40-millimeter, Cragg noticed sparks flickering from the flamethrower nozzle slung beneath the Long Tom's graceful barrel. Instinctively he stepped inside the plated shelter. At that instant Gideon squeezed the handle that controlled the volatile fuel flow, and a huge jet of incandescent gas roared across the water, like a runaway fireball. In its flaming wake, for more than thirty yards, the lagoon sizzled and boiled.

Although safely out of range, a native pirogue came to a splashing halt, and its two wild eyed occupants dived overboard. They began to swim frantically for the nearest shore, away from *Mohican* and its fiendish apparatus.

"Our first chance to light the Zippo," Gideon explained apologetically as Cragg stomped toward him. He brightened. "But it worked swell, didn't it?"

"You win this month's prize for psychological warfare," Cragg snorted. "There isn't an unscared Thiet within five miles of Bien Goa. They'll be yammering about the fork-tongued white devils for the next twenty years."

"That's half the idea, skipper. Remember the naval article you showed me about putting flamethrowers in PTs? Most of the fighting's done at 'grappling-hook distance,' it said, so we need something to jolt 'em off balance, while we close for the kill."

"You've got it," Cragg stated. "Just don't fire off any more napalm around here without my special okay."

"In writing?" Trump Gideon asked, once more his elegant self.

"Go to hell."

Bathed in the capricious yellow glow of rush torches, the moldering temple seemed even older than its nine centuries, and its tumbled pink blocks resembled soft pumice. Near the dark maw that had once been the main entrance, a headless gray gargoyle stood watch, with a native rooster perched upon its severed neck. The rooster was staring balefully at the noisy celebrants of Quyen Dhu who had disturbed his rest, impatient for the dawn, yet afraid to leave. Beside the gargoyle loomed a tall figure carved of some pale stone that had weathered the years better than the material from which the temple itself was fashioned. His hands were clasped before him, in the priestly manner, and his face was downcast. Bird droppings had whitened his conical stone hat, until it gleamed like alabaster.

In the raised forecourt, seated upon the bulkiest pieces of tile and green-lichened rock that had fallen from the temple's square colonnades and curved roof, were the people of Bien Goa.

Cragg regarded them curiously from his own superior vantage atop a thatched dais which he occupied, kinglike, with Hercule Panache.

Several score in all, the villagers had arranged themselves in a partial circle, leaving open a small segment so the dancers could enter the ring from the temple, which served as their dressing room. There seemed to be a definite social order at Bien Goa. The first row was occupied by Papa Panache's household staff, turbanned young men and women, whose skirted Annamese costumes shone like polished jade and old gold in the flickering torchlight. Behind them crouched the lowlands tribesmen and their mates, wearing pantalons and blouses, their short black hair in braids, and with hammered silver ornaments draped about their swarthy necks. Most of the women had tied plastic tooth-brushes to the metal circlets, like lavalieres. These were very precious to them, Cragg supposed, although it seemed improbable from what he had observed of the tribesmen's stained teeth that the brushes were ever used for dental hygiene.

The final row, composed largely of standees, belonged to the *montagnards* who had been invited down from the Fantastic Mountains for the night's frolic. Tall, dour, frizzy-haired, aboriginal, they clustered on the outer fringes, still gleaming with sweat after their long march. The males were clad in *sampots*, a diaper-like breechclout, and the females wore loose-fitting sarongs that left them as shapeless as rice sacks. Some of the men, Cragg observed, carried bolt-action rifles. They leaned their fierce chins upon the upturned stocks while waiting for the fun to commence.

With an anguished creak of the wicker fanchair, Panache squirmed his gross body toward Cragg.

"You have seen the guns," he said. "I provided these weapons, and taught them how to shoot. In recent weeks a piratical species of guerrilla has appeared in the hills, that owes allegiance neither to the Thiets nor the Kong. When the *montagnard* chief sought my aid against these brigands, I was pleased to comply." Panache wiped his moist face with a silk handkerchief. It was a humid night, and a faint mist had begun to drift inland from the lagoon. He added complacently: "As a result, I have acquired a splendid new source of information. Mountain natives, M'sieu Cragg, have powerful legs. They travel very far and very fast. They learn a great deal about many things."

"You have discovered the secret of true charity," Cragg said in mock admiration.

Papa Panache beamed down at his flock. He belched contentedly. It had been a magnificent dinner. Lucullan, in fact, by any criterion, including the Paris *haute cuisine* he'd almost forgotten after thirty-odd years. Of course, the native spices, with which the sauce for the roast boar had been seasoned, were highly calorific, and contributed to the evening's heat. So did the copious drafts of strong rice liquor which he had taken each time the huge bowl was carried up to the dais. He had been amused at the way Cragg sipped at the bitter brew, handling the communal bamboo drinking tube as if it were some unfamiliar woodwind, and consuming only what politeness required. Unlike M'sieu Torgerson, who was curiously abstinent tonight, the captain did not appear to be a bibulous man. Rather, Cragg seemed to be rationing himself, both physically and emotionally, like a pugilist at rest before the final round of a fight that had not gone to his satisfaction.

With a sigh, Panache glanced toward the empty chair that stood between him and Cragg. It was regrettable, although hardly surprising, that Mlle. Legére had chosen to leave the festival after the dancers finished their hour-long performance, without waiting for the chess tourney. She was remarkably puritanical, for one who had been exposed to the candid vagaries of Southeast Asian culture during her adolescence and early womanhood.

Beyond question, Mlle. Legére had even taken offense at the uncovered bosoms of the innocent girl dancers who enacted the final tableau. For the life of him, however, Panache could not

imagine a veritable mating dance performed in the same elaborate vestments worn by the glum-faced portrayers of ancient
temple rites. Brocaded jackets, ankle-length trousers, and pagoda
hats suited the latter, as did the rice powder with which they
brought their arms and faces to such a ghostly whiteness.

Papa Panache favored his subjects with another benign smile.
Actually, the mating dance was only a prelude. The traditional
chess game, played with living pieces upon a giant board,
heralded the antic fun that would commence when the village
darkened at the stroke of midnight.

Panache frowned at the chronometer strapped around his
thick, hairy wrist. It was already past eleven. Then he dropped
his gaze to the steps of the dais, upon which sat three of the four
Americans who had joined Cragg's bizarre enterprise against the
Kong. Only the man named Duke was absent, guarding their PT
boat with Colonel Toyon.

"Unlike the sensitive Mlle. Legére," said Panache, "your Mafia
quite obviously relishes our small entertainment." He paused,
then added, " '*Ave Caesar—*' "

Cragg finished the quotation. " '*Morituri te salutant.*' "

"You are also a student of Latin, m'sieu?"

"Only the military parts. Caesar's Gallic Wars. Virgil's *Aeneid.*
That sort of thing." Cragg shrugged. "But why the Roman
gladiators? They were performers, not spectators."

"It is all one," Panache said cryptically.

Cragg waited, but the Frenchman did not elucidate. He was
quiet for a full minute, staring pensively at the courtyard stage,
which was now being readied for the chess game. His pitted
cheek, silhouetted by the undulant flares, resembled a miniature
cratered moon.

Finally Panache spoke. "It is time for the chess, *mon capitaine.*
Allow me to explain how we shall play, you and I, for the
delectation of our audience. As the game progresses, you will
note that there are certain rewards for your brave gladiators,
commensurate with their master's skill."

Now the musicians had moved offstage to the courtyard steps.
When they reassembled with their instruments, and resumed

playing, the tempo was not so wild, frenetic, as it had been during the sensual dance. It was almost stately. Bamboo flageolets, slim pear-shaped lutes, metal gongs, and drums made of four-foot palm boles and buffalo hide combined to produce a haunting sound that was not unlike a classical minuet. In a moment the plaintive voices of the villagers picked up the melody. Although Cragg could not understand the words, he remembered something Denny had told him earlier, shortly before she left the festival.

"These unhappy people sing always about their past, never about today or tomorrow. That is because, to them, the past seems best."

Occupying the whole of the stage was a giant chessboard, its sixty-four squares defined by pale coral and dark volcanic sand, alternately sprinkled between bamboo strips. All the chess pieces were native girls. Obviously proud at having been chosen for this climactic honor, they confronted each other across the rude parquet, like grave-faced dolls.

The smallest of them were the pawns. They were bare above the waist. Those who represented the Whites had dusted themselves with rice powder, and they wore saffron yellow skirts, fastened beneath their navels by gold clasps. The exposed bodies of the Black pawns, unpowdered, were burnished copper in the torchglow. Their low-slung skirts, however, had been dyed to a deep carmine with vegetable juice. Gardenia pompoms for the Whites, pink hibiscus for the Blacks, completed the scanty costumes of these shock troops. Each of them carried a tiny dagger.

Behind the impassive pawn line stood the rooks, knights, bishops, kings and queens, clad according to the pieces they personified. All except the queens were accoutered as warrior-males, and even the bishops brandished spears instead of mitres, in open defiance of clerical custom. Taller than the others, including the kings, the queens were unashamedly, exquisitely feminine, their full-breasted torsos as naked as those of the humbler pawns.

Cragg's attention was drawn to the Black Queen, a statuesque creature, whose smooth body gleamed like carved teak. Her graceful neck and shoulders were adorned by a collar, or amulet, hammered out of what appeared to be pure gold and studded with semiprecious stones. A jeweled armband glittered above each rounded elbow, and both her delicate wrists were encircled by filigreed gold bracelets. A blood-red gem shone darkly from the royal navel. The skirt, caught about her narrow waist with a gilded sash, was purple brocade. In lieu of a sceptre, she lightly held a curve-stemmed lotus blossom, whose color matched the crimson of her long fingernails. She might have been twenty. Certainly no more. Thietvannese women ripened early.

Torgerson leered up at Cragg from his seat below the dais.

"That," he pronounced in a loud voice, "is the juiciest piece I've seen since 'Frisco."

Panache gave him an indulgent smile. "If your captain plays adroitly, he may capture this 'piece,' as you say. Under our tournament rules, m'sieu, the winner disposes of his trophies in whatever manner he chooses. Perhaps he will be generous."

"Christ!" Torgerson's voice bordered on reverence. "When I think of all the time I futzed away on stud poker when I might've been learning chess. . . ."

Cragg smiled. He was feeling more kindly disposed toward his exec. The Swede had resolutely, even pointedly, declined the potent rice liquor each time the wassail bowl came around. As a consequence, Torgerson was in a cold sober, calculating mood, not unlike a hungry tiger whose appetite had been whetted by the unexpected sight of a plump gazelle mincing along a jungle trail.

"Chess," observed Cragg, "is a gentleman's game."

Panache corrected him. "On the contrary, my friend, chess is a strategist's game, and the best strategists are rarely gentlemen. Successful planning involves too much double-dealing. N'est-ce pas?"

"True enough." Cragg regarded the Frenchman quizzically. "I assume you're speaking from experience."

"Fifty-eight mortal years of it," admitted Panache. "Including several wars, a smattering of politics, and now—" with an eloquent shrug—"Thietvanne."

"My chess has gotten damned rusty," Cragg said.

"Mine also suffers from disuse, mon capitaine. There are few

good players in our lost portion of the world, and it is impossible
to teach these indigenes the finer points of the art. They have too
little patience. In fact," Panache sighed, "I have not indulged my
whim since last year's festival." He gestured the musicians to
silence. "As our guest, you shall command the Whites. It is your
first move. . . ."

Like cautious fencers, each probing to find his adversary's
strengths and weaknesses before making the lunge that would
signal the kill, they commenced the strange match. It was, of
necessity, a time-consuming affair. Native page boys relayed
written instructions from the dais to the checkered stage, where a
dark-skinned monitor would peruse the notes, nod, and ceremoniously escort the piece at issue into her next designated
square.

Despite Panache's contempt for their chessmanship, the villagers of Bien Goa were plainly fascinated by the curious tableau. They watched, grave-faced, as it slowly unfolded, breaking
their polite silence only when a piece was taken. Then they
would applaud decorously while the prize was being led into one
of the roped enclosures at either side of the board. These small
stockades, akin to the penalty boxes in ice hockey, were labeled
blanche for Cragg's captives, *noire,* for the Frenchman's. Here
the comely prisoners sat, awaiting whatever disposition the victor
might decree when the contest ended. For this night alone they
belonged to him, wholly and without recourse, and were his to
enjoy, or to share, or to give away.

Normally, Cragg himself would have played a more impetuous
game, tossing caution aside in favor of a blitzkrieg drive up the
middle toward the enemy's king row, with his White Queen
spearheading the charge. But Panache's own deliberate style,
coupled with the almost terpsichorean nature of the proceedings,
forced him to weigh his actions carefully. Hasty moves were
impossible.

Eschewing the humdrum king's pawn opening, Cragg advanced his queen's pawn two squares, thus freeing a bishop for
diagonal onslaught in the event some promising situation developed. Panache declined this challenge. Instead, after a period of

earnest beard-stroking, he dispatched his messenger with penciled orders to bring the king's pawn forward one pace. Cragg responded with his own king's pawn, whereupon the Frenchman evened matters by duplicating White's first move. Successive plays projected both White knights onto the battlefield. Panache contented himself with advancing another pawn and getting a single knight into the third row.

	White	Black
1.	P–Q4	P–K3
2.	P–K4	P–Q4
3.	N–QB3	P–QB4
4.	N–B3	N–QB3

On the fifth play the White King's pawn took the Black Queen's pawn. Cragg couldn't repress a smile of schoolboy elation at having drawn first blood, even though he knew this minor triumph would prove short-lived. Still grinning, he watched as the captured maiden was directed into the *blanche* enclosure.

Torgerson heaved his giant, stubbled head around to face Cragg. "That makes a nice *hors d'oeuvre*, skipper," he rumbled. "Now let's concentrate on the main course."

Cragg's smile vanished. "Belay it, mister. Those pawns are off limits. Too small. And underage."

"Stateside jailbait laws don't apply out here in the boondocks," said Torgerson, undaunted. "And sure as hell not to an honest-to-God queen."

Panache blandly ignored the interruption. In quick reprisal he swept a vulnerable White pawn from the board, then sank back in his chair while Cragg scribbled the note that would bring a bishop into play.

This contrapuntal maneuvering continued for another four moves. Both sides castled. They began to edge cautiously, with their armed bishops now carrying the brunt, into midfield. Each of them won a second pawn. In this brief skirmish it appeared that Cragg might again have gained a small advantage, since the piece he exchanged with Panache was an isolated queen's pawn.

But his follow-up move betrayed him, forcing the barter of a bishop for a knight, and effectively depriving him of mobility for the next half-dozen moves.

By the fifteenth, however, Cragg had managed to recoup. He offered a bishop for a knight, and when this gambit was accepted, he began to feel a little more confident.

But Panache was relentless, harrying, pummeling, never permitting a moment's respite. Almost insolently, he was the first to send his Queen into the fray, and he kept her advancing. Much to Torgerson's obscene delight, loudly expressed, she came closer to the dais, as successive orders from Panache drew her nearly halfway across the board.

White	Black
5. KP x P	KP x P
6. B–K2	N–B3
7. Castles	B–K2
8. B–KN5	Castles
9. P x P	B–K3
10. N–Q4	B x P
11. N x B	P x N
12. B–N4	Q–Q3
13. B–R3	QR–K1
14. Q–Q2	B–N5
15. B x N	R x B
16. QR–Q1	Q–B4

The Black Queen stood before them, immobile in the flickering light of the torches, serenely aware of the admiration her voluptuous body evoked. Her brocaded skirt stirred in the quickening breeze that had begun to sweep off the lagoon shortly before the game started. It was an unseasonably chill wind, with a definite hint of rain to come. Nevertheless the girl's softly curving belly, her dark nippled breasts, and her remarkably wide shoulders glistened with sweat. Cragg observed that her breath was coming quickly, too, as if she had been engaging in some strenuous exercise.

Panache caught his glance.

"Her Majesty realizes that she has been thrust into a vulnerable position," he said. "And even though she places undue faith in my protective skill, the knowledge that capture may be imminent excites her." He laughed. "Once more, *mon capitaine,* I must suggest that it is your next move."

Cragg returned to the neglected game. Like Torgerson, but in a less exuberant manner, he had been distracted by the Nubian monarch's stately march from the remotest row to her present position. Inattention to duty, he discovered, had allowed Panache to train point-blank upon the White King with two of his most powerful weapons, the castle and the proud Black Queen herself. It was a damned ticklish juncture, sure to result in quick checkmate if he failed to retaliate sharply and intelligently.

"Goddamn!" Cragg grimaced reluctant approval of the Frenchman's cleverness. "You've got me boresighted."

Panache shrugged. "Every labyrinth must have its egress, however obscure," he murmured.

Cragg bridled at the other's complacent tone. In his annoyance, he dashed off an overly simplistic command that edged the White Queen one square to the left, where she could better protect her threatened liege.

Immediately there ensued a savage trade of blows, costing White a knight and a pawn, Black a bishop and a pawn. This fusillade left Cragg still mired in his rear echelon defenses, while the Frenchman steadily pushed the advantage.

White	Black
17. Q–K2	B x N
18. P x B	Q x P
19. R x P	N–Q5

In desperation, still angry, Cragg sought to untangle himself from this worsening predicament by driving ahead with his own queen. He sent her diagonally across the fast-emptying board, deep into enemy territory. Panache promptly lined up a rook with the Black Queen, and Cragg rebutted by setting his own rook alongside the perilously exposed White Queen. Whereupon Panache threatened her with a second rook, forcing Cragg to beat a hasty retreat.

The Frenchman's big teeth glinted in the semidarkness. *"Voilà!"*

he called out jubilantly, signing the death warrant for a bishop that stood on hapless royal guard duty before the White pawn row.

White	Black
20. Q–R5	QR–KB1
21. R–K5	R–R3
22. Q–N5	R x B

Cragg leaned forward, chin on hand, to estimate the battle damage. There was little cheer in what he saw. His fortifications lay crumbling, and he'd fallen an important piece short. Conscious of Panache's watchful gaze, Cragg thought sardonically of an earlier Frenchman who had met a similar crisis, but on a much grander scale. What did legend say Marshal Foch had exclaimed during the first Battle of the Marne?

"My right gives. My center yields. Situation excellent. I shall attack."

Chess, like war, posed a series of bleak alternatives. One of these was surrender. But Cragg preferred to stand and fight a little longer.

He could, of course, have plucked off Panache's rook, which now possessed the square that had sheltered his captured bishop. It looked damned tempting. On the next move, however, Panache would doubtless have put his beleaguered king in check with a knight, and thus walked off with the White Queen.

So Cragg chose a third course, interposing his rook between the enemy queen and the Black rook which had remained discretely in the distant kings row. Inexplicably, Panache refused this tempting bait. With an inscrutable expression on his pocked face, he dispatched a curt order to fetch the Black Queen alongside the bishop-conquering rook, thus strengthening the salient which aimed directly toward Cragg's king.

White	Black
23. R–QB5	Q–KN6

Escorted by the floor monitor, the Black Queen glided across the stage and took a noble stance in front of the three residual pawns who guarded the White King. In simulated wrath, they flourished their toy daggers menacingly at her. But she disregarded them. Haughtily, unflinching, the Black Queen folded her bejeweled arms over her humid breasts and stared the confused pawns into quiescence. Cragg wanted to applaud. Not in acknowledgment of Panache's last play, which held disastrous implications for the White cause, but in honor of the Black Queen herself, who was behaving like royalty incarnate. Menaced on three sides, by the White Queen and two of the guardian pawns, she nevertheless remained aloof, a regal island in the midst of devastation.

Cragg glanced fleetingly at the prisoner stockades. *Blanche* contained seven girls, *noire* only six. Then he peered again at the mammoth chessboard, debating whether to resign, or to continue a battle in which defeat seemed inevitable.

The Frenchman's twenty-third move had been a classic example of end-play. It left Cragg with only three responses, each of them unpalatable, and two of which meant prompt checkmate. If he elected to capture the Black Queen with either of his pawns, Panache would close the trap with the Black knight.

On the offchance that prolongation of the game might cause his adversary to stumble, Cragg took a last, forlorn plunge. He had scant faith that such a break would develop. More and more, Panache impressed him as a calculating sort who didn't make mistakes, in chess or anything else.

At Cragg's written command, the White Queen sortied down the knight's row, and stepped challengingly into the square occupied by her Black counterpart. The monitor touched the dark queen lightly upon the shoulder. With her head still high, carrying the sacred lotus like a disdainful banner, she withdrew from the field to the sound of the villagers' enthusiastic applause. This time Cragg joined them, although he was well aware that the play itself was merely a delaying action.

Torgerson whirled around in his seat.

"By damn, skipper, you did it!" he exulted. "The Amazon Queen's all ours."

"It doesn't mean a thing," Cragg said. "Not a bloody thing."

"Aren't we winning?" Torgerson demanded.

Cragg cast him a pitying look. "We're getting our arses whipped, mister, by an expert."

While they were talking, Panache answered White's move by checking with his knight. As was his custom after a riposte that especially pleased him, the Frenchman relaxed into his chair, humming a Gallic tune, and keeping time by riffling plump fingers along its wicker arms.

White	Black
24. Q x Q	N–K7ch

"Check, *mon capitaine*."

Cragg assented grimly, and sent the White King into the rook's corner. Showing no mercy, Panache rode down the White Queen with his rampant knight. This placed Cragg in check again and forced the harried king back to its previous position. Panache's implacable horseman pounced next upon the exposed rook.

White	Black
25. K–R1	N x Qch
26. K–N1	N x R

Cragg gnawed his pencil, debating the feasibility of taking the invader with his king, in view of Panache's dominant position. Whereas this might give him momentary satisfacton, it was bound to be a fatuous gesture, and ultimately leave him a major piece behind. Both Black rooks remained in action against White's lone castle. What had been merely perilous a short moment ago, therefore, had now become utterly hopeless.

He turned toward his serene adversary. "You're goddamned rough competition, Monsieur Panache."

Panache stopped drumming his fingers against the chair arm and sat up straight. "It was my twenty-third move, *mon capitaine*, that delivered the *coup de grâce*."

"I know," said Cragg.

"There was a famous chess match held in Breslau more than fifty years ago," Panache went on, "which devolved around a method known as the 'French defense.' Paradoxically, an American won this game, defeating the European champion. During the course of it he made a move some have termed 'the most elegant in the history of chess.' My good fortune, m'sieu, came when you enabled me to duplicate it." Panache spread his capacious hands wide. "But after all, it *was* the French defense, and I *am* a Frenchman who has seen altogether too much defense, most of it quite stupid."

Torgerson had watched the Black Queen leave the arena and disappear into the gloom that now enveloped the stockade as the flares burned lower. He uttered a frustrated howl. Cragg grinned. For suddenly it was obvious that the hungry tiger realized he had lost his plump gazelle.

"You blew the frigging ball game," Torgerson said accusingly.

Panache demurred. "On the contrary, your leader comported himself well, although he tends to be impulsive when a crisis impends. This can breed carelessness."

Doubly amused by the Frenchman's pedantic observation and his exec's disappointment, Cragg laughed at them both. "That's a trait common to PT boaters," he said, "even the retired kind."

"It also pertained to the French military, long ago, when we believed that mere *élan* was sufficient to win wars."

"Don't you still believe in *élan*? I thought it ran in your blood."

Panache looked sad. "Once upon a time I did. But I have grown much older. And fatter. And slower. Such infirmities beget a certain caution, which some mistake for wisdom."

"You shade me by a dozen years," Cragg objected. "No more."

"Those, my dear friend, were the years that brought age, and corpulence, and sloth."

"They're also the years when France got pushed out of Thietvanne."

"True."

"And lately you've been coppering your bets," Cragg said. "Is that what you mean by caution."

"As you will."

"Do you think I'm a little crazy?"

Panache gave his beard a reflective tweak. "Not a little crazy, *mon capitaine*, but exceedingly so." His sigh was wistful. "And yet I envy you."

"Why?"

"It is difficult to say. Perhaps I wish to regain something that I have lost. Let us deposit the matter there." Panache heaved himself out of his wicker chair. "Tonight was only a game, unlike the adventure which awaits you at Phom Than. This craziness—if you insist—may yet prove invaluable. One never knows."

"No," Cragg murmured, "one never knows."

"Until that exact moment arrives," said Panache, forgiving the irony. He tilted his chronometer toward the guttering torchlight. "It is not yet twelve-thirty. The night is young. As a tribute to your sportsmanship, m'sieu, I wish to present you with an appropriate gift."

"Gift?" echoed Cragg.

"The Black Queen, *mon capitaine*, with my sincere compliments." Panache waved a plump hand toward the prisoners' enclosure. "I have seen your appreciative glances. As a connoisseur of such delicacies, you will find Her Majesty a most agreeable partner."

"That's damned generous of you," Cragg said. "But I haven't time for any more fun and games. Sorry."

Panache was astounded. "Not even to essay a short bout, *mon ami?*"

"Negative. I've got to touch base with Harris. Read the radio traffic. Find out what the Kong are doing. Figure the weather. Plot our next course. See if *Mohican*'s shipshape."

"You are indeed a strange man," marveled Panache, "for an American."

Torgerson cut in. "Try me." He grinned. "Remember what the Duke always says—we can't let the side down."

"What about *Medusa?*" Cragg asked.

"She'll be four-oh, skipper. You can depend on it."

"I bloody well am," Cragg assured him. "If that mudscow isn't seaworthy by dinnertime, you'll start paddling back to the States, and without waterwings."

Torgerson reached inside his T-shirt and scratched the heat rash on his chest. "Aye, aye, sir!" His wolfish grin widened as he turned to the Frenchman. "On behalf of Cragg's Mafia, I accept your handsome offer. *Allons!*"

Panache made a slight bow in the direction of Trump Gideon and Mario DelGrado. "And would you gentlemen also care to sample these pleasures? The Black Queen has a delectable entourage."

They consulted each other mutely. DelGrado shook his head. Then Gideon said: "No, thanks. We'll take a raincheck. Lars can handle the stud detail for the whole crew."

But Torgerson was already striding toward the stockade. "Screw you bastards," he called back genially.

As they approached the plantation house enroute to the guest quarters, picking their way along the trail with flashlights, a slim figure detached itself from the shadows near the steps. Cragg aimed his beam. It was Denny. She had, he correctly surmised, been there since quitting the festival, alone in the darkness, awaiting their return. After a brief exchange, Gideon and DelGrado departed.

"You're up awfully late," Cragg said.

Denny stifled a yawn. "I could not sleep."

"Have you tried?"

"No."

"That's what I figured."

She was using both hands to shield her eyes against the harsh light, so he could not make out the expression on her face. But her tone was disdainful. "Did you find Monsieur Panache's revels to your taste, Cragg?"

"It was a nice party."

"I am astonished that you abandoned it so soon." Suddenly her voice became very small. "One might have imagined it would take more time to . . . enjoy your . . . your winnings."

He chuckled. "Hell's bells, *bébé,* I didn't win a goddamned thing. I got slaughtered."

"And if you had won?"

"Papa Panache is a generous host as well as a gracious winner. He offered me a consolation prize. Very delicious. But I declined."

Denny took her hands from her face. There were tears in her eyes, and on her cheeks. "For that, Cragg, I am grateful. . . ."

Scant minutes after he turned in, it seemed, a rude hand snatched away the sheet which Cragg had pulled around his neck as protection against *Mohican's* air conditioning. He turned upon the intruder, ready to blast the Thiet messenger for arousing him at this ungodly hour with some minor problem that Duke Harris should have handled as duty officer. But he found himself gazing instead into the unsmiling countenance of Hercule Panache.

"There is bad news," the Frenchman said, doffing his soiled topee.

Cragg swung his legs off the bunk. Not yet fully awake, he glanced at the clock, then back at Panache. It was only three A.M. Illuminated by the shaded sixty-watt bulb, the planter's cratered moonface looked drawn and gray, and his fierce eyes were red-rimmed from fatigue.

"What's wrong?"

"Two hours after they left the festival for their village in the hills," said Panache, "my *montagnards* returned. Some of them, that is. More than half had been killed in a guerrilla ambush. I dispatched scouts along the trail to determine whether this was merely an isolated incident, or the precursor of a general attack against Bien Goa."

While the Frenchman spoke, Cragg was getting dressed. "Have they reported?" he demanded.

"Yes," Panache said bleakly. "We can expect an assault at any time."

"How big a force?"

"Perhaps a hundred men. Or more."

Cragg struggled into his field boots. "Tell Torgerson to get *Medusa* launched. He'll have to finish the repair job after they're underway."

"M'sieu Torgerson has not yet come back from his rendezvous."

"Then send somebody after him!" Cragg exploded.

Panache tugged at his beard. "This I have already done. But M'sieu Torgerson flatly refuses to leave until his 'work' has been consummated."

"All right." Cragg made for the door. "If the son of a bitch isn't here by the time *Medusa* is ready to sail, he stays behind."

"I understand," said the Frenchman, following him. "But you may need help in loading the inflammables you have requested."

"Can you lend me a stevedore gang?"

"Of course." Panache produced a paper from the pocket of his white lined jacket. "Here is what I have arranged for you. These materials are awaiting your disposal in my warehouse."

Cragg scanned the list hurriedly in the light of his hand-torch. Fourteen barrels of pitch. Three hundred pounds of sulphur. Seven kegs of black powder. Twelve ten-gallon cans of kerosene. Three dozen sticks of dynamite. One bale of oily waste. And a drum of high-octane gasoline.

"The aviation fuel," said Panache, "is what you Americans would call a bonus. It is the residue of a small supply I kept available for transient planes, until the Kong made private flying too dangerous."

Cragg headed for the passageway. "You're a goddamned genius, papa," he said admiringly.

It was Panache's opinion that their best strategy would be a rolling defense based initially on the temple, where the chess game had been played. As the enemy pressure mounted, they could stage a gradual withdrawal to the plantation headquarters, and finally to the top of the trail leading down to the lagoon. It wasn't a cheap plan. They were certain to take casualties in the process, being so badly outnumbered, but Panache contended that it was the only way they could hold the Kong at bay while *Medusa's* work-party loaded the incendiary stores and the repair gang completed its chores.

Cragg reluctantly agreed.

"How many troops can you muster, papa?"

The Frenchman figured rapidly. "Perhaps twenty," he said, "including the returned *montagnards* and my personal staff."

Most of the villagers, Panache added, were already evacuating Bien Goa, bound for the fancied safety of hamlets farther down the coast. Their departure, however, was no great loss. Unlike the *montagnards*, whose avocation was fighting, these placid people had little stomach for a quarrel, much less for actual combat. If anything, they would be a hindrance, rather than a help, once the battle joined.

By mutual consent, Panache assigned a half-dozen of his huskier mountain men to the stevedore detail, while Cragg dispatched an equal number of Akim's riflemen to replace them on the hastily drawn defensive perimeter.

Under Trump Gideon's temporary command, *Mohican* had orders to cruise just offshore, employing her fixed guns as cover for the retreat. *Medusa*, now afloat, was moored with her stern toward the beach. This would permit the junk's after 40-millimeters to join the protective barrage.

"And you, *mon capitaine?*" asked Panache. "Where do you propose to take your station?"

"Where the action is, papa," Cragg replied. "At the temple."

"Do you wish to lead the defense?"

"Negative. As long as we're ashore, you're the boss."

The Frenchman drove both fists against his hips, and favored Cragg with a grin that made his ugly face almost handsome.

"In the holy name of all the saints whose names I never learned," he cried, "you are indeed as astonishing man!"

"Why?"

"Because you prefer to remain here, when it would be so much safer on board your boat."

"I'm impulsive," Cragg reminded him dryly. He patted the Browning automatic rifle which he had drawn from *Mohican's* arsenal. "Besides, I'm a fair hand with a BAR, and you'll need all the fire-power you can get."

Together the two men walked slowly up the graveled trail toward the ancient temple. Behind them marched the *montagnards*, the plantation staff, and Akim's six-man detachment. After the small force was properly emplaced in sheltered positions around the ruined statuary, Cragg allowed himself the luxury of a cigar. He studied Panache's bearded profile in the brief light of the struck match.

"You'd have been a hell of a lot safer, too, if you had bugged out," he said, "like the rest of the villagers."

"*Vraiment.*" The Frenchman gave him an impassive look. "But what would be the use? It is plain that my arrangement with the Kong has been terminated. Whether or not their attack succeeds, Bien Goa is finished as a trading post." He shrugged. "When such a delicate political membrane has been broken, one cannot repair the damage."

"So where does this leave you?"

"It is my desire," Panache said gravely, "to accompany your expedition."

Cragg smoked in silence for a moment. Then: "Those native pirogues seem pretty seaworthy to me. You could still escape, you know."

"Perhaps."

"Why this sudden urge to get involved?"

Panache considered the matter carefully. "One might cite several reasons. Probably I have remained too long aloof from my adopted country's travail. Or possibly it is for the neglected glory of France." He emitted a short, humorless laugh. "It might also be that you are entitled to a return match in chess, or any other test of strategy that appeals to you."

Cragg regarded the Frenchman's shadowy face, probing his masked expression for evidence of sincerity.

"We carry no idlers in *Mohican*," he said. "Even the girl works."

Panache drew himself to his full height. He was taller than Cragg had realized, over six feet, and built like a linebacking center. The huge arms that extended from the short sleeves of his jacket, grasping a rifle, were well muscled beneath the padding of fat.

"Whatever is required, *mon capitaine*, I can do."

"There's one other thing," said Cragg. "Once you step aboard my ship, I *am* the captain. It's not just a courtesy title. My orders are law. No arguments, no reservations, no delay after they're issued. *Comprenez?*"

"*Je comprends—mon capitaine.*"

By five A.M. the task of readying *Medusa* was almost completed, and DelGrado sent word from her hold that another hour should see the basic repairs effected, at least to the point where she could put to sea at reduced speed. There had been no sign of the Kong. Now, with gray dawn beginning to show, the *montagnards* were getting restless. It would be preferable, their leader told Panache, to ambush the Kong deeper in the jungle, before darkness was gone, rather than wait passively for them here.

But the Frenchman demurred. As a longtime student of guerrilla tactics, he could assure them that the enemy would have reconnoitered the area, brought up reinforcements, and then made ready for one of their traditional attacks at daybreak. Not knowing the strength of the Bien Goa defenses, they were playing it cautious, until they had a proper chance to sample the opposition.

"We cannot sustain a prolonged engagement," Panache went on. "So the more we delay this showdown, the better for our purposes. Do you not concur, m'sieu?"

"Anything you say." Cragg took a practice sighting along the barrel of his BAR. "You're in command of the goddamned infantry."

The Kong attacked minutes later, emerging wraithlike from the screen of trees beyond the courtyard, in a spread-out formation. The *montagnards* started firing at once. But their hasty aim was poor, and the enemy managed to approach within a hundred yards of the bulwarked defenders before the more accurate response from Cragg's BAR and the rifles wielded by Panache and Akim stopped them. Three Kong bodies were left in the clearing.

After a short lull, they charged again, and got closer. This second attempt cost them another four killed.

For the next assault they split into two waves, coming at the temple from right and left, in a flanking move. Sweat was plainly visible on the face of a Kong who made it almost to the headless gargoyle, behind which Cragg was crouching, and it took a concentrated volley from the BAR to stop him. The Kong dropped at Cragg's feet, his denim-clad torso burst open like a ripe pink watermelon, the sweat still flowing.

"We must withdraw," warned Panache. "The next time they will overwhelm us."

"After you, papa."

With an agility remarkable for a man of his bulk, the Frenchman led them swiftly toward the plantation house, stooping low and taking advantage of the intermittent cover afforded by thickboled palms. The *montagnards* brought up the rear. Occasionally, on the quarter-mile retreat, those farthest back halted, whirled around, and fired blindly at the foe. But it was a heroic gesture at best. Six of the rearguardsmen, who tarried too long, were picked off by the sharpshooting Kong.

When he reached the comparative shelter of the house, Cragg checked his watch, and was surprised to discover how little time had elapsed since the first attack. It couldn't have been more than twenty minutes. This meant they must somehow hold the enemy at bay for another half hour, to let the repair crew finish its job.

Making his way to the seaward verandah, Cragg looked down at *Medusa*. There on the lofty poopdeck, he saw Lars Torgerson. The Swede was brandishing a tommy-gun and shouting something he could not understand because of the renewed firing.

Then he suddenly perceived what Torgerson was driving at. Both *Mohican,* prowling close to the beach, and the anchored junk cut loose with their artillery. The twin barrage was directed toward the heavily foliaged area between the vacated temple and the house. Like a many-bladed reaper, it chopped methodically away at the unseen Kong, who were first demoralized, then driven back by this unexpected fire-curtain.

Panache stumped around the corner of the thatched porch. He had been wounded in the fleshy part of his upper arm, and his beard was caked with dirt.

"The *bâtard* who shot me was killed immediately by your man Akim," he rumbled. "An excellent marksman, that one, I owe my life to him."

"Are you badly hurt?"

"No."

"Then we'd better make a run for it," said Cragg, "while we still have a chance. Those jokers will damned soon make another move to outflank us."

Panache nodded. Sadly, with bloodshot eyes, he surveyed his threatened castle, staring for the last time upon its woven walls and thatched roof, before signaling his men to leave.

During the few minutes it took them to descend the trail the enemy had already regrouped, and for the final fifty yards they came under brisk fire from the hill overlooking the lagoon. Seven *montagnards* and two of Akim's gunners were hit. How many were killed, how many wounded, could not be determined. The survivors pressed on, unable to stop and aid the fallen. At Cragg's shouted command they thrashed through the hipdeep water, and scrambled up the rope ladder, while Torgerson was hoisting anchor. The junk moved away from shore. Behind her, face-down on the placid surface, floated the bodies of another five sniper victims. Three of *Medusa's* crew and two Bien Goan cargo-handlers lay dead on the deck. A couple of wounded were hobbling painfully toward the midships hatch.

"Head for the entrance," Cragg ordered. "We'll join *Mohican* outside."

By the time they reached the flowing gap in the reef, the plantation house roof was beginning to smolder, and small tongues of flame could be seen nibbling along its dry eaves. The sacking of Bien Goa had commenced.

Cragg did not address Torgerson again until *Medusa,* under power but without her sails, was well clear of the narrow passage, aimed on a converging course toward *Mohican.* Nor did the Swede himself seem anxious to revive the events of the previous night. Naked to the waist, as always, he stayed at the wheel, single-handedly working the enormous rudder, with a studied disinterest in what Cragg might be doing or thinking.

At length, in a voice laden with sarcasm, Cragg asked softly: "Was she worth it, mister?"

Keeping his face averted, Torgerson muttered: "Hell, they're all worth it." He attempted a defiant laugh.

"Balls."

"Sure. Balls. That's my problem, doctor. I get horny."

"Horniness is your exclusive department," Cragg said. "Also boozing and going A.W.O.L. Believe me, fella, if we weren't so shorthanded, I'd throw your ass in the brig. *Tout de suite!*"

Torgerson ducked his balding head in feigned repentance. "Lars was a bad boy. Lars won't do it again."

"Lars is a horny alcoholic," Cragg growled. "And Lars bloody well won't have another chance."

The exec swung around to confront his accuser. In a more conciliatory tone he said: "Hell, I got here, didn't I?"

"When?"

"Before the action started, in time to take over the launching detail."

"But you were told to come back earlier."

Torgerson removed one fist from the helm and rubbed the blond furze on his head. He grinned. "So I didn't believe the gook bastard who came after me. I figured he was just running scared, like they all do."

"While I take over the wheel," Cragg said coldly, "you can handle the burial detail. Get those men over the side."

Torgerson obeyed without protest.

After he'd left, Cragg reshaped their course slightly, to compensate for the fact that *Mohican* had hove to about five miles beyond the barrier reef. While the junk slowly overhauled the motionless PT he mentally computed the losses they had suffered ashore during the brief, furious engagement. Ironically, as nearly as he could figure it, the Bien Goan newcomers now aboard exactly balanced the number of dead among *Medusa's* crew. Therefore he still commanded twenty-one men, overall, in both vessels.

No. Make that twenty-two. He'd forgotten Papa Panache.

Immediately after *Medusa* closed with *Mohican,* and the two craft were riding coupled, Cragg went aboard the PT. With a curt wave, he indicated that Torgerson should accompany him. Then he summoned the Mafia, Colonel Toyon and Hercule Panache into a council of war in the wardroom.

"Our original plan," Cragg said, "called for a three-day run between here and Dokoro, with a rendezvous each night at Points *Echo, Foxtrot* and *Golf.*" He surveyed them grimly. "It's apparent the Kong know a lot more about this layout than we'd figured. So we'll have to make a quick switch."

Torgerson gave him an insubordinate leer, and started to say something about security breaches in high places, but Cragg silenced him with an icy glance.

"Even without our itinerary, they would realize that Dokoro is the next logical fueling stop. Now we've got to throw them off stride." Cragg slapped the banquette table. "We'll skip those first two junctions. I'm going to take *Mohican* straight into Dokoro. Torgerson can follow at *Medusa's* best speed, and meet us off Point Hospital three midnights from now. Savvy, mister?"

"I savvy," the exec acknowledged glumly.

"For several reasons," Cragg continued, "I'm going to cut down *Mohican's* complement. If the Kong get the jump on us, we might wind up with a rescue operation, and want the extra space for mission personnel."

As finally decreed, the PT's minimal crew consisted of Trump Gideon, Mario DelGrado, Papa Panache, Denny, and Loo, the English-speaking Thiet helmsman. It was chopping uncomfortably close to the manpower bone, Cragg admitted, but that's how it had to be.

He cast a meaningful look at the girl. She had accepted his hint of possible trouble at Dokoro with a white-lipped stoicism.

"If my father should acquiesce to the need for evacuating the mission, where would you transport him, and my mother, and the hospital staff?" she asked.

Cragg rubbed a reflective hand over his stubbly chin.

"You'd have to pick the safest place," he said, "and we'd drop them off. Anywhere south of Dokoro, as long as it's within a single day's run, so we can make the turnaround and finish our business at Phom Than before Friday."

"I do not understand," she said wonderingly. "This is not your concern. My parents mean nothing to you."

"Panache would chalk it down to my impulsiveness," Cragg grunted. "That's probably as good an answer as any, unless you want me to be practical about it, and remind you that we're damned well counting on the fuel supplies there. I don't want them destroyed."

Denny shook her head. "It must be more than that, Cragg, when one lays deliberate plans for such an act, knowing the consequences of what he intends to do."

"Listen," he said harshly, in a sudden burst of candor, "and listen damned hard. Let's not kid ourselves. Your people may be in deep trouble. So you'd better brace yourself, in case things turn out worse than we think."

"I understand perfectly," she said. "And with God's help, I am prepared."

7

"Never Look Back"

CRAGG NUDGED BOTH throttles forward. Slowly at first, then more quickly, the PT veered away from *Medusa*. He glanced back. Duke Harris and Colonel Toyon were waving from the junk's lofty taffrail. From his place at the wheel, Torgerson evinced no sign that he knew or cared that *Mohican* had finally gone. The Swede was bitter at having been left out of the excitement that portended at Dokoro, and his cold demeanor showed it.

For more than an hour Cragg held on course-090, due east, to lay a safe margin between *Mohican* and the coast. When he turned northward again they were a good twenty-five miles offshore. This distance, combined with the raincurtain that drooped from the low clouds, would provide ample cover while they negotiated the curving coastline. Except for a few hopeful scavenger gulls that had followed them from Bien Goa, and an occasional flying fish which escaped briefly from the ocean's darker depths, they were alone on the spectral sea.

Cragg scanned the iron-gray skies ahead of them for any sign of a break. Seeing none, he motioned to Loo, who had remained tenaciously at his side since their departure.

"Take over the wheel, fella."

The little helmsman gave a delighted yelp. "Aye, aye, *mon capitaine!*" He peered at the gyro-compass card. "Course-045?"

"Check."

"For how long, sir?"

"Five bloody hours, until we come around to 030 for the second leg. We'll stay on that heading for another hour, and wind up on course-315. Reckon you can hold out?"

"Loo will try."

"Well," Cragg grinned, "Loo won't have to handle the whole job by himself. We'll divide the watch. Four on, four off."

Before he went below, Cragg fixed his critical attention upon the graygreen combers that rolled down from the northwest, seeking to determine whether their endless, regular pattern signaled a delay in the storm's arrival, or merely a tentative lull before it struck. He estimated that the front was still a dozen miles away, moving so deliberately as to seem almost anchored. Occasional flashes of lightning forked below the squall line, and there was a vague brimstone aura about the dank wind that blew across *Mohican*'s plunging bow.

"From the looks of things," he told Loo, "we've got about an hour more of this half-baked weather. After that it'll start kicking up. If the storm hits sooner, and you have trouble keeping her nose pointed, just press the buzzer."

Loo nodded. "Aye, aye, sir."

From the charthouse the ladder led directly into the officer's wardroom, a five-by-eight compartment which could seat six persons in a kind of banquette, as in a short-order café. Cragg stood there for a moment, still gripping the rungs, while he sought to get the hang of *Mohican*'s interior roll-and-pitch. After several motionless hours topside, he'd long since learned, he had to acclimatize himself in this lubberly fashion to the different footing belowdecks. Until his encounter with the Nip shell, Cragg had not found it necessary to pause, even briefly, before quick-stepping down a companionway. But his locked knee had deprived him of his agility, leaving scars on his pride that matched the physical damage to the limb itself.

Mohican was behaving in confounded unladylike fashion, as if resentful of her need for buckling down to the long haul to Dokoro. There was scant comfort to be derived from a 'tween-decks sojourn, aside from escaping the driven spume and sharp wind that made any protracted topside watch damned rugged after a few hours. True enough, you could inhale the rich coffee aroma from the porcelain pot on the miniature galley cookstove, but you also had to accept the diesel stink from Mario Del-Grado's other domain, the engine room, which lay barely five yards aft, behind a thin bulkhead.

Since Delgrado refused to leave his precious power plant untended, Cragg guessed that Denny had brewed the coffee herself, in the French manner, black and bitter. She was sitting beside Hercule Panache, facing forward and cupping a heavy chinaware mug between her two slim hands.

Neither she nor the Frenchman seemed eager to talk. Denny was shrouded in her own bleak thoughts. That portion of the Frenchman's moonface which showed above his beard had a greenish tinge, reminiscent of the sick color Cragg had seen on the faces of the dilettante millionaires he'd taken fishing off the Farallones, when the rogue sea began to assert its independence.

Cragg grinned compassionately. Panache looked up.

"I am not a sailor." His puncheon shoulders quivered in what might have been a shrug. "My *poilu* training. . . ." He let the thought expire, and lifted his cup.

"Coffee helps," said Cragg.

"Mlle. Legére produces a robust blend," Panache agreed, more animatedly.

Denny asked quietly: "When should we sight Dokoro?"

"Around midnight, with luck, and if the sea doesn't rise."

"Do you expect these waves to grow larger, Cragg?"

"They generally do."

Panache groaned. *"Merde!"* Then to Denny: *"Pardon, mademoiselle."*

Disregarding both the obscenity and the apology, she said: "When we reach the mission, there will be many things to do. Unless you have other orders for me, I shall retire to my room." She slipped out of the banquette, and stood before him, waiting for him to speak. He said nothing, staring at the rosary that was clutched tightly in her right hand. Taking his silence for consent, Denny moved across the galley toward the master's stateroom. At the doorway she paused. "Please call me . . . if there is any news."

Cragg turned to Panache after she was gone.

"How is she holding up?"

"Corporeally, much better than I. She has a strong stomach, that one. Spiritually?" The Frenchman's shrug became more pronounced. "She prays a great deal." Panache struggled to his feet. "I, too, feel the need of repose. May I use one of your beds?"

"Bunks," Cragg corrected him gravely. "Up forward, past the galley, you'll find eight of 'em in the crew's quarters. Pick one that strikes your fancy. They're all goddamned uncomfortable."

Not at all distressed at finding himself alone, Cragg left the table briefly to get his Thietvanne coastal chart, which he kept locked up in his rarely used stateroom desk. He unfurled the chart and anchored each of its four corners with salt and pepper shakers.

Dokoro did not concern him now. Until they arrived there, fourteen hours hence, he could make no sensible plans. It was something that had to be improvised, and no amount of advance agonizing would make an iota of difference. *Hang loose,* as his old squadron commander used to say, *and wait for targets of opportunity.*

But Phom Than, the ultimate, the payoff, was another matter entirely.

Cragg glowered at the stained expanse of linenbacked paper. Their goal lay more than two hundred curving miles beyond Dokoro, at the apex of the Pregnant Woman's globular right breast, past Point India and Point Juliett, above their final rendezvous at Point *Kilo*. On the chart, *Kilo* was formally identified as Quang Duk, a jutting headland, upon which stood a lighthouse whose lamp had long ago been extinguished by a sharpshooting Thiet gunboat. It never was restored. As a consequence, the Kong steered well clear of Quank Duk's treacherous shoals, although this meant a wide swing into the Gulf of Kan-Tong after leaving Phom Than harbor, before they could safely return to coastal waters. The Kong capital itself occupied eight constricted miles along the base of the Fantastic Mountains. Its seaward portal was guarded by a pair of islets, called the Khandos. Once these were passed, however, the harbor widened sufficiently to accommodate a sizeable amount of shipping.

He had pasted a ten-year-old *National Geographic* photograph of Phom Than on the back of the chart. Written twelve years earlier, when a united Thietvanne was still resisting the rebellion that sundered it at the 17th parallel, the magazine caption observed nostalgically: "Phom Than's landlocked bay gave the author a sense of complete remoteness, as if it were shut off from the rest of the world." Along the beach, in this idyllic scene, the fishermen's shacks squatted upon the same sort of pilings that supported the thatched huts at Bien Goa. Behind them rose the narrow, stuccoed city. And in the foreground could be seen the fisherfolk themselves, mending their hempen nets, and patching the sails of the junks that rode the serene blue surface a few score yards offshore.

Cragg wondered how many of these peaceful craft had been pressed into combatant service by the Kong. For all their apparent innocence, they looked damned tough, ranging in length from a modest thirty feet to a stalwart ninety-odd, with ample freeboard and a girth that betokened plenty of space belowdecks for the lethal cargo they must now carry.

During the remainder of the long day *Mohican* continued to log a solid twenty knots as they drove ever more deeply into the translucent gloom of the monsoon front. At three P.M. Cragg found it necessary to light the binnacle lamp so that he or Loo, whoever had the helm, could read the compass card.

Around seven P.M. Gideon announced they were nearing Point

Foxtrot, as best he could judge from the terrain contour showing on his radar screen. There was a peculiar headland off the port bow, in the shape of a dog's leg, which corresponded to a promontory just below the site originally marked for a rendezvous with *Medusa*.

Three hours later, when he was smoking a cigar between sessions at the wheel, Cragg was hailed by Panache. The Frenchman had dragged himself topside sometime during the early evening, and had been sitting with Duke Harris in the chartroom, listening to shortwave chatter. Now he stood at the open hatch.

"I wish to report a matter of concern," Panache said earnestly, "relative to Dokoro."

"Spill it."

"For the past five years Dr. Legére has made it a regular custom to transmit certain weather and local news items to the area served by his mission. He always goes on the air at precisely ten P.M. Tonight there was no message from Dokoro, although his power signal has been clearly audible for thirty minutes."

"You think Dr. Legére's in trouble?"

"I do not know what to think," Panache spread his hands in a helpless gesture. "Yet I am greatly worried. And I should like permission to seek a shortwave contact with Dokoro."

"If something's already happened," said Cragg, "that wouldn't accomplish a damned bit of good. But it might alert the Kong, if they're monitoring that frequency."

"Very well, *mon capitaine*." Panache turned to reenter the chartroom. "I understand."

"I'm sorry, papa."

For the next five hours they ran close to the shore, disregarding the danger, to conserve precious time.

And at one-twenty A.M., well ahead of Cragg's most optimistic estimate, Gideon sang out from the charthouse that Dokoro had come into view on the radarscope. It was a positive fix, he said, because Panache and the girl had both been helping him monitor the set for the last half-hour, and they were in agreement that the jagged concavity at the upper end of the screen was indeed the mission harbor.

"What's the range?"

"Twenty-three miles," replied Gideon. "And we're right on course."

Cragg paid brief tribute to DelGrado's overworked diesels. Assuming they held up, it would require another fifty-five minutes to close Dokoro. Maybe less, since they were now traveling in the lee of the big peninsula that thrust seaward from Point Foxtrot.

Once more he blew into the engine-room tube. When DelGrado answered, Cragg said: "Gideon's got Dokoro locked on. About twenty miles away. How are they doing?"

"Bad, bossman, goddamned bad. They've been overheating for the last couple of hours."

"Apply an icebag till the fever breaks," Cragg advised grimly. "But don't let 'em quit on us."

DelGrado made a grunting sound at his end of the tube. "Any chance of slacking off a hair?"

"Negative. What I really want is another three knots."

"You must be off your friggin' rocker!"

Cragg looked at the horizon, dead ahead, beyond which lay Dokoro. He saw, or thought he saw, a faint red glow just above the ocean's darker rim. Before putting his night glasses to it, however, he responded brusquely to DelGrado's anguished roar.

"We're all crazy, *amigo*, or we wouldn't be here."

Observed through the binoculars, which magnified eight times, the luminous patch was very real. It had a distinctly crimson cast. And as Cragg strained to identify the source, it appeared to undulate, growing perceptibly larger, then subsiding, only to flare again.

"You are observing the fire, *mon capitaine?*"

Cragg gave Loo a surprised glance. The Thiet pilot had become so dependable, such an integral part of *Mohican's* smoothly functioning apparatus, that Cragg tended to forget that he was always there, chinhigh to the wheel, with never a complaint about his seemingly endless watches.

"How do you know it's a fire?"

"It cannot be otherwise," said Loo. "They all look the same, these fires, when they feed upon the wooden houses of Thiet-vanne."

Mohican was narrowing the gap at twenty-three knots, now, with Loo still at the wheel.

Cragg felt no hesitation in ordering them straight toward the blaze, since Dokoro's harbor lay wide open to the sea, unprotected by the usual barrier reef. When they came within five-mile range, it was evident that two separate fires were raging. Cragg handed the nightglasses to Denny, who had been standing mutely beside him for the past half-hour.

"Look," he commanded. "Tell me what you see."

The girl took the binoculars from him without comment, adjusted their focus, and peered into the inferno. After a moment she said in a dull voice: "The hospital is burning, Cragg. But I cannot discern the school, among those flames, so I suppose it has already been consumed."

"What's the other fire—beyond the mission?"

Denny swung her gaze right, past the mission, where a second outbreak was clearly visible and spreading rapidly.

"That must be the fuel dump, Cragg."

"Give me those glasses!"

As he refocused the lenses, Cragg discovered that his hands were sweating. He swore under his breath. This had been inevitable from the beginning, so it shouldn't surprise him now. Once having put the torch to Dokoro's main facilities, the marauders were bound to extend their sabotage to the oil supplies, if only for the purpose of creating a more spectacular bonfire.

Through the glasses Cragg could see several figures milling around the perimeter of the dump, which had not yet become fully ignited. He assumed they were hunting for strategically situated drums, which they would then hack open, and light, to hasten the destruction. Had the stored fuel been aviation gasoline, rather than diesel crude, this wouldn't have been necessary. The dump, along with everything else inside a hundred-yards radius, would have blown skyhigh long ago. Lacking the volatility of gasoline, however, the heavy oil burned slowly, and it required much coaxing to achieve the pyrotechnic effect which the saboteurs obviously craved.

Cragg abruptly laid aside his binoculars. He reached for the engine-room speaker tube. But before he could speak, Mario DelGrado anticipated him.

"I've got her parked on the front step now, bossman. There ain't no more left."

"Back her down," roared Cragg. "Full reverse."

"Shoals ahead?"

"Negative, fella. Gunnery practice."

Almost immediately *Mohican*'s forward surge began to ease. Within the space of fifty yards she slewed to a halt, dead in the water, about three miles offshore.

"Get Gideon out of the charthouse," Cragg told Denny. "Also Panache." She darted away, relieved to be doing something useful.

During the thirty seconds it took Trump and the Frenchman to disengage themselves from their radio gear and reach the bridge, Cragg finished his computations. He had already made up his mind. All that remained was how best to implement a damned chancy decision, one that might save a few precious barrels of fuel by scaring off the brigands, or else backfire upon him by coalescing the raiders into a solid defense force. It was a toss-up, Cragg conceded grimly, whether the buggers would haul-ass or give battle, after *Mohican*'s 75-millimeter shells started bursting among them.

It was also a toss-up, he knew, whether even Trump Gideon could lob the high explosive packages accurately enough to do the job, with only his manual skill to train the Long Tom. Three miles wasn't extreme range, by any means, but it wasn't exactly point-blank either, for a weapon that had no proper sighting equipment.

Cragg glanced at Denny. Having taken her place beside him again, she was staring toward the enflamed shore with an expression of quiet, disbelieving horror on her small face.

"Here," he urged, proffering her the glasses. "Try these."

But the girl merely shook her head. Like himself, thought Cragg, she would have known that his unspoken caveat about

Gideon's marksmanship was a futile precaution. In this fratricidal war few survived, innocent or not, once the battle was joined.

Trump was calling to him from the starboard splinter shield. His voice sounded unnaturally loud in the sudden quiet that had fallen upon the PT.

"What's the drill, skipper?"

"You and Panache unlimber the seventy-five," Cragg said, "while I keep our tail pointed toward the beach." He prodded Loo. "You'll be their loader. *Allez!*"

"Targets of opportunity?" asked Gideon.

"Christ, no! Drop your eggs on the south side of the fuel dump. That's where the bastards are concentrated. But don't clobber the dump itself. Or hit what's left of the mission."

"I'll try, skipper," Gideon said.

"Trying's not good enough, mister," Cragg bellowed. "You'd damn well better do it."

Gideon's irreverent retort was lost in the night as he started aft with Hercule Panache in tow.

For more than twenty minutes *Mohican* lay hove-to off Dokoro, while the Long Tom methodically pumped shells into the narrow corridor between the stored oil drums and the fire-gutted settlement. Gideon interspersed his tracers with high explosives, at a ration of one-to-three, in a manful effort to obey Cragg's well-nigh impossible dictum. The first of these flaming guides landed short and fizzled out in the wet sands below the fuel dump. The second arched a bright trajectory that ended midway to the compound. But the third, fourth and fifth came progressively closer. As a result, the trio of HE shells which followed each tracer appeared to be blasting a deep trench toward the startled raiders, very slowly, very deliberately, and with an impersonal relentlessness that gave Cragg immense satisfaction.

It was, he ruminated pleasurably, a splendid performance.

Cragg timed their next series of shots. From tracer to tracer, they were arching shoreward at the rate of one every ten seconds. Although six per minute was a sharp comedown from the four hundred which a modern gun could deliver in this same period, it wasn't too bad for an outdated weapon manned by a pickup crew, and mounted on the unstable stern of a PT that couldn't supply enough electric power for a fully automatic cannon, anyhow.

A quick glance at his watch confirmed that it was now three A.M. *Mohican* had, Cragg figured, posted about one hundred steel-jacketed messages at the enemy, the last dozen or so of which should have been fairly convincing. Unless the marauders carried nightglasses as standard equipment, thus enabling them to identify the PT, they might well have gotten the mistaken idea that a Thiet governmental warship had sped to Dokoro's rescue. It seemed unlikely, though, that even the Kong boasted such sophisticated equipment.

Cragg trained his own treated binoculars upon the fuel dump, where he had last seen the cluster of torch-bearing figures. None were visible. And although black, viscous smoke continued to rise from the scattered drums, the flames had died down.

He snapped open the voice tube.

"Rev up, fella. The fireworks are over. We're going in."

"You want her back on the front step?" asked DelGrado.

"Affirmative. And all the way into the goddamned parlor, if that's possible."

Over his shoulder, Cragg said: "Turn on the searchlight, Loo, and aim it at the mission."

"You wish them to see us coming, *mon capitaine?*"

"I wish them to know that something's definitely headed their way, fella, without baring all our little secrets."

Loo scuttled around to the portside of the bridge, peeled the canvas cover off the twelve-inch lamp, and trained it forward. He reached for the switch. As the white beam suddenly probed the dark void which separated *Mohican* from the approaching beach, Cragg crossed his fingers, and kept them that way over the wheel for an instant. Although the three-mile range was too great to gain much practical advantage from the searchlight, he was gambling that it would dazzle the eyes of any shorewatchers who might be hanging around after the miniature bombardment. With their vision impeded, Cragg hoped they'd continue to mistake the PT for an onrushing Thiet gunboat.

Always assuming, of course, that this happy illusion had succeeded in the first place.

At two miles, using his right hand to manipulate the nightglasses while keeping his crooked left arm firmly locked around the helm, Cragg tried to discern whether Dokoro's single loading pier had been spared. Unless the wooden jetty remained, they would be forced to anchor, then free the life raft which was lashed over the forcastle, and paddle ashore. Such a cumbersome procedure would leave them wide open to small-arms fire during the entire time they were inching toward their destination.

But the probing beam still fell short, and beyond its reaching finger a heavy smoke pall further obscured the goal.

Cragg glanced around him as he let the binoculars drop back across his chest. Gideon and Panache had abandoned the Long Tom when *Mohican* made its further use unfeasible by heading once more for the beach. They were huddled behind him, in the narrow space between the bridge and the dayroom superstructure, prepared to man the .50-caliber machine guns if Cragg issued the orders. Mario DelGrado remained with his hardpressed diesels. And Denny, silent, immobile, stood in the remotest corner of the bridge, staring straight ahead. Cragg couldn't see her face. But the girl's slim shoulders were erect, in a manner that suggested she had reached some inward accommodation, or found some fresh source of strength, which now sustained her.

The dock had not been destroyed. Like the outstretched arm of a partially incinerated corpse, it jutted a full hundred yards into the black waters of Dokoro harbor, below the burned-out rubble which only a few hours earlier had been a slumbering mission village.

Without reducing speed Cragg conned *Mohican* toward the pier. It was his plan to fetch them alongside fast, slam the engines into reverse, and drag the craft to an abrupt halt with her bow and stern lines. Loo and Gideon were on station, inch-thick manila at the ready, for this maneuver. On the starboard quarter, where *Mohican's* hull flared wide, Panache squatted with a woven hemp fender in his brawny fist. This would be their only safeguard against the jarring collision that was certain to occur, despite Cragg's best seamanship, when the undermanned PT sidled into the jetty. But Cragg had no choice, as he saw it, than to make a crash approach. Creeping in gingerly, the way the book prescribed, would give the enemy too much thinking room. This bold gambit might confuse the bastards to the point where they overestimated the paltry manpower arrayed against them. Moreover, the searchlight kept the pier under such harsh surveillance that anybody waiting there to greet *Mohican* would be half blinded and unable to take good aim.

At least that was what Cragg was hoping for.

Mohican hit hard.

For a crazy instant, caroming like a fifty-ton billard ball off the stout pilings, she broke free. But then Gideon and Loo got their lines emplaced. As the hawsers drew taut she returned sluggishly and came to rest against a weatherbeaten ladder that gave access to the dock itself. This was a distinct break. Cragg had been resigned, if necessary, to sending Loo aloft with a rope ladder, a contrivance which he heartily detested.

Instead, Loo was issued a tommy gun, with curt orders to guard the boat with his life.

"You'll also stay aboard," Cragg told Denny, "until we check things out."

She shook her head. "I am going with you."

"It's an order, *bébé*."

Her small chin lifted in quick defiance. "Now that I am home, Cragg, I no longer must obey your commands."

"Okay," he relented. "Come along. But you'd damned well better carry a gun, like the rest of us, and stay in the rear."

Denny did not reply. Gathering up her skirts, she stepped daintily over the PT's starboard coaming, and planted her right boot upon the lowest rung of the ancient ladder.

"Stop!" roared Cragg.

But the girl was already halfway to the top, climbing nimbly despite her cumbrous garments, and a moment later she vanished from sight. For a split second Cragg glowered in angry amazement. Then he deliberately tightened his webbed gunbelt and made sure that his long-bladed knife slipped easily in its sheath, before he swung around to face Gideon, DelGrado and Panache. "Follow me," he snapped, "*and* the lady."

By the time Cragg could wrangle his way up to the dock, doubly impeded by a clumsy automatic rifle slung across the shoulders and by his stiff knee, Denny had begun to climb the graveled road that led toward the station. She was running erratically, as women run, with her elbows flat against her sides. Aware of his reckless folly, without pausing for reinforcements, he started in limping pursuit, expecting at any moment to become the target of a concealed sniper.

But no shots rang out. The only sound Cragg heard, as he galloped down the planked decking, was the uneven thud of his own two feet and the rasp of his own breathing. Nobody lay in ambush for him, either on the pier, or immediately ashore, or along the sloping road, or within the debris-strewn compound itself. All was silence and desolation.

The others overtook him at the outskirts of the village. Together they formed a skirmish line and moved, briskly yet cautiously, past the skeletal remains of tiny shops, minuscule houses, and a somewhat larger structure that must have been Mme. Legére's school, toward the devastated hospital.

The wind-fanned blaze had raced through the settlement, consuming everything in its path and giving the inhabitants little chance to escape. Cragg played his flashlight beam from side to side as he walked. He counted a dozen or more blackened corpses among the embers, legs and arms outflexed, as if they had been trapped in flight. Several Dokorans, he noted, had managed to elude the flames. But they were dead, too, murdered in cold blood before they could reach the imagined security of the waterfront.

There was ample evidence of systematic looting. Along the corridor that comprised the village's main street were strewn random pieces of household gear and personal belongings which the heavily burdened raiders had dropped in their haste to leave, or abandoned because they had found more valuable items. Cragg saw remnants of earthen jars, a few dented kitchen utensils, torn pieces of garish-hued cotton cloth, bits of brass jewelry, and a bag or two of rice burst at their seams and stamped with the U.S. aid imprimatur. But nothing of real value, save an occasional chicken that had escaped the looters, and a lone pig.

They came at length to what looked like the village commons, hardly more than a slight enlargement of the narrow street, in the center of which stood a well. Beside its circular stone base, with his hands tied behind his back, lay an old man. He was sprawled face down upon the sandy ground. Only his blood-splattered white hair was visible above the faded blue gown which he wore like a monk's robe.

Cragg gave Panache an inquiring glance.

"Legére?"

The Frenchman knelt and rolled the gaunt figure over on its back. Two sightless eyes stared up at them. And in the center of the old man's wrinkled forehead, there was a neat bullet hole, rimmed with powdergrime. The rifle that made it had been fired at close range. Death must have come instantly to the old man.

Panache stood erect.

"This is not Dr. Legére." He muttered a Gallic oath. "It is Trang Kai. I knew him well. He was the elected mayor of Dokoro."

Cragg gestured toward the body. "Whoever killed His Honor knew exactly what he was doing. That's a damned professional job."

"Yes," agreed Panache. "Most professional." He jabbed the butt of his tommy gun against the low stone wall. "And it proves beyond doubt that something which I have long been fearing has now taken place. Conditions, *mon capitaine*, are far worse than I had believed possible."

With his own tommy gun, Cragg indicated the shattered buildings around them. "What could be worse than this?"

"The undeniable fact that the Kong have made common cause with the barbarians."

"How can you tell?"

Panache ran a grimy hand across his unkempt beard, as if weighing the matter, before he replied. Then: "The brigands would not have dispatched Trang Kai in this fashion. True, they would have slaughtered him, as they did his people, to eliminate a hindrance while they went about their looting. But here you see the classic handiwork of the Kong, designed to terrify any provincial Thiets who dare accept public office."

"So it puts them in Dokoro. But where do the other bastards fit in?"

"Although they live off the land," Panache explained, "the Kong never burden themselves with more food than they can eat in one day, or with useless goods such as were stolen tonight." The Frenchman looked past the square, in the direction of the fuel dump. "Nor would they have set fire to those drums, considering their desperate need for oil to run the trucks that bring their supplies down from Phom Than. Ah, no. Credit for that belongs to the outlaws." He shrugged. "Let us now proceed to the hospital."

Cragg turned to Gideon. "You and DelGrado hightail it down to the dump. Maybe they missed a few barrels. Separate 'em from the burned stuff, and if you can find a shovel, bury 'em."

The ghostly silence that had settled upon Dokoro seemed even deeper, more pervasive, in the ruined confines of the mission hospital. Panache went through the shattered doorway first. He paused beside the charred remains of the reception desk, flashing his torch around the anteroom, before he proceeded toward the sagging stairs that led to the second floor. As Panache strode through the darkness, he shattered the unnatural quiet with a torrent of futile, angry words which Cragg could not understand, but which he knew were directed at the wanton assassins of a peaceful village.

Breathing heavily, Panache climbed the stairs and pushed past a tangle of overturned chairs, tables and carts, to the room in which his old friend kept the mission's shortwave radio. He had been here often. In fact, long ago he had helped Legére install the set and shown him how it functioned, so that he himself would have somebody to talk with, during those lonesome nights at Bien Goa when he couldn't sleep.

The louvered door was closed. But through its horizontal

apertures shone the fitful glow of a kerosene lamp, which eased the blackness outside sufficiently for Cragg to perceive the expression on Panache's bearded face. It was a study in controlled, implacable fury.

Then, surprisingly, the Frenchman knocked upon the door.

"Mlle. Legére?"

There was no immediate response. He knocked again. In a voice that came to them from far away Denny called very softly, "You may enter, m'sieu."

Cragg followed Panache into the room. The girl sat on the bare floor, cradling a woman's head in her lap, stroking the matted hair that fell across the upturned face. The woman had been crudely, barbarically slain, almost disemboweled by an intruder who did not consider her worth the expenditure of valuable bullets, and who had used his machete instead. Nearby, slumped alongside the table which held the wreckage of his cherished radio, lay Dr. Legére, shot twice in the head, once in the chest. He had fallen with his right hand still groping for the shortwave microphone.

"They have killed my parents," Denny said, like a child repeating a statement she finds difficult to believe.

Cragg stepped to her side, and leaned down.

"Let me help you."

Like a sleepwalker Denny allowed herself to be lifted upright. She remained standing, passive, while he took off his khaki jacket and covered the woman's mutilated torso.

Panache said, "Let us go. We can return later to do what is necessary."

With the girl between them, half-carrying her, they left the silent room and made their way slowly back to the pier.

At the first pale light of dawn, which broke less than an hour after they had deposited Denny in her stateroom aboard *Mohican*, Cragg called his crew together for a council of war. Disregarding the exhaustion that showed in each man's drawn face, he announced gruffly that there were bodies to bury before the tropical sun made Dokoro unlivable, and a defensive perimeter to be established against possible sneak raids during the three days they must wait for *Medusa*'s arrival off Point Hospital. Although Hercule Panache declared positively that neither the Kong nor their brigand allies would return, having reduced the village to little more than scorched earth, Cragg was not convinced.

"Maybe the bastards will remember they forgot something," he said sourly, "like a rag doll, or a dried haddock, or a teapot. Maybe they'll come back just to see how this goddamned graveyard looks by daylight."

So the defenses were readied. They used the dock as a base, complete with barbed wire, two .50-caliber machine guns taken from the PT's deck arsenal, and a searchlight mounted on the shoreside railing of the pier, in case the enemy attacked after dark. All this was Trump Gideon's responsibility as gunnery boss. He was assisted by the Frenchman.

Mario DelGrado and Loo drew the grave detail. As they trudged off, long-handled shovels slung over their shoulders, Cragg saw that Loo was carrying a rosary wrapped around his thin wrist. Their orders were to take care of the Legéres first. In a brief lucid interval before she succumbed to the Seconal capsule which Cragg had given her, Denny whispered that she wanted them buried together in the hospital courtyard, under a single white wooden cross. Later she would go there by herself and recite a prayer for their souls.

It was Sunday.

When he was satisfied that work had gotten properly under way, Cragg went below to get the Pregnant Lady from his desk. After pouring a mug of coffee, he came topside once more, and spread the chart across the dayroom superstructure. Even though the sun was only sixty minutes old, its teeth already had a sharp bite, so he stripped to the waist before lighting his first morning cigar.

For a long while, unable to focus his mind upon the fresh threats that confronted his ill-starred enterprise, Cragg sat smoking and moodily contemplating the desolation ashore.

Dokoro had been a placid place, away from the mainstream of the ugly little war that engulfed Thietvanne, buttressed against evil by an abiding faith that should have saved it, yet couldn't, when evil eventually arrived. It boasted no industry. For years its people had remained largely self-sufficient, tilling their modest plots of buckwheat, maize and potatoes, raising a few pigs and fowl, and letting an abundant nature supply the rest. With the spread of guerrilla warfare, however, had come increasing demands from GaiSong for able-bodied men. So lately Dokoro had been populated mostly by women, children, and old men like Trang Kai, the mayor, and the village priest. Now even they were dead, all of them.

Cragg looked past the row of sloping palm trees that grew along the beach, with huge boles that made great humps in the white sand, toward the compound itself. Here he could see reminders of the Dokoro preparations for the Feast of Quyen Dhu, five days hence. There were heaps of trochus shell with which they had planned to make ornaments honoring their hero; gay flower garlands for draping across the thatched eaves of houses that now were blackened rubble; barbecue trenches deep and broad enough to accommodate whole wild pigs that weighed three hundred pounds apiece.

As Cragg caught sight of the roasting pits, a macabre thought struck him. These excavations would make the job of digging mass graves a lot easier for DelGrado and Loo.

With a profound sigh for the futility of life, and for the senselessness of death, he tossed away his cigar and gave his attention to the Pregnant Lady. It was indeed Sunday, although no bells tolled, and he had much to do.

The problem, as Cragg saw it, was twofold. *Item:* How to administer the immediate, dubious affairs of a twenty-three-year-old female orphan, whose filial grief had rendered her in such a state of quiet hysteria that she'd probably have to be coddled like an infant. *Item:* How to bring the Mafia together, under drastically altered circumstances, for the final strategy huddle that was prerequisite to any surprise assault upon Phom Than.

Despite their seeming disparity, these questions were interlinked, like the ups and downs of a crossword puzzle, and neither could be answered without reference to the other.

Cragg scowled down at the chart. He had folded and refolded

the linenbacked paper so many times that its creases were beginning to tear. Stains of sweat, grime and oil almost obliterated the geographical indices and depth markings along the fructile Lady's upper torso, until she resembled a bad tattoo job, done in haste by a Hong Kong artist who used cheap ink and a very dull needle.

Where in God's name could he desposit the girl?

If Hercule Panache was right, none of the places that might have sufficed earlier would be adequate now. Cragg cursed the offending map. The devil of it was that he had no reason to doubt the Frenchman's flat assumption of a Kong–outlaw alliance. Panache understood the country and its weird people the way Cragg himself understood the waterfront bums and beatniks of Sausalito. Between the Pregnant Lady's navel, which was Dokoro, and the tip of her mammoth right breast, the village of Xuan Luu, where he planned to stage their last rendezvous, stretched two hundred miles. There wouldn't be a cove or inlet safe enough to shelter *Mohican,* much less a village where Denny might seek sanctuary. Even by reversing course and taking the girl south it was unlikely they'd find anything suitable within a day's run.

He grimaced helplessly. The solution was obvious. They must keep Denny with them until they reached Xuan Luu. There, willy-nilly, she'd have to debark, so the Mafia could proceed unhampered upon its essential business. Casting the girl adrift was cruel, yet necessary. So once again, without any real alternative, he bowed to the inevitable.

Then, having made his difficult obeisance, Cragg stopped agonizing. He hoped that Denny would be able, somehow, to find her own way back to GaiSong. For he knew that the likelihood of *Mohican's* return to Xuan Luu was remote, after they'd accomplished their mission at Phom Than.

Bending over the map, Cragg mentally erased Point *India* and *Juliett* as rendezvous sites for *Medusa* and the PT. When the junk arrived off Dokoro on Tuesday night, he would order Torgerson straight into Xuan Luu, where next day they'd hold their last council of war before engaging the Kong fleet.

More than ever, it was imperative for them to reach the enemy capital before the Feast of Quyen Dhu. Until now manpower had been the rebels' chief shortcoming. But that deficiency would damned soon be remedied. Having made a pact with the brigands, the politically sophisticated Kong were certain to dominate their new allies, whom they would weld into a massive combat force capable of challenging General Kwo's tired army in open warfare. Nor would they lack for weapons, once the supply armada unloaded its cargo upon the Dalagong delta lowlands, where the ultimate battle must be fought.

Cragg had finished his cigar.

For a moment he considered going ashore and lending a hand with the armament detail. But he discarded the notion. Gideon and Panache seemed to be getting along quite well, and he was personally goddamned pooped, content for once to accept the ancient truism that Rank Hath Its Privileges. In this indulgent mood, therefore, Cragg stretched himself full length upon the warm planks, face to the midmorning sun, and let its rays bathe his boneweary frame. Caressed by the heat, soothed by the soft slapping of the waves against *Mohican's* tethered hull, he fell asleep.

A half-hour later he was aroused by the sound of heavy field-boots clumping across the deck as Gideon came toward him, waving his filthy hands and grinning broadly.

"Auditioning for sunstroke, skipper?"

Cragg sat up, still slightly dazed, and wiped perspiration from his eyes. "I must've corked off," he said, not at all embarrassed at having been caught napping.

"You're getting damned red," warned Gideon. "Better cover up that manly bosom."

Panache stepped off the ladder.

"Thietvanne is not the French Riviera," he added. "Its sun is treacherous to white skins."

Cragg gave him a surly glance. "Like everything else in this Godforsaken country," he growled, reaching for his wrinkled shirt.

Panache took no offense. "True," he agreed sadly. "Most true."

Gideon looked at the chart. "Been cerebrating?"

"Sort of."

"So what's the latest word on the Word?"

Cragg explained. After he ended his gloomy recital there was an uncomfortable pause, while Gideon and Panache digested the full import of what he intended to do.

Finally the Frenchman said: "It is a harsh choice, m'sieu."

"They're all harsh," Cragg rasped. "Every frigging one of 'em. And they'll get a lot worse before they get better."

"Suppose mam'selle won't buy?"

Cragg stared coldly at Gideon, but made no reply. Instead he demanded: "Are your guns properly emplaced, mister?"

"Almost."

"That's not good enough." Cragg checked his watch. "Eleven hundred. I want the job finished by noon."

Gideon tugged at his sweaty forelock in a burlesque imitation of humility. "Yassuh, boss," he said abjectly. "After papa and I slake our thirst with some of *Mohican*'s warm, lovely, sluttish water we'll tramp back to the cottonfields."

Below, Gideon and Panache were seated at the pulldown mess table, sipping the hot tea which the Frenchman had wisely suggested instead of ice water, and relaxing while they got their second wind. Beyond them, in the galley, stood Denny. Having brewed the tea, she was now preparing for noon chow, working silently over the miniature cookstove, with a remote expression on her profiled face.

Unseen by either the men or the girl, Cragg stepped quietly into his stateroom and thrust the map back into its steel pigeonhole. Then, seated at the desk, he riffled through the pages of a dog-eared magazine, staring vacantly at the pictures, while he waited for Gideon and Panache to go away.

Presently he heard their footsteps outside the door, and Panache's guttural voice replying to something Trump had said. Soon they were gone.

At his approach Denny looked up from the saucepan into which she was blending slices of tinned meat, dried onions and spaghetti with a can of tomato soup. Beside the stove, on a chopping board, was a penciled recipe. Cragg recognized Mario DelGrado's fine Italianate scrawl.

He asked somewhat inanely, "How do you feel, *bébé?*"

"Now that I have slept a little, and prayed much, the pain is less." She bent over the saucepan. "I am grateful, Cragg, for what you have done."

"But I didn't do a bloody thing," he said bitterly. "We got here too late."

"You tried." Denny raised her head. "Although it meant risking your plan."

Astonished by her composure, Cragg made no comment. He had expected, when she emerged from shock, that the girl would react to her tragedy with a delayed show of grief. There should have been tears, and wild lamentations, and perhaps a violent outburst against the marauders who had slain her parents. Instead, her voice was serene, devoid of passion.

He said, "I told Mario and Loo how you wanted things arranged at the hospital."

"Thank you, Cragg."

"Because of what's happened," he continued, watching her narrowly, "we can't let you stay here."

Denny directed her attention to the bubbling saucepan, stirring abstractedly, before she murmured: "I understand."

"I've gone over the chart," Cragg said. "There's no place south of Xuan Luu where you'd be safe. And we can't retrace our course toward GaiSong."

"Again I comprehend. The fuel."

"Yes. Gideon says they managed to salvage fourteen barrels. That's seven hundred lousy gallons, barely enough to fill up before we leave Dokoro—and then replenish for the run home after we've finished at Phom Than." Cragg felt that he was being overly defensive, too voluble, in outlining the situation. Nevertheless he plunged on, uncomfortable under the girl's calm gaze, in his effort to explain. "Trump and DelGrado buried the drums. We'll dig 'em up later."

He stopped, conscious of the inept imagery of his last remark, as her eyes grew clouded.

Then Denny gave him a faint smile. "It is all right, Cragg. I know this place, Xuan Luu, and I do not mind remaining there for a time. Two years ago my . . . my father took me with him to assist when an epidemic struck the village. Some will surely remember his visit, and a few may even remember his nurse." She paused. "I have good reason for going to Xuan Luu. It has a church, and there can be no mass for my parents without a priest."

Cragg had intended to state the case briefly, bluntly, without equivocation, and then depart, leaving Denny alone to adjust herself to the dismal prospect of what lay ahead. But now he was enmeshed in his own words. And it came to him, surprisingly, that the girl was trying to help soften the blow, to reassure him of her willingness to obey.

Aware that he was implying a possibility which did not exist, Cragg warned: "We might not be able to put into Xuan Luu on our way back."

"Please do not fear on my account, Cragg. You have many more important matters to resolve. I will manage." She hesitated. "The danger is very great at Phom Than, is it not?"

"Yes."

"There will be much killing?"

Cragg shrugged. "Whatever the job requires."

By midafternoon the perimeter defenses were established to Cragg's grudging satisfaction, although not until he had personally supervised the protective sandbagging of the transplanted .50s, then sighted their muzzles along the curved beach, so they covered a full 180 degrees. Gideon heard him muttering, in a voice unmeant for subordinate ears, that these emplacements might prove damned uncomfortable, and untenable, if the Kong decided to enfilade the pier from the nearby mission heights.

"We can always haul ass," offered Gideon.

Cragg grunted. "And cruise around for the next two days, wasting fuel, until *Medusa* shows up?" he asked scornfully. "Negative, mister. We've got to take our chances right here. Meanwhile consider yourself off duty, fella. Hit the sack till 1800. After dinner you can resume the communications watch." Beckoning Panache to follow him, he added: "Let's you and I find out what Radio Phom Than's got on its agenda."

"Who'll man the guns?" asked Gideon.

"DelGrado and Loo will take the sentry detail, four on, four off, until we're damned sure Papa's crystal ball works."

As they started down the pier toward *Mohican,* the sound of aircraft engines halted them, and they peered upward, shielding their eyes against the sun's rays. Panache spotted the plane first, flying at two thousand feet, on a course that would fetch it directly overhead. When it came nearer, they saw that it was a twin-motored scout-bomber of World War II vintage, with blue-and-red South Thietvannese stripings on the tailfin.

It passed over them, made a steep-banked circle around the ruined village, then headed seaward once more, climbing as it went. The trio waved. But the craft gave no acknowledgment, although it could not possibly have failed to observe the moored PT, and the men themselves, from such a low altitude.

"You blind bastard," Gideon yelled disgustedly, as it disappeared southward.

Panache was more charitable. "When he found the airfield inoperative, the pilot doubtless concluded it would serve no useful purpose to delay further."

"He could have waggled his goddamn wings."

"Maybe he was afraid they'd fall off," Cragg suggested. "It's an old crate."

"Balls." Gideon began clambering down the ladder. "Why did he come in the first place?"

"To learn," said Panache, "precisely what he has now learned, my friend. That Dokoro is dead. And that we have arrived safely."

In a mournful, saccharine manner that was intended to convey the Kong's deepest and most mendacious regrets, Radio Phom Than went on the air at five P.M. to make the first official announcement concerning the "reduction" of Dokoro.

It had been apparent for some time (said the guileful voice) that the mission was being increasingly put to less-than-humanitarian purposes. Despite repeated warnings by the People's Republic, military units of the South Thietvanne government persisted in using Dokoro as a sanctuary, while deploying there for drives against the Kong liberation forces. Beyond question, Dr. Legére and his hospital staff knew what was occurring, yet they made no effort to direct the warlike flow elsewhere. As a result, on Sunday last, Dokoro surrendered its immunity as a medical mission and was placed on the reprisal list.

Such a grave step (said Radio Phom Than) was not taken lightly. Far from it. The decision to "eliminate" Dokoro was made only after the most careful analysis of the evidence at hand, including verified reports that a Thietvannese destroyer had anchored in the harbor, and was preparing to refuel from the missions oil supplies.

Naturally this could not be permitted.

So, with the efficiency that marks every Kong operation, an assault was launched against this *de facto* stronghold. Our warriors (said the sad voice) performed heroically in the face of treacherous counterattacks by armed civilians, while under merciless bombardment by the enemy warship. Their gallantry prevailed. The bone has been plucked from the Liberation Army's throat. Dokoro no longer exists.

And the Thiet destroyer, its guns forever stilled, lies at the bottom of the sea.

From all this (said the voice, getting tougher) the leaders of South Thietvanne would be well advised to reconsider their defiance of the People's Republic. They cannot win. Therefore, the only sensible course for them to follow would be to abandon their fruitless opposition.

Of course (the voice turned persuasive), it need not be surrender, but rather a meeting of minds, a coalescing, a pragmatic arrangement whereby even General Trang Kwo's regime might have a role. The alternative was the total destruction of GaiSong itself.

As its *bona fides* in making this generous offer, the Phom Than government recommended an unconditional cease-fire, starting on the Feast of Quyen Dhu. The general's response must be delivered no later than Thursday midnight. . . .

Cragg switched off the shortwave.

"Those lying bastards. Who in God's name do they think they're fooling with that crap?"

"We know it is untrue," Panache said dryly, "but others don't. Like ancient Carthage, Dokoro is gone. *Delenda est.* There are no voices left to contradict Radio Phom Than."

"Except ours."

"But you forget, *mon capitaine,* we have been sunk."

"Even they don't believe that." Cragg gave him a fiercely questioning glance. "Do they?"

"One believes what one chooses to believe," said Panache. "The Kong wish us sunk. Their guerrillas inform them that we have been sunk. *Voilà!*"

"Simple as that."

"Perhaps," Panache observed meditatively. "Then again, perhaps not. . . ."

"General Kwo knows we're still afloat."

"Ah, yes. His Excellency is indeed aware that the expedition survives." The Frenchman's tone was gently ironic. "This assurance must afford him great comfort in his hour of trial."

Cragg snorted. "It seems the case has been called up a lot earlier than he expected. What'll the son of a bitch do now?"

"*Qui sait?*" Panache hunched his ponderous shoulders. "Phom Than has offered what you Americans term a blank check. But if Kwo reaches out for it, they will snatch it away, inscribe the amount, cash it, and then laugh in his face." The Frenchman shrugged again. "Yet Kwo has always considered himself a wily fellow, able to outguess his opponents. Perhaps, aware that defeat is imminent, he will decide to take the gamble."

"Before we've done our job?"

"Ah, no, my friend. Afterward." Panache gave Cragg a saturnine look. "Thus the good general inhabits the best of both possible worlds. Should your mission fail, as he believes it surely will, he can insist that Toyon acted contrary to orders, and so disclaim responsibility for the illegal attempt. But in the improbable event that you succeed, his hand will be vastly strengthened for dealing with the Kong."

"Either way he'd buy the truce."

"Probably."

"Great."

"Might I suggest," Panache said, "that we postpone further theorizing until we have conferred with Colonel Toyon?"

"Why?"

"He is no mere equerry, m'sieu. Kwo has kept him on a tight leash, always within arm's reach, because this odd little man holds a unique appeal for those who wish to fight the Kong to the finish. The general fears that Toyon might one day galvanize this hard-line faction—the hawks—and he knows that if such a time ever comes, Kwo would no longer rule Thietvanne."

"So why did he send the colonel with us?"

"Obviously, *mon capitaine,* to guarantee a potential rival's death."

"At a cost of $50,000!"

"For what His Excellency has in mind," said Panache, "it was an unparalleled bargain."

"I think," said Cragg, "we'd better break camp a little earlier than scheduled, and go after *Medusa.*"

Dawn broke in a singularly unpromising fashion, mist laden, dismal, foreboding, as if a watchful Providence knew precisely what *Mohican's* crew had planned, and did not approve.

To Cragg, supervising the tedious business of refueling, and the restoration of the .50-caliber machine guns to their midships baskets, the new day was neither good nor bad. Despite the rain threat, it was simply an oppressive condition under which they must operate, like damp turf for a crucial football game, or a muddy track for the Derby. You learned to live with it, hoping that the other guy, the enemy, would find it even less to his taste.

All morning they worked earnestly, with minimum conversation, at their assigned tasks.

Because they were demonstrably the strongest, Panache and DelGrado drew the thankless chore of hauling the oil drums across the field and down the long slope on a peddler's wagon the Frenchman had found among the village ruins. It took six 50-gallon barrels to top off the PT's bunkers. The remaining eight were left buried in the blackened earth beside the fuel dump, against their return, hopefully, four days hence.

Shortly before nightfall Cragg pronounced *Mohican* in all respects ready for sea.

8

"Only Fools
Aren't Scared"

THEY INTERCEPTED *Medusa* a half-hour before midnight. Deferring to Cragg's seniority, Torgerson, Harris and the colonel made the difficult transfer from the junk to the PT, while Panache and Loo strove to hold the pitching vessels at safe boathook length. High above them, at *Medusa's* wheel, Akim watched the watery proceedings with unmistakable joy in his one visible eye. By the time the three had groped their way down the rope ladder to *Mohican's* deck they were thoroughly drenched.

When they were fairly aboard, Cragg swung the PT clear, and relinquished the helm to Loo.

"Stay parallel to *Medusa*," he said, "about two hundred yards distant. We're going below for a talk. It might take a while, and I want to keep moving." He motioned toward Harris and Toyon, who were shivering in the chill wind. "You fellows go first and start thawing out. You look like drowned rats."

Torgerson flashed his mocking grin. "Hell, skipper, we needed
a bath anyhow. That frigging mudscow doesn't have your hotel
comforts."

Cragg waited until the others had disappeared through the
chartroom hatch before he spoke directly to the exec. Torgerson
seemed oblivious to the night wind, although his huge naked
torso glistened with salt water.

"Growing soft in your dotage?" Cragg taunted. "Or does
hobnobbing with the Bien Goa nobility spoil a man's appetite for
the rugged life?"

"Screw you," said Torgerson, his insubordinate grin widening.
"Don't tell me this joyride has ended, and we're finally going to
see some action."

"That all depends on the colonel."

"What's that little orangutang got to do with it?" the exec
demanded. "He's just along for laughs."

Cragg explained. "So maybe," he concluded, "we've been
mothballed."

Still muttering scornful disbelief, Torgerson shambled after
him, down the ladder, along the passageway, and into the wardroom. Trump Gideon and Mario DelGrado had joined the others.
The three Mafia brethren were grouped on one side of the
banquette, facing Toyon and the Frenchman, stolidly drinking
coffee. Denny had brewed tea for Panache and the colonel.
Having withdrawn once more to the galley, she was now watching them, like a child hidden at the top of the stairs, listening to
the grown-ups talk.

"You know about Dokoro?" Cragg asked Toyon.

Since this was more statement than query, the colonel merely
gestured toward Panache, indicating that the Frenchman had
informed him of the tragedy, and that further discussion would
be inopportune with the girl present.

"But M'sieu Panache has only hinted at the extraordinary news
from Phom Than," said Toyon. "He preferred to wait for you."

Cragg took a seat beside the colonel. At close range the Thiet
seemed more leathery, wrinkled, and emaciated than ever, as if
the voyage had prematurely aged and shrunken him. As Cragg
was detailing the offer made by the Kong, Toyon stared past him,

his dark face focused on something that lay beyond the small compartment, beyond *Mohican* herself. There was little expression on his face, except for the look of inchoate sadness which Toyon habitually wore, both in good times and bad.

"And so," Cragg finished, "it boils down to this—should we proceed, or stand by to see whether Kwo accepts the truce bid?" He stopped, waiting for Toyon's comment, but the colonel was silent. So he added: "We can make it back to GaiSong in four days. That way you wouldn't even miss Friday's festival."

"Friday would be too late, Mr. Cragg. I would have to be in GaiSong tonight, now, to exert any influence upon His Excellency's decision."

"So what's your wish?"

Toyon regarded him strangely. "Are you not in command?"

"Yes. But it happens to be a political judgment, colonel, and politics is your game, not mine."

"Conceiving this attack, over the general's intense objections, was not politics. It was our only chance to save Thietvanne."

"What if our fancy power play backfires?"

"So be it," said Toyon. "We shall have tried."

"Then you want to continue?"

"Definitely!"

Cragg peered around the crowded compartment, at the others who were listening so intently to his dialogue with the colonel, and who were now awaiting his own decision.

Lars Torgerson, lolling against the galley doorframe, seemed the least expectant. Backlighted by the single overhead bulb, his thin furze of blond hair gave him a deceptively haloed look. The Swede was whistling softly through the gap made by his missing front tooth.

Across the dropleaf table sat Duke Harris, Trump Gideon and Mario DelGrado, their faces carefully blank, giving no hint of what lay on their minds. Harris was toying with the strands of lank dark hair that straggled down the back of his otherwise bald skull. Gideon was tapping out a soundless tune with his right hand, absently, precisely, like a pianist practicing upon a dummy keyboard. Equally unaware of what he was doing, DelGrado fondled the crucifix which he wore around his tunsized neck.

Cragg shifted his gaze to Hercule Panache. As always, when lost in meditation, the Frenchman was gently stroking his grizzled spadebeard, as if he were appraising the value of Bien Goa's autumn rubber harvest, and finding it less than he had hoped.

"Very well, colonel, let's carry on."

Toyon inclined his head in brief, solemn acknowledgment. "Thank you."

Cragg beckoned to Torgerson. "Okay, tiger. You and the colonel go back to *Medusa*. Harris stays here. We're setting course for Point *Kilo*. After sundown tomorrow we'll rendezvous at Quang Duk lighthouse. But take it smooth. It's a tricky passage. And there's no candle in the window."

"Quang Duk?" repeated Torgerson.

"Affirmative. It's a little summer resort about 25 miles below Phom Than. But the season's over. Nobody visits Quang Duk anymore. Ever since the light was shot out, Loo says, the Kong figure it's been haunted by evil spirits." Cragg grinned at him. "So consider yourself a resident ghost."

"Why Quang Duk?" Torgerson persisted.

"Because," said Cragg, "it's the last place in God's world they'd be looking for us. And we need an uninterrupted twelve hours to get things in shape for D-day."

After *Mohican* and *Medusa* had rendezvoused, and parted again, Cragg lingered topside for a few minutes to clear his lungs of the 'tweendecks stuffiness. The sickle moon had broadened into a butcher's meat cleaver. Only a scattered tracery of clouds remained high overhead, and the lambent sky held a promise of good weather. Cragg frowned. For the cutthroat crime they were about to commit, he would have preferred monsoon conditions, evil, ugly, replete with wind and rain. No. On second thought, belay the rain. A downpour at the wrong instant, at the quivering brink of zero-hour, could wreck everything. But lowhanging scud, fog, or heavy mist would be just about perfect, providing the cover they needed for their excruciatingly slow swing around the Quang Duk headland, past the fortified Khandos

Islands, and thence into the cul-de-sac that was Phom Than harbor.

Cragg swore softly, and mentally revamped his schedule. If the weather stayed clear, they would strike an hour before dawn, instead of at first light, as he had originally planned. This would make the job a lot tougher, causing them to labor in pitch blackness as they applied the delicate final touches to an operation which must be carried out with split-second timing. But it couldn't be helped.

"I'll relieve you in twenty minutes," he told Loo, "after I've seen Mlle. Legére."

The Thiet helmsman exposed stained teeth in a cocky smile. "No sweat, *mon capitaine*." Lest Cragg charge him with insubordination, he hastened to add: "That is what M'sieu DelGrado always says."

Denny was washing the last of the coffee cups at the metal sink when Cragg entered the galley. She glanced up, mildly surprised. But she did not stop working. Panache had gone to bed.

"When you are finished," he said, "come to my stateroom."

"Yes, Cragg."

"I have something to show you."

"Very well," she assented placidly. "I shall only be a moment."

He turned and limped across the short passage to his seldom-used quarters. Leaving the door ajar, he seated himself at the desk, pulled open the drawer, and began to sort through a jumble of papers. Finally he found what he sought, a yellowed newspaper clipping. When Denny came into the room, he handed it to her without comment.

She regarded him curiously.

"Read it."

"Aloud?"

"Why not?" He nodded toward the unmade bunk. "Sit there."

Denny began in a low-pitched voice: " 'Everyone will now be mobilized, and all boys old enough to carry a spear will be sent to Addis Ababa. Married men will take their wives to carry food and to cook. Those without wives will take any woman without husband. Women with small babies need not go. The blind, and those who cannot walk, or who for any reason cannot carry a spear, are exempted.'" She looked up, puzzled. "What is this strange document, Cragg?"

"Go on."

"'Anyone found at home after receipt of this order will be hanged.'"

"Now I'll explain, *bébé*. It's the order Haile Selassie gave his people when Mussolini invaded Ethiopia in 1935. It's what total war can mean." Cragg reached for the clipping. "It also fits our present situation. You're a 'woman without a husband,' and you can cook. So you meet the basic requirements."

"Still I do not. . . ."

"You're mobilized," he said. "Drafted for active duty in the flagship of the free Thietvanne navy. Or what's left of it." When her perplexed expression deepened, he added: "Under the circumstances we can't waste time in a way stop between here and Quang Duk, so you'll have to stay aboard *Mohican*. Now do you understand?"

"Yes. But it was not necessary to approach this matter in such a complicated fashion, Cragg. I am not a child." She smiled faintly. "At GaiSong I told you I had learned how to care for the wounded. Remember? Now I have witnessed two battles . . . and seen the results of a third."

"Our chances of survival aren't very good," he pointed out. "In fact, they're infinitesimal."

"My own survival is of small concern, and it does not greatly interest me, although I wish you well for Thietvanne's sake."

"What about mine?" he asked. "And the others?"

She hesitated, seeming to weigh his words, before replying. "Does such a foolish question deserve an answer?"

"Even a mercenary likes to believe that his life is worth something," he said, "to somebody."

"I have never stopped praying for you, Cragg."

"Assuming we do come out of this, where will you go when it's all over?"

Denny shrugged. "Who can say? There will always be other wars for you. But for me . . . ?" The sentence went unfinished.

"Other wars? Hell, *bébé*. I've had it." He gave a short, harsh laugh. "They've priced themselves out of the market."

"*Comment?*"

"This crazy exercise was worth $50,000. Part down, the rest held in escrow in GaiSong, or in Quid Kwo's Swiss bank account. In either case, we'll never see it. So now we're working for love."

"Love of what, or whom, Cragg?"

He laughed again. "Damned good question. A few months ago I could have answered it easily. I was fed to the teeth. Bored stiff. Useless. When Toyon showed up, it looked like the break I'd been waiting for, a chance to get away, and maybe turn the clock back to a time when things had a meaning." He leaned forward in his chair, trying to make the girl understand. "You live all your life inside a building. The façade grows older, but you're always looking out through the same window at the same view. So sometimes you think you are the same, too; that you haven't changed or grown older. Except early in the morning when you've awakened and it's dark and you can't see anything, except inwardly, and then you know how it really is." He stopped. "That doesn't make much sense, does it?"

"What do you see, Cragg, when it is not dark?"

"It's been a lousy view, mostly. I've never liked it much." He grinned. "Oh, it's not all that bad, *bébé*. Not when I'm doing the things I want to do. Sailing. Fishing. Usually alone."

For a moment Denny was silent. Then she asked in a soft voice: "Why do you call me *bébé?* Is this not an affectionate term, even in the American argot?"

"It can be," he said cautiously. "But sometimes it's used for waitresses and barmaids, if they're cute enough."

"Perhaps I should go to America."

Cragg arose. With grave ceremony, he held out his right hand, and pulled her erect. "That sounds like one hell of a fine idea . . . *bébé*." He brushed a kiss across her forehead, gently, before turning into the passageway. He did not look back.

Loo confronted him with a broader-than-usual grin.

"Did it go well, *mon capitaine?*"

Cragg rewarded his temerity with a scowl that would have

daunted a lesser man, but the Thiet's confident grin persisted. "Did what go well, fella?"

"Your talkings," said Loo.

"Yes." Cragg relented slightly. "I suppose you might say the talkings went well."

Loo stepped aside to let him take over the wheel. "Does this mean we shall indeed sail against Phom Than?"

"Affirmative. Right down the bloody gunbarrel." Cragg gave him a curious glance, noting for the first time that the helmsman was wearing a bandanna over his tiny skull, knotted at each corner, like a prayerful Buddhist. Maybe Loo was trying to reduce the odds, too, petitioning help from an older Thiet diety as well as from the strange Christian God to whom he had been introduced at Dokoro Mission. Not at all embarrassed, Loo removed the kerchief and thrust it into the hip pocket of his dungarees.

"Do not inform Mlle. Legére," he said solemnly. "She would not comprehend."

"Whatever you were doing is your own business," Cragg assured him. "Let's hope it works." He regarded the Thiet for a brief moment, then urged gently: "Tell me, mister, what sort of message you were relaying Upstairs."

Loo grinned again. "I asked Him to keep those Kong junks in Phom Than harbor until we arrived."

Cragg staggered him with an admiring thwack across his skinny right shoulder. "You weren't just praying for rain, Noah. You were asking for a flood."

Loo looked perplexed. "I spoke only of the Kong ships. There was nothing about rain in my prayers."

"Figure of speech," said Cragg. "Forget it."

"Aye, aye, sir." Loo hesitated. "At what hour does *mon capitaine* wish to be relieved?"

"At o6oo, mister, with a red-hot cup of coffee."

Loo saluted and left. Alone at the wheel, Cragg checked the compass, satisfied himself that *Mohican* was aiming straight for Quang Duk on course-285, and adjusted the throttles for fifteen knots. Then, settling his back against the bridgetub, he lit a cigar. It was a routine Philippine stogie rather than a crisis Upmann, because the real moment of truth had not yet arrived, and wouldn't for another twenty-eight hours. In point of fact, he'd discovered earlier that only one of General Kwo's contraband Cuban cigars were left in the box. This he intended to smoke as dawn broke Thursday morning, at the very instant when the Mafia launched the attack. Cragg remembered his old PT squadron leader's favorite saying, an exhortation with which the grumpy bastard concluded every pre-mission briefing. *Okay, men, let's go bite the frigging bullet!* He shaped a wry grimace with his salt-cracked lips. As a bullet to bite upon, when the pain started, Quid Kwo's last Upmann would be unbeatable. Appropriate, too.

That notion, and Loo's ambivalent theologizing, had fathered a whole new train of thought. Cragg was suddenly struck by the bizarre symbolism which seemed latent in everything the Mafia was doing out here, in this bereft corner of the world. If it weren't so goddamned hopeless, it might have been funny: a spavined Chinese junk teamed with an obsolete Yankee torpedo boat, both of them manned by polyglot crews, toiling toward a desperate objective like characters in some never-the-twain-shall-meet charade. They were mismatched, unfitted, implausible.

Cragg narrowed his gaze, sighting across the windscreen, to take a hard look at the canvas-hooded 40-millimeter gun on the foredeck. He wondered how Mlle. Legére would react, with what horrified Gallic exclamations, if he were to announce that her battle station was the saddleseat of this horrendous weapon. Briefly, humorlessly, he laughed aloud at the absurd idea of Denny cranking the pointer's wheel, trying to train the lethal barrel upon some live enemy target that needed killing.

No. The girl would stay below. She could bandage and suture. That way, if *Mohican* caught a bad one, she'd never know what happened, because it would be over so quickly, as it always happens with PTs. But if she were really lucky, and they survived, her virginal noncombatant status would remain unimpaired. Hell. Denny wouldn't even have to explain to the priest, next time she entered the confessional.

Cragg drew deeply on his cigar. The malodorous smoke streamed aft, borne by the breeze, and he didn't laugh again. His mordant humor had passed. Deliberately, he let his mind go blank, except for that small automaton brainlobe which devoted itself to the simple business of steering the fifty-ton vessel.

When he saw it in the daylight, as gray dawn broke, Cragg was very pleased.

Quang Duk couldn't have been more deserted if an atom bomb had wiped out the station's one-time inhabitants. The lighthouse itself stood useless guard at the apex of the low-lying point, windows smashed, stuccoed walls cracking under the alternate impact of heat, damp and cold. Perhaps sixty feet tall, the columnar structure looked for all the world like a dismantled rocket shorn of its launch scaffolding.

Inshore from the lighthouse a narrow causeway connected the peninsula with the mainland. At high water this became flooded, making Quang Duk a veritable island. Now, fortuitously, was the time of neap tides, during the final phase of the moon's first quarter. Because the rise and fall was minimal, the causeway remained constantly under several feet of turbulent water, inaccessible to vehicular or even foot traffic.

Cragg gave the abandoned facility an approving nod. It was even better than he had expected. In a way, Quang Duk reminded him of an old lighthouse on the California coast, near San Simeon, called Piedras Blancas. That beacon was also set on a sandy peninsula, and it lost contact with civilization at every high tide. Although Cragg had seen Piedras Blancas often during his meanderings along State Highway 1 in the straphooded Morgan, and had wondered what life was like in that lonely place, he had never paid it a visit. Now he wished he had.

Picking up his binoculars, Cragg gazed once more around the bleak countryside that lay west of Quang Duk, and once more he was impressed by the growing resemblance of the Thietvanne coast to the California he knew, both in flora and terrain. Those stunted pines could have been Monterrey cypresses, and the queer subtropical gorse might have been the same rank saltweeds that grew along the Pacific sandspits. In the dim distance the Fantastic Mountains, loftier here than in the south, seemed not unlike the Coast Range where it dipped down toward Big Sur.

Viewed close at hand, of course, there were certain basic differences. Back home you never found chinhigh nettles whose heart-shaped leaves held enough poison to incapacitate a man for a week. Nor was there an impenetrable cover of rattan and bamboo beneath the tranquil forests that lay across the wide ocean.

In fact, Cragg concluded, there was nothing friendly about these desolate slopes that climbed uncertainly toward the far-off peaks, their drab brownness relieved only by an occasional trail and a few scattered huts. California was a million miles away. He let the binoculars drop against his bare chest. Except for some unidentifiable animals skulking at the edge of the brush, and a gaggle of long-legged waterfowl standing sentry along the beach, he had seen no evidence of life within the five-mile arc that came under his scrutiny.

Why, Cragg wondered, would men fight to hold, or capture, a land as patently inhospitable as Thietvanne. Out here on the enemy's threshold, even the goddamned birds seemed hostile!

Their rendezvous was accomplished without incident. Having made voice-radio contact a dozen miles below Point *Kilo* shortly after sunset, Cragg had sent *Medusa* into Quang Duk ahead of the PT, with orders to moor in the lee of a rock jetty that extended a few hundred feet seaward from the southern flank of the sandy point. According to his chart, the breakwater offered a modicum of shelter for shallow draft vessels bringing supplies to the lighthouse.

Mohican followed at a discreet interval, and made fast against the junk's outboard flank. In this coupled fashion Cragg hoped to achieve maximum security for his miniature flagship. Despite the pitch-blackness, he dispatched a Thiet workparty under the direction of Akim to chop a load of tranh grass and palm fronds, which they arranged across *Mohican's* armament-laden deck. In the unlikely event that an intruder chanced to stray down the unserviceable road and spot *Medusa*, the PT might be mistaken for a bumboat, fetching supplies to a presumptuous nautical wayfarer. As further guarantee of privacy, at daybreak he also positioned Akim's sharpest rifleman at the water's edge, where the causeway emerged, with instructions to look as though he were fishing, in case an enemy plane moved in to investigate.

"Shoot any sons of bitches that show up," Cragg snarled, "and save the foolish questions for the inquest."

By seven A.M. they were ready to commence the task which had brought them to Quang Duk. They labored all morning, Thiets, Mafia and Papa Panache alike, to arrange *Medusa's* incendiary cargo the way Cragg wanted it.

The seven barrels of black powder remained belowdecks, in the geometrical center of the junk's cavernous hold, lashed together with heavy line and interlinked by a swift-burning wick fuse which, in turn, ran along the rough planks to the foot of the main ladder.

At carefully spaced intervals from the butt-end of the foremast to the engine-room door Cragg placed six of the dozen cans of kerosene, and built a hillock of oily waste around each. He had the remaining five-gallon containers taken above, where they were similarly dispersed, three to a side, along the port and starboard rails. The rest of the inflammable waste material was strewn like wadding from a split mattress between the kerosene tins.

"Just make damned sure a couple of sharp axes are kept handy, up here and down in the hold, so we can breach these jugs in one hell of a hurry," Cragg told Torgerson.

The Swede scowled, but said nothing.

All fourteen barrels of pitch were wrangled topside through the loading hatch to the welldeck, then decanted into buckets. Cragg gave long-handled swabs to the half-dozen Thiet seamen whom Akim designated as best equipped for masthead work. With pails slung around their shoulders they went aloft, led by *le capitaine* himself, and started smearing wood tar over the hemp rigging and the unfurled canvas sails. Satisfied that the Thiets knew their job, Cragg clambered awkwardly back down the starboard mainmast ratline to take charge of the next assignment.

The drum of aviation fuel—Panache's bonus—was suspended over the fantail like a tipsy lifeboat, with the screwcap kept easily accessible.

"So what's the big frigging deal?" Torgerson demanded, obviously puzzled, and not enjoying it.

Cragg paused to catch his breath. "After the whole hand's been dealt," he said, "I'll explain the rules. Right now all you need to know is that you're elected to take the rubber boat into Phom Than harbor, and handle the underwater demolition caper. That's the key assignment. Okay?"

"Okay." Torgerson relaxed. "Have it your way—skipper."

"Good."

The issue settled, Cragg proceeded to divide the three hundred pounds of sulphur into lesser sacks, which he distributed strategically along *Medusa*'s deep scuppers. These, in turn, were linked with a continuous fuse that terminated at a stanchion near the great flat steering wheel.

Finally he instructed Trump Gideon, as chief ordnanceman, and Panache, as a practical expert in tree stump blasting, to pass a miracle with the thirty-eight sticks of dynamite.

"Plastic bombs would have been a lot handier," Cragg admitted. "But GaiSong wouldn't part with any. So we'll make do with what we've got. Find a way to convert that stuff into underwater bombs. I don't give a damn how you do it, as long as it's done. The whole show might depend on these packages going off at exactly the right second."

Gideon whistled softly. "That's a hell of an order, bossman."

"This is a hell of a war."

"Granted." Trump looked at Panache. "D'you have an alarm clock, papa?"

"Yes."

"So do I. We'll need four more. And a batch of those pliofilm cold locker bags." Gideon shook his head doubtfully. "Maybe it'll work."

"Possibly," agreed Panache. "But I should not wish to stake my life on it."

Cragg uttered a grim chuckle. "Better make 'em good, papa. You've just placed the chanciest bet since they invented Russian roulette."

Duke Harris, who had emerged from *Mohican*'s stuffy chart-

254 THE SKY SUSPENDED

room for a breath of air, overheard Cragg's deep-voiced admonition. He called up to the junk.

"Haven't changed a ruddy bit since the Solomons, have you, chief?"

"Old seadogs never change," Cragg said equably. "They just hobble away into the sunset." Suddenly serious, he contemplated the radioman's Pickwickian face for a moment. "Tell Denny to report on board *Medusa.* I've got a job for her."

Ten minutes later the girl appeared at the top of the accommodation ladder that led from *Mohican's* forecastle to the junk's waist. Her dark hair was disarrayed, and her face was flushed.

"You sent for me, Cragg?"

"Yes." He regarded her curiously. "What have you been doing?"

"Preparing lunch."

"Forget it. This is no time for hotel service. We'll eat cold C-rations."

Denny shrugged. "As you wish."

He gestured toward the clutter of wooden chicken coops and pigpens on *Medusa's* lofty poop. "But don't let the galley stove go cold. I want every one of those hens killed, cleaned, boiled, and stowed away in the cold locker. They're our grubstake for the return voyage. . . ." He almost added, *if we make it,* but he left that thought unspoken.

"And *Monsieur le Coq?*" she asked ironically. "Do we spare him?"

Cragg laughed. "The rooster's reprieved. Too tough even for short rations. After we leave, he'll help colonize Quang Duk, along with the pig."

"Why not barbecue the goddamned hog," Torgerson rumbled, "instead of wasting all that good pork?"

"Sure, why not? And invite every Kong in the country to join the party, after they spot the smoke." Cragg gave him a withering glance. "But I'll tell you what you *can* do."

"What's that, skipper?"

"Grab an axe—and start slaughtering those chickens. Then help Denny pluck feathers."

Torgerson showed angry disbelief. "Hell, have DelGrado do it. He's a goddamned farmer. I'm not."

"Get cracking, mister. That's a flat order."

For a moment the exec seemed on the verge of mutiny, until Cragg's uncompromising stare fetched him to his senses. It came to Torgerson, then, why he had been given this menial chore. Cragg had waited a long time to punish him for his sins at Bien Goa. But when the right opportunity arrived, the sly bastard had seized it the way a fox pounces upon a rabbit.

Under the wide-eyed gaze of the Thiet work crew, who were taking unconcealed delight in this hazing of their much-feared boss, Torgerson stalked aft. For the next half-hour the shrieks of dying fowl provided a weird obbligato for the normal workday sounds aboard *Medusa*. Even when they sat down to munch their C-rations, the Thiets continued to grin, their appetites not at all diminished by the massacre. They were, indeed, professionally intrigued by the exec's murderous skill with a double-bladed axe.

One had to concede that this terrible man was most adept when it came to killing. He did it with a flair. Moreover, he enjoyed it.

They spent the entire afternoon rendering both vessels shipshape enough to stand the test of Cragg's meticulous final inspection.

Deck weaponry had to be overhauled. Trump Gideon was charged, in particular, to make certain that *Mohican*'s Long Tom and its flamethrowing appendage were in tiptop working order. Behind closed ports, *Medusa*'s six .50-calibers were put through a dry run by the Thiet gunners, under Akim's impassive, one-eyed scrutiny. Where the livestock cages had stood, more tranh grass and palm fronds were stacked high, completely covering the 40-millimeter stern rifle. The junk's bow cannon lay hidden under similar camouflage.

Shortly before nightfall *Medusa* was the very model of an oriental Q-ship: innocent to behold, yet heavily armed, and impregnated with volatile fuel, incendiary materials and explosives.

Mohican remained what she'd always been: a deadly, if somewhat modified, vestpocket warship.

Convinced that his two-unit squadron was as ready as dedicated effort would ever make it, that nothing else could be done, Cragg ordered all hands to take a sixty-minute break for relaxation and another cold meal. At seven-thirty P.M., they would assemble in the windowless ground level of the lighthouse, where Loo had prepared a driftwood fire on the hearth. Although the fireplace wasn't large enough to barbecue a pig (he added for Torgerson's benefit), using it might take the chill off the night air.

"Are we going to stage a community sing?" scoffed the exec. "Or maybe a wienie roast?"

"Neither." Cragg stretched himself full length on the canvas cushions that were heaped on the junk's upswept stern. "Now that the cards are dealt, we're going to memorize the rules of the game." He closed his eyes. "It's a goddamned tricky one, fella, so come to the party sober."

The pulsating throb of aircraft engines awakened him before the hour was half gone. Raising himself to a sitting posture, he saw the plane, an ancient twin-motored Tupolev. It was about a half-mile distant, bumbling toward them at treetop height, its blunt wings silvered by the last rays of the setting sun.

Cragg twisted on his stiff elbow. Beside him, frantically tearing at the camouflage that shrouded the 40-mm. stern rifle, was Torgerson. Two Thiets were assisting him.

"What the goddamned hell d'you think you're doing?" Cragg bellowed.

The Swede flung the answer over his shoulder. "Unlimbering this popgun so we can clobber the bastard on his next swing."

On his feet now, Cragg hobbled across the narrow deckspace which separated him from the three men. "Belay it!" He began replacing the palm fronds.

Instinctively, he ducked as the World War II vintage TU-2 swept overhead. The Thiets threw themselves flat. But Torgerson remained erect, gaping incredulously at Cragg.

"Have you gone nuts?"

Cragg watched the enemy plane climb seaward. It had already started a wide banking turn before disappearing in the eastern dusk. Then he whirled upon Torgerson.

"You crazy son of a bitch," he said in an ominous voice that impressed the exec more than the roar which had proceeded it. "We're stupid peasant-fishermen. Remember? We're holing up at Quang Duk for repairs because nobody told us about the lighthouse spooks. And we're unarmed."

Torgerson stepped back a pace. "You're going to let the bugger off scotfree?"

"Affirmative. Now park your tail against the rail, fella, and pretend you're a native. When that plane comes back, wave your goddamn arms off!"

They waited tensely for the Tupolev's second run. Barely high enough to clear the beacon, sufficiently close for them to see the pilot's begoggled face peering from the canopied cockpit, it thundered above the nested vessels. Cragg flung his good arm aloft in a gesture of friendship. Reluctantly, Torgerson followed suit.

The bomber was lost to view again, over the purpling foothills, and they remained frozen to give it plenty of time for a third reconnaissance. But the droopnosed plane didn't return.

Cragg exhaled audibly. He felt as if he'd been holding his breath for a long while under water.

"Maybe the joker was satisfied with his double take," he said.

"More likely we'll have company pretty soon." Torgerson gave him a baleful scowl. "*Then* can we start shooting?"

"Yes, mister, you can start shooting if the Kong show up. But first you'd better get acquainted with a born loser named George Custer. He blundered into a situation like this, once, and found that being a trigger-happy hero didn't help a bloody bit. . . ."

Cragg turned away from the exec. Leaning his elbows on *Medusa*'s waist-high rail, he brooded toward the serrated western horizon, where the sun had finally vanished in fire-opal splendor. The color faded quickly, leaving the twilight aftermath a brooding gray. This pleased Cragg. It meant, providentially, that tomorrow might also be gray, nasty and mean.

He glanced at his wristwatch, before he swung slowly around to face Torgerson.

"Damned near 1930," he grunted. "Better whistle up the troops."

Only the Thiet sentry was absent when they assembled in the circular ground floor of the lighthouse. Although it offered serious drawbacks as a meeting hall, the room was considerably more convenient than *Medusa's* dank hold, and *Mohican* had no space large enough to house their entire complement: the five Mafia, a Frenchman and a Frenchwoman, and the fourteen Thiets. Moreover, Cragg had decreed a total blackout for the junk and the PT, since deck lights would be certain to attract the unwelcome visitors who might have missed them by day.

Taped above the mantelpiece of the small hearth was a chart of Phom Than harbor, which Cragg had laboriously hand-sketched, about three feet square. A portable spotlight played upon it. Otherwise the room's sole illumination was the hungry driftwood fire, which Loo kept fed from the half-cord stack he had accumulated during the afternoon.

Despite the blaze there was a definite chill in the air. Cragg saw that Denny had once again swathed herself in the ugly brown duster.

"I'll make it damned brief," he began. "For anybody who knows how Sir Francis Drake beat the Spanish Armada with fireships, the plot will sound familiar. I've updated it, that's all."

Cragg indicated a series of red crayoned X's with his dagger-bladed utility knife. "The Kong are moored here. From what we've learned, there may be sixty junks, give or take a few, tied up along the waterfront. They'll probably lie three or four deep, in a long column, because the berthing space is pretty limited.

"From Quang Duk, here, to the inner harbor it's a good 25-mile haul. Two fortified islands, called the Khandos, guard the entrance proper. We don't know exactly what they've got in the way of firepower, but it's bound to be considerable.

"I'll take *Medusa* in first. We'll hug the mainland, where it bellies out toward the Khandos, to lay maximum distance between us and the fort. Weatherwise, we're lucky, with a low overcast that might thicken into fog, gusting winds, and only a quarter-moon to worry about in case it clears up.

"The way I make it, *Medusa* should pass the islands about two hours before daylight." Cragg glanced at the exec. "You'll get another small break, fella. The tide's coming in, running fast through the channel, so you two will have an easier time negotiating these last six miles."

"Two?" Torgerson echoed the word in an irate voice. "What the hell d'you mean? This is strictly a one-man show."

"Negative," said Cragg. "I'm giving you Akim."

"Horsecock! I don't want company."

"But you've got it anyhow. Unless you reach the Kong with enough darkness to spare for the UDT exercise, the whole thing breaks down. Savvy? So Akim goes along for extra paddlepower."

Torgerson surrendered ungraciously. "Have it your way, skipper."

"Thanks," Cragg growled. He lit a cheroot before resuming. "*Medusa* will stay hove-to for ninety minutes, then get underway again at zero-minus-thirty. Meanwhile Lars will have secured his dynamite to the Kong hulls here—" he speared the X's that denoted the vanguard of the enemy fleet—"and swum back to where Akim is holding the raft." Cragg touched the chart once more. "This particular X is goddamned vital. Nail it down. It's the point where *Mohican* will pick them up in mid-harbor."

Looking at Gideon, who would be commanding the PT, Cragg added: "Once *Medusa* has made contact with the Kong, I'll break radio silence and give you a solid fix with the TBS. At that time we can forget about secrecy, anyhow, so I want this to be letter-perfect. Get me?"

"Got you, bossman."

"As *Mohican* draws alongside, Akim will heave a towing line to your bow hands, and they'll haul the raft aboard. That way you can keep rolling."

When Torgerson's first charges exploded, Cragg would put *Medusa* to the torch and start his final run. The Thiet gunners, who'd have been tending their clandestine machine guns below-decks, would hustle topside to take over the fore-and-aft 40-millimeters.

The gunpowder in *Medusa*'s hold would detonate as they neared the leading Kong vessels. Then, and only then, positive that she was irreversibly on-course, would they abandon their flaming ship.

"Everybody will wear life jackets," Cragg said. "The minute you hit the water, start swimming like hell toward Torgerson's raft. He'll flash a light for us."

How the escaping crew, half-blinded by the flames and stunned by the dynamite blast, would be able to locate this incandescent pinprick was left unexplained. Nor did Cragg describe the horror that might engulf them, if the jettisoned aviation fuel spread flaming across the harbor's choppy surface, and caught them before they could escape into midstream.

Once again Cragg paused. He regarded them quizzically through the pale smoke of his Manila stogie. Yet nobody posed a question, not even the two Thiet motor mechs who kept *Medusa*'s venerable diesel operating, and who might have been justified in demanding how they would escape from their tiny compartment once the explosives went off.

So Cragg continued.

Mohican would stay discreetly beyond the Khandos' range during the preliminaries, ready to start rolling the instant her lookouts spotted the distant fires.

"I want at least twenty knots," he told DelGrado, "by the time you pass those goddamned islands."

Mario nodded. "You'll have 'em, skipper."

"Okay." Cragg caught Loo's eye across the room. "And I'm counting on you, fella, to steer straight for the target without wasting any time. The Kong may try to break out, and *Mohican*'s got to be there to stop 'em."

He turned to Trump Gideon. "Use the Long Tom on any mavericks who cut loose from the herd—and give 'em an extra goose with the flamethrower if they don't keep burning the way they should." Cragg jabbed his knifepoint into a red crayoned X that denoted their rendezvous with Torgerson. "On your way in, pick us up here. We'll be waiting for you."

As for the others: Colonel Toyon would embark in *Mohican,*

along with Gideon, DelGrado, Harris, the girl, and the four
Thiets who had been eliminated from *Medusa's* skeleton crew.
Anticipating a protest from Toyon, Cragg said briskly: "Your
real job isn't at Phom Than, Colonel. They'll need you later at
GaiSong. So we can't take any unnecessary chances."
"Thank you, Mr. Cragg." Toyon bowed. "I shall endeavor to
make myself useful as a gunner."
"Good." Cragg turned finally to Hercule Panache. "And you,
papa—"
"You cannot deny me the pleasure of your company, *mon
capitaine*. After all it is my *matériel* which fuels your fireship. I
must make sure that you utilize these valuable stores properly."
"It's your funeral."
"*Merci.*"
"Now that you've seen the general outline, what d'you think
about the plan?" Cragg asked. "As our resident chess champion, I
mean."
Panache played a brisk tattoo upon his bent knees, ruminating
a moment, before he replied. "In this game, I am a piece, not a
player."
"You'd make one hell of a big pawn."
Panache's teeth glinted through his ferocious beard. "Not a
pawn, *mon ami*. Perhaps an heretical bishop, or a knavish knight,
but never a pawn."
Cragg sheathed his knife. "In the Solomons campaign it took a
thousand rounds of .50-caliber to sink one wooden barge, and
sometimes five hundred rounds of 20-millimeter, pumping away
for ten minutes at point-blank range. Sure, the 40-millimeters are
an improvement, and the Long Tom is even better. But we've
got a hell of a lot of junks to contend with, all of 'em tougher
than those Jap barges. So conventional firepower won't work."
"*Hélas,*" agreed Panache. "Too true."
"You still insist on going with me?"
"Yes, *mon capitaine*."
Cragg contemplated the nineteen men and the girl who were
arrayed closely around him, intently listening.
"You'll do," he muttered. "You'll have to."
Still pondering his enigmatic remark, they were dismissed with

orders to make *Medusa* ready for a three A.M. departure, so that she could arrive off the Khandos islands by four. *Mohican* would sail an hour later.

Cragg lingered by the fireplace as they started filing through the narrow door. It was obvious that he intended to stay there, alone, after they left. Loo hung back, waiting to see whether *le capitaine* desired more driftwood placed over the dying embers. But Cragg motioned him away.

Denny was the last to go. At the door she hesitated, turned, and spoke in a timid voice.

"Cragg?"

He interrupted himself in the act of relighting his dead cigar. "Yes, *bébé?*"

"May I remain for a few minutes?"

"Certainly." He beckoned her to the hearth. "Come here where it's warm."

As she walked slowly toward him, Denny began unbuttoning her long cloak. When she reached the fireplace, she removed the drab garment and spread it over the broad stone hearth. "Sir Walter Raleigh did this for his sovereign, *n'est-ce pas?*"

Caught offguard by this unexpected action, Cragg said gruffly, "Raleigh was a man. An Englishman. He didn't want his queen to muddy her shoes."

"And I," said Denny, standing proud in her workstained skirt and blouse, "am a woman. A Frenchwoman. I would not want my captain to soil his trousers on this reprehensible floor."

"You'll get cold," he objected. "Besides, they're already filthy."

She sank gracefully onto the cloak, like a ballet dancer at curtain call, and smiled up at him. "You could revive the fire, Cragg."

Baffled by her mood, so alien to what he had known, Cragg loaded his arms with logs from the driftwood cache. He laid them carefully on the coals, taking his time, not looking at the girl. Her gesture with the cloak had been singularly appealing. Cragg waited curiously to see what would come next. He did not confront her directly until the salt-encrusted wood was well ablaze.

"Please sit down beside me," Denny pleaded in a voice no longer coquettish.

He obeyed. "You're more scared than cold, aren't you?"

"Yes, Cragg, I am afraid. But is not everyone afraid?"

"Only damned fools aren't scared of battle. Or types like Torgerson, who don't give a hang whether they live or die." He eased his webbed gunbelt. "Where would you rather be tonight? GaiSong, perhaps?"

"No. GaiSong is not a good place. Its people have lost their spirit."

"Paris?"

"Again, *non*. The French no longer understand, or care about what is happening. Now they think mainly of themselves."

Stretched upon the cloak, her head cradled by one freckled arm, staring frankly at him, Denny had lost the schoolgirl ingénue air that accompanied her first remarks. The varicolored fireglow gave a maturity to her recumbent figure, enhancing the curve of her slim hips and the soft rise of her breasts.

She mimicked his earlier question: "And you, Cragg, where would *you* rather be tonight?"

"In Sausalito, California, rigging a diesel clipper for a weekend albacore charter."

"Is that such a good life?"

"The best." He twisted his body so that he was also full-length upon the hearth, facing her. "Any mistakes a man makes are his own. The only thing he fights is the weather."

"It must be very nice, this Sausalito of yours, where the people are not afraid, and there is peace."

"Don't be confused by the kind of life I led," Cragg said. "Most Californians don't understand, either, any more than the French do. They just happen to be farther away. Which makes them imagine that their world is a sort of private preserve, and nothing can ever happen to them."

"Tell me again what brought you to Thietvanne," she asked abruptly.

"It's been so long that I've forgotten. If I ever knew. Maybe getting out of a mile-deep rut. Money. Plain damned foolishness. . . ."

"And now?"

"We're committed. Once you're committed, you can't turn back."

"Committed to what, Cragg?"

"Finishing a job. And trying to save our own blasted skins."

"But commitment also requires involvement. You are involved, *mon cher*, far more than you know."

"There's only one involved man aboard, in the way you mean it, and that's Toyon."

"Ah, yes. *M'sieu le Colonel* qualifies. One day he will be a great man in his country."

"If he survives."

"I have never met a man like you, Cragg."

"Count your blessings. You're damned lucky."

"Why do you say that?"

"We inhabit different worlds, *bébé*. When mine touches yours, there's bound to be trouble. Somebody gets hurt. Like now."

Denny bent toward him. He caught the faint scent of her hair, and the delicate woman odor, which the fire's warmth had accentuated.

"I said once that you are a decent man," she murmured. "I find no reason to change my mind. Truly. You are an instrument for good."

"A damned blunt instrument, like one of those fireplace stones."

"In our own ways, all of us are instruments. My father taught me to be self-sufficient, so that I could do the things that had to be done at the mission."

"You didn't seem very self-sufficient at GaiSong, when you were begging a ride."

"But I knew where to seek assistance, did I not?" she reminded him with a faint smile.

Then the smile faded. Denny shut her eyes. As if the question had triggered an emotion she could not control, she suddenly buried her face against his chest, groping with blind fingers for his unshaven cheek. He heard the sound of muffled sobs.

Half rising, he seized her shoulders in an iron grip and forced the girl to look at him. "You've damned near had it, haven't you, *bébé?*"

"D-damned near, Cragg."

"Uncork." He stroked her eyelids tenderly, as one soothes a distraught child. "It'll be good for you."

"I'm such a fool," she raged helplessly. "An utter, abominable fool." As he released her, Denny opened her eyes, but she remained huddled against him, softly weeping. "Have you perhaps a handkerchief?"

"Here." He pulled the red bandanna from his hip pocket and offered it to her gravely. "It's big enough for you to use as a bath towel."

"Thank you." She wiped her face. "I'm sorry."

"You were overdue for this," he said, "by about three days."

Denny shook her head. "These are not tears of grief, or of fright, as you might think."

He ran his calloused hand over her tangle of dark hair. "I understand."

"But you couldn't!" She drew back, and peered into his seamed countenance. "It is not possible."

"Why?"

"Because if you really comprehended, Cragg, you would know that I love you."

Cragg supposed he should have been startled, caught unaware as he was by this simple declaration. Instead, he felt unaccountably sad, as if something precious, which he'd wanted very much and for a very long time, had been offered him too late. He also felt rather old, and quite weary.

"You'd better reconsider," he said, trying to ease the moment. "Hell. I'm a burnt-out crock. Damned near kaput. You're a young girl. . . ."

"No, no! Tonight I am more ancient than this lighthouse, and as alone." She reached out imploringly. "I need you, Cragg."

He pulled her gently toward him. "Christ knows, *bébé,* I need you, too. But first we've got to live past tomorrow."

They lay there, not speaking, while the fire guttered and died. Before she fell asleep in his arms, Denny sighed once, contentedly, and nestled against his lean body. At length, convinced that she was slumbering peacefully, he disengaged himself. Taking his canvas windbreaker from a peg alongside the fireplace, where he had hung it during the briefing, he spread it over her. After a final searching glance at the small figure on the hearth, Cragg limped slowly out.

A heavy overcast, which seemed almost to rest upon Quang Duk's sightless beacon, had obscured the quarter moon and its attendant stars. There was a hint of breeze, too, in the silent darkness.

Looking aloft, Cragg could discern tendrils of fog, vaguely lighter than the blanketing night itself. He was pleased to note that they were sweeping in from the east. Should the offshore wind hold, or better yet, rise, it would add a couple of knots to *Medusa*'s headway during her clumsy dash past the Khandos batteries.

As he walked stiffly down the path that led to the jetty where the two boats were docked, Cragg found himself hoping for one more providential advantage: a further dropping of the overcast, until it blotted out all surface visibility. The risk of negotiating the mile-wide passage between the fortified islets and the mainland through a pea-soup fog was far less, in his judgment, than the hazard that would befall them if the Khandos gunners opened fire, and thus alerted the whole Kong fleet. Even considering how he'd punched a hole in *Medusa*'s hull off Bien Goa, and damned near lost her, Cragg was willing to take his chances in another game of blind man's buff. Besides, racking up the junk on that coralhead had been an act of sheer stupidity, one which he wouldn't repeat.

At the pierside edge of the gangway he was peremptorily challenged by a Thiet deckhand, flourishing a businesslike carbine.

"Who goes?" demanded the sentry.

"Cragg."

"Okay." The Thiet lowered his weapon and stood aside. "Pass."

"You're on your toes, fella."

Although he did not fully grasp the compliment, the Thiet bobbed his kerchiefed head, displaying snaggled teeth in an appreciative smile. "*Merci, mon capitaine.*"

Cragg threw a ceremonial salute at *Medusa's* taffrail before he stepped across the bow. This instinctive gesture amused him. Being accosted by an officer of the deck, even a ragged Thiet, had triggered an old naval ritual. Somehow the act gave him a nostalgic moment of security, as if he'd just boarded PT 387, ready for a mission against the Tokyo Express.

He went below.

In the harsh beam of two converging spotlights, Trump Gideon and Hercule Panache were putting final touches on the submarine bombs.

They had discarded the alarm clocks as too unreliable, Gideon said, in favor of a technique used by modern underwater teams, which he had found in one of Cragg's *Naval Institute Proceedings*.

The six dynamite packages were connected by a series of detonating cords, each thirty feet in length, and from the set that would be attached last hung an even longer cord. To make Torgerson's task easier, explained Gideon, these heavy parcels would be buoyed up by a flotation arrangement consisting of two Mae West jackets, which the Swede would inflate shortly before he took to the water.

"It's jerrybuilt as hell," Gideon confessed, "but it should work."

"Should!" snapped Cragg. "It's damned well got to. It's the key that'll open the whole can of worms."

"Well, skipper, there are a few Jesus factors to contend with."

"Such as?"

"Stringing these Mickey Mouse gadgets under the Kong hulls without jerking loose any connections. They're fixed to explode together, after Lars swims clear and activates the detonator."

Cragg scowled across the compartment, to where Torgerson had laid out his black foam rubber wet suit, his black gloves, his black swimfins, his black-rimmed face mask, and the black belt from which depended a longbladed knife. The exec, who was seated nonchalantly upon one of the powder kegs tinkering with a scuba unit, waved back at him.

"Have a nice happytalk with the little lady?" Torgerson gave him a lewd grin. "Get lots of good sleep?"

With an effort, Cragg checked his temper and managed to

keep his voice calm. "Belay the comedy, mister." He threaded his way through the tangle of barrels and boxes for a closer look at Torgerson's UDT gear. "That's a pretty crazy Hallowe'en costume you've got there."

"Like everything else in this frigged-up circus," the Swede said bitterly, "it'll have to do. But it could be a damned sight better."

"What's the problem?"

"This!" Torgerson brandished the scuba. "I wanted a semi-closed circuit rebreathing outfit, and had to settle for this half-assed air-gobbler." He exploded a profanity. "It's dandy for abalone diving, when you don't mind leaving a trail of bubbles, but it sure as hell isn't built for reconnaissance."

"From the looks of the weather," Cragg consoled him, "we'll have pitch-darkness."

"Sure. And if we don't, maybe the Kong will mistake me for a mermaid."

"Chickening out?"

Stung by Cragg's calculated insult, Torgerson tossed aside the oxygen device. He stood up, glowering. "Have I ever let you down?"

"Not since Bien Goa."

"That was fun and games." Torgerson flexed his gigantic biceps, as though to prove his undisputed strength. "Listen, skipper, I'll finish the job if I have to dog-paddle from here to Phom Than, holding the blasted stuff in my teeth!"

Cragg felt oddly contrite. Torgerson was right. When the going got rugged for the Mafia of old, he'd never failed them, whether it meant toting fuel drums on his bare back, or single-handedly manning a deck gun, or delousing a hot torpedo that refused to function.

"Very well, mister. So we'll assume everything is four-oh."

"I didn't say that," Torgerson growled. "I just said I'd finish the motherlovin' job. Period. Over-and-out!"

Akim was already on the poopdeck, carefully wiping moisture from the great horizontal wheel. Under strict orders, the sentry had routed him out the instant Cragg came aboard. Now the one-eyed helmsman was demonstrating his efficiency in the only manner possible, since little more remained to be done before *Medusa* got underway, except hoist sail.

Cragg sniffed the dank air. It was saltier, and palpably heavier, than it had been the previous hour.

"Nice for playing hide-and-seek."

The tall Thiet blinked his visible right eye. Cragg's remark meant nothing to him, although it plainly signified that *le capitaine* was in a favorable mood, in itself a promising omen, considering the magnitude of the task that lay ahead. So Akim summoned up a proper acknowledgment from his limited store of English.

"Most beautiful."

"Beautiful's the word, fella." Cragg looked at his watch. "It's two o'clock. Better sound quarters."

Akim lifted his bosun's whistle and blew three shrill blasts. In a moment the Thiets, who doubled as gunners and foremast hands, burst through the main hatch. Shortly thereafter Torgerson emerged, followed by Gideon and Panache.

Cragg turned to Trump. "All ashore who're going ashore."

"Hell! I live right next door."

"I'd forgotten, mister. Then we'll be seeing a lot of each other, won't we?"

"That's right," Gideon thrust out his hand, and Cragg shook it solemnly. "Starting along about 0500."

"One last thing."

"Name it, skipper."

In a low voice, so Torgerson would not hear, Cragg said: "Wake Denny. I left her asleep in the lighthouse."

9

"You Just
Keep Going"

L IKE AN ENORMOUS stalking cat, with only the sound of
a rusted bell buoy to bid her lonesome farewell, *Medusa* slipped
her hawsers and crept out of Quang Duk's barricaded shelter at
three A.M. The fog clamped down almost immediately, leaving
the Mafia waving at opaque nothingness from their stations on
Mohican's low-slung deck before the junk had gone two hundred
yards. As the murk engulfed them, Cragg saw Denny, standing
a little apart from the others, and holding aloft his big red bandanna. He raised an arm in response. But it was too late.

Cragg turned slowly away. "Hold steady on course-010 for
twenty minutes," he instructed Akim. "Then left to 280."

"Aye, aye, sir!"

The Thiet helmsman adjusted the piratical patch over his right
eye, spat on his calloused hands, and braced himself for the task
of plowing a straight furrow with this unwieldy, broad-beamed,

ninety-foot vessel. Although he'd have one of the seaman-gunners to help him, the responsibility was his alone. For this implacable captain would accept no excuses for a crooked wake, not even a plea that the quartering sea sometimes caused *Medusa* to yaw like a bloated cow, or that the torque of her spinning propeller upset all normal calculations.

Unaware of Akim's self-doubts in the presence of a master mariner, Cragg moved away from the binnacle, satisfied that *Medusa* was firmly on course. He found a wind-shielded corner of the poopdeck, laid out two cushions, and knelt down to study his Thietvannese coastal chart in the dim glow of a blue flashlight.

It would take *Medusa,* progressing at top speed under the combined force of wind, current and diesel, one hour to raise the first of the Khandos. Those sixty minutes should give Torgerson, aided by Panache, ample time to make certain that the underwater charges were operative—or as potentially reliable as any such impromptu devices could ever be. They would dry run the simple circuitry, test the detonator cords, check the fuse caps. After which, thought Cragg, they'd better damned well chant a few mystic incantations for added insurance.

Once more he studied the narrow channel that twisted between the Khandos and the jutting mainland. On the chart it looked harmless enough, not unlike a segment of the Sacramento River, northeast from the Bay. Unless the weather stayed foul, though, and held visibility down to a groping nil, it could turn into a one-way passage to Hell. As things stood, the visual range would likely double because of the early morning offshore breeze, once they came about and left the open sea for their westward tack past the sentinel islands. By remaining in midstream, therefore, they should keep several hundred yards of protective murk between *Medusa* and the Khandos guns on the starboard side, and any possible coastwatchers to port.

It would have been a lot simpler and safer to mount a night attack, Cragg knew, following Drake's ancient script. Certainly they'd have a better chance to escape with a modicum of their singed hides intact, under cover of darkness, than in the fog-shrouded hours after daybreak. But there was always the chance the Kong, too, could break free of their trap. Blind man's buff works two ways. Despite its undeniable hazard, a dawn strike was surer, since their objective was total destruction of the Kong fleet.

Cragg hoped Denny was praying for bad weather.

She might also, he thought randomly, ask the Man to sharpen the eyes of *Medusa's* bow lookout as well as his own tired brain cells.

He peered down the ski-sloped deck toward the waist where three crewmen were vaguely discernible, going about the routine business of tightening sail under Akim's low-voiced command. None of them impressed Cragg as being dependable enough for the lookout assignment. He still had a rueful memory of the near catastrophe at Bien Goa.

"Akim," he called softly.

"Sir?"

"When we make that left rudder turn I'm going to plant myself partway up the foremast ratlines. I'll be watching through my night glasses. So listen damned closely for orders. *Comprenez?*"

"*Oui, mon capitaine.*"

"And the minute I signal that we've passed the Khandos, heave to and start helping Mr. Torgerson with his gear. I'll come aft as fast as I can."

"Should we drop anchor?"

"Hell, no! Once you're both launched, we'll keep moving—in tight circles—in case of trouble."

"Aye, aye, sir."

Gingerly, ponderously, like an overweight boxer essaying his rusty footwork after long retirement, *Medusa* moved along the crescent-shaped corridor. Thirty feet above the forecastle, eyes glued to his binoculars, Cragg kept vigil, while the junk crept toward the relative safety of the fogbound harbor. As a judicious afterthought, he had elected to bring them closer to the mainland than to the menacing Khandos. This posed the calculated risk that any inquisitive Kong would take them for just another stupid coaster who was eager to visit Phom Than for tomorrow's Feast of Quyen Dhu.

Much depended upon how the Kong themselves behaved on this festival eve.

If they were like their southern enemy cousins, they'd probably have begun celebrating twenty-four hours early. Rice wine can give a man a glorious hangover and effectively dull his senses if he imbibes deeply enough and with proper enthusiasm. Moreover, in honor of the legendary Quyen Dhu himself, who'd reputedly finished his chess game before marching against the Manchu overlords, the Kong might be indulging in their own updated version of fun and games. Especially, Cragg thought, with General Kwo's proffered truce so firmly in sight.

Only once did he lower the night glasses long enough to relieve his aching eyes, during *Medusa's* slow transit of the winding strait. At that instant Cragg again cursed himself for not providing the junk with radar.

But their luck held. After what seemed endless hours, though it was hardly more than fifteen minutes, he called out to Akim in a hoarse whisper: "Bring her into the wind, mister!"

By the time Cragg had clambered down and groped his way back to the welldeck, Torgerson was already in the rubber life raft, settled among the packaged explosives, ready for entry into the dark water. Akim had relinquished the wheel to the seaman-gunner and was donning his own wet suit.

The exec resembled a monstrous black knight in his UDT costume, armored *de pied en cap* with helmet, breastplate, cuisse, greaves, gauntlets, and finned sabatons. As he crouched there, Cragg noted sorrowfully, he betrayed signs of an unmistakable belly. The Swede had been too long out of training and was slowing down, although he had a long way to go before he'd become a gimp-legged, stiff-armed relic. Torgerson had not yet lowered the mask over his huge grinning face.

When he saw Cragg approach, he hoisted a mammoth rubber glove and spread his fingers in a V-for-victory sign.

"Great weather," he exulted, "for us ducks."

"Made to order," Cragg agreed somberly. "Everything ship-shape?"

"Affirmative."

There was much more that Cragg wanted to say. But the exec's matter-of-fact demeanor discouraged foolish sentiments at that awkward juncture. It was not unlike the old Mafia days in the South Pacific, when they'd roared off into battle with only a casual flip of the hand, or a jovial obscenity, to mark their awareness that this might be their ultimate mission.

Then Akim crawled aboard the raft, which had been hoisted on davits, and grasped the forward lines.

"Ready, fella?" asked Cragg.

"Check," Torgerson grunted.

"Lower away!"

The raft hit the surface with a muffled splash. Its original orange color, intended for easy spotting by aerial searchers, had been overpainted a dull black. Although designed to carry four men, the craft was deep-laden now with demolition equipment, and it got underway rather sluggishly as Torgerson and Akim dug in with their twin-bladed paddles. Within five minutes it was lost to view.

Cragg stared toward the place where the raft had disappeared. When the deed was done, that inadequate cockleshell must also accommodate *Medusa*'s survivors. Some of them would be badly wounded, and therefore unable to cling to its outside lines. But others among the ten-man crew would be very dead, and hence no problem at all during the pickup attempt.

Panache was waiting for him on the poopdeck, beside the helm, with a report that *Medusa* could be put to the torch whenever the captain desired.

"It's almost four-fifteen," said Cragg. "Torgerson will need an hour to reach the Kong, and another fifteen minutes to fix his charges. At five sharp we'll head in." He gave Panache a speculative look. "Can you and I handle the arson detail by ourselves?"

"Easily, *mon capitaine*. I've arranged it so that only six firings are necessary. Besides," the Frenchman added quickly, "igniting the powder in the hold."

"Good. Then we won't have to draft the gunners."

The seaman-gunner to whom Akim had delegated both the wheel and his authority said in a proud voice: "I have already given my men their orders. They will continue shooting until they are told to leave the ship."

"Suppose we run out of targets?" Cragg suggested.

"Surely *le capitaine* jests."

"He does."

"Ah." The helmsman relaxed. "The noise of our weapons will cause much fright among the Kong, and make it more difficult for them to think clearly."

"That's what I had in mind, fella." Cragg nodded approval. "You would make a fine platoon leader."

For the better part of forty minutes *Medusa* executed a series of taut circles in the area adjacent to Torgerson's jumping-off point, her sails slatting, engines throttled low, while Cragg mouthed curses at the abysmally slow passage of time. A faint lightening in the east, past the still-shrouded Khandos, signified that daybreak was less than an hour below the horizon. The fog had begun to thin, too, and visibility was now a full half-mile.

At 0445 Cragg announced: "Okay, gladiators, let's parade into the ring!"

While Panache watched curiously, he extracted a cigar from his breastpocket, and with elaborate care cut a small notch in one end with his sheath knife. Then he held the fragrant cylinder to his nose, as a connoisseur might lift a wine goblet, and inhaled deeply.

"The last," said Cragg, "of His Excellency's Upmanns. I've been hoarding it."

"For good luck?"

"Yes."

"Each of us has his *tiki*." Panache stroked his whiskers. "Mine is this ugly beard. As long as I can hide behind it, I am invisible, and therefore quite secure."

"That's a damned comforting thought," Cragg said. "I hope it's true."

Panache dropped his bantering tone. "So do I, *mon ami*."

After lighting the Havana, Cragg jammed his duckbilled cap down over his ears and told the helmsman to fetch the junk due west to course-270. It occurred to him again that this absurd engineer's cap had also been regarded as a lucky symbol by the Mafia, having brought the stubborn head that wore it safely through a dozen Pacific battles. Except the last engagement off

Okinawa, of course, for which he had paid so dearly. *Last?* Any warrior worth his salt needs one more battle, one more chance to prove himself.

They were about to commence that battle now.

For another twenty minutes *Medusa* plowed steadfastly onward, while the false dawn gleamed dully, turned dark again, then threatened to become a muted opalescent sunrise. They were not challenged. With a scant mile remaining, the Kong fleet still veiled behind the fogbank, Cragg summoned the Thiet gunners from their stations belowdeck, with orders to man the fore-and-aft 40-millimeters.

They obeyed briskly, tossing the palm frond camouflage into the sea, like schoolchildren released for a rare holiday. When the weapons were uncovered the Thiets ran through a fast drill, expertly spinning the pointer wheels and training the long-snouted barrels, while Akim's assistant surveyed them pridefully from the helm.

"Okay, *mon capitaine?*"

"Okay."

At that precise instant *Medusa* broke briefly through the curtain. Before them, arrayed four abreast in a column that extended the length of the Phom Than waterfront, lay the Kong armada. The inboard ships, Cragg observed, were moored only a few yards from the shore. Through his glasses he could count a dozen quadruple sets of them, all heavy-laden, and beyond these loomed the dim shapes of still more tethered junks.

Their lights were ablaze.

It was evident that the enemy, caught up in the excitement of the impending festival, had totally relaxed their vigilance. With a casual disregard for security the Kong crews were gathered in jovial groups, drinking, dancing, gambling, moving at random among the ships of the close-knit fleet, like merrymaking delegates at a peacetime convention.

If the surprise held for another ten minutes, while Torgerson finished his business and *Medusa* closed the gap, it might prove to be just as Cragg had prophesied at Bien Goa: shooting fish in a barrel.

He gave the enemy a last calculating appraisal before he descended to the main cabin, where the voice-radio was switched on, humming softly, ready for use. Cragg unhooked the microphone.

"*Mohican?* This is *Medusa*. Come in."

Trump Gideon had been guarding the frequency. Across the intervening twelve miles his voice sounded eager. "I read you five-by-five, bossman."

"We've got the bastards boresighted. Start rolling."

"Stand easy a couple of seconds while I take a fix." Cragg waited. Then Gideon said: "Check."

"Make it awful fast, horntooter."

"Wilco. Twenty-two knots. Over."

"Over," said Cragg, "and out."

Medusa continued to ghost toward the unsuspecting armada. She was intermittently in the dubious clear, but more often veiled by the fog tendrils that clung to her like vast cobwebs.

When the range had dropped below a thousand yards, Cragg decided it was time to abandon all pretense and promote a diversion that would effectively turn attention away from Torgerson during this crucial phase of his underwater chore. The Swede intended to mine the lead echelon of junks. *Medusa*, therefore, would strike for the succeeding quarter.

Cragg spoke to the helmsman. "Point straight for the yellow junk, the big one, that's fourth in line."

"Aye, aye, sir."

"And tell the gunners to open fire."

"Will do."

In a quieter tone Cragg told Panache: "Strike a match, papa."

The Frenchman started forward with a kerosene-soaked swab, touching off every segment of rigging and sail he could reach on the portside, just as both deck guns opened up. Their loud reports gave impetus to his waddling gait, and he was halfway down the welldeck before Cragg began his own incendiary task along the starboard rail.

The tarsmeared hemp and canvas caught briskly. Within

seconds *Medusa's* upperworks were blazing like trees in a tur-pentine forest, as the intense heat bore the flames skyward.

Cragg overtook Panache on the forecastle. "Go below and light the rags," he said. "And in sixty seconds, the powder fuses!"

The Frenchman waggled his behemothic head. Somewhere between the taffrail and the bow he'd lost his protective topee. Red-hot cinders had seared his eggbald scalp. He was drenched in sweat, winded, beard singed, but dead game. His teeth glinted in a fierce smile.

"Oui, mon capitaine!"

Cragg crushed out a smoldering place on his own rolled-up trouser leg. It was time now to kindle the sulphurous waste strewn below the rails, which in turn would feed the kerosene that sloshed along the scuppers. Two flicks of the torch sufficed. Like a questing snake, the rivulet of fire raced aft, hissing, spewing sparks, sheeting upward to link with the flames in the lower tackle.

Through the fiery haze Cragg saw Panache stumble once, catch himself, then disappear through the open welldeck hatch.

Pointing toward the stern, he shouted to the three Thiets who were directing a steady stream of incandescent tracers and explosive shells from the bow gun: *"Allez, allez!"*

They went.

Close behind them, battling his way between the two walls of fire, limped Cragg. When *Medusa's* death throes began, her towering poopdeck would become the last refuge for the twelve men aboard. Or those few, he thought grimly, who had survived until then.

The helmsman freed one hand from the wheel long enough to indicate something in the middle distance, off the port quarter.

"There is a boat coming toward us, *mon capitaine!*"

Cragg wiped ashes from his eyes and peered out. Awake at last, the Kong had dispatched a patrol sampan to intercept them, a big one, mounting a machine-gun on its blunt prow and loaded with troops. It was closing fast. Its purpose was plain. The Kong intended to grapple and board.

At less than two hundred yards, closer than point-blank range, a 40-mm. cannon is a monstrous weapon, even when manually operated. Now, its long snout depressed, *Medusa's* stern gun poured a lethal, if ragged, stream at the onrushing craft. But the sampan kept doggedly on course despite the raking fire that was slaughtering its close-packed occupants. Still afloat, it careened against the junk's sloping waist, as the survivors made ready to board.

At Cragg's relayed command, the Thiets who had been relieved at the bow seized automatic rifles, and aimed amidships, toward the low rail over which the invaders would momentarily leap. They began shooting even before a Kong showed. In the teeth of this barrage the first enemy pair lasted barely three seconds, then dropped out of sight. The Thiets continued to hammer away until the Kong stopped coming.

There was a short hiatus while the unseen foe regrouped.

In that sudden lull, something exploded just inside the taffrail, near the 40-millimeter. Cragg whirled.

Two of the Thiet gunners lay sprawled on deck, ripped and bloody, while a third staggered blindly down the canted deck, holding spread fingers over his smashed face. He screamed once before he collapsed in a gobbety heap.

With his automatic at the ready, Cragg stalked aft toward the place from which the grenade had been lobbed. He reached it just as the Kong, having climbed the straked planks to the lofty poop, raised his head cautiously above the rail. For an instant they glared savagely at one another. As the Kong leveled his own revolver, Cragg squeezed the trigger of the heavier forty-five.

A jagged hole appeared in the Kong's forehead. He soared backward, outward, like a diver launched from a highboard. But he made no sound.

"Splendid marksmanship, *mon vieux.*"

Cragg turned. Panache stood there, panting, with a BAR cradled in his arms. He waved its muzzle toward the welldeck. "This has been a day for good hunting. Our visitors have been eliminated."

"For now," Cragg grunted. "What about the fuses?"

"They are burning."

"How long before the powder kegs blow?"

Panache computed rapidly. "Perhaps five minutes."

"Did you tell the engine-room gang to secure?"

"Yes."

Cragg gripped the rail. "So we're all set." He noticed that the teakwood felt hot to his touch.

Still on target, although enveloped in flames, *Medusa* had closed within a scant quarter-mile of the belatedly aroused armada when the largest junk in the front echelon rose like a surfacing whale, poised for a moment on a crest of dirty water, then sank back tiredly. An instant later the three adjacent ships also went up. The dull sound of a multiple submarine blast reached *Medusa* as flames started to lick along the waterline of the stricken vessels.

Cragg loosed an exultant war whoop. "Right on the goddamned button, you great big beautiful bastard!" He craned far out over the port rail, as if by so doing he might somehow assist Torgerson.

Behind the shattered vanguard he could see the crews of the next four junks, frantically chopping at the lines that coupled them to their doomed comrades. The entire formation, in fact, seemed more intent on escaping from its immediate predicament than on wreaking revenge on whoever, or whatever, had caused the devilish explosion.

Even this blazing apparition which had emerged so mysteriously out of the dawn murk, and was now bearing down upon them, drew minimal attention. Most of the Kong, farther back in the ruck, had missed the patrol sampan's abortive effort to halt *Medusa*. As a result they apparently took her for one of their own, which had simply caught it earlier and was careening out of control around the harbor while her crew fought the flames.

Someone in the third row of tethered junks, however, must have guessed what was up. There was a smattering of small automatic weapons fire, sporadic and poorly aimed. As Cragg had anticipated, most of the Kong transports and freighters were lightly armed, although the mined vessels must have been carrying ammo, to judge from the way they blew.

Medusa sustained one more casualty during her final approach. A seaman-gunner, loading shells into the reactivated 40-millimeter, took a bullet through the left breast. He died instantly. But another Thiet took his place, and the undermanned gun kept up its enfilading fire at the yellow junk, which now loomed before them like a stalled boxcar.

Cragg peered through the eddying smoke toward the spot in mid-harbor where Akim should have brought the raft, while waiting Torgerson's underwater swim to safety. All that was visible in the area of Point X, however, was the shadowy form of the ruined Kong sampan with its cargo of corpses.

He spun around as Panache tapped him on the shoulder. "The powder should go any moment, *mon capitaine.*"

"Okay. Tell all hands we're going to abandon ship."

As Panache repeated his order in a stentorian bellow, Cragg gave *Medusa* a last overall scrutiny. Flames had enveloped her from the Evil Eye painted on her bow to the squat mizzenmast, and were finally threatening the upper poopdeck, where the crew had gathered.

Although scorched and shaken, the Thiet motor mechs, who had managed to escape the holocaust below, were helping the helmsman secure the wheel with quarter-inch line. Keeping *Medusa's* rudder frozen slightly to starboard, even after she struck, would guarantee that she'd continue her incendiary run down the length of the Kong fleet.

Everyone had obeyed his order to don life jackets the moment Panache lighted the fuses.

Everyone, that is, except Cragg himself. He'd damned well forgotten. And now his equipment was God-only-knew-where, having been tossed aside when he got engrossed in the arson detail. No matter. So he'd swim unencumbered. At least a stiff knee and crooked elbow posed no handicap to his rough Australian crawl.

Cragg motioned toward the distant sampan.

"Jump!" he roared. "And swim like hell for that boat!"

The two surviving gunners took the twenty-foot plunge first, closely followed by the two mechs, and then the helmsman. But the Frenchman hesitated, straddling the rail, frowning down at the turbid water. Huge in his kapok vest, he looked like a circus bear, reluctant to obey the ringmaster's command.

"For Christ's sweet sake, papa—jump!"

The Frenchman heaved outward. He hit the surface with a mighty splash, emerged, and began to paddle after the others.

Cragg let a full half-minute elapse. This would give them godamned little time to break clear, yet it was more than he could spare. He watched. The helmsman was doing fine. He'd pulled out in front of the pack. But the others, especially Panache, were lagging badly.

With a sigh that was almost a groan, Cragg tossed away his long-dead cigar, and walked to the fantail where the drum of aviation fuel hung on its davits, and wrenched the screwcap free. Then he lowered one end of the barrel until it was suspended nearly upside down, to make sure its entire contents would spill out.

The volatile liquid flowed swiftly. Mating with the water, it created a thin film, an invisible Rorschach blot, which encompassed Medusa and the yellow junk. Its unseen tentacles also reached out toward the five swimmers, who were moving even more slowly now that they had encountered the full force of the incoming current.

A fraction ahead of schedule, as Cragg reached three in his silent fifteen-second countdown, the powder kegs exploded. With her vitals ripped asunder, dark smoke gushing from jagged holes in her amidship timbers, Medusa finally closed the gap. She rammed the tall stern of the yellow junk, clung there for an excruciating instant, then began caroming along the outboard flanks of the Kong fleet, igniting whatever she touched.

Cragg's final act, before he leaped, was to snatch up a piece of burning sailcloth. Impromptu torch in hand, he inhaled a deep breath and plummeted into the widening expanse of high octane film. The gasoline flared up immediately. Within seconds it formed a spurting, crackling lake, deadly to anyone trapped inside its borders.

He had been stunned by the double shock of Medusa's internal blast and the subsequent collision. But his brain cleared fast as he plumbed the chill waters beneath the incandescent surface. He leveled off at twenty feet. Husbanding his strength, conserving precious oxygen, he started to swim away from the anchored ships, toward what he hoped was safety. He proceeded underwater for a full ninety seconds before his tortured lungs forced him to come up.

Cragg looked over his shoulder.

Although he had outdistanced the fire for the moment, he felt nakedly exposed in its fierce glow, a patsy for sharpshooters on the enemy junks. But there were no retaliatory gunbursts.

The Kong were too preoccupied with this fresh peril to strike back against a lone swimmer. So the burning gasoline remained his prime concern, the true foe. Cragg saw that its rate-of-advance had eased. When it met the swift tidal current, he figured, it would halt.

With deliberate, steady strokes, pacing himself, he began to swim in the direction of the sampan which he'd last seen about three hundred yards off *Medusa's* flame-swept starboard bow. Very soon he overtook Panache. The Frenchman was laboring, making slow work of it, as if the unfamiliar effort had turned his great thews into unresponsive lead.

"Step it up, papa!" Cragg thrashed his hand toward the rim of fire. "The bastard's gaining!"

Panache gurgled something unintelligible and strove to comply. But when the flames had crept within twenty yards of them, he gave Cragg a look of patient despair.

"It is futile, *mon capitaine.*"

"Goddamn it, keep trying!"

Cragg seized Panache by the collar of his life jacket, and began to propel him faster through the choppy sea, away from the encroaching fire. Either this slight added impetus, or the sudden realization that only a superhuman effort could save them both, now that Cragg was committed to succoring him, seemed to give the Frenchman fresh strength. His weary arms lashed out. Together they fought their way clear of the sheeting flames, and together they reached the derelict sampan.

Two pair of lean brown arms reached down to assist them. Panache went first. After the Frenchman was aboard, Cragg allowed himself to be hoisted up, then dumped unceremoniously onto the waterlogged deck, before he reached for his sheath knife, rolled over on his back, and prepared to defend himself against whatever Kong had survived *Medusa's* devastating shellfire.

But it wasn't the enemy that stared down at him. One of the men was Akim, the other was the seaman-gunner who had taken over *Medusa's* helm. Akim crouched anxiously above him while Cragg labored to regain his breath.

"Where's Torgerson?" Cragg gasped.

The one-eyed Thiet gestured mutely toward the elevated stern. Cragg twisted his head. Stretched out prone beneath the tiller, which idly slatted back and forth over his sideturned face, lay the giant Swede. He had a collapsed appearance, like that of some creature flushed too quickly out of the saurian depths. A bloody froth flecked the corners of Torgerson's battered lips, as he breathed with painful effort through his half-opened mouth.

Shaking off Akim's proffered help, Cragg lurched aft, and knelt down beside the wounded exec. Torgerson gave him a look of glazed recognition.

"The frigger blew too soon," he said weakly. "The blast caught me before I could get away. I'm all busted up inside."

Cragg set his hand on the Swede's hot brow. "You did one hell of a job, mister."

"'Above and beyond the call. . . .'" Torgerson essayed a twisted smile. "Maybe I'll rate another medal." Then he shut his eyes, and Cragg turned questioningly to Akim.

The Thiet explained. Despite his grievous internal injuries, Torgerson had somehow managed to bull his way back to the life raft, which Akim had brought within a few hundred feet of the exploding Kong ships. Under scattered rifle fire from the enemy, Akim had hauled him aboard, then began to paddle toward the midstream rendezvous point. Several random shots hit the inflated cockleshell, however, and punctured its rubber sides. It was obvious the thing would never stay afloat long enough for *Mohican* to pick them up, even with only themselves to support, much less the others who should soon arrive from *Medusa*.

They were starting to founder, said Akim, when this sampan

drifted by. So he hitched the raft to the patrol boat's outer side, where the foe would be less likely to spot it, and wrangled the semiconscious exec into the comparative shelter of the larger craft.

Cragg beckoned to the seaman-gunner. "Did any others make it?"

"None. None at all."

Halfway to their goal, he said, they'd become confused and started veering back toward shore. Although he yelled at them, they kept swimming the wrong way. He shrugged despondently. It was evident that his four companions had fallen prey either to the gasoline flames, or to the Kong.

Cragg offered no comment. He regretted their loss. But what had happened to Torgerson was a worse blow. The mighty Swede's absence from the lineup would be sorely felt.

Thank Christ, though, he'd saved Papa Panache, whose prowess with a gun was amply displayed on the bloody boards of the sampan. Twelve dead Kong sprawled in grotesque disarray near the bow, where the Frenchman had methodically chopped them down before they could invade *Medusa*. A thirteenth lay beside Torgerson, under the useless tiller, and a fourteenth had been killed while trying to revive the boat's stalled engine.

Cragg directed his attention to the carnage along the waterfront. *Medusa* had done her job nobly. He counted more than fifteen furiously blazing junks, and at least seven others with incipient flames licking at their upperworks. Only a handful had succeeded in disentangling themselves from the melee. Several of these were encountering a different kind of trouble, crashing into one another and winding up with hopelessly tangled spars and rigging. Like cattle penned in a burning barn, the rest of the Kong, perhaps twenty in all, were unable for the moment to break free. They comprised the second and third inboard files. Helplessly, as the fire began to devour them, they awaited their chance to leave the treacherous moorings.

With hands telescoped around his smarting eyes, Cragg swung his gaze away from the hellishly lit harbor and tried to pierce the offshore murk for some sign of *Mohican*. The PT should have reached them by now. If Trump Gideon didn't come soon, they were certain to attract the attention of the first Kong junk that happened along, after which it would be only a matter of time before Torgerson's blackclad form was glimpsed among the jumble of Thiet corpses. By then the enemy, having recovered from his initial shock, would be hell-bent on revenge.

As he peered, Cragg sensed rather than saw the burgeoning sunrise. It was true dawn, now, albeit gray and foreboding. But the sun had risen above the horizon so imperceptibly, so stealthily, that its initial rays did little to cut the formless gloom which marked the limits of his perception.

The Khandos remained invisible. Cragg hoped they'd stay that way.

After a short while he thought he heard the distant chortle of diesel engines. He waited, listening hard. The sound grew louder, and in a few minutes *Mohican* broke through the curtain, driving at top speed, a white bone in her sharp teeth. When the PT had closed within a quarter-mile Cragg was able to make out the Thiet guncrew guarding the 40-mm. on the bow, and Loo at the wheel. Beside the tiny helmsman stood Gideon, studying the sampan through binoculars. Only their faces showed above the bridgeshield. But they looked damned purposeful.

Cragg peeled off his sodden shirt. Hopeful that Gideon wouldn't mistake his lean torso for that of a Kong, he balanced himself precariously on the afterdeck rail, waving the khaki garment like a truce flag.

There was no room for miscalculation. *Mohican* had to identify them as friendly, snatch them aboard, then proceed at once to intercept an enemy junk which had freed herself from the rearmost echelon and was already maneuvering for combative action.

Mohican began slowing as she drew within a hundred yards.

From his station on the port wing Gideon answered Cragg's frantic signal. The PT surged to a halt, both engines at full reverse, as Loo laid her adroitly alongside the crippled sampan.

"Get us up," bellowed Cragg, "fast!"

Between them, because of their own exhaustion and Torgerson's

dead weight, he and Panache were barely able to carry the
exec across to the starboard side, where Duke Harris, Colonel
Toyon and two Thiets took over. Cragg fashioned a stirrup with
his cupped hands, and propelled Akim swiftly aloft. It was more
difficult to raise Panache to *Mohican's* deck level, but somehow
he made it. Before the rescue operation had ended the PT was
once more under way. Cragg felt the cold lash of seawater
against his naked feet as he was swung across the widening
gap.

"Is the sickbay ready for casualties?" he demanded.

"Denny's got the wardroom set up," said Gideon. "If she needs
help, DelGrado's on call."

"Good." Cragg spoke to Akim. "We're clearing for action. Have
two of your strongest boys take Mr. Torgerson below."

"Aye, aye, sir."

"Hand me your binocs, Trump."

Gideon relinquished his glasses. Cragg focussed on the liber-
ated enemy junk. She was roughly a mile distant. At their
combined speeds, the Kong's probable six and *Mohican's* average
twelve from a standing start, the two vessels would close in less
than four minutes.

"Is your flamethrower limbered up?"

"Check," said Gideon.

"Then hit it!" Cragg addressed Akim again. "Are you feeling
okay, tiger?"

"Yes, *mon capitaine,* for anything."

"Go with Mr. Gideon." Cragg turned next to the colonel. "I
want you on the starboard .50-caliber. We'll need it for close-in
work." And to Panache: "You can work the portside."

Up forward the 40-mm. was already beating out a deaf-
ening tattoo as the Kong ship converged upon them. From a
half-mile, dimly perceived as through a gauze curtain, she looked
bigger, fatter, and more sluggish than she actually was. But her
decks were lined with armed troops. If she closed within grappling distance, where her superior manpower could prevail,
Mohican's clean-up chore would be abruptly terminated.

Steadily, with a kind of pachydermic obstinacy, the foe kept
advancing, disdaining evasive action. At six hundred yards the

junk began to return their fire. It was immediately apparent that she was one of the convoy's armed escorts, equipped with automatic weapons, crewed by men who knew how to use them. Enemy tracers stitched a white seam along the iron-gray surface as the Kong tested their aim. A moment later bullets chipped at the PT's plywood deck.

Now it was Cragg's option, whether to spare *Mohican* through evasive tactics on his own part, or to persist until he could bring the flamethrower to bear upon his lumbering adversary. The decision had to be made immediately, in full awareness that a lucky shot from the Kong might disable the PT and thus permit the enemy to ram. What Cragg needed was about a half-dozen yards of open sea between *Mohican* and the junk, enough to keep the Kong from swarming down upon them, yet not too much for Gideon's purposes. It was a narrow, delicate choice.

Cragg tightened his grip on the wheel. *Mohican* didn't deviate a com ass point.

Suddenly the 40-millimeter in the bow stuttered, ejected a few more rounds, then went quiet. Cragg tore his eyes off the target for a fleeting instant, long enough to observe that two of the Thiets were hanging dead in their harnesses. The third, badly hurt, was trying to crawl aft. He made it almost to the chart-house.

From both sides of the bridge the .50-calibers were pouring a steady hail of lead at the towering junk. Once the enemy barrage faltered. But only once. The Kong had ample reinforcements. Their weapons resumed firing after the briefest of pauses.

Something struck Cragg in the left shoulder, flattening him momentarily against the bridgeshield. He clapped a hand over the place, felt a gush of warm blood, and gave silent thanks that the wound wasn't lower, or on the right side where it would have affected his good arm. He put his hand back upon the wheel. Let the bastard bleed! He shook his head to clear his vision, and stared up at the junk, which was barely fifty yards away.

Her gunners were having trouble depressing their barrels sufficiently to engage the lowslung *Mohican*. Only small-arms fire greeted the PT as Cragg plowed within thirty feet. He spun the helm abruptly, to give Gideon's nightmarish weapon free rein from the faintail.

"Now!" he yelled.

The pressurized gas erupted, sparked, flared, and roared against the Kong's lofty flank like an incandescent jetstream. Gideon elevated his nozzle. The murderous spray crept upward, incinerating planks, rails, the riflemen perched upon them, and the rigging above their blackened skulls.

Within five munutes the junk's entire portside was aflame from bowsprit to poopdeck.

Mohican moved off.

Beyond the burning junk Cragg saw another Kong refugee. This one was smarter, less belligerent. Having witnessed the massacre of her comrade, she was fleeing in the opposite direction, toward an auxiliary exit north of the Khandos.

Cragg gave chase.

Mohican intercepted the foe halfway to presumed safety, and quickly reduced her to a blazing hulk. Two other Kong junks, which had been preparing to follow suit, abruptly changed their minds. To make sure they didn't recant, Cragg pursued them back into the inner harbor and gave them each a scorching, before they deliberately ran aground.

By this time *Mohican* had come under fire from several shore batteries. But the confusion and the capricious visibility made accurate shooting impossible. Nor was their aim improved by the fact that they had originally been installed for anti-aircraft defense, so their hasty conversion to lateral uses was a haphazard affair at best.

Cragg breathed thanks for yet another providential favor as he conned *Mohican* once more around the smoking harbor, in search of residual targets. But there was none worth the final risk. Of the sixty-odd imprisoned junks, only those four had succeeded in breaking entirely free, unscathed, after *Medusa* completed her blind, pyromaniac journey. The gambit had prevailed beyond all idiot expectation.

It was now time to escape, if they could, from the inferno they had created.

Cragg wheeled *Mohican* around and set course for the passage that angled south of the fortified islands, with no definite plans for their withdrawal other than to haul-ass, in the words of the immortal Halsey, as fast as DelGrado's laboring diesels would allow.

He scowled at the indistinct puttyball that marked where the sun was threatening to emerge through the murk, beneath which spread the hostile Khandos. At their present rate of advance they would come within range of the fortress guns in about twenty minutes. Until then he could do little, beyond making sure that *Mohican* was again ready for action, this time purely defensive.

Acutely conscious of the pain in his torn shoulder, Cragg stumbled around the corner of the bridgetub to take a census of their topside casualties.

There were four dead, he quickly learned, including the 40-millimeter trio, and one of the Thiets who had been assisting Gideon on the fantail. Besides himself, there were two others wounded: Akim, with a superficial crease in his swarthy scalp, and Toyon, with a sniper's bullet in his left thigh.

Thus far the expedition had lost twelve out of an original complement of twenty-two, all of them Thiets. No. Make that twenty-seven. He'd almost forgotten the five men killed at Bien Goa. As always, war was harsher on the indigenes than on the interlopers.

Cragg paused beside the starboard .50-caliber. For a man who didn't have much to start with, Toyon had lost a remarkable quantity of blood, and he was sagging against the circular steel rail of his machine-gun mount, barely conscious.

"I believe, Mr. Cragg, that I shall require help in getting down from here," he said in an apologetic whisper.

"Take it easy, colonel."

But as he reached up for Toyon, Cragg belatedly caught the full impact of bone marrow fatigue caused by his long ordeal in the water, the strain of the past half-hour at the wheel, and the weakening effect of his own massive bloodleeching. However manfully he tried, he couldn't wrap his uninjured right arm around the waist of the small figure on the saddleseat. His left hung useless, caked with dry blood, numb from shoulder to fingertips.

Panache, having witnessed his difficulty, strode across the

deck, bringing with him one of the Thiets from the 40-millimeter. Together they carried Toyon below.

Cragg followed them down the ladder, after first issuing orders to cast the four bodies over the side. Whatever obsequies were required would have to be conducted later, *in absentia.* There might be others, he thought grimly, for a mass funeral at a more convenient hour.

They placed the colonel on the wardroom banquette, opposite the transom on which Lars Torgerson lay. Denny looked up. She had been testing the exec's pulse. When she released his left hand, it dropped stiffly, and the gnarled fingers seemed to grope for the blackrubber scuba suit piled upon the deck near his uncovered feet.

The girl answered Cragg's questioning glance.

"I am truly sorry. Mr. Torgerson is dead."

Limping across to the transom, Cragg stared down at the exec. Even in death, Torgerson was a formidable figure. From the defiant expression on his battered face, Cragg guessed that the Swede had gone out fighting, as usual, against Higher Authority.

"It's been a damned long cruise, old buddy," he muttered. "Wait around. Maybe I'll be seeing you." Then he turned and said curtly: "Better take care of the colonel. He's in damned bad shape."

"What about yourself, Cragg?"

"I'll survive. Toyon won't, though, unless you get at it."

Denny bit her lip, but said nothing more. Swiftly, expertly, she stripped away the colonel's bloodsoaked trousers. Cragg watched silently while she cleansed around the wound, then probed for the spent bullet with the handle of a sterilized teaspoon. Toyon had been given a morphine shot. He did not stir. Finally Denny dressed the wound and straightened up.

"Now, Cragg?"

"Now."

She helped him remove his shirt. He gritted his teeth as she applied an alcohol swab to the anterior opening in the flesh where the shell had penetrated below the shoulder blade. Although she was very gentle and exceedingly deft, it hurt like hell.

"Turn around," she commanded. Cragg obeyed. "You are

indeed fortunate. The bullet passed cleanly through. There is nothing inside."

"Good."

"But I must tape the arm against your side," Denny said. "Otherwise the wound may burst open again."

Cragg shook his head. "Negative. Just fix the blasted thing so it'll work. Later I'll drop by for a complete overhaul." Suddenly, off the port bow, he heard the unmistakable crump-crump-crump of heavy gunfire. "And make it goddamned fast."

On certain occasions during the war the Mafia had been called upon to duel with larger foes that outgunned and outclassed PT 387 as much as fifty to one. Even against a Jap destroyer, however, they had maneuverability on their side, and the prospect of unleashing a torpedo spread at the ultimate moment. They could, in short, fight back. They had a chance of winning.

But this time there would be no retaliation. It wasn't even a duel. It was an elemental matter of staying live during their passage of the strait that led past the Khandos, where batteries of six-inch guns, manned by a thoroughly aroused, coldly vengeful enemy, would be hammering away at them with only the slightest chance of absorbing a return blow. By hugging the headland, putting a full mile between Mohican and the guns, they might somewhat lessen the danger. Provided, of course, the whimsical fogbank didn't come apart at the seams.

If there had been two of them, Mohican and a sister PT, they might have cut cards to see which survived. The loser, naturally, would have to lay a protective smokescreen for the winner, as in the old days.

But Mohican was alone. And Cragg himself had never felt more solitary, more nakedly exposed, in all his forty-five years. Instinctively, he felt for the breast pocket of his shirt, where he habitually kept his cigars, and touched the bandage that covered his naked chest. Hell. He wouldn't even have a goddamned Philippine stogie to comfort him.

Cragg cast a sharply appraising glance to starboard, toward the Khandos. The larger of the two islands lay approximately abreast of them. Its cannon were engaging them now. From here to the outer jaws of the trap, where the smaller island's guns would take over, stretched some five miles of exposed sea-lane. Having ebbed, the tide would be flowing outward, thus adding slightly to *Mohican*'s 23-knot maximum speed.

He looked skyward. The sun had disappeared and the ceiling had lowered. Not much, yet perceptibly, to less than a thousand feet. And the ragged fog curtain was self-mending its worst torn places. Where the murk spread heaviest, Cragg noted, it was like a temporary screen protecting the base of a statue, a kind of tarpaulin cover, before the unveiling. Ahead of *Mohican* he could see a half-dozen or so of these low-hanging shelters, intermittently spaced, with a god-awful expanse of wide-open water between them.

Although the initial bursts from the nearby fort had fallen short, the pair of white geysers that marked the second volley were measurably closer. Cragg nudged Loo.

"I'll take over," he said. "Hustle yourself up forward and keep an eye peeled for shoals. We're going to rub elbows with the mainland."

"Aye, aye, sir."

Giving his cherished wheel a reluctant last look, Loo saluted and scuttled along the slippery deck to the prow. There he threw himself prone, with his face craned far over the stem, so that he could scan the subsurface immediately ahead of the pounding craft. As a skilled helmsman, Loo knew that the briefest of warnings was all the captain required to whip *Mohican* into a safer course, should an obstacle be sighted.

Cragg eased the PT a point to starboard, then another, and still another, while cupping his ear for a sudden shout from the man at the bow.

Mohican crept closer to shore. The third round of shell splashes seemed no nearer than the second. Then Loo called, "I can see bottom, *mon capitaine*," and that was the end of the running room. Cragg swung the PT hard to port, leveled off, and waited grimly for the next salvo.

On the fantail, which squatted low in the water, Gideon, Akim, Panache and the lone remaining Thiet gunner were struggling to train the Long Tom toward the fort. But it was a chancy business. Even though *Mohican's* speed was barely half that of a full-fledged PT, they found it impossible to use both hands for their complex task. Like bronco riders in a rodeo, they had to keep one fist gripped on the saddle, simply to hang on, as their eighty-ton mount plunged toward the open sea. And the target itself was obscure. Only the occasional gunflashes that winked against the dark side of the fortified peak disclosed where the batteries were concealed.

Nevertheless Gideon somehow managed to bring his long-snouted rifle to bear upon the enemy.

Mohican's response was erratic, hardly calculated to disable the fort. But it did serve a useful purpose. The Kong, who hadn't figured on retaliatory fire from anything as impressive as a 75-millimeter, hesitated for almost two minutes after the PT's first shell exploded in their general vicinity. This was the margin Cragg needed to pass out of their limited radius. Although it merely meant exchanging the rocks of Scylla for the whirlpool of Charybdis, he reckoned himself fortunate, for the gauntlet was now half run.

Things had gone well so far. Too goddamned well. And the next phase was bound to get a lot rougher. The offshore batteries were doubtless already profiting from these previous errors in judgment, computing their range more carefully, and taking small vows to ignore the popgun on the insolent marauder's stern.

The principal advantage *Mohican* had gained, Cragg realized, was having finally reached the mouth of the V-shaped opening to Phom Than harbor. Whereas the margin between the PT and the larger island had been a mile at most, he could now count upon a solid two miles of leeway from thin-skinned ship to cannonading shore.

Their respite was short-lived.

As *Mohican* began to veer slightly southward, striving for safety around the protective headland, the Kong opened up. This time the geysers erupted in quadruplicate. Cragg inched the PT a few yards nearer the rocky coast, listened for Loo's monitory shout, heard it, and flattened out again.

He called into the engine-room tube: "Are you giving us the limit, Mario?"

DelGrado's tired voice came back immediately. "The absolute bloody limit, skipper, plus five."

"Very well." Cragg held his lips over the mouthpiece an instant longer. "Better stand by in the wardroom. If we catch one you may have to help Denny get the colonel topside."

"What about the engines?"

"Wire down the throttles," Cragg said, "so I won't have to worry about 'em."

"*Madre de dios!*"

Cragg closed the tube as another salvo burst off their bow. Great gouts of seawater cascaded over the deck, temporarily blinding him. When he could see again, *Mohican* was recklessly close to shore. He jerked the wheel to port. The PT heeled, swung, and headed almost for the menacing fortress itself.

His reflexive action saved them for the moment. The ensuing four-shell spread pocked the graygreen surface thirty yards to starboard, where they would have been had *Mohican* stayed on-course. Before the Kong gunners could compensate for their quarry's sudden turn, the fourth round dropped well astern.

But Cragg saw more peril than profit in continuing on that tack, which would have fetched *Mohican* into suicidal proximity within a half-minute. So once more he aimed for the beach.

There was an agonized scream from the fantail. He glanced around. The Thiet gunner, already shaken loose from his precarious perch on the Long Tom by the first unexpected maneuver, had been catapulted over the side by the ensuing abrupt turn.

Cragg saw the man come up, arms flailing, then start swimming slowly toward the nearby land after a hopeless look in the direction of the PT. He was probably a lucky bastard at that, thought Cragg, although he didn't know it. At least the Thiet would have a one-in-a-hundred chance of escape once he hit the beach, whereas the salvation odds of those he'd left behind were down to an irreducible nil.

Ten seconds later the fifth salvo exploded even closer than the second. *Mohican* lurched like a dumdummed rhino. Cragg waited for the sound of cracking timbers, and braced himself to hold the wheel firm against the inevitable slewing motion that must follow. But *Mohican* kept plowing ahead, as if undaunted by the near-miss.

He was preparing to congratulate himself on yet another miraculous escape when the speaker tube whistled. DelGrado had quit his wardroom post and was back in the engine room, with a report that *Mohican* was taking water through a break on the portside waterline.

"Is it repairable?" Cragg demanded.

"In a drydock, sure. Out here, Christ knows."

"Start the pumps," ordered Cragg. "And do what you can."

DelGrado was briefly silent. Then: "At this speed, skipper, we may tear off the whole side."

"Are the throttles still wired down?"

"Affirmative."

"Leave 'em that way. We've got another three miles to do before we're out of range. Then we'll take inventory. Meanwhile I'll send Harris down to help."

"Tell the Limey to hurry!"

Cragg ungripped the wheel long enough to make a megaphone of his two hands, "Duke," he roared, over the diesel whine and the wind's howl.

Harris appeared at the charthouse hatch. "Paging me, old boy?"

"Get below and join the damage repair detail. We're taking water from that last near-miss."

"Right-o," said Harris. "As soon as I switch off the bloody radar." His Pickwickian head vanished.

At that instant the enemy gunners found the mark with their sixth round. Three shells rumbled close above the fleeing PT. But the fourth, a fraction lower in its trajectory, struck the cubicle which Harris had just reentered. The plywood bulkhead offered too little resistance for the armor-piercing projectile to explode. It rocketed cleanly through the charthouse, and a split-second later it heaved up a tall white pillar in the roiled sea beyond *Mohican*'s starboard flank. There was little to indicate the PT had been hit. A wooden shard, chipped from the frail topdecking, brushed Cragg's face. Once more he felt blood, this time from a deeply slashed left cheek.

He called Harris again. But no reply came.

Then Cragg yelled, "Loo!"

The small Thiet had not taken his gaze off the waters ahead when the shell perforated *Mohican.* Now he looked back hastily.

"Yes, *mon capitaine?*"

"Belay the lookout detail. Take over the goddamn wheel."

When Loo was firmly set at the helm, with orders to stop following the coast and aim straight for the open sea, Cragg scrambled around the sheltered bridge to the charthouse. Using the splintered overhead for a trapeze bar, he swung on one arm through the open hatch and landed alongside the radarscope. It was still glowing. But Duke Harris was dead, decapitated by the Kong shell, and his torn body lay upon the red-glistening vinyl deck. Cragg reached across to turn off the machine. The screen went black.

He gently spread a gray navy blanket from the transom over the small, mutilated form. It was inadequate covering, quickly soaked with Harris' blood, but he could do nothing else for the moment. His first concern was for *Mohican,* which had begun to assume an unmistakable bow's-down attitude, and was moving sluggishly as a consequence. Cragg glanced around the charthouse. The shortwave set had fared worse than the radar. Before it egressed near the base of the low-slung bulkhead, the shell that slaughtered Harris had also demolished the two-way radio.

Cragg was assailed by a brief sense of guilt for the thought that the machine was worth more than the man, and he left the chartroom without looking again at the huddled figure on the bloodstained deck.

"I'm going below," he informed Loo. "Stay on this course."

"Aye, aye, sir."

Then Cragg peered hurriedly aft. Gideon and his two-man crew were still pumping futile iron at the fort, which now lay almost astern of them. The Kongs' last salvo—their seventh, unless he'd lost count—had fallen slightly short. Maybe by as much as thirty yards. He supposed their fortuitous error had resulted from *Mohican*'s abrupt shift from shore-hugging to a flat-out dash for open water.

Before descending the ladder, Cragg took advantage of a lull in the Long Tom's ragged bursts to issue a shouted command. "Cease firing, and make smoke!"

Gideon waved acknowledgment with his free hand.

Cragg lurched down the ladder. When *Mohican* lay parallel to the Khandos there had been no purpose in touching off the chemical smokepots. But now that she'd tucked her tail between her lean legs, running away like a scared mongrel, this camouflage might do some good. It was worth a try. God knows the Long Tom was no longer having any inhibitory effect on the receding fort.

DelGrado and the girl were waging a losing battle against the sea that kept pouring through the breached hull, despite their best efforts with mattresses ripped from the forecastle bunks. Cragg sized up the situation. The bilge pumps would soon be inundated, and the deadly tide would engulf them within a few minutes. *Mohican* needed major surgery, not a superficial bandage.

Cragg heaved his weight against the wardroom table, once, twice, thrice, until he felt the anchoring screws come loose. On the fourth try the metal legs broke free. Holding the bulky table in front of him, he bulled his way through the hatch that led into the crew's quarters, and ordered DelGrado to remove the water-logged mattresses.

Although it was by no means designed for *Mohican*'s flared side, the tabletop fitted reasonably well over the hole, reducing the flow by half, and making it feasible for them to complete the patch with another set of dry mattresses.

"It'll do," grunted Cragg, "until we can heave to for repairs."

DelGrado stood back, panting. His dark eyes were mournful. Suddenly he beat his naked chest. "Goddamn it, skipper, I should've thought of a simple thing like that."

"Forget it, mister. You tried. Hell's bells. Even experts blow it sometimes." Cragg regarded Denny. "How's your morale, *bébé?*"

The girl rendered him a faint smile. She was drenched. The

linen skirt and silk blouse, blood-smeared from her surgical duties, were molded against her slim figure. In the harsh light of DelGrado's emergency lantern Cragg could plainly discern the outline of her narrow ribcage, and her young breasts, as she stood before him, shivering in the cavern dankness that had enveloped the forecastle.

"One has no time to consider morale," she said.

"True," he agreed somberly. "You just keep going."

Cragg followed her into the wardroom. From his hospital couch, the banquette which had served the ripped-out table, Colonel Toyon contemplated them through heavy-lidded eyes. His voice was weak, yet surprisingly steady.

"Are matters progressing badly, Mr. Cragg?"

"They could be a lot worse. We're still afloat. And we're damned near out of range."

Toyon glanced at Torgerson's shrouded form. "And the casualties?"

"Bad. One more of your men. And Duke Harris."

The Colonel asked softly, "It is a terrible thing to ask, my friend, but what of the radio equipment?"

"Destroyed."

"I see." Toyon closed his eyes. "So now we cannot raise GaiSong."

"Not until we reach Dokoro."

"When will that be?"

"We'll either get there within forty-eight hours," said Cragg, "or never."

"Regrettable," murmured Toyon. "Most unfortunate."

Trump Gideon had the pots billowing full-blast when Cragg returned to the bridge. Rising upward to meet the lowering clouds, the smoke interposed an opaque screen between *Mohican* and the batteries, behind which the PT crawled toward the gray expanse beyond the Khandos. He had been forced to reduce speed, lest the pressure of seawater against their ripped fore-quarter rip away the haphazard poultice. DelGrado was right. They could damned well lose an entire section of laminated wooden skin. If that happened, *Mohican* would sink like a tossed brick.

Cragg rewarded the lowering sky with a nod of pure approval. He estimated the ceiling at less than eight hundred feet, now, and dropping fast. In a few more minutes even a flathatting Kong MIG would find it impossible to give meaningful pursuit.

He intended to hold *Mohican* on an easterly course until she was a full hundred miles out from the jutting peninsula where Quang Duk's lighthouse stood, before heading due south for Dokoro. He checked the chronometer on the saltcrusted instrument panel. It was almost ten-thirty. With luck they should reach the turning point around dusk. That would give them time to strengthen the hull patch, and still leave most of the night to extend their tenuous safety margin.

10

"They Were All Good Men"

T HE SLAG-COLORED SKY had already begun to darken, a little before five P.M., when Cragg signaled for slow-speed. *Mohican* eased from the twelve knots she had been logging steadily since midmorning to a minimal four, just enough to keep her bow against the oncharging waves and prevent her from slipping broadside into a trough from which she might never recover.

Leaving Gideon and Akim to man one of the midships .50-calibers, in the improbable event a stray Kong fighter plane might scout them through a hole in the murk, Cragg summoned Panache and made his way belowdecks. It was the Frenchman's first opportunity to view the damage. He waggled his grizzled head, and clucked disparagingly over the *michel souris* repair effort. Thereupon he opined that he, Hercule Panache, would apply certain woodworking skills acquired as a plantation owner toward creating something more durable.

"That," Cragg said dryly, "is why I brought you down here, papa. What d'you need?"

Panache wanted the framework and slatting from the transom berths in the captain's and executive officer's staterooms, plus whatever usable lengths of wooden deck could be pried loose without seriously impairing *Mohican's* walkability. Also a saw, hammer, nails and caulking compound. Cragg directed that these be obtained forthwith. After satisfying himself that the Frenchman did indeed know what he was doing, Cragg left DelGrado in his charge and beckoned to Denny.

"Come with me," he said. They went to his torn-up quarters, where he pointed at the cabin's single chair. "Sit."

"Thank you, Cragg."

"Do you happen to own an English language Bible?"

"No. But Mario has one." She smiled faintly. "It is not your Protestant version, however. It is a Douay."

"Aren't they pretty much alike?"

"Although the language may differ," she agreed with gentle irony, "the essential message is the same."

"So it doesn't much matter," he said.

"Why did you ask, Cragg?"

"After the repairs are finished, and the night's run is over, we've got to hold burial services for Torgerson, Harris and the others."

"Burial services?"

"At sea," he explained in a bleak tone, "you can't dig a nice neat grave. We sew the bodies in a canvas sack, weight their feet, and consign them over the side. Usually they're covered by a flag. It stays on board." He paused. "I don't know about the Duke. But that's how Torgerson would have wanted things done."

"And the Bible, Cragg?"

"There are some passages that ought to be read," he said, "although I don't remember which ones."

During the war, Cragg went on, his squadron commander had once been called upon to conduct a simple burial service in the absence of the chaplain. Although the PT crewmen who had been killed in action were laid to rest in the moist earth of the Solomons, the Old Man performed the rites according to what he'd remembered from his midshipman days abroad a training cruise ship in the 1920s.

"Will you recite the verses I choose?" asked Denny.

"Yes." Cragg studied his weatherbeaten hands. "But you'll have to make the shrouds."

"Very well." She stood up. "Give me the materials, and I shall go to work at once."

"There's plenty of time," he said. "We can't hold the ceremony until dawn tomorrow."

All that evening, while Cragg and Loo divided two-hour watches at the wheel, *Mohican* continued southward on course-180. This heading carried them ever closer to the bellying coastline, and it would require only a slight westerly adjustment at the final hour to fetch them into Dokoro harbor. Although he was pleased with Panache's repair effort, Cragg remained dubious about the fractured hull, and he held the PT to her previous twelve-knot speed. There was another advantage in keeping *Mohican* reined in. At this rate she would conserve fuel and wouldn't arrive at Dokoro with bone-dry bunkers, should they find it unsafe to stop at the mission. Exactly what they'd do in that event Cragg didn't know, nor care at this point. He saw no profit in worrying about alternatives, considering their immediate predicament.

To be sure, Colonel Toyon was unhappy as hell, down in the wardroom, fretting because *Mohican* had a good ten knots going to waste up her diesel sleeve. For some reason, which he apparently preferred not to disclose, it was vital that they reach Dokoro at the earliest possible moment. Cragg supposed the Colonel's manifest impatience sprang from his utter isolation, here on the fleeing PT, now that the radio was silent. Understandably, Toyon was burning to find out what had happened at GaiSong when news of the victory in Phom Than harbor burst upon the Thiet capital.

How GaiSong reacted, of course, bore heavily on Toyon's own future.

"What if the homefront news is bad?" Cragg asked him during the midwatch break, when Loo had the helm.

Although it was almost one A.M., and he was unable to sleep because of the pain in his wounded thigh, Toyon had stubbornly refused the sedative urged upon him by Denny. Propped up by pillows, he reclined on the upholstered banquette, inscribing his private thoughts in a diarylike book. The colonel stopped writing and contemplated Cragg with a pensive eye.

"Then we shall see," he said. "Perhaps we will begin again, somewhere, but I do not think that will be necessary. What you have done, sir, has given my people fresh courage, new heart."

Cragg turned away from the tiny figure on the bench, toward the transom upon which Lars Torgerson had died seventeen hours earlier. DelGrado and Akim had carried the Swede's giant body aloft, into the crew's dayroom, where for the moment it lay beside Duke Harris's.

Now Denny occupied this selfsame transom, laboriously engaged in fashioning a seam in the thick canvas which Cragg had brought from the supply locker. It had originally been earmarked as a jury rig, if they ever got desperate enough to outfit *Mohican* with sails. He'd drawn the pattern himself after figuring the dimensions required for the burial shrouds, and had cut the cloth with his sheath knife. Even using a sailmaker's padded glove, Denny was finding it difficult to thrust her needle through the heavy fabric. But she persisted. And the forbidding garment that was designed for Lars Torgerson began to take shape.

Belatedly, Cragg responded to Toyon's last remark. "Although it might have seemed large, colonel, our success is only a small detail of the whole picture. You know that."

"True," Toyon said gravely. "Yet we have had few such achievements. None, in fact, since the Americans left. Thus we are doubly grateful."

The colonel turned back to his notes. As Cragg prepared to leave, Denny glanced up from her sewing, and gave him a profound look, in which was blended much compassion, pride, and a curious sort of respect.

"I have found those passages you wished for the service," she said. "Do you want them now?"

"No. They can wait. Finish what you're doing, *bébé*, and grab some rest. Dawn comes in another four hours. I'll see you then. . . ."

Mohican's long night was uneventful. By first dim light, shortly after five A.M., she had traveled better than a hundred miles since veering southward off the Khandos. Which meant, according to Cragg's chart, that roughly another one hundred stretched ahead of them. Moreover, these would be the critical miles, with their safety dependent on a number of factors, none of which was susceptible to modification by his own effort, skill or judgment. If the weather stayed constant, low-ceilinged and squally, their chances of slipping unnoticed into Dokoro harbor would be reasonably good. If the Kong outsmarted themselves, by figuring that *Mohican* wouldn't dare seek this too-obvious haven, the odds would improve even more. And if the mission remained as they had left it, totally abandoned, they could refuel quickly and get the hell out, before the enemy was any the wiser.

God knows they stood no chance at all against a determined land assault. On the other hand, they might be able to counter a random air attack by a couple of MIGs at the nether end of a search run. Except for her bow gun, *Mohican's* anti-aircraft battery was intact. With Loo at the wheel, they had adequate manpower to serve the surviving 40-millimeter and the paired .50-calibers.

Now the sun was definitely showing above the eastern horizon, off their port beam, and Cragg took heart at its evil reddishness. Unless the portents were wrong, they should enjoy another day of ugly weather. He felt into his hip pocket for the sheet of foolscap which Denny had given him a short while earlier. On it, in her precise, almost Spencerian hand, were penciled the eight verses she had chosen from the New Testament for the ceremony he would soon conduct. He studied them for the fifth time. They would do. In fact, they suited the occasion admirably.

On *Mohican's* cramped afterdeck, between the stern and the crew's dayroom, rested the bodies of Lars Torgerson and Duke Harris, their shrouded feet close to the rail. Each was covered with an American flag. The Swede lay beneath the riddled ensign that had flown from the radar mast during the battle. The spare flag, which would be bent onto the halyards and hoisted after the service, was draped over Harris.

Cragg blew into the engine-room tube. "I want all hands on deck," he told DelGrado.

"Even the colonel?"

"If you can manage it."

"We'll manage," DelGrado said.

Within minutes, borne upon a stretcher constructed out of two boathooks and the residue of the jury rig canvas, Toyon was brought topside. DelGrado and Akim placed him carefully upon the boxlike dayroom superstructure. Toyon looked older than his thirty-seven years, frail and shrunken, with his thin torso swathed in a blanket stenciled USN. But his eyes were fixed unwaveringly upon the waiting captain.

While the colonel was being deployed into position to observe the proceedings, Cragg surveyed his depleted ship's company.

Papa Panache, drawn up straight, stood at Toyon's side. As always, when he bothered to think about it, Cragg was surprised to note that the Frenchman matched his own six-foot-one height. Panache's immense girth, the heft of him, tended to diminish the effect of tallness. His spadebeard was rimed with salt. He wore his spare topee, shielding his vision against the red rays that sloped toward *Mohican*'s damaged left flank, and his pitted face was very solemn.

Trump Gideon, no longer dapper, was finding it more difficult than the brawny Frenchman to hold himself fully erect. Exhaustion had etched dark crescents below his pallid eyes. And once, while Cragg watched covertly, he stretched out a hand to steady himself against the 40-millimeter frame. Gideon had placed himself near Torgerson's head, so that when the proper moment came he could reach down and seize the flag, just as the body was tilted over the side.

DelGrado was similarly posted alongside Harris's body. His full Sicilian lips were shaping strange words which, Cragg guessed, betokened some Latin ritual for the dead, and his fierce brows formed a single thatch above his huge jib of a nose.

Denny stood between the two of them, facing forward, but unlike DelGrado she kept her lips tightly compressed. Only her freckled hands, clasped at her waist, suggested that she, too, was composing a private prayer. She had not donned her linen duster. Instead, she wore one of Cragg's old pea jackets as protection against the dawn chill. The morning breeze had ruffled her dark hair, and blown a vagrant lock across her tanned forehead.

The two Thiets remained apart, Loo at the wheel, Akim beside him, staring impassively toward the silent group on the after-deck. Akim's good right eye betrayed no more emotion than did the dark patch that covered his blind left one.

Before he began speaking, Cragg fought back a brief surge of pain from the neglected wound in his shoulder, a wave of nausea, and then he resolutely ignored it. There was a curious roaring in his ears, like distant surf, and his own voice seemed very far away, mocking him. After a moment, however, it passed. The phrases from the Douay Bible came easier to his tongue than those of the archaic King James edition which his mother had made him read aloud, long ago, when he'd been fetched home by the cops to be punished for some juvenile peccadillo.

"The wind blows where it will," he read, "and thou hearest its sound but dost not know where it comes from or where it goes. So is everyone who is born of the Spirit . . . Jesus therefore said to them, 'Yet a little while the light is among you. Walk while you have the light, that darkness does not overtake you. He who walks in the darkness does not know where he goes.'"

Cragg stopped and looked at the flag-draped figures before he went on.

"'Greater love than this no one has, that one lay down his life for his friends. You are my friends if you do the things I command you. . . . Watch, stand fast in the faith, act like men, be strong. . . . I have fought the good fight, I have finished the course, I have kept the faith.'" Once more Cragg hesitated. He stole a quick glance at Denny, who gave him an almost imperceptible nod. Then he finished swiftly: "Jesus said . . . 'I am the resurrection and the life; he who believes in me, even if he die, shall live. . . .'"

Cragg signaled to Gideon and DelGrado. They elevated the two bodies by the shoulders, preparatory to sliding them into the sea. He dropped his hand. There was a double splash. The shrouded corpses vanished into the gray depths, and *Mohican* pressed on, oblivious.

As Gideon and DelGrado stepped back from the rail, clasping the flags, Cragg regarded them thoughtfully, even affectionately. He observed in a quiet tone: "So that does it. We're all that's left of the Mafia. Just us three, after twenty-seven years, and we're still a long way from home." He paused. "Before you go to work, I've got a few more things to say. It won't take long. But maybe there won't be another chance."

Cragg raised his voice so that Akim and Loo could hear him more clearly.

"This includes you." He looked at Toyon and the girl. "And also you, colonel, and Denny." Toyon responded with a courtly inclination of his head from the improvised stretcher. "Those words I've just read are meant for all the men we've lost thus far, the five killed at Bien Goa, the *montagnards,* and the twelve others who died with Torgerson and Harris at Phom Than. The Mafia is proud to have served with you."

Cragg flexed his stiffened shoulder. "We should raise Dokoro in about four hours. Carry on!"

There was no need for further orders. Quietly, efficiently, they resumed their various assignments. DelGrado and Akim carried the colonel below. Soon afterward the Thiet emerged through the hatch, to join Gideon at the 40-mm., where they began a meticulous inspection of its hardworked mechanism, preliminary to test-firing. Denny went back to the galley. Out of their drained stores, somehow, she must coax the Spartan meal that *Mohican's* crew would eat at their posts, standing up. Loo took over the starboard .50-caliber.

The weather front, which Cragg had hoped would screen their approach, failed to materialize. Instead, it turned into one of those deceptive mornings, flatlighted, when the ocean seemed dry, and the spume off the cresting waves blew like Sahara dust. They sighted land shortly before eight A.M., thirty miles away, through a haze that cleaved the Fantastic Mountains horizontally, separating the tallest peaks from the great mass below.

Through his glasses Cragg searched out a particular cone-

shaped summit, which lay directly west of Dokoro, and aimed
Mohican for this remembered landmark. If their luck held, they
should reach the mission pier in another two hours. He resisted
an impulse to ring for more speed. The torn hull was leaking
again, and DelGrado had started the pumps. Although the last
thirty minutes would be the most critical, bringing them within
potential gun range of the beach, Cragg knew that even then
they couldn't risk a further weakening of the patch.

It was highly unlikely, moreover, that any Kong search planes
would intercept them before they entered Dokoro harbor. The
real danger lurked ashore, in the gutted village, or in the jungle
that surrounded it. For this reason Cragg had taken Gideon off
the 40-millimeter, and ordered him back to the Long Tom, with
Panache and Akim as handlers.

Still unchallenged, escorted only by the carrion seagulls that
had flown out to meet her, *Mohican* forged ahead. By nine A.M.
the slanting palm trees which rimmed the crescent bay were
visible through the binoculars, and a half-hour later they commenced the final run.

There was no opposition. Dokoro looked as totally deserted, as
utterly lifeless, as when they had left it.

Cragg swung *Mohican* alongside the moldering dock and
moored her against the same steep ladder to which she had been
tied a week earlier. For the remainder of the morning, and for
much of that afternoon, he drove his five-man crew without
mercy. It was a nightmarish reprise of the hours they had spent
during their previous stay at the mission: wrestling the .50-
calibers loose from the deck fittings, emplacing them at the head
of the pier, establishing *Mohican*'s big searchlight where it could
command the beach approaches, strengthening the barbed wire
entanglements, rearranging the sandbags which were doubly
heavy because of the rains. All this had to be done, said Cragg,
before they reconnoitered the village itself. The fact that the PT
had made her landfall and docked without incident was no
guarantee that Dokoro was free of Kongs. They could be lying
doggo, wary of *Mohican*'s firepower, awaiting a chance to bush-
whack the intruders at a more favorable moment.

If the village assayed clean, they would make an immediate

survey of the airstrip. Toyon had urged top priority for this. Three days after their departure from Dokoro, he said, a Thiet labor squad should have arrived on the scene to repair the damaged runway. There would be a DC-3 standing by in Gai-Song, ready to take off the instant he flashed word that *Mohican* had returned. When Cragg suggested that General Kwo might countermand such an order, the colonel smiled and remarked quietly: "His Excellency knows nothing of this plan."

Next on the agenda was putting the mission radio back into operation, as a substitute for the PT's wrecked equipment. Because the hospital transformer had been sabotaged during the original attack, *Mohican's* four standby batteries would provide the necessary power. DelGrado and Akim had instructions to find a cart or wheelbarrow and transport them from the dock to the administration building.

Given ideal working conditions, Panache guessed he could restore Dr. Legére's transmitter in about three hours, using parts cannibalized from the shipboard set. GaiSong would get the news by midevening. Once the message was acknowledged, said Cragg, they'd retire to their beachhead until the plane arrived. It would be a bloody long wait, he warned, since the DC-3 couldn't possibly land until daybreak.

Leaving Loo behind as sentry, Cragg led Panache, Gideon, DelGrado and Akim up the steep slope toward the mission compound. They trod warily, in skirmish formation, with their Browning automatic rifles at the ready. He had stubbornly insisted on taking the point, despite Gideon's plea that any of the others would be a lesser casualty to the expedition if the enemy opened fire.

"Forget it," Cragg retorted. "I've brought us this far. But now it's just a matter of survival. There's no reason why I should rate any special favors."

There were no Kong in the village. The cluster of gutted shops and hovels was as lifeless as when they had come here before, and the rubble along the pathetic little main street was undisturbed. Near the well around which had centered the Dokorans' neighborly enterprises, however, they found evidence that a detachment of moderate size had recently used the commons for a bivouac. The fire-pits, four of them, were cold. But Panache, after probing the ashes with his fingers, estimated the fires hadn't been extinguished more than a couple of hours. It appeared likely, he said, that whoever had built them broke camp about the time *Mohican* hove into sight off Dokoro.

"How many would you figure?" asked Cragg.

The Frenchman studied the pits. "Perhaps forty."

"Kong?"

Panache nodded grimly. "Beyond all doubt. These are too cleverly fashioned to be the handiwork of an outlaw band."

Cragg appraised the pallid sun, which had sunk low over the charred village roofs, and slung the BAR across his unwounded shoulder.

"They'll sure as hell sneak back after it gets dark," he growled. "Let's roll."

At six-twenty P.M., like the lowering of an opaque curtain, the subtropical twilight abruptly faded, giving way to pitch-black starless night. For another hour Panache pursued his intricate task in the glow of a kerosene lantern held by Gideon, while Cragg and DelGrado stood armed guard at the window of Dr. Legére's second-floor office. Akim had been posted across the compound, with instructions to squeeze off a single burst from his rifle if he detected any movement beyond the village boundaries, and then rejoin them at the beachhead.

At length, with a satisfied grunt, Panache announced that the radio was ready for testing. He placed the earphones over his huge head, spun the dials, and after a few minutes he turned toward Cragg, grinning.

The receiver had brought in GaiSong, loud and clear, and he was pleased to relay the news that the capital had subsided into restless quiet following several days of rioting. General Kwo, said Panache, had closeted himself in his palace, refusing to heed the demands of his subordinates for a follow-up drive against the Kong, now that the reinforcement threat posed by the enemy armada had been blunted. Only one thing seemed certain. Colonel Toyon was the man of the hour, an authentic hero, in a city that had almost forgotten the nature of valor. Exactly how this noble business had been accomplished at Phom Than remained something of a mystery, as did the colonel's whereabouts. But the entire citizenry was eagerly attending the return of this gallant officer and his comrades.

It was obvious that Radio GaiSong no longer reflected the views of General Kwo.

"That's great," Cragg said brusquely. "Now try the goddamned transmitter."

Panache complied. When he sought to raise GaiSong, however, his repeated call went unheard. After fifteen minutes of futile effort, he wrenched aside his headset and beckoned to Gideon.

"Once more the lantern, *mon ami.*" The Frenchman sighed. "It may take time to locate the source of the problem."

For another quarter-hour Panache struggled with the balky transmitter, sweating and angry, and then he tried again to contact GaiSong. Still there was only the empty crackle of static in reply. He exploded a Gallic curse.

Suddenly, through the open window, came the sound of Akim's single warning shot. Cragg heard it echo against the flanking hills.

"Okay," he snapped. "That's it."

Panache remained seated. "Permit me to stay here, *mon capitaine,*" he urged. "I am certain that this difficulty can be resolved promptly."

"Negative, papa. You're needed on the pier."

Unwillingly, with a helpless backward glance at the recalcitrant set, the Frenchman shambled after the others, who were already hurrying down the dark stairs. As the four men reached the crown of the ridge that loomed above the wharf area, Akim's BAR spoke again, this time in a chattering tirade. It was still arguing with the Kong when Cragg led them through the barbed wire and into the dockside perimeter.

By prearrangement, Loo and Gideon took over the fixed .50-calibers, leaving Cragg, DelGrado and Panache as mobile marksmen with their Brownings. It was a damned thin red line, Cragg thought, whose only hope lay in superior firepower. Assuming, that is, the guerrillas themselves hadn't brought up a machine-gun or two, for placement on the overhanging bluff. When morning came, though, the pier would be vulnerable as hell to snipers, who could keep the defenders pinned down behind their sandbags while the larger Kong force massed for all-out assault.

For a few minutes they listened to the intermittent barking of Akim's gun. Judging from the sound of it, their one-eyed rear guardsman was slowly retiring from the compound toward the waterfront. Occasionally, in the intervals between his volleys, they heard the lesser crackle of small arms fire.

Then, abruptly, there was silence, carefully followed by a spaced series of rifle shots.

Cragg counted off a full ninety seconds before he said: "Aim the searchlight at the notch where the road starts downhill."

DelGrado complied promptly. None questioned the command. It was evident, beyond any doubt, that Akim's pursuers had overtaken him despite his best efforts with the BAR. Perhaps he'd run short of ammo, or been caught from the rear. Whatever, those final shots unmistakably signaled a deliberate *coup de grâce*, administered to a fallen victim. Akim no longer needed the enshrouding darkness for his escape.

Shortly thereafter the first Kong made their appearance at the top of the slope, a quarter-mile away, picked out by the bright finger as they loomed over the brow. There were five of them. Without waiting for orders, Gideon and Loo opened fire with their .50s, and the enemy vanguard melted away, screaming.

"Douse the light," said Cragg. "They've got the idea."

Cragg had shut his eyes before issuing the command. When he reopened them his vision was already acclimated to the darkness. He lifted his night glasses with his unshackled right hand. Peering through the gloom he could see a dozen or so Kong scrambling for sheltered positions along the ridge.

"There'll be a slight intermission," he said, "while the bastards regroup. But brace yourselves for a charge."

Cragg rested the snout of his BAR against a sandbag and wished he had a cigar. It was a thoroughly fanciful notion, of course, but it brought home the futility of their plight. He might just as well wish for a cigar, he told himself grimly, as for a miraculous lifting of the hopeless siege which had now begun.

Belatedly, too, Cragg realized he should have left Panache with the radio, on the offchance that the Frenchman could get the transmitter operating, and alert GaiSong to their arrival. Insisting that papa accompany them to the beachhead was a goddamned stupid blunder, committed on the age-old military theory that you don't divide your forces when you're outnumbered.

The ironical thought also occurred to him that he hadn't wanted Panache to stay behind and face certain death at the hands of the Kong. Here death was equally certain, although it might be briefly delayed by a vigorous defense. He'd done papa no great favor by inviting him to join Custer's last stand.

During the tenuous lull, Denny climbed the steep ladder from *Mohican* to the pier, and walked swiftly through the darkness toward the revetment. Cragg did not see her approach. He whirled, startled, when she spoke to him.

"Cragg?"

"What are you doing up here?" he demanded angrily.

"Colonel Toyon wishes to know whether you were able to contact his friends before the Kong came."

"We weren't. Now get the hell back into the boat. This place is about to turn into a shooting gallery."

He resumed his vigil with the night glasses. Denny stared at the ridge toward which his binoculars were pointed and asked in a steady voice: "Do we have much chance, Cragg?"

"Probably none," he said, "unless the Kong lose their nerve after we blast 'em a few times."

Panache had overheard Cragg's remark. "We can survive the night," he rumbled. "But the dawn. . . ."

"What shall I tell Colonel Toyon?"

"To start thinking whether he intends to surrender or defend himself. You know where the guns are kept. Find him a pistol, in case he decides to make a fight for it—when the Kong overrun us." Then Cragg added in a curiously muted tone: "Better arm yourself, too, *bébé*."

"It would be useless," she said. "I could not kill a man."

"That isn't what I meant." He lowered his glasses, turned, and looked deeply into her face. "I wouldn't want you captured by the Kong."

"You wish me to kill myself, Cragg?" she asked wonderingly.

"If the worst happens."

Denny shook her head. "A Catholic does not take his own life. Suicide is a mortal sin."

"For a woman," he said, "it wouldn't be suicide, using a gun to escape the Kong."

Once more she shook her head. "There are some things you do not understand."

"Several million," he agreed sorrowfully, "and no time left to learn."

She prepared to leave. "*Au revoir,* Cragg."

"So long, *bébé.*"

The Kong made their first move a half-hour later. They poured down the narrow road in a manner reminiscent of the *banzai* attacks the Japs had flung against the Marines of Guadalcanal. As they charged, yelling, DelGrado flicked on the searchlight, and the harsh beam followed them the whole distance, down the hill, along the causeway, and up to the edge of the sandbagged redoubt. So did two .50-calibers wielded by Gideon and Loo. Before the reckless charge ended, Cragg counted six enemy killed, and twice that many more wounded.

"Finish 'em off." he roared.

Methodically, like twin firehoses extinguishing stray embers after a blaze is quelled, the machine-guns sought out those who had fallen, but were not yet dead. The job was soon finished. Within five minutes uneasy silence again prevailed over the narrow battleground.

As Cragg was about to cut the searchlight, a sharpshooting Kong saved him the trouble. There was a splintering crash, a sudden incandescent fury, and then the beam winked out. He swore. Although this was bound to happen, and he'd been gratefully surprised that the enemy had taken so long to destroy the light, its loss was a grievous blow to his defenses.

Cragg called to DelGrado. "Back to your tommy gun, mister."

But Mario did not respond. Cragg strode across the deck to the searchlight stand. DelGrado was kneeling, as if in prayer, against the stanchion, his head swiveled toward the menacing hill, with an astonished look on his swarthy countenance. But his eyes were as blind as the shattered beacon above him. In seeking out the light, the sniper had made several near misses before he found his mark. One of the shots had penetrated DelGrado's left temple. Still striving to guide the beam, Mario had collapsed into this oddly natural attitude before he died.

Panache came lumbering through the darkness.

"He is dead?"

"Yes."

Laying aside his BAR, the Frenchman helped Cragg dispose DelGrado's body on the rough planking, and straighten the lifeless limbs. Then he announced in a firm voice that brooked no dissent: "I am detaching myself from your command, *mon capitaine.*"

Cragg stood up. "You're crazy, papa. There's no place else to go."

Panache glanced at the ridge. "It is my intention," he said, "to return to the hospital."

"You'll never make it."

"One can only try." The Frenchman stroked his beard. "Unless we achieve communication with GaiSong, *mon ami,* all hope is gone."

"I know," muttered Cragg. He awaited Panache's justifiable recrimination for his earlier tactical mistake. But none came. So he said: "You'd better take Loo along."

The Frenchman grinned. "As you would say, *mon capitaine,* negative." He jammed his singed, greasy topee down over his head. "But you can wish me luck."

"*Vaya con dios, amigo.*"

Panache went to the edge of the dock, dropped upon his haunches, and propelled himself clumsily onto the sandy beach below. For an instant he hesitated. Then, with a flourish of his BAR, he struck out along the shore, staying close to the breaking waves, in the direction of the burned-out fuel dump. The Frenchman's huge form was quickly lost in the opaque blackness. Cragg squinted at his wristwatch. It was nine-forty P.M. By taking this circuitous route, and treading with extreme caution, Panache should reach the hospital in about thirty minutes.

Now there were only three of them manning the barricades, the two who remained from the old Mafia, and the scrawny Loo, confronting an unknown number of guerrillas. The girl didn't count. She would not, or could not, bring herself to bear arms, even against an enemy as implacably savage as the Kong. And Toyon was a total debit. In fact, to Cragg's mind, it was highly possible that the Kong knew of the colonel's presence in Dokoro. If this proved true, the likelihood of their withdrawal before they had killed or captured the perpetrator of the Phom Than outrage was less than nil. Moreover, their own intelligence would have informed them that Toyon's imminent return was being eagerly heralded in GaiSong. To reverse the triumph by parading the miscreant through the streets of the Kong capital, bound in chains, would therefore be an outcome devoutly sought by the injured foe.

Cragg spoke to Gideon. "You and Loo fire a couple of rounds at short intervals. Maybe it'll divert the bastards' attention away from Panache."

Trump nodded. "We'll keep 'em occupied, skipper."

"That's the general drift." Cragg laid his BAR on an ammunition crate. "I'm going down to *Mohican* and give Toyon the word."

"Straight?"

"Yes."

"And Denny?"

"She already has the bad news. But she might be trying to keep the old boy from worrying."

Turning, Cragg made his way along the dock, moving in a half crouch, down the ladder to the tethered PT. As he descended, he heard the sound of whispered voices, and when he reached the deck he was greeted by Toyon. The colonel was gripping Denny's right arm with one thin hand, and further supporting himself by using a boathook as a cane.

"I waited," he said simply. "And when the Kong did not burst in upon us, I concluded that you had driven them back."

"For the moment. I can't guarantee the next time."

"Mlle. Legére has assisted me thus far, Mr. Cragg. But she cannot do more. If you will carry me to the pier, I should like to join your men at the revetment. It is possible, you know, to aim a gun quite accurately from a sitting position."

Cragg weighed the request briefly. Then: "Are you strong enough to hang onto me while I climb the ladder?"

"I shall manage."

"Very well."

Cragg bent down, and the colonel grasped him around the neck. The pressure applied against his wounded shoulder made him clench his teeth to forestall a cry of pain. Together they began the precarious ascent. Having only one arm free to negotiate the rungs, Cragg made slow work of it. The colonel's hundred pounds had become a dead weight ton before they reached the top. But Cragg did not relinquish his burden there. Instead he continued along the pier with Toyon still fastened limpet-like to his back, and finally deposited him within the sandbag shelter.

Despite his brusque orders to the contrary, Denny accompanied them. Just as firmly, she had told Cragg that if it were going to end here, in this fashion, she wished to remain beside him. The girl stated her intention in a calm manner, unsmiling, without heroics.

Her resolve seemed to falter momentarily when she saw DelGrado's body. But she quickly recovered. Crossing herself, Denny knelt down to retrieve the tiny gold cross which Mario wore on a chain around his neck. She arranged his hands over his chest and placed the cross between them, murmuring a prayer as she did.

Toyon regarded her somberly. "Another life in the cause of Thietvanne," he said. Then he settled himself against the revetment, with DelGrado's BAR propped between his legs, to begin the seven-hour vigil until dawn.

Papa Panache's half-hour was long gone. It was almost midnight. There had been no distant gunfire, nor any startled outcries, to indicate that he'd run afoul of the Kong during his circumnavigation of their siege-line along the bluff. Everything was quiet, abnormally so, except for an occasional burst from the defense guns on the dock, and an admonitory retort from the nearby enemy.

"D'you suppose he made it?" asked Gideon.

Cragg replied to this purely rhetorical question with a shrug and a grunt. But Toyon observed: "Panache is a man of many parts, Mr. Gideon. Personally, I believe he did."

"We won't know," said Cragg, "until it gets light."

"True." Trump rubbed his tired eyes. "I was just making smalltalk."

"Okay, tiger."

For a long while after that they sat in silence, spelling each other with the night glasses, striving to stay awake. Only Denny slept. She had lain down in the lee of the sandbags, in a spot which Cragg designated as relatively safe from shoreside fire, with her face upturned to the sky. A few stars were discernible through the ragged cloudblanket, and she fell asleep counting them.

At two A.M. Cragg got stiffly to his knees, and crawled across to where Loo was nodding at his .50-caliber post. The Thiet snapped out of his semi-trance with a guilty start.

"Rest easy, fella." Cragg gave him a reassuring thump on the back. "Nobody'll court-martial you." Loo's slight frame relaxed. "It's just that I've got a job for you."

"Yes, *mon capitaine?*"

The job, explained Cragg, was seeing to it that the irreparably damaged *Mohican* could be set afire at an instant's notice so the Kong wouldn't be able to make use of her salvageable parts.

"After we leave?" asked Loo.

Cragg nodded. "One way or the other," he agreed enigmatically.

"It is a sad thing," the Thiet said. "But it shall be accomplished."

"There's some butane left in the galley stove tank." Cragg went on, "and another canister of the stuff in the ammo locker. Get it out. Pile everything burnable you can find around them. Then return here. Later, when I give the signal, you'll hightail back to the boat, turn on the gas, scram the hell out, and toss a match down the galley vent. *Comprenez?*"

"Yes, *mon capitaine.*"

"So move."

Loo scuttled away. Cragg timed him. He was absent exactly twenty-five minutes. On his return he reported with an air of melancholy pride that all had been done as the captain instructed. *Mohican* would never aid the Kong.

By Cragg's best reckoning, dawn was due to break at five–fifteen. Shortly before first light, through the perverse blackness that was the harbinger of arriving day, he crept to Denny's side and awakened her. His face was very close when she opened her eyes.

"It's that time, *bébé.*"

She smiled at him. "Kiss me, Cragg."

He raised her head with his uninjured arm and solemnly obeyed. Her lips felt cool.

"They'll be attacking damned soon," he whispered.

"Do you love me, Cragg?"

"Yes." His voice was taut. "Christ knows I do."

"Then I am very happy."

He released his arm, and the girl sat up. "Don't move from this place," he commanded. "No matter what happens."

"If you are hurt," Denny said, "I shall come to you. Nothing on earth can stop me."

He gently touched her dark hair. "It's your life, *bébé.*"

"Not mine, Cragg. Ours."

The night glasses were no longer necessary to keep watch on the Kong. In the quickening light the defenders could see them gathering for the final assault, half-hidden behind trees and rocks, and could plainly discern the smoke from campfires which had until now burned unnoticed below the escarpment. If Panache had been right in his original estimate, the enemy still numbered about thirty men, down a third from the forty-odd who had bivouacked in the village before *Mohican's* arrival.

But first, of course, the Kong would endeavor to wear out the defenders with enfilading fire from the summit.

"Keep your heads low," Cragg said, "and don't shoot unless you've got a goddamned solid target in your sights."

It was an essential order. The first engagement, and the sporadic fusillades which were designed to cover Panache's mission, had seriously depleted their ammunition. Cragg figured they might be able to repel one more major onslaught. After that, if the Kong persisted, they'd have nothing to throw but sandbags.

For the next quarter-hour the four men and the girl remained huddled close against the shallow revetment, pinned down by sniper fire. Neither Gideon nor Loo had an opportunity to use their .50-calibers. The machine-gun emplacements were too vulnerable. Only the BARs wielded by Cragg and Toyon could be brought into occasional play, through slits in the sandbagged wall, when a Kong showed himself along the skyline.

Finally, either because they had lost patience, or believed the defenders were cowed by their persistent snipery, the Kong launched a charge. They were partway down the slope before Gideon and Loo could scramble back to their .50s. In the pink dawning Cragg counted almost fifty Kong, and the idiot thought struck him that Panache had badly underestimated the foe's strength.

It was a brief wild melee that cost the Kong another eleven killed. But it also reduced Cragg's pitiful force by one-quarter. The enemy had advanced under cover of the hilltop gunners, whose uncertain aim was bound to improve eventually, and at the very moment of turning back the Kong wave Trump Gideon was hit.

Cragg saw him topple to the deck. But there was no time to give aid. In a quiet rage, he redirected his BAR against the temporarily confounded foe, and kept squeezing the trigger until the Kong once more withdrew to lick their wounds.

When he could turn his attention to Gideon, he discovered that Denny had already reached the stricken man's side. Trump tried to say something. But it wasn't intelligible. He had been shot twice, in the chest and neck, and all he could manage was a bubbling gasp, before he went limp.

Cragg glanced over the ragged parapet. Only the enemy dead remained. All the living had fled. But the sniper fire was stepping up, ominously, making it more lethal than ever to man the .50-calibers.

Now, at this excruciating moment, was when *Mohican* should have been destroyed. They could not withstand another assault. Cragg was positive of that. Yet it would be suicidal for Loo to attempt the run down the pier. He wouldn't get fifty feet. So the order was not given.

It was then that they heard the throb of distant aircraft engines. Denny detected them first. They came from the southwest, growing steadily louder, and a few minutes later a pair of ancient prop-driven fighters appeared low over the headland that formed one arm of Dokoro harbor.

Toyon said in a remarkably restrained voice: "Those are ours, Mr. Cragg."

Yes, and Trump would never know that Papa Panache had made it, Cragg thought bitterly.

The planes flathatted across the bay and opened up with their wing guns as they neared the ridge, snuffing out the sniper fire almost immediately. Cragg let a minute elapse before he arose from his crouching position. Then he limped to Gideon's abandoned weapon and began methodically to outline the undulant profile of the hill with .50-caliber bullets.

Between bursts he yelled over his shoulder to Loo: "Do your duty, mister!"

The Thiet threw him a hasty salute, spun, and loped for the ladder that led down to *Mohican*.

After several passes, the fighters banked sharply toward the southwest, to pick up a transport plane that had hove into view while they were giving their attention to the Kong. It was a lubberly DC-3. But it looked more gorgeous than a PanAm clipper, drabclad in khaki and showing the bright sunburst insigne of the Thietvanne republic.

Cragg pursued it with his binoculars. It made a leisurely wing-down circle around the harbor, as if to give its occupants a thoroughgoing chance to inspect the compound, the waterfront, and the three persons who were waving at them from the little fortification on the jutting pier. Then it leveled off for a landing.

"The crazy bastards!" Galvanized into action, Cragg started toward the beach, BAR in hand. "The Kong will slaughter them!"

"Wait, Mr. Cragg!"

But Cragg paid no heed to the colonel's shouted protest. Cursing his crippled leg, angrily aware of the weakness caused by his untended shoulder wound, he fought his way up the steep slope. As he reached the brow, he could see the scattered remnants of the Kong force slipping through the dense foliage beyond the compound, plainly intent on picking off the DC-3's crew after they landed.

Cragg knew he probably couldn't overtake them. He knew, too, that if he somehow did, it would represent a futile gesture at best. The Kong would cut him down before he uncorked a half-dozen shots with his BAR.

Sobbing for breath, he halted alongside the well in the village commons and impotently watched them melt into the jungle that surrounded the airstrip. He caught a glimpse of the transport as it dropped out of sight behind the matted trees. He heard the engines rev once before they stopped. And then he heard the unmistakable chop of a Browning automatic rifle, wielded by a practiced hand, and the screams of men caught in its murderous fire.

Cragg began running again with clumsy strides toward the airstrip. But now he was buoyed up by fresh hope, the certain knowledge that Papa Panache had established himself as a one-man ambush, after having made radio contact with GaiSong. When he reached the field, the Frenchman was already accepting the felicitations of the two Thiets who had brought the DC-3 into Dokoro. Overhead the fighter planes maintained a close watch for Kong stragglers.

Panache uttered a mighty bellow as Cragg emerged from the bush. "*Mon capitaine!*" He laced a proud arm around his unhurt shoulder. "This," he informed the pilots, "is Colonel Toyon's naval commander."

The senior Thiet bowed, then asked anxiously: "What of the colonel?"

"He is waiting at the pier."

"Is he all right?"

"He's been badly wounded. But he'll be okay."

"Let us go to him," said the Thiet airman.

Cragg asked, "Where's the rest of your crew?"

"We came alone, just the two of us, thinking your people might require all the available space."

"That won't be necessary," said Cragg. "There are only five now, including the girl."

The pilot's eyes opened wide. "Girl, m'sieu?"

"Mlle. Denise Legére."

"You found the mademoiselle here—alive in this forsaken place?"

"No. She's gone the whole route with us."

"*Incroyable!*"

"I concur," Cragg said. "It's goddamned *incroyable.*"

While he and Panache remained on guard at the airstrip, the Thiets went after Toyon. Cragg told them to pick up the wheelbarrow which had been used to haul *Mohican's* batteries from the dock to the hospital. It would, he explained, serve as a mobile litter for the colonel. Rude, but adequate. He asked them also to help Loo bury the dead.

After they left, Cragg lowered himself painfully to the ground, and sat against the bole of a palm tree. He found that he was feeling lightheaded, somewhat dizzy, and he wanted to clear his brain. But he held his BAR at the ready across his bony knees.

"We sure as hell missed you, papa."

Panache regarded him with mournful acquiescence. "I did not succeed in raising GaiSong until three A.M.," he said. "It was not a satisfactory contact even then, so it took me another half-hour to convey our message. By that time it became readily apparent that the Kong were in full control of the waterfront. Since it was impossible for me to rejoin you, I did what I could, and prepared for the arrival of the aircraft."

"It was a smart decision," said Cragg.

"Who else has been killed?"

"Trump Gideon."

The Frenchman blinked rapidly. "He was a good man."

"They were all good men."

The Thiet pilots wheeled Toyon alongside the DC-3 and lifted him from the barrow. Panache helped them bundle him into the plane. Using blankets, they fashioned a bunk for the colonel along three bucket seats. He thanked them with regal dignity.

"Sir," said the chief pilot, "it will take two hours for the return flight. We should reach GaiSong at approximately nine A.M. You will be met by the Thietvannese defense committee. Thereupon an armed motor convoy will escort you directly to the palace, which has been designated as your headquarters."

"And what of General Kwo?" Toyon asked quietly.

"When M. Panache's signal was received, a deputation from the committee visited him." The pilot's lips twitched in a peculiar smile. "It was arranged that the general be transferred to a more suitable location."

"Where, lieutenant?"

"GaiSong prison, sir."

With that, both airmen strode forward, leaving their passengers to brace themselves for the takeoff from the abbreviated runway. Because the ancient DC-3 was unequipped with safety belts, Cragg and Panache knelt at Toyon's side, gripping the metal girders that arched above his recumbent body, to keep him securely on the bunk. Opposite them crouched Denny and Loo, holding fast to the rail which formed the outer edge of the shallow bucket seats.

Cragg glanced into the pilot's compartment. As the craft began to lumber along the hastily repaired strip, the senior Thiet craned his head around and looked through the open hatch. He shaped a reassuring O with his thumb and forefinger. The DC-3 gathered speed. At the excruciating nether end of the tarmac, it lurched skyward. The fronded tops of the palmgrove clawed at them, missed, and fell away.

Out of the dirt-encrusted porthole Cragg caught a glimpse of the mottled smoke column that arose from the burning PT. Then the transport banked steeply, swung south, and in a few minutes the smoke was no longer visible, because Dokoro lay astern.

After the plane reached its altitude, Cragg moved to the seat beside Denny. She, too, had been staring back at *Mohican*'s pyre.

"It is indeed a sad ending, Cragg."

"When a man loses his home," he said, "it's always rough. Even though it mightn't have been a particularly good one. And now I've got to find another foxhole."

She looked again through the misted port. "Perhaps you will remain for a little in GaiSong."

Cragg cupped the girl's chin with his right hand to bring her solemn face closer to his, and peered into her questing eyes. His expression was also grave.

"Not long ago you told me you wouldn't want to be in GaiSong. Remember? You said the people there had lost their spirit."

"Yes. I remember. But it is different now. Perhaps they have rediscovered something that had been forgotten."

Ignoring the others, oblivious to their attentive gaze, Cragg kissed her.

"Very well, *bébé*, GaiSong will do—for a start. . . ."

THIS BOOK WAS SET IN CALEDONIA

AND ATF BASKERVILLE TYPES.

IT WAS PRINTED, AND BOUND BY

AMERICAN BOOK—STRATFORD PRESS.

TYPOGRAPHY AND DESIGN ARE BY

LARRY KAMP.